The
Intermission

Elyssa Friedland

BERKLEY
New York

BERKLEY
An imprint of Penguin Random House LLC
375 Hudson Street, New York, New York 10014

Copyright © 2018 by Elyssa Friedland
Penguin Random House supports copyright. Copyright fuels creativity, encourages diverse
voices, promotes free speech, and creates a vibrant culture. Thank you for buying an authorized
edition of this book and for complying with copyright laws by not reproducing, scanning, or
distributing any part of it in any form without permission. You are supporting writers and
allowing Penguin Random House to continue to publish books for every reader.

BERKLEY is a registered trademark and the B colophon is a trademark of
Penguin Random House LLC.

Library of Congress Cataloging-in-Publication Data

Names: Friedland, Elyssa, author.
Title: The intermission / Elyssa Friedland.
Description: First edition. | New York : Berkley, 2018.
Identifiers: LCCN 2017009974 (print) | LCCN 2017014882 (ebook) |
ISBN 9780399586873 (ebook) | ISBN 9780399586866 (print)
Classification: LCC PS3606.R55522 (ebook) | LCC PS3606.R55522 I58 2018
(print) | DDC 813/.6—dc23
LC record available at https://lccn.loc.gov/2017009974

First Edition: July 2018

Printed in the United States of America
1   3   5   7   9   10   8   6   4   2

Cover design and illustration by Adam Auerbach
Book design by Tiffany Estreicher

For William, who is simply the greatest

ACKNOWLEDGMENTS

The idea for this book came about when I was watching my beloved husband load the dishwasher. It took him nearly twenty minutes, as he was very precise about the placement of each dish and glass, treating the entire chore as though he were competing in a Jenga tournament with a million-dollar prize. I do everything quickly (he would say haphazardly), and so it was nearly unbearable for me to watch this drawn-out process. I am beyond blessed to be married to my best friend, and so I can honestly say this is the worst it gets for us—neither of us can watch the other load dishes. But it got my gears cranking. What if there were a couple with problems, of both the monumental and trivial variety, haunted by secrets they've kept from each other, and they put their marriage on pause to reevaluate if they are right for each other? So Cass and Jonathan Coyne were born right in my kitchen. Therefore, my first debt of gratitude is to my amazing, delightful, adorable husband, William. Please keep doing chores slowly and inspiring my books.

The team at Berkley was enthusiastic and passionate about this book from the start. Kerry Donovan, my talented, patient, perfectionist editor, was always ready and willing to hash out these characters and their issues until both our throats were sore. You totally "got" Cass, and I love you for it. For my gorgeous and striking cover, I have the talented Adam Auerbach to thank. The marketing and publicity departments, specifically Lauren Burnstein, Tara O'Connor and Fareeda Bullert, threw their muscle and passion behind this book. My agent, Stefanie Lieberman—ahh, where would I be without you? I honestly feel like you are more my soul sister than literary agent. You are the best advocate, counselor and friend any writer could possibly ask for. I could discuss novels with you for hours . . . and hours . . . and hours. Molly Steinblatt, thank you for being such a careful reader and thoughtful contributor to my work.

My mom was a superb lay editrix and an available ear at all times. Love you, Mom! I am so lucky to have incredibly supportive parents and in-laws and siblings-in-law and the coolest batch of nieces and nephews. My children—Charlie, Lila and Sam—make this writer at a loss for words to describe how much I love them . . . but I will try. You are what ice cream, perfect weather, cozy sweatpants, an amazing book and the funniest comedian would be if they were combined. Thank you for being patient with me every time I yelled at you, "Shhhh, I'm working!"

I'm fortunate to have a fierce girl gang of writers at my side. Cristina Alger, Lauren Smith Brody and Leigh Abramson, I learn so much from you and love how we all support each other. Many thanks to all of my other friends who read early versions of this book and shared their insights and suggestions. Jenna Segal, thank you for explaining the world of Broadway marketing to me. Daniel Goldin, thank you for your medical knowledge—I definitely prefer discussing lung cancer and car crashes with you when the patients are fictional!

Finally, a genuine thank-you to my readers. In a world that moves too fast, where everyone seems more concerned with likes and follows than genuine dialogue and getting lost in a story, I am so appreciative of those who take the time to read books.

I fell in love with her courage, her sincerity, and her flaming self-respect. And it's these things I'd believe in, even if the whole world indulged in wild suspicions that she wasn't all she should be. I love her and it is the beginning of everything.

—F. Scott Fitzgerald

◆

*Thanks again for saving me.
Someday I'll save you too.*

—Zelda Fitzgerald

◆

*When a match has equal partners
then I fear not.*

—Aeschylus

act one

TOGETHER

PROLOGUE

Five Years Earlier

JONATHAN AND CASS Coyne watched as the bride opened her mouth to receive the first bite of wedding cake, a four-tiered monstrosity covered in fondant roses and edible pearls. The groom, intoxicated, jammed the fork in too deeply and the bride gasped as the tines probed the back of her throat.

"Christ," Cass said, reaching for Jonathan's elbow. "These two need to work on their coordination. That first dance was nearly an amputation below the knee."

Jonathan laughed. "Be nice!"

Jonathan and Cass had been married for just three months and had already attended four weddings since their own. They were at the age when their peers were coupling at rapid speed, and so the newly married Coynes were often bopping to "Celebrate" and clinking champagne glasses on the weekends. They'd developed a wicked party game (Cass's invention, though Jonathan happily played along) where they would bet on how many years the bride and groom would last. They would record their bets on one of the monogrammed cocktail napkins and keep them in a locked desk drawer at home. Neither of them had yet to come up with what the prize for a correct prediction would be, other than the obvious satisfaction of accurate fortune-telling.

"I think these guys have ten years tops. They can't dance, he's a drunk and she looks like she wants to murder him for shoving that buttercream flower down her throat."

"Disagree," Cass said, facing her husband. "She used to be really overweight and is still insecure because of it. And he was super awkward when he was younger—I can tell by the high school friends. It's a perfect match."

"That's quite a calculated analysis, Mrs. Coyne," Jonathan said. "So you're going fifty-years-plus?"

"Correct," Cass said. "Just like us."

"Just like us," Jonathan said, handing Cass the pen from his inside suit pocket. "Though hopefully we stick for better reasons."

"Of course," she said. Cass sounded certain. But he noticed she didn't offer any window into what sort of virtues might fuel their marriage for the long haul.

"You don't suppose anyone's ever bet on us, do you?" Jonathan asked. He hated to think of people from his past judging him or judging Cass—or worse, judging what they had together.

"I hope not." Just the thought made Cass ill, as though suddenly she was a nude model in art class and everyone around her was sketching her most objectionable flaws, the ones she habitually lied about.

The Coynes looked at each other for a moment. Separately, they reflected on what would be exposed if their own lives were examined under a microscope, or a walk down memory lane. And then they both shifted their gazes to their place settings, where generous slices of cake had been placed before them.

Cass took the napkin on which she and Jonathan had scribbled their predictions and crumpled it up.

"This is mean, isn't it?" she asked her husband.

"Agreed," Jonathan said. "Though we're still fifty-plus."

"Totally." Cass lifted a forkful of cake and artfully placed it between Jonathan's waiting lips. "We are totally fifty-plus."

1. CASS

CASS COYNE WAS thinking a lot about her marriage lately. Particularly, she found herself wondering how much joy she should derive from it. Or maybe joy was ambitious, and it was really complacency she should be after. She just didn't know what was normal to expect to feel on a daily basis. It didn't seem correct that after five years of marriage she was evaluating her relationship with her husband like it was an item in the grocery store she was considering purchasing. A melon probed for firmness. Sweetness. Or that she sometimes pictured her marriage like a snow globe, the delicate flakes inside representing the past, present and future, and that no matter how it all shook out, it didn't seem to settle properly.

These weren't questions that could easily be raised with her friends, some of whom would give their right arm for a husband like hers. Others would think the mere question was childish—their modus operandi was to get up, go to work, make dinner, have sex, maybe make a baby, rinse and repeat. Besides, "normal" was too relative a term about which to have a meaningful discussion. So was "happiness." Cass just wanted to know, in the recent days where minutes stretched into hours and weeks blurred into months, if it was normal (there was that word again) that at times (only rarely!) she wished she was single. That she'd never married Jonathan Coyne. That she'd never clinked beers with him at Paragon, where the serious types at Brown went to get wasted. That she hadn't called out to him on Park Avenue and flung her arms around him six years later. But how could she help it? He was the answer to everything.

Her husband—before he became that—used to remind her of a nearly ripe farm-stand peach, a project almost completed. He was someone in need of finishing touches, a man who would be so grateful to her for getting him a better haircut and jazzing up his apartment that he'd fail to see that she was truly the one in need of finishing. And that day on Park Avenue? When they *finally* came face-to-face? Well, he had flashed her the warmest of smiles when the recognition set in, sending a heat coursing through her chilled body. At that fateful moment, she marveled at how a person could literally transmit electricity to another person without even touching. Lately, though, she wondered if her body had just been responding to a spike in temperature after leaving the artic chill of the office tower where she was working. Maybe excessive air-conditioning was to blame for the subsequent trajectory of her life. Of course she didn't really believe that. She had charged into her marriage with eyes wide open. Back then, Jonathan was a doorway with an inviting threshold, one she had no inclination to sidestep. After all, she'd beaten a path right to it.

In their king-sized bed (a bed of her own making, she thought wryly), Jonathan snored peacefully. *Snoring.* It was caused by a narrowing of the upper airway during sleep. Just the thought of it made her feel like she was choking. But every night, Jonathan snored comfortably next to her. He'd always snored, or at least she thought he had. Thinking back over the course of their relationship was surprisingly like gaping at something through foggy glass. It was just that now, the snores were deafening, and still Jonathan managed to look at ease as he sputtered out those throaty *chaaaa-shoooo*s. Sometimes she had to wonder if he was faking it. *I'm trying to sleep; don't talk to me,* his pretend snores were conveying. Well, that was fine. She did that too sometimes. He would tap her on the shoulder and whisper, "Cass," wanting to chat or maybe have sex, and she'd utter something unintelligible in return, while in her head she held back a perfectly logical response. When did that pattern of theirs start? Another thing she couldn't quite remember.

She looked up at the blurry red numbers dancing on the ceiling. Jonathan had insisted on buying one of those alarm clocks that project the time upward. He adored gadgets—it went along with his penchant for science, math, numbers—anything with a concrete solution and logic behind it. She argued that the new device would make their room look like a spaceship. Who was too lazy to rotate their head? In truth, she loved it, smiling to herself each time she didn't have to turn over to make out the time on the night table. Especially now that she wasn't sleeping well, watching the numbers tick by on her back was almost hypnotic. Not that she ever told Jonathan how much she liked that glowing metronome in the dark, choosing instead to add her tolerance of it to a growing stockpile of bargaining chips she maintained. Was that normal too? That she treated their marriage like an accountant maintaining a ledger of checks and balances? She was hardly in a position to do anything of the sort.

Relief took hold of her when she saw it was 5:00 a.m., and she anchored the spindly tips of her shoulder blades more deeply into the Tempur-Pedic mattress. What a funny thing, a Tempur-Pedic. A way to share without having to compromise. If only all things in life, in marriage, were that easily reconciled. It was morning enough outside—sharp slivers of light attacked the crevices between the curtains and the window. Five was much better than three, the time she had grown accustomed to waking recently. Why was it that when she had to get to work, the sound of her alarm clock at seven thirty was the most excruciating noise, rousing her from a sleep that felt almost drug-induced it was so deep and so pleasurable? But since she'd stopped working, sleep had evaded her, wakefulness creeping up on her in the still of the night like it never had before. It had to be anxiety, that menacing beast.

Cass eyed Puddles sleeping in his usual spot, stretched on his back like a hysterical lady on a fainting couch. He was covered partly with the pilled cashmere throw ornamenting the otherwise useless arm-chair in the corner of the room. Their snooty decorator, Carmel, had talked them into it. Apparently having a master bedroom with only a king-sized bed and a television did not qualify as a room, so a cozy club chair was purchased. Puddles loved to sleep in their room, even though his crate and toys were set up in the spare bedroom, where he happily watched Animal Planet during the day on an enormous flat-screen TV. It was a bit absurd, she knew, the way they had tricked out the adjacent room with a bone-shaped area rug, canine wall decals and felt baskets overflowing with chew toys. The minute they had a baby, Puddles would be displaced and "his room" would be transformed into a light blue or light pink paradise, but not until someone was hired to clean it with hazmat-level intensity. The poor guy didn't realize how soon that day was coming.

"You're up," Jonathan said, but it sounded more like a question. She hadn't noticed his snoring had quieted.

"Yes, I'm up. Was I stirring too much?"

"It's fine. I'll be able to fall back asleep."

Of course you will, she thought. *You'll just press your "sleep" button and drift back into dreamland.* Lately, Cass found herself resenting good sleepers the most, even more than loud talkers, slow orderers and unwanted touchers (the ones who plucked your loose threads or a detached eyelash without permission). Now it was those people who could get a reliable eight hours of shut-eye each night who had become the most detestable, even if that included her harmless husband.

"I'm gonna take a shower now. I'll be quiet." She slipped out of bed and drifted toward the bathroom. This morning she chose to stand smack-dab in the center of the shower, letting the rainfall faucet pound her evenly all over. Hot drops rolled down her face like molten tears, minus the saltiness. She licked her lips.

"We have sex once a week," she said out loud, but quietly. She liked to speak to an imaginary therapist every now and then. It was cheaper than real therapy, not that she needed to be terribly worried about such an expenditure. The freedom to spend money still managed to surprise her every time she swiped her AmEx for an overpriced latte or a new pair of heels at Bergdorf Goodman. How could it not, when she grew up in a home where the cable and electricity were turned off regularly and Cass, by age six, could recognize and decode the colors of the eviction notices stapled to their front door? A green notice was a threat but still vaguely friendly—as if to say everyone over at the sheriff's office was rooting for you to get your shit together and pay what you owed. Yellow meant you had thirty days to scrounge up the rent; red—well, red meant Cass should start packing up her room immediately. Red meant she and her mom were closer and closer to ending up in one of those trailer parks near the highway. God, she hated that color. Didn't have a stitch of red decor in the apartment she and Jonathan shared and she even avoided using it at work when possible. Marketing the revival of *The Scarlet Letter* had proved especially difficult. Her boss had chewed her out for the first time ever when she presented the poster with the pink *A*.

She didn't love her husband *because* he made a very good living (or for the comfortable nest egg his family provided), but she sure found it attractive that being Mrs. Jonathan Coyne meant that her mail was a stack of *Architectural Digests* and not letters from collection agencies. That she didn't have to try a dozen pieces of plastic before sales clerks said to her, relief and pity in their eyes, "Okay, that one went through." There was no shame in appreciating her lifestyle: on the contrary, she was proud. Up until recently, she had been contributing nicely too. And she'd continue to do so again, once . . . once . . . next steps were decided upon.

The waning of their sex life, among other things, was worrying her, though she was resistant to visiting a shrink to talk about it. For one thing, Jonathan was dismissive of talk therapy. When she told him about a coworker starting couples counseling, he sniggered and said how grateful he was that Cass was *so* not the type to drag him to anything like that. And going alone to talk through things on a couch didn't seem like it would yield much of a solution. Her friends told her their weekly sessions were essentially monologues, and you just had to pray the entire time you weren't going to run into anyone you knew in the waiting room. How would she respond when the therapist inevitably asked, "What brings you here?" Could she really answer, "I'm not sure," and then expect him to tease it out of her? Was there even anything to tease? A subtle layer of confusion clouding her everyday routine. An anxiety that shook the sleep out of her. The persistent revisiting of her past actions. Yes, it seemed there was most definitely something to be discussed, but once the genie was out of the bottle, restoring it and locking it back in the deep folds of her subconscious would be impossible. Talking to a bar of soap had fewer repercussions.

"Actually, it's more like once every two weeks," she continued aloud. If she was going to unburden herself, even if only to the glass door getting soaked by the showerhead, it might as well be the truth. "My husband works a lot. I used to as well."

Tell me more about that, the therapist responded. Or he didn't. It was always a he in her mind.

"There's nothing more to say. I just thought you should know. It seems to be an important subject." Cass looked at her waterproof watch, saw it was 5:10, and decided the session was over. Another advantage to an invisible shrink.

She worked the fragrant shampoo with the Le Bristol label on the mini bottle through her hair, scrubbing her scalp more vigorously than usual. How many bottles of that shampoo did she have left? She had filched about a dozen on her and Jonathan's trip to Paris a year ago. He'd had to go for work and she had tagged along. He didn't want her to bring home the bottles, bellyaching that airport security would think it was some kind of liquid bomb, and even if the bottles were cleared, they would surely leak in their suitcase. His undertone: *If you want fancy bath products, just go buy them—in America.* She acquiesced, but stuffed them in her luggage at the last minute anyway. They never discussed it when they got home, though Jonathan could hardly have missed the tidy row of them in their shared medicine cabinet. Lemon verbena. It smelled nice. She'd still never looked up what "verbena" was. A plant, probably. Something for rich people.

What kind of rebellion was it anyway to provoke her virtuous husband by stealing toiletries? Was it just to show him she wasn't embarrassed about where she came from? She *was* embarrassed, so what kind of move was it to try to convince him otherwise? Her insecurities fed her need to prove something to Jonathan, and though she recognized the vicious cycle, she simply couldn't break it. What was it about feeling unworthy of Jonathan that brought out the worst in her? Basic common sense would dictate that she should be her best self around him: compassionate, loving and agreeable when it came to shampoo. But the repressed sense of inferiority—the depths of which only she knew—made her constantly feel the need to test her husband, who deserved none of this in his life. She wanted to pinch herself to make it stop—this gruesome habit of playing with fire. Sometimes when she laid her head on her pillow at night, after Jonathan said his ritualistic "Night, love you," she'd swear to herself that the next day she'd be different. She'd pour his orange juice, kiss him tenderly before he headed for work and tell him how lucky she knew she was.

2. JON(ATHAN)

He was standing in front of a Bloomberg Terminal in the hallway when the new girl approached.

"Mr. Coyne, can you review these memos before I include them in the investor packet? I looked up several years of precedents before drafting, but I'm happy to make any changes you'd like."

"No problem. Just leave them on my desk. I'll call you after I look them over."

"Thanks," she said with a friendly smile, pivoting in the direction of his office. He started to watch her figure, tight and curvy, get smaller as it retreated down the hallway, but quickly looked back at the screen, out of the danger zone. So he checked out other women—every guy with a pulse did. And he didn't think he should feel particularly guilty about it. Still, it was safer to focus on stock prices after a few seconds of instinctive fantasizing.

Laurel, he thought her name was. She was a new hire at Winstar, still eager and a bit tentative, calling him "Mr. Coyne" and defending her work product. He found the vulnerability, and her desire to impress him, appealing. It would go away soon. Winstar Capital was an informal place, only twenty analysts (mostly junior, a few equity), one very rich owner, the requisite support staff, and a small investor relations team. That's where Laurel fit in—another pretty girl to keep the clients happy. They rotated through Winstar like ripening crops. Somehow hearing "the returns *have* been disappointing" was more tolerable coming from a twentysomething with perky tits and a gravity-defying ass. Laurel was fresh out of Duke and had been assigned to help manage Jonathan's clients. She was cute, with a ponytail of dark reddish hair and a Southern drawl like dripping molasses. Cass was more sophisticated, of course, her personality as layered as a mille-feuille. Simplicity could be attractive, but complication had a certain devastating allure. At least for him. He believed life would be easier if he was a meathead like so many of his college buddies and colleagues, married to Stepfords who did Pilates and shopped all day, but he couldn't change his nature.

He popped into the small office kitchen, with its flashy onyx countertops and stainless-steel everything, and made himself an elaborate cappuccino. *What was Cass doing now?* he wondered. It was strange to think of his wife at home all day. Unlikely she was enjoying her time off with daytime television. Judge Judy or Steve Harvey would make her skin crawl. Many things did, actually. It made pleasing her that much more satisfying. He never set out to love that type of woman, the kind requiring so much work, but it seemed to be his fate. To have married anyone else would have been like trying to swim upstream. Right now, Cass, his predestined bride, was probably reading Playbill online or palling around Central Park with Puddles. Their beloved Choodle (half Chihuahua/half poodle) came from a shelter because of Cass's "concern" for the neglected animals of the world. She had opposed going to the breeder his family had used for decades. Maybe it was unfair, the way he put air quotes around her concern.

She would have his balls if he ever did that in public. He just hoped she wasn't thinking about Percy all day. He blamed Percy, or rather the absence of her beloved boss, for her sleeplessness and their recent lack of intimacy.

"Women are all a lot of work," claimed his rowing buddy Anders, the first of Jonathan's friends from Brown to get married, over drinks one night after he and Cass had been out a couple of times. Jonathan already knew at that point she'd be complicated. He'd been Jon until he was twenty-eight years old. Then, after one date with Cass, he'd been rechristened Jonathan. The weird thing was, he was okay with it.

"Has anyone ever called you Jonathan?" Cass had asked, making a show of dipping her french fry into ketchup and letting it linger on the trip to her mouth like it was on a sensual journey. They were at Burger Joint in Le Parker Meridien hotel, a kind of hole-in-the-wall that was cool for its randomness. He'd settled on that choice after deciding against trying to impress her with Boulud or Gramercy Tavern, feeling somehow that would strike the wrong chord. Cass ate a lot on their first date, which he liked, but he couldn't shake the feeling she was doing it for his benefit. It was a classic first-date move, the hoping-to-impress-by-attempting-not-to-impress act. He normally hated them (first dates)—their awkwardness was reason enough to settle down—but this encounter was going better than most, even though they'd both obviously put in some thought about how to play things.

"No, why?"

"It's nice," she'd said. Simple as that. She never said, *I'd like to call you Jonathan*. Or, *I dislike nicknames*. Just "It's nice." And he, the fool, the romantic, the sexually charged, had responded, "You're right. I think I'd like to try being Jonathan."

Headboard-gripping, doggy-style sex followed a few dates later. Maybe she wasn't that hard to please after all.

His mother, another woman for whose approval he'd worked overly hard (until Cass came along and siphoned off all his energy), was less enthused with the change. You'd think she'd be happy. She named him Jonathan, after twenty-seven hours of grueling labor with a failed epidural. He was supposed to be Christopher, like his dad, but Betsy thought it was pedestrian—the handyman who tended to her parents' Fisher Island home was named Chris—so she declared naming rights while the doctor stitched her level-four tears. Jonathan Edward Coyne: it got written so quickly on his birth certificate that his father, the man who was meant to become Christopher Sr., barely had a second to quibble. By grade school, he was Jon, and Betsy never put up a fight. She'd won the war; the battle was beneath her.

Betsy had scowled sharply the first time she heard Cass call him Jonathan. This was noteworthy because Betsy DeWalt Coyne did almost everything with subtlety. If you didn't stare at her intently, you could almost miss the dismissive eye roll, the gentle shrug of disapproval or the quick pursing of her lips. Big emotions, loud voices—those were crude, decidedly "ethnic," according to his mother. So the scowl, which darkened her face so fiercely that it seemed like a rain cloud had stationed itself above her head, was significant. It meant his mother's reaction to Cass was so visceral that even she, the queen of composure, couldn't hide it.

Fucking women. Whoever said, "You can't live with them, you can't live without them," was a true genius.

He glanced at his watch as he returned to his office, frothy drink in hand. It was past eleven. If she'd gone to the gym instead of trolling the Broadway blogs, she'd surely be back by now. He thought about what Cass had declared just the other day—that she would use her time off to get into the best shape of her life. Said she'd spin, lengthen, tone, crunch, and stretch the days away. He didn't say what he wanted to say: that he didn't understand how that goal fit in with their other stated goal. Because Cass said a lot of things, and didn't mean half of them. His marriage ran a lot smoother once he realized that. Maybe he'd give her a call at home now, just to check in. As he picked up the receiver, his boss, Jerry, walked in with his usual burst of self-importance. Jerry was the kind of guy who got off on people's automated responses to his arrival: phones slipped back into pockets, sucking candies discreetly tossed, spines stacked more uprightly. But he'd earned it—a self-made man was always entitled to have swagger—and Jonathan didn't mind straightening his tie when his boss came in.

"Jonathan, the energy gods are smiling on us. Ginny called to say she caught enough of CNBC this morning to know she could go crazy in the stores today." Ginny: the prototypical Stepford. "You've done well, son," he continued.

Jerry's use of "son" was unique. It wasn't particularly parental or avuncular, but it wasn't condescending either. It was something else, a Jerry-ism, and since Jonathan's own father never called him "son," he took it for what it was—some measure of affection, however attenuated. And Ginny. She was a first wife, *surprise, surprise*, but had nipped and tucked herself into someone who could easily pass as a second. Jonathan loved that Cass was nothing like Ginny, fitting into some prefab mold like Jell-O, but then again he was no Jerry either. Jerry's meteoric rise from son of an oil rigger in Texas to one of the highest-paid energy traders (the poetic symmetry duly noted) was nearly apocryphal, while Jonathan's own ascending career was rather less newsworthy. His father and both grandfathers were investment bankers from Boston, back when shoes were white and gin was a lunchtime staple. To get where he was, all Jonathan had to do was not screw up in any material way. Which he had, actually, but he was lucky that it occurred in that halcyon era just before every incident and rumor were documented for posterity online. Cass made a point of reminding Jonathan that he owed his professional success to no one but himself, that he'd turned down a courtesy title at his father's firm in favor of an independent path, even if it was in a related industry. (That part couldn't be helped—numbers were in the Coyne blood.) She'd identified his weak spot and chosen to massage it. He loved her for it, and hoped one day he could do the same for her. What were her weaknesses, though? Sometimes he thought he knew Cass inside and out, while other times the words that fell from her mouth made his wife seem like a total stranger. In the same vein, sometimes Cass could seem like the most confident woman in the world, and then she'd be petty and insecure a beat later. When he was a younger man, newly married and without a clue, he tried to match up these mood swings to her cycle, but found he wasn't so lucky as to be able to predict her volatility with any type of regular rhythm.

"It's been a good quarter so far," Jonathan agreed, with the innate modesty to which he attributed his success at Winstar. He got the feeling he was Jerry's favorite analyst, if such things could be measured by the number of office pop-ins, backslaps and those "sons." Other guys around him got ahead with relentless self-promotion, some of them even stealing credit for Jonathan's own conquests. But he preferred to keep a lower profile. And he found that even at a hedge fund, some old-fashioned humility could still be rewarded. Yes, he was a hard worker and exhaustively researched all the tips and noise that came his way, but his whole presence at Winstar could be boiled down to an accident of birth if you looked back far enough. More importantly, it could all just as easily crash, and when it went in the other direction— as it always inevitably did—he didn't want to be held responsible the way he was credited for the uptick.

"Keep this up and you'll be an equity analyst in no time. How's Cass? She find a new job yet? Not that she needs one now."

"Not yet. I'm not sure she's looking all that hard, to be honest. We're thinking about a kid. It's time."

Jerry nodded approvingly.

"Ginny would love to take Cass to lunch. I'll have her give her a call." His boss turned away, strutting toward his corner office.

Lunch with Ginny Winston. That would probably rate even lower than daytime television for Cass. But it had to be done. At least he and

Cass would have a lot to talk about afterward. They called it "dissection," their analysis of conversations and interactions with other people, acting as though they were lab partners probing a foreign body.

He leaned back in his chair. Four monitors showing the Asian, U.S., Latin American and European markets blazed green and red wavy lines across his desk, like an EKG report. Oil prices were soaring. Copper was up too. He lifted the memos Laurel had left on his desk and gave them a good read. He barely had any changes. Smart girl. Maybe he'd talk to her about revising the quarterly packets they sent to investors. He'd had it in his head for a while to trim them and simplify the language. But it was probably a better idea to make Peter, a newish analyst, take the first bite at it rather than asking Laurel. Temptation was always showing up unannounced—he didn't need to give it a personal invitation.

He moved his gaze over to the wedding photo perched on his desk, sunlight bouncing off the elegant frame. He brought it closer to appreciate the wide, gummy smile on Cass's face. Her dress, strapless, straight, simple, was exactly what he'd expected her to pick. It went along with her pared-down aesthetic, which crossed over from her design work. The gown had no train in need of bustling, no frivolous beading or lace. Back when Cass was on the hunt for her dress, she'd printed several pictures of Carolyn Bessette on her wedding day for inspiration. He always wondered if that made him a John-John—is that how Cass saw him? Probably not, she just liked the simple dress. Cass wasn't the kind of woman who played "wedding" with her dolls. Her childhood best friend, Tiffany, whom he'd met on one of their infrequent trips back to his wife's hometown, told him a story of Cass leasing her the Barbie convertible she received for Christmas after she grew tired of playing with it. Apparently the terms were fair: a bag of Twizzlers and a pack of Garbage Pail Kids every month, no interest.

He glanced at his calendar and saw only two meetings scheduled for the afternoon. Sneaking out early was a possibility. Maybe he and

Cass could grab a bite instead of their usual scrounge-or-Seamless routine. But then he remembered he was meeting Leon at Starbucks on 112th Street at six. He couldn't bail on Leon. His Little Brother had specifically asked Jonathan for help reviewing his college essay after their last group outing. Oh well, he'd have dinner out with Cass another night. She would understand. Cass loved Leon.

Five years of marriage. The days were long but the years were flying by. Or maybe the days were short but the years were dragging. Somehow the rhythm of their lives felt askew—maybe because they weren't marking it with children's milestones yet (#twoweeksoldtoday or #teddysfirstsmile). Jonathan wasn't quite sure why, but it felt like loving Cass could somehow warp time.

3. CASS

"THEY'RE REALLY, REALLY cute, Jem," Cass said with a mouth full of guacamole and chips. Burn four hundred calories in spin class, consume eight hundred calories three hours later when her insides felt like they were eating themselves for survival. That was the latest pastime of her sabbatical—finding sense in the nonsensical.

Jemima vigorously nodded her agreement, looking at her children like they were the Second Coming. It was love so entirely pure and all-encompassing that Cass couldn't help feeling jealous. *Count your own blessings,* she reminded herself. It had become something of a daily chant for her lately.

"I'm not supposed to say it, right? That they're so adorable? But you don't have your own yet so I think I can."

Cass tried to follow that logic, not that she should be critiquing anyone's stream of consciousness. Her own looked like a Rorschach test.

"Jasper? Blakey? Come hug Mummy."

The twins, newly three, borderline obedient, trotted over and jumped onto Cass's couch to nestle into waiting arms, their salsa-stained hands leaving drops like fresh blood on the Ultrasuede. It was washable. Carmel the decorator, for all her insistence on unnecessary chairs and insufferable references to channeling Coco Chanel's atelier, was exceptionally good at picking easy-to-live-with materials. And for that Cass was grateful, considering she hadn't wanted to use a decorator in the first place and only did so because Jonathan suggested it and she was getting crushed at work at the time (two national tours of hit musicals, three new plays each with questionable subject matter at the Public) and didn't have the bandwidth to devote to the apartment. So while Cass could have chosen a pleasing palette and designed an efficient furniture plan, she didn't have a clue about thread counts and dye lots and durability and the difference between calacatta and terrazzo. Carmel had worked with enough young couples to know how to poop-proof and snot-proof chicly. Their decorator didn't have to ask Cass and Jonathan about whether they planned to have children in the apartment. One look at them, the smiling and strapping Coynes holding hands in the design meetings, and procreation seemed inevitable.

Before she moved in with Jonathan, Cass lived in a fifth-floor walk-up in the West Village. She did a decent job fixing up the place—and the daily hike up and down gave her a killer ass—but there was only so far she could go with her starter salary, most of which was going directly to pay down her college loans. She could repaint an Ikea cabinet and repurpose it as a bar cart, but it was still a few cheap slabs of particle board screwed together. She was reminded of that fact when it started to fall apart after only a few months. It would have been nice if her father, a contractor by trade, could have helped with the assembly. The instructions might as well have still been in Swedish. But her subpar accommodations didn't matter that much to her—she was out every night seeing a show or working late in the office, and it just felt so good to be on her own. She had been de facto "on her own" since childhood, but, as a working woman, it finally felt like her independence and stage of life were appropriately aligned. She was never going to get visits from her parents to see her apartment or to take her for a trendy brunch in the Village, but at least she wasn't alone, cowering in the library, on Parents' Weekend.

The first time she and Jonathan met with Carmel after their engagement to discuss redoing his bachelor pad, Cass had to keep pinching herself under the table to confirm it wasn't a dream. She was choosing fabrics that cost three hundred dollars a yard, and someone else was paying for it without blinking an eye. She'd known that Jonathan's career was going well—thank God she'd never considered settling down with one of the theater guys from college who were all probably on unemployment now—but still, this was almost too much to take in. When the decorator's snarky assistant asked them for a deposit for the living room sofa, Cass had asked, innocently enough, for the details of the layaway plan. "No, honey," he'd said, hand on hip, "this isn't a payment plan. It's standard to pay the atelier 50 percent up front for a custom piece." Jonathan had squeezed her knee gently. It was a gesture of reassurance. His touch meant, "I don't care that you don't know about crap like this." But Cass had wanted to shrivel up and disappear behind the marble breakfront—another exorbitantly priced object headed to their home. Yes, she was thrilled the days of layaway and wearing dresses with discreetly hidden tags only to return them the next day were over, but she hated the way she couldn't shake feeling like trailer trash, that she was nothing without Jonathan. The contrast between them was too vast. And there was just so much for her to learn. Always.

Cass edged closer to Jemima and the twins, cozily scrunched together on that very same couch, and let her forearms brush up against the huddle. What she liked most about her neighbor's children was the feel of their skin. It was buttery soft and supple, the smoothest thing she'd ever touched in her whole life. That thought made her sad. Thirty-four years old and the best things she'd ever stroked were the alabaster cheeks of the toddlers in Apartment 16E. The closest second was the ikat fabric Carmel covered everything in.

"It's so much work, though," Jemima volunteered as Blake shoved a football-shaped cookie into her mouth. "These kids suck the living daylights out of me. I almost never get a break. Even with Manuela and the part-time nanny, I'm washing, cleaning, calming or playing with something or someone the entire day. You'll see soon enough. We"—she leaned in conspiratorially and covered the twins' ears (the outer ears with her hands, the inner ones by suctioning them together, forcing a shriek out of Jasper)—"basically never have sex. We're too tired."

"Neither do we," Cass said, but the words lodged in her mouth so that all that actually came out was a cross between a groan and a mumble. Better that she didn't say it anyway. Her mother was perhaps the opposite of a fountain of wisdom, but she had wisely advised Cass not to air dirty laundry—probably because she herself had so much of it. Besides, people were so weird about sex. Yes, intimate details were shared. Gaggles of girls whispered over dirty martinis at overpriced restaurants, "He couldn't find my g-spot with a map" or "Anal was an utter disaster for us." But the deep, dark truths, the ones that could reveal weaknesses in the fibers of a relationship, those were kept subterranean, and so you never really knew when you heard "We never have sex," if that meant no more than once a week, or whether long, dry months had passed, causing condoms to expire and converting NuvaRings into vestigial body parts.

It is worth it, though, isn't it? Cass wanted to ask this deep and pressing question of her neighbor, whose answer might be a simple "Of course" or a cascading litany of trade-offs and hedges. Cass had always imagined that sacrificing her sanity and energy to have children who charged at her when she came through the door and always seemed to smell like baby powder and lemon zest was a no-brainer. But what about work? Cass wondered if Jemima missed it—their shared industry, so full of passion and creativity and, yes, glamour at times. But she couldn't really ask now. Not in front of the twins. Maybe she'd ask Jemima the next time they were alone—she theorized it happening post–spin class, when they were both sweaty and ready for truths to spill out of open pores, or over manicures while the technicians were distracted. Though really, she knew the chances of her probing this topic with her friend were quite low. Again, honesty would be an issue, hers and Jemima's. Besides, Cass's concerns with parenthood would be wholly unrelatable to Jemima. Hers were borne of unique circumstances that belonged solely to her and Jonathan.

Across the living room, on low-slung Barcelona chairs, the other halves of these theoretically sexually deprived couples sat. Jonathan had a cold beer in his hand, a monogrammed linen cocktail napkin wrapped around it to catch the beads of condensation. It was a ridiculous sight, the Amstel covered in an E. Braun napkin that probably cost a fortune and took two months to make if you believed the whole "handmade in Florence" bit. But didn't she love that? That Jonathan knew about "good" napkins but didn't care enough to treat them with any particular respect? Nothing could be a further image from her upbringing. Her mom took one-ply napkins from the McDonald's dispenser and stuffed them in her purse. The only time Cass saw ketchup come out of a squeeze bottle was at a playdate. Otherwise, it arrived in tiny packets pilfered from the condiment bar. Maybe that's where her Le Bristol shampoo kleptomania came from. She could bring that up at her next shower therapy session, while she worked the stolen goods through her roots.

Next to Jonathan, Jemima's husband, Henry, sat with his paunch of a stomach spilling over his thighs, his shirt pulled so tightly across his chest a button was sure to pop off before the fourth quarter. Something good happened on the screen. Both men screamed, jumped up, hugged wildly, then peeled apart like one of them had told the other he had leprosy. Men were so strange about physical closeness, particularly her husband, who spooned her after sex for less than thirty seconds before rolling over or, worse, hopping in the shower. She didn't want to complain about it, though, to become one of those wives bemoaning a lack of intimacy. She wanted to be above clichés. At least she knew not to take the lack of warmth personally. It was Super Bowl Sunday and her husband couldn't embrace his friend without shame after a Giants touchdown. Correction: a field goal tying up the score. Cass really couldn't give a crap. But it was better than sitting alone with Jonathan on the sofa, Chinese containers stinking up the apartment and her caring not a lick about the game. In those circumstances, she'd have ended up doing both of Puddles's nightly walks in the freezing cold because the Super Bowl was sacred, an automatic pass for husbands. So she invited the Wentworths instead. Jonathan was thrilled. And she'd had an excuse to hire the dog walker: *entertaining.* What would her mother, or Tiff, or anyone else from home say if they caught wind that she shelled out forty bucks to have someone else scoop the poop for one evening? She'd been walking Puddles during the day since leaving her job without any trouble, but the night walks on the icy streets, those she particularly hated.

Luckily, Jemima wasn't judgmental and knew virtually nothing of where Cass had come from. They knew each other from work and had a long history together as far as friendships formed post-college went. They'd worked on the same show several years before Jemima gave birth to the twins, a revival of *Cat on a Hot Tin Roof* that Cass was marketing and for which Jemima was designing the costumes. The wardrobe choices were impeccable. Cass had never seen a more sensual and explosive Maggie. After seeing the show in previews, Cass felt compelled to reach out to the costume designer. She was a newcomer named Jemima Bartlett who had recently brought her talents Stateside from the West End. A friendship bloomed and they met frequently for lunch in the Broadway district and dished about the bitchy insiders they both had to contend with. A few years later, Jemima was fixed up with Henry Wentworth, also a Brit, and got pregnant on their honeymoon. They left their Upper West Side rental for Brooklyn in search of square footage and a small backyard, even though it meant a harder commute for both of them.

The Wentworths were initially charmed by Park Slope, even admitting to joining the famously high-handed food co-op, where the couple had mandatory shifts peddling bee pollen. But when Jasper and Blake were only two months old, Cass received a frantic email from Jemima detailing a harrowing scene at a breastfeeding support group that she attended strictly to make friends. The truth was that the feeding was going fine for Jemima—she'd stick a kid on each tit and watch *Kathie Lee & Hoda* at ten, *Days of Our Lives* at one, *Ellen* at four and *Jeopardy!* at seven. According to her, it was the least guilty she'd ever felt about her TV addiction. Still, she needed a mommy crew to roll with now that she'd taken an indefinite leave from her job, so she googled "mastitis" and headed for the pretentious Bend & Bloom yoga studio with her double stroller. There she found, in her words, "Bloody preschoolers demanding milk from their mums. I told Henry, to hell with the tiny excuse for a backyard we have. We're moving back to Manhattan where children who can talk drink cow's milk." Cass had felt her nipples tingle at their conversation. She wanted to think it was a sign of readiness, but more likely it was a biological reaction to the memory of hearing her mother say to friends that it had been easier and cheaper to breastfeed Cass than to bother going out for formula.

On impulse, Cass had told Jemima that their next-door neighbors were moving to the suburbs and vacating a lovely Classic Six if the Wentworths were interested in having a look. She didn't think Jem would actually bite, but she and Henry jumped on the F train, each of them clutching a twin and oohing and aahing the next day over what would be the twins' room and the kitchen's southern exposure.

Cass never appreciated just how talkative and unguarded Jem was until they became neighbors. Only then did she notice how her friend was eerily similar to a well-shaken soda can, prepared to bubble over if someone pulled her tab. This was especially true after a few drinks. Initially it made Cass nervous to be around someone who shared so much. She worried about having to give after all that take. But several years later Jemima still seemed content with the one-way nature of their relationship, and everything Cass had vaulted didn't seem to be in any danger of getting out. Henry and Jonathan got on well enough. Between sports and the Dow Jones, they didn't seem to lack for conversation. The Wentworth twins lived for Puddles, and Cass approved of anyone who appreciated Puddles's supremacy over all other dogs. It was a happy living arrangement, not quite Melrose Place, but with Jemima's unwillingness to acknowledge that American football was a real thing and Cass's utter disinterest in sports, having them over for the Super Bowl was pretty ideal. The way their neighbors interacted— Henry often saying something inappropriate (misogynist comments were his jaw-dropper of choice, though he got away with it more than he should have because of his charming accent), Jemima swatting at him but secretly loving his irreverence—would give her and Jonathan so much to discuss over leftover pigs in a blanket once their guests left. *Dissection*: their favorite.

"More wine?" Cass turned to Jemima, the bottle of Sancerre in her hand sweating onto her friend's leather pants. Jem nodded appreciatively. She claimed her alcohol consumption tripled after having the twins, meaning a ratio of 1.5 drinks per child. Cass was already gently lying to her internist about her own drinking habits. Intake form: *How many drinks do you consume per week?* She'd scribble a five that could all too easily be mistaken for a three. She couldn't imagine where her drinking would go after childbirth, especially on the heels of nine months of forced sobriety. Jonathan almost never drank to excess—she'd marvel at how he'd manage to leave over half a glass of wine at dinner when she'd gulped hers down before the appetizer arrived.

"Mummy?" Blake said, looking suddenly green-tinged and hollow. "I'm not feeling so good."

Jemima rolled her eyes at Cass while stroking her daughter's back. "It never ends," she mouthed.

"Henry, we have to go. Blake's stomach again."

Cass watched as Henry rose slowly from his chair, the expression he shot to Jonathan clearly indicating that he didn't understand why that meant he should have to leave too.

"Now," Jemima snapped.

Blake tugged wildly at her mother's hand, signaling an urgency that frightened Cass. A moment after the door to their apartment shut and certainly before the Wentworths made it the ten paces to their home, the sounds of violent retching could be heard.

Jesus, was that going to be her soon? Cass wondered. Mopping up puke, leaving parties early, sniping at her husband about shared responsibilities. Perhaps, but it would also be her French-braiding silken fine hair and securing it with satin ribbons, ordering Brown onesies online, lending a hand to assist those first wobbly steps. Those moments would surely eclipse the grunt work, she assured herself as she settled back onto the couch and gazed at her husband, wondering if any of these thoughts were running through his mind. For her at least, having a child was an opportunity to do everything so much better than she'd had it. Maybe so for Jonathan too, to a lesser extreme. They would make good parents, she and Jonathan, just so long as she could keep her head out of her ass and appreciate how good things were. But the reality was that having a child with Jonathan would mean increased dependence on him. And that wasn't something she could easily abide after so many years of going it alone. She was scared to need someone so acutely.

As she surveyed the shipwreck conditions of her apartment, her cell phone dinged.

Sorry about that, Jemima wrote. **Hoping that you'll come to the twins' bday party next weekend. It's at Chelsea Piers. I promise to serve wine.**

Cass stared at the text. She really should go—she saw those kids almost every day, or at least she heard them through the plaster walls of their adjoining apartments. But birthday parties brought back the very worst of her childhood, and she'd need more than wine to get through this one intact. For sure Jemima and Henry would pull out all the stops for Blake and Jasper—probably two cakes, two sets of decorations, two tables overflowing with presents. Through age nine, Cass had never had a birthday party. Her mother would buy a Duncan Hines cake mix that Cass would be tasked with making, except there'd always be some essential ingredient missing, like the eggs or the vegetable oil. *Nota bene: Do not substitute canola oil.* Finally, for her double digits, her mother promised her a party at Miss Louise's Dance Studio in the nearby and exclusive town of Bloomfield Hills. In this, Cass felt the effects of her extra leverage that was due to her parents' recent split. For weeks in advance of the party, Cass went over every detail with Tiff, whose father was a known drunk and whose mother had abandoned the family years earlier. She was maybe the only person to whom Cass felt lucky in comparison. She and Tiff discussed ad nauseam what games would be played, what the favors would be, and who would be invited—both Melanie R. and Melanie B. had said yes! Cass tried on her party dress a dozen times—a bit small on her but still stylish—and twirled around in front of the mirror every night until she was dizzy. And then, three days before, when the anticipation was mounting so much that she could barely concentrate on homework, her mother came into her bedroom looking solemn. "What's up?" Cass had asked, though she had a sinking suspicion what was coming.

"Listen, Cassidy, the landlord said if I don't get him the back rent by Friday, he's going to kick us out. We just can't have your party. He's being a real son of a bitch," she added, as though it was their humorless landlord who was to blame. Cass looked up at her mother. The black streaks that Donna swiped across her top and bottom lash lines every morning had smudged into puddles of coal. She looked like a witch.

That night Cass waited until her mother was asleep, then used the kitchen phone to call her father. She explained the situation to him, begging him to help her out. She knew that his new girlfriend was already pregnant and that money was tight, but her father had an ego and she used a mixture of flattery and supplication to convince him. "You got it, baby girl," he said, and she exhaled fully for the first time since her mother had dropped the bomb a few hours earlier. But her relief didn't last long. The next day her mother came back up to her room after work and said, sharply, "Next time, talk to me before going to your father for help. Miss Louise said there is no chance she'll host your party if your father is paying. He subbed in shitty parts last year during her renovation and left her with a leaky roof and warped doors. She said he was lucky she didn't sue." And with that, Donna walked out of the room before seeing her daughter collapse in a fit of tears. The rest of the night was devoted to scheming up a cover story to hide the shame of her canceled party. She settled on telling her classmates that she'd twisted her ankle at gymnastics (as if her parents would ever pay for an after-school class) and couldn't dance. Cass spent the next two weeks getting around school with a fake hobble. And the thing was, the kids bought the excuse, helping carry her books and sitting with her on the bench during recess. By age ten, Cass had learned the simple and useful art of lying.

Of course we'll be there, she texted back to Jemima. Hope Blake feels better.

When was Luna coming to clean? she asked herself, studying the aftermath of the twins' visit. They had pillaged drawers, spilled juices, pulled off every pillow and somehow managed to go through at least six plates and four cups each. Hopefully their cleaning lady would show by Wednesday.

Cass disliked a mess. Unfortunately, just not enough to do much about it.

4. JONATHAN

"THANK YOU" WAS definitely not what he planned to say to Cass after he rolled off of her, peeling the condom off carefully so as not to drip on the sheets because his wife hated the wet spot. Sex with a latex barrier between them. It was like high school all over again. He was in the music room at Exeter and had come, once again, way too quickly with the captain of the girls' field hockey team and his first, if not true love, then at least infatuation.

He wanted to say to Cass, *That was great.* Or, even better, *I love you.* But instead he said, "Thank you," like he was some pathetic teenager. Maybe it was the condom, the déjà vu of it all, wreaking havoc on his mind-to-mouth neural pathways. Or maybe it was just that they hadn't had sex in a while, and he was genuinely grateful and wanted his wife to know it.

Cass had been off the pill for more than a month already. By the spring, they would start trying, when the hormones were definitely out of her body. He didn't even mind the wait—the timing could mean a

Christmas baby. So for the time being, it was condoms. Why he felt like a pervert when he bought them at CVS he didn't understand. Or maybe it was more that he felt pathetic. Like the checkout girl with the overflowing breasts and the tongue ring gave a shit whether he had to wear protection. He made sure she took note of his wedding ring, swiping his AmEx awkwardly with his left hand. Only on the way home did he realize the stupidity of that move. It was much worse to be married and wearing a condom than to be some single guy running out to the pharmacy while a hot body waited in his bed.

Cass giggled at him. "Anytime," she responded, pulling down the Brown T-shirt that was hiked up to her shoulders. He wanted her so much more when she wore a ratty tee to bed than when she had the whole lacy getup on. Made him feel like he was in a porno, where people were always having sex at unexpected times: borrowing milk from a neighbor, buzzing the nurse to adjust the light. Sometimes he liked to be reminded of her grittiness.

It had been thirteen days since the last time they'd had sex. Jonathan could rarely remember what he'd had for breakfast, or how many times a day the vet said to give Puddles his reflux medicine, and certainly not whether he had locked the front door. But Jonathan could always pinpoint the last time he and Cass had had sex. Before tonight, it was after they came home from a fortieth birthday dinner for one of his colleagues. Cass had had three basil Bellinis, he'd had two scotches—double his usual; both were primed and ready the minute their apartment door slammed shut behind them. Cass was adventurous early on, but things had definitely taken a turn for the routine. Maybe they'd just run out of things to try. No, that definitely couldn't be—there was a world of kink and experimentation that he and his wife had never so much as approached. Twice he'd suggested that they try "the back door" and both times Cass brushed it off. Once she emitted a nervous laugh, trying to play it off like he was joking. The second time she'd just pretended not to hear him.

So they tended to stick to missionary, and foreplay was often forsaken in favor of watching *Shark Tank*, but what disappointed him most was the occasions on which they had sex. After a dinner party. On their anniversary. When he got his bonus. It was so . . . so . . . so not the kitchen floor at 10:00 a.m. just for the hell of it. Still, he wouldn't quite say he was bored, not yet anyway. Sex was like pizza. Even when it was cold and soggy, it was still good.

"I think Jemima had Botox," Cass said, and Jonathan understood at once why she was so forgiving of his embarrassing show of gratitude. She wanted to get to her climax—the gossip. "She's all, I used to live in Brooklyn, Jasper and Blake have never eaten a goldfish cracker, but I swear her eyebrows are no longer moving."

"I thought she looked good," Jonathan said, realizing his mistake a second too late.

"Really?" Cass said, propping herself on her side, primed for battle. "You like that cellophane look?"

"I like your look," he said, disarming her. "I like your little chin, your eyes, your tiny nose, your smell, your everything." He meant it. Cass was soul-crushingly beautiful. She knew it—the way she could turn heads—but it wasn't a crime to own your own power. That day six years ago, when he ran into her at Park Avenue and 52nd Street, she had literally taken his breath away, doubly so when he realized who she was. In college, his vague recollections of Cass were that she was something of a tomboy. She wore cargo pants, Converse high-tops and simple tank tops—clearly not an L.L.Bean shopper like everyone else he knew. Her top half was lithe (breasts barely jutting out farther than her flat stomach), but her bottom half was round and full, making the boyish-girl thing never fit her quite as believably as perhaps she hoped for. But professional Cass, the one standing outside the Seagram Building looking for a taxi, was a different story. She was wearing tight black pants, high heels and a sleeveless top with a pair of oversized sunglasses perched atop her shorn and highlighted hair.

Jonathan was sure he liked what he saw—so did all the guys in his group, from what he could tell. When she smiled, he noted with pleasure that she hadn't fixed the imperfection of her two front teeth (the left slightly encroaching on the right) that he remembered from that night at Paragon. And now this gorgeous creature, evolved better than Darwin could have imagined, while still possessing enough nuance to make her approachable, wanted to talk to him. She hugged him. Asked him to have coffee! The woman had a face he knew he could look at for the rest of his life and be content. A thousand-watt smile that could literally serve as his power source. Yes, he would have coffee with her.

"You spoil me," Cass said, but he knew she would have been happy for him to go on.

"Tonight was fun," he said, after Cass settled herself back into the crook of his arm. "Thank you for having Henry and Jemima over." Damn it, he'd thanked her again. They were married five years already. When would his constant need to praise and thank his wife for every little thing start to subside? If the answer was never, well, that was a large pill to swallow.

"They're my friends too," she said, stiffening just the slightest bit in his embrace.

"I know, of course. It's just I know Henry can be a jackass sometimes, when he's not being hilarious. Tonight he was decently behaved, I thought. His fund closed down 20 percent. Maybe his shitty Christmas bonus is fostering some humility."

"Well, your fund is up, what, like a billion percent? Is that going to make you an asshole?" Her words were harsh but her voice was sweet, teasing.

"You know it's not, Cass. Anyway, their kids were pretty cute, up until Blake's stomach explosion. Jasper must have rubbed Puddles's back for the entire third quarter."

At hearing his name, Puddles rolled over and let out a screechy bark.

"It's great that kids love our dog. Actually, even better that Puddles loves kids. Jem told me her doctor said she only had to be off the pill for two months before they tried. Maybe we can start sooner."

"That'd be amazing. Oh—Ginny wants to take you to lunch. Sorry, but you gotta go. Jerry really goes in for this Winstar family stuff."

"No, it's fine. I've been starving from all this damn exercise. I'll suggest we eat at the Cosmopolitan Club. They do a decadent lobster lunch on Wednesdays. If we're going to be trying, I might as well just get fat now anyway. I'll tell Ginny I have an appointment right around the club. Trust me, she'll pounce on the chance to show off her protégée in the dining room. Because Jerry's kept her around, she thinks we're supposed to take her word as gospel. You're not the trade-in type, though, at least I don't think." She jabbed him playfully in the ribs, then looked up at him in expectation of more praise.

"Definitely not," he said, happy that was at least true. Whatever his misdeeds, he'd never *seriously* entertained trading Cass in for anyone. "Besides, you're practically like Sybil. I already feel like I have multiple wives." He liked that answer. Normally Cass was the quick one. And he was happy to hear her say she was ready to bulk up in anticipation of the baby. He felt reassured knowing they were on the same page.

"Very funny. One of my other personalities feels like reading now," she said, reaching for the hardcover on her bedside table. It was a biography of Harry Truman. He found it sexy that Cass read only nonfiction, that she liked documentaries, that she was amazing at trivia. The trouble of course was her memory, which rivaled the wisest of elephants. It would surely come to bite him in the ass one day. Telling Cass something and hoping she'd let it slide to the outer recesses of her mind was impossible. Everything seemed to stay front and center. Her institutional memory of every play and musical performed in the past three decades was a valuable asset at work—but at home, her recollection of every one of his missteps was less beneficial. It was the price he paid for a wife with a mind on steroids.

At that moment, Cass leaned over unexpectedly and planted the gentlest of kisses on his cheek, which left residue from her fragrant lip balm. It was sticky and he thought to wipe it off, but he liked going to sleep with a piece of Cass on him. He felt his eyelids grow heavy with happiness. It wasn't the end of the world that his wife left her glasses, books and the TV remote in the bed every night instead of putting them on her empty night table. Those were nothings—just tiny spikes in his blood pressure. And he knew he had plenty of annoying habits too—though come to think of it, Cass was vocal about his, whereas he generally kept mum.

He wished he could stay awake a few minutes longer, to fully enjoy this precious time with Cass, her curled up next to him, the melody of their chatter punctuated with only a few car horns and the purring of the radiator. In this moment he was sure they were happy, still capable of making each other laugh after six years together. It wasn't that much time in the grand scheme of life, but a divorced friend once told him he knew on his wedding day that he was making a mistake. Jonathan had taken that to heart, always finding comfort in his lack of wedding-day jitters. And what about Cass? Had she been nervous in the moment? There was definitely a tense look on her face that he caught when he glanced over at her during his toast—but he was fairly confident it was because of her family's presence, which could send anyone's orbit into a tailspin. His family wasn't much better, though proper behavior at weddings was not something he needed to worry about. If anything, that type of thing was their forte.

"Great. Love you, Cass," he said as he rolled away from her. "Can you please—"

"Done. It's set for a quarter to six. Love you too," she added softly.

He noticed her looking up at the ceiling, probably calculating how many hours of sleep she could get if she fell asleep right then. Why couldn't she sleep well anymore? he wondered again, hoping it was Percy and nothing more. He turned on his side, his back to Cass, and in no time he was out.

◆ ◆ ◆

THE NEXT MORNING, Cass's side of the bed was empty when Jonathan blinked open his eyes at sunrise.

"Cass?" he called to the blankness, and got no response. He pulled himself out from the covers and ambled over to the laptop they shared, which was open atop their dresser. The screen was all hard bodies and glistening muscles. He squinted and made out the schedule for Core-Train, one of these crazy hybrid workouts Cass had told him about. Looked like she'd set out for the 6:15 class. Hadn't she just said the night before she was ready to give it all up since they were going to have a baby? He couldn't shake the feeling at times that he was only hearing 50 percent of what she was thinking.

When she threw him for a loop, like this morning, he always went back to their origins. Cass didn't seem particularly withholding when they first got reacquainted, the bits and pieces of her backstory flowing to him in a steady tide. At their first coffee, she told him all about her job on Broadway, triggering the memory of her telling him years earlier that she was a theater arts major and that she took classes at the Rhode Island School of Design. She said it was why she had chosen Brown, and that puzzle piece clicked nicely, but years later he overheard her explaining to one of the Big Brother kids that Leon hung with that Brown had offered her the most generous financial-aid package of the Ivy League schools, after she had been admitted to an embarrassing six of eight. Why didn't she tell him that the first time they met, Jonathan had wondered, and what else was she keeping from him? And did he exude such an obvious elitism? It was like the Coyne travel schedule—the summers on Martha's Vineyard, the winters on Fisher Island—was printed across his goddamn forehead and not just noted in his mother's datebook. After he'd worked so hard to beat back any latent propensity for snobbery in high school, here was this interesting girl who still chose to stay silent about her upbringing.

Maybe his mother's hoity-toity affect was hereditary. No, then it wouldn't be an affect. It would be imprinted in Betsy's DNA, and she was too deliberate about her every move for that to be true. Maybe Cass's lack of candor had more to do with using one's youth to try on different identities. Jonathan told Cass, on that first night in the bar, that he chose Brown over Harvard just to piss off his parents. Though it was true he was accepted to both schools, his proffered reasoning for choosing Brown was false. He wondered if lies—little ones, big ones—were a part of every relationship. A necessary part, even. Certainly in his case they were.

Five years into his marriage, he still found himself surprised by the things Cass said and did. There were benefits to having some layers unshared. It was the consequence of their spontaneous meeting. They hadn't had adequate time to prepare the versions of themselves they would proffer. But it was worth it. To bump into his wife in a city of eight million—especially when he'd been feeling so low—was a gift. One he shouldn't be rethinking.

5. CASS

THREE IN THE morning and her mind was a runaway train. All day she'd done nothing but tire herself out with mindless errands—tailor, three Puddles walks, returning a sweater—in the hopes that she'd be able to break her sleepless spell. But it was the middle of the night and she knew it was fruitless. All she wanted was to reach for the materials stashed in her night table, but she knew if Jonathan were to wake up, she'd be busted. Instead, she quietly padded toward the kitchen and opened the fridge, looking for anything that might calm her nerves. Chocolate pudding, a wheel of Brie or, better yet, wine. An open bottle of white was lying on its side. She took a large glass off the shelf and went to pour. Only a single drop rolled out, and there was no more wine in the house either. She'd taken the empty bottles lining their countertops to the recycling bin just that evening.

She was sure Jonathan had been the one to put that bottle of white back the other night. He'd offered to clean the table while she sorted through their mail and, out of the corner of her eye, she'd seen him put the Chardonnay in the fridge. He always did stupid shit like that, shelving cereal boxes with ten lousy flakes remaining or not replacing a toilet paper roll with one square left. Why wouldn't he when, in his childhood home, fresh cereal and full rolls of toilet paper were magicked into existence? The sitcom version of her would have gotten him back by emptying his aftershave or favorite ice cream. Even if she didn't have the energy for such antics, she wanted at least to be the Cass who practically skipped down the aisle five years ago, because that woman would never pick a fight about a silly thing like an empty wine bottle put back in the fridge.

God, had she wanted to marry Jonathan Coyne back then. Throughout their engagement, at the dress fittings getting nicked by pins, stuffing her face with veal loin at the tastings, proofreading in the calligrapher's office, she'd sometimes get asked, "Any cold feet?" *Not even chilled,* she'd answer. In fact, her soles were ablaze, ready to run down the aisle at their wedding in the four-inch white satin Louboutins that she'd splurged on. "Prick me!" Cass wanted to yell at the dressmaker. "So that I know this is real."

She couldn't wait to loosen her father's half-assed hold on her elbow when she reached the altar and to toss the orchid bouquet to all the single ladies like it was a hot potato. In the beginning, Cass even loved Betsy and her cluster of pearl-choked, martini-swilling friends: Louisa, Cecile, the Susans. The whole crew from the Cheshire Golf & Tennis Club made Cass feel elevated, like she suddenly existed on a plateau where the worst problem she might encounter was a back-ordered tablecloth. These ladies *loved* throwing showers. They *loved* inviting their daughters to meet the "new girl," watching with pride as their offspring taught Cass how to make a hat out of ribbons and told her where to get the best stationery. And the daughters themselves were as sleek and invulnerable as a pack of young swans. They'd never had to watch the family credit cards get snipped in half by sniggering supermarket clerks or pretend they were dieting when their moms packed them a dented can of SlimFast for lunch instead of a sandwich.

Cass was genuinely over the moon as she sat in an oversized floral armchair with ornate wooden handles at her bridal shower (thrown by her future mother-in-law, of course), opening her fourth salad spinner. Because it meant she was marrying Jonathan Coyne, security at last. Love too, but sometimes Cass felt that part was ancillary. The last page of the novel was read, she'd carefully written the beginning, and all she had to look forward to was enjoying the middle.

There were girls, she'd known them all her life, who just couldn't stand to be alone. So they went from boyfriend to boyfriend, trying out mates like they were shoes in a department store with a good return policy. Not her. Watching her mother marry and divorce three times and keep the company of dead-end boyfriends in between was all Cass needed to comprehend the value of independence and of waiting to settle down. Seventeen years of parental neglect did a lot to prepare her for the lonely stretches, to teach her to find satisfaction in the quiet of her own company. She was solo throughout Brown, kissing—sometimes screwing—whomever she felt like, but waiting patiently for the right person to come along before she honed in. Jonathan was it. She was certain. It just took him longer to realize how perfect they could be together.

She knew after their first encounter. At the college bar, after they exchanged their first real conversation after a hundred imagined ones, and Jonathan stood under a fluorescent Coors sign that made his dark hair glint and fished with strong hands through his worn leather wallet to pay for their drinks, something seismic happened to her. Then even more spark when he kissed her in the snow outside her dorm before sauntering off with the crooked gait of a tipsy college student. The current started in the tips of her fingers, the neurological origin point of chemistry, then spread to the pit of her belly, and finally erupted in the quickening of her heart. The work she'd done to make this moment come about had been worth it.

And then he didn't call.

It bothered her for an entire month, much longer than she'd let any other guy unnerve her. Checking her email every five minutes, asking her roommates timidly if anyone had called—it was humiliating, like she was back in high school vying for the pretty, rich girls to look at her. There could be no denying that she and Jonathan clicked, exchanging easy banter with the ring of sitcom dialogue, laughing at each other's jokes and trading stories like Halloween candy. He copped to seeing her around campus, and she thought she did an excellent job of playing coy about it, even while he did his best to figure out which course they may have taken together. And, boy, was he pretty. Long lashes, a narrow jawline, brown silky hair she ran through her fingers when they kissed. His tan was even, save the sunglass outline in white. There was mostly Irish and Italian in her stock, with a sliver of Eastern European Jewish (a "mutt," her father used to call her, even though the word made her blood boil), and the ability to tan evenly would be something she'd envy in others her whole life, using it as a misguided decoder of social class. She'd never come across a guy who looked like Jonathan back home. Men in her hometown of Hazel Park, Michigan, wore tattoo sleeves instead of Izod; they grew mullets instead of letting the wind sweep their hair into whatever good thing Jonathan had going on.

All signs had pointed to him asking her out. He wanted to know which joint she thought had the best pizza in Providence, what her plans were for Christmas break (he was going to Round Hill, Jamaica—a place she had to look up later; she was reluctantly off to her aunt's house in Delaware), and even inquired about past relationships. Cass, trying to play it cool, said she was doing her best to focus on school and not get too distracted with dating. She shared that she was majoring in theater arts and minoring in history, an impractical combination, but it suited her, and she saw Jonathan nod approvingly. She made sure to mention that if she met someone worthwhile, she'd find the time to juggle dating and schoolwork, *hint hint*. He said there'd been someone, his high school girlfriend, Brett, two years his junior, but they'd broken up quite a while ago. She didn't like the face he made when he said her name or the way he hung on to that last *t* in her name. There were obvious traces of wistfulness, which she prayed was just high school nostalgia. Guys like Jonathan, the preppy boys, always came to college with a girlfriend from home. Someone sweet who visited campus for football games and fraternity parties wearing a Tiffany heart necklace, who pasted pictures of her far-off beau on the inside of her locker. The only certain thing about these relationships was that they never lasted long. As for Cass, on her high school graduation day, all she could think of as she looked at the crowd piled into folding chairs while she gave her valedictory speech from the podium was that she couldn't wait to leave them all behind the minute she got to Brown.

Her break from home happened more quickly than she'd anticipated. She'd worried for weeks about navigating campus on move-in day with her mother, who would certainly say and wear all the wrong things, leaving Cass on a bad footing from day one. But her fear was for naught, as Donna announced Cass would be moving herself into college. Patty, Donna's best friend from work, was getting married and her bachelorette shenanigans were taking place during move-in weekend. How did these women in their late forties not realize they were too old and weathered for bride-to-be sashes and penis-shaped shot glasses? For Cass, it turned out to be more embarrassing to drag her own ratty suitcases and street-bought halogen lamps up four flights of dormitory steps like an orphan than to be shadowed by her brash and irritable mother.

"Where are your parents, dear?" her freshman-year roommate's mom asked, a look of pity in her eyes that went right through Cass. She was a bustling woman, thick in the middle and wearing a "Brown Mom" T-shirt, who agonized for nearly twenty minutes over where her daughter should hang a silly Eiffel Tower poster.

"Venezuela."

It was the first thing that popped into Cass's head, and much like her twisted ankle from grade school, it proved to be a surprisingly effective cover. She spent the next few weeks concocting fictional stories about her parents having to be in South America for a distant family member's wedding. Was it any wonder she was so determined to seek out a suitable mate? Someone with whom she could build a life her children wouldn't need to bury beneath a protective coating of lies, an art form she'd been forced to perfect over the past decade?

Since breaking it off with Brett, Jonathan said he hadn't had a serious girlfriend, lamenting that the girls on campus lumped him in with the rest of the athletes. He told her that was why he was at Paragon that night, and Cass was all ears, nodding with sympathy, the implication being that she would never stereotype him like that. She tried not to look at the crossed oars on his T-shirt peeking out from his unzipped hoodie. Later, on school break watching the Lifetime channel in Delaware and picking at leftover fruitcake, she'd wonder why someone would bother to trek across campus to reinvent himself and then wear a team shirt. She believed him to be a kindred spirit, someone also trying to shed an outer layer, it was just that he was less adept at it than her.

A few weeks of bad TV movies about stalkers, domestic violence and stolen babies coupled with a lonely Christmas with her mom, who was sullen due to an uncommon single patch, and her reindeer-loving aunt and uncle helped a little to beat back the romantic notions from her brain, but she was unable to vaporize Jonathan. She never stopped keeping tabs on him well after graduation, using social media, word of mouth and the alumni mailings to monitor his whereabouts and goings-on. She dated here and there, but mostly to fulfill her sex drive, which was a vibrant, forceful thing in her early twenties, and to remind herself there were straight men outside the entirely gay world in which her professional self existed. Once Jonathan made his way to New York City, she quit the diversions and made up her mind not to sleep with anyone but him from that day forward.

It happened on their third date after getting reacquainted. Cass had been with enough men by then to appreciate just how good it was with Jonathan. Before they even made it to her bedroom, his pants dropped around his ankles while he leaned against her refrigerator. That pretty-boy face, contorted with pleasure, brought her nearly to orgasm. It was important to her that he realize just how stupid he was not to have called her in college. She'd always be able to offer him something more than the Lilly Pulitzer girls. And it was true—their sex life had a wild character to it for a while, multiple times a day, in public bathrooms, and even once with a camera propped up on a tripod in the corner of the bedroom. She'd made up her mind then and there that if things progressed with Jonathan to where she wanted them to, she would never turn down sex. She might not be the full package, but she'd always have that. And when it came to satisfying a man, *that* was no small thing.

Brunch the morning after their first time sleeping together was at Balthazar. Over poached eggs and cappuccinos, it went unspoken that they were now a couple. Or so Cass hoped. He told her about his new job at a hedge fund called Winstar; she raved about her boss for maybe a little too long, but the guy was amazing. Percy Zimmerman had founded the largest theatrical ad agency in the country single-handedly and she was damn proud to work for him. She never expected such a high level of job satisfaction, what with her prior professional experience consisting of restocking shelves in the Brown library and working the Baskin-Robbins counter during the summer. And she wanted to tell Jonathan all about it.

Percy was a theater legend, with more than thirteen Tony credits to his name. Producers at all the major stages relied on PZA (formally the Percy Zimmerman Agency), and by extension Cass, for advice on scripts, staging, casting and—Percy's forte—length. "Cut!" he would yell out unprompted during rehearsals when he felt the twitch of "ants in his pants." Cass was less of a chopper, though she'd quietly suggest to her boss, if they were in a one-act play that seemed to be dragging, that it would benefit greatly from an intermission. Few things couldn't benefit from pressing pause and letting people gather their thoughts. To let the suspense percolate and have the audience guess at what would be revealed in the next act. Or simply take a deep breath and prepare for the next phase.

Everything about PZA was cool—from its hipster workforce of theater geeks, to mandatory Ping-Pong breaks, to the freestyle desk arrangement where oddball props sat proudly like trophies. "Sit anywhere," Percy would say, bounding into the office each morning rolling his electric blue bike alongside him. "Better yet, do jumping jacks." He hired Cass, who at the time was working for a seventy-five-seat dance theater in Harlem, over email, and she basically worshipped him from that day forth. After she and Jonathan got Puddles, Percy not only let him come to work with her, he encouraged it. Puddles was an excellent playmate for his labradoodle, Shirley. On most days, Cass and Percy would run Puddles and Shirley over to the dog park in Chelsea for some frolicking after lunch. While they strolled with their pooches, they dished about their lives. One of the first things he'd said to her after she told him about her new boyfriend, Jonathan, was, *Good, because you deserve someone who you can totally be yourself around.* Had her boss suspected something about the nature of her budding relationship and offered this cautionary piece of advice? Or was it just a mindless thing people say when they are trying to sound wise? If it was the former, what had she done to create the impression that she was anything but genuine at all times? She dressed how she liked, expressed her views on work-related matters in earnest alignment with her opinions, and didn't overthink her words when engaging her coworkers in office banter. Still, Percy had looked at her in a certain way when he'd said it that made her feel he knew everything about her and what she'd done.

She'd often wonder what else Percy could intuit about her. Did he know how much she pondered why married sex was a shadow of its former self, absent of showmanship and commingled sweat, pulsing hearts and body-quaking groans. Yes, she still came regularly, but when she did, the psychological effect was the same as paying a bill that had been sitting on the desk too long: *So glad I got that done.* And what of her promise to herself to never say no? Ha! She and Jonathan still had bodies that were young, fit and able, and she wondered sometimes how the sex would be when their skin puckered like prunes, veins rising to the surface like flotsam. Her vagina would dry out—she knew this from her mother, who overshared with her about menopause whenever they spoke—and Jonathan's erection would no longer be counted on. Would Jonathan pop a pill and take on a lover, someone younger with no grays and an upright rack? Would she find someone even older than her who would appreciate that her parts were still more or less in the right places, no errant hairs on her chin, no uncontrollable flatulence? So far Jonathan had asked her for anal sex twice but she'd managed to deflect it without saying no. Maybe that would be their next "thing." It was important to keep things spicy, but it was harder than she'd anticipated. She couldn't pinpoint the exact moment when sex had become a chore for her, but it didn't really matter. The important thing was that her husband should never feel that way.

Even if she contemplated him straying from time to time when her imagination really got the best of her, Cass truly believed that Jonathan would never cheat on her. But then she'd remind herself, grimly, that he didn't know *her* as well as he imagined he did. Maybe it was impossible to ever really know someone fully, and she shouldn't feel so guilty. Marriage shouldn't mean becoming one person, with each spouse swimming inside the other's private thoughts. No, the best relationships were built like Venn diagrams of two overlapping circles, where the only variable was how big the shared part was and how much remained for the individual. The real question was how much overlap was enough. Cass worried constantly that she and Jonathan had a smaller shared circle than most. If this was true, Cass knew she alone was to blame. Her early scheming might have robbed them of a shot at a fatter intersection. But if they could get through this bumpy patch, raising a child could very well change that and she'd have a chance to redraw the lines.

All signs pointed to the timing being right for Jonathan and Cass to start trying. Work for her was on pause, Jonathan was crushing it, and they'd been married for long enough to know it was sticking. Adding to their family was a case of simple math. One unemployed wife plus one successful husband plus five years of a pretty decent marriage equals baby.

Why wasn't she working? Because Percy, her professional idol, was dead. Just nine months earlier, he came into work one day looking uncharacteristically somber and called a firm-wide meeting. Due to the nature of the workspace, an all-hands powwow meant the fifteen of them sitting cross-legged on the floor of the "ideas zone." It was there that he dropped the bomb: he had stage-four pancreatic cancer. Six months to live. Percy's partner, Emmet, a former chorus boy who was a regular at the office, was making his husband close up shop. A competitor had offered to purchase PZA's database and buy out its contract with the largest billboard company in New York City, and Emmet was making Percy take the deal. There was no obvious heir apparent at PZA. Cass overheard Emmet say those exact words shortly after the doctor delivered the news. "PZA is Percy. No one else here has half his magic." The words weren't meant to wound, but they did.

Cass visited Percy in the hospital every night on her way home. Sometimes she'd stay for five minutes—just long enough to drop off his favorite German gummy bears—and sometimes she'd sit by his bed for hours before she could tear herself away. She always brought her game face and an arsenal of the choicest Broadway gossip—the latest understudy to sleep with a director, which new show had a set malfunction on opening night. But Percy barely smiled at the bawdy stories that once would have had him rolling with laughter. He was so fragile by then, barely an outline of the man he was before cancer, that Cass couldn't bring herself to ask him why he didn't think she was capable of taking over.

Percy used most of his remaining strength to ensure all of his employees would be able to keep their jobs after the buyout. He took his last breath just a week before Christmas as a soft, powdery snow was falling and the city was at its most magnificent. Cass remembered being upset that the weather wasn't mirroring the blackness she was feeling. Then she quit a hot second after collecting her year-end bonus, two days after Percy's funeral.

It was okay, this being unemployed for the first time in ages, tolerable because she'd gotten the motherhood bug, a welcome feeling after what had happened two years earlier that left her feeling like an empty vessel. Percy's illness reset something intrinsic inside her, and suddenly she became obsessed with creating life in the face of death. Whereas she used to walk down the street staring only at her phone, now she was on permanent baby watch, peeking into strollers and estimating ages to the nearest month, because having a kid meant life was going to be measured in entirely different units of time. She was fawning over those tiny socks that looked like shoes, which seemed to be all the rage. Girls wore Mary Janes; boys wore ones that looked like Converse. She had her eyes on one of those tall Swedish strollers that supposedly kept the baby from sucking in car exhaust, and she'd even poked her head into Rosie Pope Maternity, just to see how bad things would be once she popped. To her surprise, the pregnancy clothes weren't half bad, and she almost tempted fate by purchasing a fun vacation dress with horizontal stripes.

She had made an appointment with Dr. Levin, her ob-gyn, on her first morning of freedom and practically skipped down the block to his office. She didn't know he would tell her to wait for the birth control hormones to be out of her bloodstream. "Two months is sufficient." That's what he'd said, but she'd decided to stretch it to three just to be safe by the time she saw Jonathan that evening. She didn't want to take any chances of something going wrong—even though she positively detested getting her period every month, which was why she'd been on the super-strong pill Seasonale, making her period come only four times a year. More than two decades had passed already, and still she couldn't shake the terrible feeling each time she saw those first few drops of blood in the toilet when it was her time of the month. She was staying at her father's for the night when she bled for the first time. Thanks to obsessive readings of *Are You There God? It's Me, Margaret,* Cass knew exactly what those bright crimson drops were when she saw them. But the smell, sour and faintly metallic, scared her. She had nothing with her—no sanitary pad packed in her overnight bag, even though she'd been smart enough to swipe a few from her mother to stash in her school locker. She snuck into the master bathroom, but found only tampons in Trish's medicine cabinet, and she had no idea what to do with those. Well, she knew what to do, but she didn't know how to do it. Having no better option, she wadded up toilet paper, scratchy sheets of one-ply, and layered them in her underwear. Then she tiptoed down the stairs carefully and tapped her stepmother on the shoulder. Trish was watching the lotto numbers get announced on TV with a pen in one hand and a cigarette in the other.

"Hang on, Cassidy," Trish grunted, putting her smoking hand in Cass's face. "Damn it, another loser," she said, thrusting down her lotto tickets next to the ashtray on the coffee table.

"Sorry," Cass stuttered. "About losing. I was wondering if you could help me out." Knowing she wouldn't have the words to describe the kind of help she needed, she slowly brought out a tampon from behind her back. "It's my first time. I don't know what to do," she squeaked out.

Trish smiled, and for a moment Cass thought she was going to rescue her. It would be awkward as hell, but Cassidy would get through the night. But then Trish said, "Honey, you better call your mother. I didn't sign up for this when I married your father." And she swiveled her head back to the TV, leaving Cass to stare at the aerosol-locked frizz of her bleached blond hair.

Cass slunk away and went for the kitchen phone. She asked the operator to connect her to McGinley's and, after speaking to two different bartenders, her mother came on the phone.

"What is it?" Donna asked, yelling over the annoying trill of "Bad Girls."

Cass had no choice but to yell to be heard. She explained the situation.

"Fine, I'll be right over. Make sure to be waiting by the front door so I don't have to see Trish or the asshole." Thirty minutes later (even though McGinley's was only ten minutes away), the headlights of her mother's car shone through the windows in the living room and Cass hopped up, careful not to jostle the toilet paper she'd arranged in her underpants, and left with no explanation. Trish could tell her father what had happened.

Unlike other bad memories from her childhood, which Cass had the ability to push aside for the most part, this was the one that dinged her every twenty-nine days like clockwork. The vision of Trish smiling before turning her back on Cass; the knowledge that her mother waited to finish her drink or get some loser's phone number before picking her up. Those consistently filled her with rage and sadness each month until finally she heard about Seasonale on a TV commercial and was able to cut back dramatically on these nightmarish flashbacks. And now even that reprieve was gone.

If Cass had known her OB was going to tell her to wait for the birth control to fully flush out of her system, maybe she'd have stayed at work a bit longer, collected a few more paychecks instead of dust. Now she was home all day, overthinking everything: Jonathan's annoying habit of biting his nails, why Percy never once mentioned her taking over PZA, how cancer was such a bitch, what kind of mother she would be, and why Jemima decided to get Botox. She found herself self-flagellating for noticing other men more than she used to, wondering if they found her attractive, and questioning when Jonathan had become so entrenched in his routine. He'd wake up, get to his desk by 7:15 (except for Tuesdays and Thursdays when he jogged with Puddles through the park and would arrive at work closer to 8:30), eat Shake Shack for lunch at his desk, come home around eight, watch one TV show, then go to bed. The only deviations from his routine occurred when he had a Big Brothers Big Sisters event or a work dinner. He really was a Boy Scout, down to his 4.9 Uber rating. A month earlier Cass had suggested to Jonathan that they go to a rock concert downtown—he looked at her like she had two heads.

Cass pressed her thumbs into her temples and massaged in a circular motion. Doing nothing was proving more exhausting than going to work each day. Without the fulfillment of her job, she spent her time reevaluating settled matters—specifically her marriage and whether it was strong enough to sustain the trials that parenthood would inflict upon it. Whether she and Jonathan would do a number on an innocent little being who hadn't asked to be born. Then she'd remind herself that of course her marriage was solid and that if she pretty much did the opposite of what her parents did, their kid stood a solid chance.

These gripes she had—they were clearly annoyances masking something bigger. But it was easier to fixate on the small stuff than to dwell on what was really bothering her. Especially when she was going crazy from all this free time, picking fights to force up her blood pressure, goading Jonathan just to get a reaction. After all, she loved that he kept to a schedule. And that he was a mentor to an underprivileged kid. Who else did she know who was so selfless with their time? Jonathan had yet to miss one of Leon's basketball games. Did she honestly want a husband that she had to track down, whose absence in the evenings made her question his whereabouts or sneak glances at his text messages? Certainly not.

So what difference did it make how she and Jonathan had gotten to the place they were in? They were here now, they were happy, and that was all that mattered. If only he hadn't given that toast at their wedding, the one where he went on and on until there wasn't a dry eye in the room about fate and timing and how the sweetest things in life are usually born of serendipity. It was that stupid toast that kept her awake in the wee hours, agonizing over what-if. What if he knew how she'd zeroed in on him like a chomping Pac-Man after the cherry?

As she'd grown accustomed to doing, she pushed her guilt to the side, like an unwanted vegetable mucking up an otherwise great meal, and tried to focus on the future. Anything to bring about the restful night's sleep she so desperately needed.

"MORNING," JONATHAN SAID, pecking her on the cheek. She was doing the *Times* crossword at their kitchen counter, grateful it was a Wednesday when she had a shot even on little sleep. The kiss felt jarring, like being approached by a close talker. The night before, they'd grabbed dinner with Jemima and Henry at some ridiculous fusion place. Even though they'd each had a few cocktails, they still didn't have sex when they got home. It felt to her like the absence of intimacy was a third person in the room with them, hovering just out of reach. Maybe it was all the talk of the twins' various issues—constipation, night terrors, speech delays, biting—that had ruined the mood. Not that they were off condoms yet and *needed* to have sex—that was still a few weeks away.

"You slept well," she said, knowing he'd get her meaning.

"Snoring again?"

"Every night. You really need to see a doctor. Remember Marcy from PZA? You met her at Percy's Christmas party? She went to the sleep clinic at Columbia and it's only one overnight where they hook you up to a monitor to observe you. So not a big deal. It's probably a deviated septum or whatever it is that people say they have so that insurance covers their nose jobs. But you really have it."

"I'll go, I'll go. I'm sorry if it keeps you up—I noticed you were missing from bed in the middle of the night. Work has just been insane." He grabbed a bagel from the brown bag on the counter, smothered it with full-fat cream cheese and took a huge bite. His ability to eat whatever he wanted and not gain weight made Cass hate him just a little bit. She'd so wanted to believe that marriage would mean the calorie counting could stop, and in some ways it was true. Jonathan would hardly mind if she gained five or even ten pounds—especially considering a pregnancy was hopefully imminent for them—but still she couldn't bring herself to give in to the temptation she faced in every bakery window. Because she still wanted to be her most attractive self, to turn heads, to have other men want to take her clothes off. What did that mean? It wasn't necessarily a red flag waving the notion that she and Jonathan wouldn't go the distance. There were plenty of women wearing wedding bands sweating it out at CrossFit who would probably rather be home eating bonbons. But maybe that was because their husbands, unlike her own, expected them to keep a certain figure. That just made Cass feel worse about her vanity. For so long her looks felt like a possession no one could take from her. Her parents' fighting got worse, but she got prettier. The popular kids at school got new clothes, but she had clear skin and nice cheekbones. Was it any wonder she wanted to keep up her appearance?

"It's fine. Oh, I got you the smoked salmon you love from Sable's yesterday. Eat it while it's fresh." She loved watching the gratitude he felt for her simple gesture spread across his face as he went to the fridge. To watch the effects of her love take hold was a beautiful thing. But why did she have to see her generosity self-referentially? That felt like a failure, undoing all the goodness.

"What's a four-letter word for 'a boring knife'?" She'd already cracked the clue, but sometimes it was just fun to test him.

"I don't know, babe. Thanks for the salmon. When's Luna coming back?" He gestured grandly to the mess of dishes spread across their countertops and piled high in the sink, a move Cass didn't appreciate one bit. It was annoying that he was neater than her, probably because she attributed it to his coming from a meticulous household, unlike the revolving pigsties she grew up in.

"I'll text her." She scrawled in D-U-L-L, which intersected with the easiest clue in the puzzle for her—nine across: L-E-S-M-I-Z (Victor Hugo show, for short).

"It's fine, I'll load the dishwasher." Jonathan took off his suit jacket, draped it over a stool and rolled up his shirtsleeves. Before she could protest, he got to work scrubbing remains off the blue-and-white Willow dishes they'd received from Betsy at their engagement party. "Heirloom," she'd said, watching Cass unwrap the boxes and peel through layers of tissue.

"Then I'll serve tomatoes on them," Cass had said, with a little smile. Betsy didn't smile back. She didn't appreciate wordplay. Not when it came to the good china.

"The big plates go in the back, honey," Cass now said, looking up from the paper after a few moments of considering ten across. "Plus you should be putting the knives in facing down. And a few of our mugs have chips, so you shouldn't clutter them together."

Silently, Jonathan shifted the dishes, replaced his suit jacket and said something to her she couldn't decipher over the hum of the booted-up Miele.

6. JONATHAN

"*What three things do you want most out of life? You know, like, for us?*" *he asked Cass, coiling locks of her wheat-colored hair around his index finger. He was leaning up against the headboard with his legs spread, she was propped against his chest like a neighboring book on a shelf. They had been engaged for six hours. The ring still looked like a third person in their relationship.*

She exhaled deeply, letting him know she was giving the question the thought it deserved.

"One: I want to be with you forever.

"Two: Beautiful babies. Two or three little us-es.

"Three: I never want to be petty."

Her words drifted to his ears like a cloud of baby powder raining on him softly.

"I couldn't agree with you more."

◆ ◆ ◆

UN-BE-LIEVABLE, HIS WIFE. He's got to get to work and she's home all day doing God knows what. But he's the one loading the dishwasher because she hires some college student with a trust fund to be their maid. Luna Spiegel's father, Marty, was one of the wealthiest producers in Hollywood. He was half of Spiegel Productions, which he started out of his garage in the San Fernando Valley with his cousin Eli Spiegel, and which had produced more Oscar-winning films in the past thirty years than any of its competitors. Jonathan knew because he'd looked up the whole story on Wikipedia. And Marty's daughter, Luna, from his first marriage to the soap actress Bella Criss, cleaned Jonathan's toilet every week. It was more like every other week, actually. If Luna had an audition or a midterm, she would just fail to show up and, if she felt so inclined, would text Cass two days later to apologize. That's what you got for hiring a maid who was probably four times richer than you.

Before Cass moved in, he'd had a woman named Manuela clean his apartment once a week. She was married to the building super, kept his place meticulous, and replaced vacuum bags and Swiffer pads like an invisible fairy godmother. Jonathan couldn't even remember ever interacting with her. There was probably a handshake or a head nod at some point, but after that, Jonathan just left $150 in an envelope on the coffee table every Monday and he'd come home to a note saying something like "Mr. Jon, I bought Scotchgard with the petty cash." That was the extent of their interaction and it suited him perfectly fine. She ironed his Turnbull & Asser shirts properly, cleaned out the fridge periodically, and mopped away any crumbs left over from his ordered-in dinners throughout the week.

Enter Cass, with her artistic hours and her flair for shaking up things that didn't need changing. Percy told his staff at PZA to come in when they felt "energized" enough to work. The thought of his boss saying anything like that was downright laughable. He'd say, "Son, you come in as soon as there is money to be made." That meant approximately 7:30 a.m. for most of his team. Cass would typically leave for work around ten, after three cups of coffee, a scroll through Facebook (where she was a voyeur, not a poster) and reading several sections of the *Times*. Apparently, those were the things that "energized" her enough to design billboards and web banners and strategize on how best to get the blue-hairs to train it in from the burbs for lunch and a show. The result was that she and Manuela overlapped in the early morning. Unlike Luna, Manuela actually came to work, and punctually. She'd arrive promptly at eight thirty and start cleaning, exactly as she was paid to do. It was all too much for Cass, apparently.

"I can't stand it, Jonathan," Cass moaned to him one day. He could tell from the echo that she was holed up inside their shower stall making the call. "The guilt is killing me. Here I am drinking ridiculously expensive European espresso and doing sudoku, and Manuela is vacuuming under my feet. I see her scrubbing our toilets and I want to cry. If things were reversed, and I was the one born in Guatemala, you know I'd be doing the dirty work. She'd probably be a surgeon. I don't even feel that comfortable having a cleaning lady to begin with. I certainly never grew up with one, and this just feels wrong."

So try to clean the place yourself if you're home, is what he was tempted to say. And—*All you do is complain how disgusting your mother's place is when we visit.* But he bit his tongue, as he'd grown accustomed to doing. He probably had a permanent indentation in it by now.

"What do you want to do, Cass? Fire her because you feel sorry for her?" He gave an exasperated sigh and hoped she heard it. Hoped it made her feel as ridiculous as she sounded. "You could just leave for work earlier."

"That's not the point. You know what Percy says. He'd be mad if I showed up before I was my best self."

Don't I deserve the same courtesy as Percy? Jonathan wondered, though he wouldn't want his wife to treat him with any kind of forced consideration, the kind that could make her feel any more distant than she already felt at times. At least he knew when he got the moody side, she was letting him in.

"The Wentworths need a cleaning lady. I'll give them Manuela."

He had to laugh, even if only on the inside. Did Cass hear herself? She was knee-deep in her high-and-mighty routine, saying it bothered her to watch another woman clean her toilet, and then in the same breath she's suggesting "giving" Manuela to their neighbors like the woman was a bag of sugar.

"Do what you want, Cass. Just make sure Manuela doesn't lose out on work."

"Of course," Cass said, the implication being, *Duhhhh! I'm the kindhearted one.*

He had to hand it to Cass, she did her research. Found a group of undergraduates and masters students at NYU called PhD Housekeepers, the cleaning equivalent of College Hunks Hauling Junk, and hired Luna over text message.

"Jonathan, she's at the Tisch School of the Arts. How great is that? Down the road, maybe she'll be interested in doing some babysitting for us." He could tell Cass could barely contain her excitement, like she had landed some fabulous intern to work at PZA for college credit. It was clear she'd already invented the scenario where they came home from dinner to find Luna and their toddler putting on an elaborate puppet show together, employing the Strasberg method. He just didn't understand the fuss. So the girl who would sweep away their granola crumbs and clean their Nespresso machine was college educated, could even hum a tune. Who cared?

The fact was that he'd grown up with two uniformed housekeepers tending to his family's every need—dusting the baby grand every other day and climbing precariously on stepladders to make sure the picture frames on the highest shelves gleamed—and his wife had known nothing of this type of life. They were coming at this argument from totally different places and he felt obliged to back down. It was better to acquiesce when the consequences were this minimal and save up reserves for when truly needed.

And that was how they came to have Luna Spiegel, heiress, daughter of Hollywood royalty, mediocre cleaner at best, working in their home. Luna was obviously going through a phase where she was hell-bent on establishing her own identity, something he could relate to, but in a far more attenuated form. For their cleaning lady, proving herself meant accepting nothing more from her father than college tuition and having a lot of tattoos, including one of those "lights, camera, action" slate boards on the inside of her wrist, leading one to question how serious she really was about distancing herself from her heritage. Esperanza, one of the caring and meticulous housekeepers he'd grown up with and who still worked for his parents, had a sister in Queens. He kept Pilar's number in his phone in case Luna stopped showing up altogether, or for when Cass came to her senses.

The whole crazy situation of Luna, their perpetually messy home and Manuela displaced to the Wentworths was made so much worse when Cass chose to do what she had done that morning—telling him how to load the dishwasher. How the hell would she know? He was nothing if not methodical, whereas Cass's underwear drawer made him break into a cold sweat. When her aunt died, the one she used to spend Christmas with before his family's traditions took over, she called him at the office and asked him to pack an overnight bag for her so she could leave for the train station straight from work. He agreed, even though it meant him having to leave work too, because Cass always had a weird thing about packing. It was all the moving around as a child—not that she'd ever said so, but he'd deduced it. *No emotional intelligence, my foot,* he thought, recalling something Cass had once accused him of. The truth was he preferred to do the packing anyway. Filling the shoe bags, preparing the Dopp kit, fitting L-shaped boots against bras shaped like camel humps. It was a little bit like do-ing a 3-D puzzle.

The entire bureau under the TV (yes, they had a TV in the bed-room, which did not signal defeat as far as he was concerned, even though they originally put it in saying it'd only be for porn and now it ran nothing but Netflix series) was claimed by Cass the minute she moved in, and in searching for her underwear that day he'd found crum-pled receipts, cell phone chargers, her rolled-up diploma and about six years' worth of Filofaxes, which he doubted she ever used past Febru-ary. How could this be the woman who was going to tell him how to arrange the coffee mugs? It didn't matter, though, this growing pile of grievances, because they amounted to nothing more than a molehill when compared with how much he loved Cass.

The night before he met Cass in the city, he'd felt particularly low. It had been a shit day at work—Jerry was pouty about an unflattering profile of him in *Hedge Fund Weekly* and he was taking it out on everyone. And while Jerry could be on the thin-skinned side (yet still do nothing toward keeping a low profile), Jonathan couldn't help but feel sorry for his boss and mentor. Jonathan was one of Winstar's first hires—the firm was only two years old when he joined—and he took the negative press personally. Winstar wasn't quite his baby, the firm most certainly belonged to Jerry, but Jonathan was at least a devoted custodian of it. The work crap coupled with the fact that dopey Russell had gotten engaged the night before to an ex-model and was walking around the office with his chest puffed out (so much so that he actually looked constipated) put Jonathan desperately in need of a drink.

So he had slipped out of work a bit early, poured himself a small scotch in front of the TV and started diddling around on his laptop. He wasn't really active on social media, but every now and then he'd mosey over to his computer and start looking people up. That night he checked in on a few friends, mostly rowing pals from college, before typing in Brett's name.

He gasped at her profile picture. There she was: smiling, sitting on the deck of her dad's sailboat, with a baby bundled in her arms. When, exactly, had his ex-girlfriend grown up? Why did he still feel like the horny kid prone to reaching under her shirt in the Cheshire game room while she'd gone all adult on him and started a family? Jonathan refilled his tumbler on autopilot so many times he lost count.

And then he saw Cass, less than twenty-four hours later. And *everything* changed. He became obsessed with the concept of fate—the idea that a single change in the day they reconnected could have meant the difference between Cass being his wife and not. It was the opposite of the way his mom and dad were strategically seated next to each other at the country club Memorial Day barbecue by their co-conspirator parents. His parents' marriage was a loveless one, serving purely functional purposes: procreation, joint filing on tax returns, someone to share the driving with on long trips. Far worse existed, and he'd believed that if that's what was in store for him, he could still lead a fulfilling life. He was lucky that he really loved his job. Marrying for love would be gravy. Cass was gravy.

Betsy didn't take to Cass in the beginning, that much was obvious. "Rogers," she said, chewing on Cass's maiden name like it was a tough piece of steak. "I don't know any Rogers from Michigan." This was followed by a larger than usual sip from her martini. A gulp. His former girlfriends, including Brett, the field hockey girls from boarding school and even most of the girls he hooked up with at Brown, all had the "of" attached to their last names. Melanie Clark *of* the Main Line Clarks; Theodora Whitley *of* the Greenwich Whitleys. He was Jonathan Coyne *of* the Boston Coynes. They were a family of functional drunks and low-level depressives, but they had lineage to spare. Open the New England Registrar and there they were: Dorothy and Edward Coyne had settled in Boston in 1712. In some ways, his mother was obsessed with the past; in other ways (like when it would cast a shadow on her children), she was awfully quick to forget it. She suggested, not too subtly, that Cass might not be interested in her son for the right reasons. He knew Cass wasn't like that and tried to tune out the noise.

His point to his parents was that it shouldn't matter that Cass's dad, Dick Rogers *of* Troy, Michigan, was a ne'er-do-well carpenter who left Cass's mom high and dry. Dick had a reputation in their town for skimming off subcontracts and padding his materials bills. He still got jobs because he was always the low bidder, and there was inevitably a steady stream of customers who believed they couldn't be fooled. At the time Jonathan reconnected with Cass in the city, Cass's mother, Donna, was giddy about her *much* younger and unemployed boyfriend, who was later mistaken at his and Cass's wedding for a waiter.

Betsy tolerated Dick and Donna with the chilly forced courtesy she offered to outsiders. Dick was largely MIA, and if Donna noticed his mother's coldness, she didn't seem to care. She was more than happy to let Jonathan's parents take over wedding planning, though you'd think she'd be full of insight after three marriages—Vegas or city hall, prime rib or shrimp scampi? Cass didn't talk much about her father and treated her mother with a resigned embarrassment, barely rolling her eyes when Donna said, when visiting their apartment for the first time, "Sheesh, they press the elevator button for you here? I'm going to call them when I need someone to wipe my ass." There were three half siblings from Dick, all of whom made it to the Vineyard for the wedding, and Jonathan noticed that Cass handpicked everything they would wear down to selecting the nail polish on the girls. This wasn't out of bridezilla tendencies. It stemmed from fear.

Cass was nothing like the other girls he'd taken out in the city, whose names always started with *J* and ended with an *a* sound. She didn't ooh and aah over his apartment's posh address, or the swanky bachelor pad furnishings, even when he bought his first real piece of art. It was a Damien Hirst print that cost him 25 percent of his bonus that year. All the other guys at work were starting to talk about "collecting" after Jerry toured them around his Hamptons home at the company retreat, dropping the name of every artist whose work they passed as his protégés trailed behind. It felt like a class trip to the MoMA. It was funny, truly, a group of binge-drinking former frat boys bragging about their Sotheby's specialists. He felt compelled to get in on the action, and chose the blue-and-bronze butterfly print because he thought Cass would like it. Correction: he thought it would impress her. She didn't say a word when she saw it, and you couldn't miss it because it hung right over the headboard. In that moment, he had to admit, he missed the sycophantism of the Jessicas and Jennas. Cass's middle name was Jessica, but she hated it. When she changed her name after they married, she legally dropped the Jessica and left only the *J.* That move said it all.

Cass was generally stingy with praise—prided herself on it too. "At least you know when I say I like something, I really mean it." He nodded his head vigorously when she told him that (it was a third-date confession of hers). He was still besotted with her then, intoxicated by the way she clubbed her pen like a preschooler, gaga watching her rub her forehead with the back of her hand before she answered a question, smitten by those slightly overlapping front teeth. These, among other minutiae that together added up to a near-perfect Cass, were driving him wild. If she were to say it to him again, what she said to him at Masa on date three, he'd respond: *It's not the worst thing in the world to make someone feel good just for the hell of it. Trust me, I do it all the time.* But what you say on a third date and after six years of togetherness rarely have much in common.

"Mr. Coyne?"

It was Laurel, popping her head into his office. There was something noticeably different about her demeanor, the way she hesitated before tapping on his door. Apprehension. The fidgety hands reminded him of Cass, at least the Cass of late. He needed to get to the bottom of what was eating at his wife, but not until he finished his report on the Brazilian petroleum company that had been kicking his ass lately. Until then he lacked the energy it would take to probe Cass about what was bothering her; the conversation would probably involve hours of late-night questioning and denial before she finally confessed the root of her malaise. She wasn't sleeping well, but that shouldn't have to cut into his precious eight hours.

"Everything all right? Have a seat," he said, wondering what made him extend the gesture. Some parental instinct, he hoped. *Brotherly,* he corrected himself—they weren't that far apart in age. There was no harm in mentoring the new kid, telling her not to feel bad that Liz, the head of investor relations, picked on her and the other girls for sport. Liz was fifty (he knew this because Russell had dug up her eHarmony profile), a good thirty pounds overweight, sardonic to a fault and agitated the minute her caffeine high wore off. Her job at Winstar was to supervise Laurel and the other pretty young things in investor relations who flitted around the office in short skirts giving all the analysts hard-ons.

Laurel slumped in one of the chairs opposite his desk, took a handful of auburn hair dangling from her ponytail and twirled it around her finger. It was the first time he noticed it—the engagement ring that was now catching the light and casting a rainbow across his papers.

"It's all going to sound very silly to you, but . . ." she started to say. He wanted to tell her not to qualify her words. Men never did that; women frequently did. *You're going to laugh when you hear this . . . Call me crazy, but . . .* Even Cass did it at times, and that's when he knew she was feeling vulnerable. It went along with her rolling her eyes back into their sockets, her unique way of avoiding eye contact.

"My fiancé and I had a big fight last night," she said, twisting the ring around her finger. It was small, round, set on a diamond band. Reflexively, he started winding his own yellow band around his finger. They sat there in silence for a prolonged moment, working their rings in infinity loops.

"About?" he asked, when he should have said, *I'm sorry to hear that.* Shoot him for it, he was curious.

"Nonsense, really. My fiancé, Walker, wants to have a DJ at the wedding. He says bands usually butcher the music, but I think DJs look cheap. And my parents are paying anyway, so it should be up to them, which means me. He says I'm being a control freak." She looked down at her lap, adding, "I know, it's dumb, and you're busy."

He had to admit, he was a little disappointed after she shared. Something a bit more psychologically complex, like *His family makes me feel like I'll never be good enough for him*, or *I don't think she understands the difference between constructive criticism and emasculating*, something a bit more Jonathan and Cass, that could have been interesting. He might have been able to give some real counsel. A tiff over wedding planning was child's play.

Laurel looked up at him from under heavy lids, as if she knew she'd let him down. Quietly, she added, "Besides, how can I be expected to be with one person for the rest of my life? I'm only twenty-two. That's like child bride age in New York City."

Now we're talking. He reclined deeper into his office chair.

"I can't really talk to Liz about this, and I don't have many friends in the city yet. Plus, my entire family is in Mississippi. If my parents suspected I had cold feet, it would put them into early graves. They got married at eighteen. Any advice? I know you're married." She eyeballed his encumbered finger. "Your wife is really pretty," she added, looking over at his framed pictures.

He straightened up, pleased to have the chance to be an authority on something, though he wouldn't have figured marriage would be the topic where his expertise would be called upon.

"She is. We just had our five-year anniversary—been together six years total. Guess that means we've got the seven-year itch in the not-too-distant future." That was definitely not what he had intended to say, especially just as Liz was passing by. She peered into his office suspiciously and stalked away with a disapproving snort.

"What did you do?" Laurel asked, both of them pretending not to
have noticed Liz.

"For what?"

"Your anniversary."

"Oh—um. Hmm, I guess we did nothing." He hadn't even realized until now that he and Cass did nothing to celebrate. Should they
have gone on a trip? Or was a piece of jewelry meant to be purchased?
They must have at least gone out to dinner. He couldn't remember.
Was it on him or on her to plan something? He really needed an in-
struction manual: *How Not to Fuck Up Your Marriage in Three Easy
Steps.* While Laurel sat across from him, he googled the traditional gift
for the five-year wedding anniversary. Wood. For some crazy reason,
the first thing that came into his head was a baseball bat.

"I'm kidding, of course, about the seven-year itch. Cass is great. I
know what you're saying about being with one person for the rest of
your life. It's scary. I was nervous too." He actually hadn't been, but it
seemed like the right thing to say to an engaged person with cold feet.
"But if it's the right person, you make compromises to make them
happy." *Like reloading a perfectly organized dishwasher. Like sleeping
with a gas mask on while a bunch of lab technicians record your breathing. Like firing a competent cleaning lady and hiring an irresponsible
heiress to clean your toilets. Like giving up on having sex three times a
week.* Cass and Jonathan actually shook on that number. It was during
their engagement, when they were up late drinking Dark 'n' Stormys
on the beach after an exhausting day of hashing out table seating and
finalizing the wedding playlist. He didn't say it to Laurel, but he agreed
with Walker. DJs were better. He and Cass had a band—a seersucker-
suited quartet making sorry attempts at "American Pie."

"We're still gonna fuck a lot once we're married, right?" Cass had
asked, her eyes glazed over from the alcohol. She dug her big toe into
his ankle and gave him a pesky scratch. She always got a little raunchy

when she drank. Whenever Cass let the dirty talk out, he could tell she was embarrassed about it the next day. Inevitably, over their morning coffee she'd bring up a *New Yorker* article she'd read or try to engage him in a conversation about world affairs while she left her glasses on longer than usual. The insecurity made his wife more human somehow, and he had the urge to hug her whenever her self-doubt crept out.

"No less than three times a week," he had responded to his soon-to-be wife that night on the beach, offering up his pinky for a swear. She looped hers around his and he thought their fate was sealed. Sex three times a week for the rest of his life. Why would anyone *not* want to get married? Those odds were certainly better than his chances when he was single.

Recently they were down to once a week. No—once every two weeks. And they didn't even have kids yet. Work got in the way, especially in the past six months when his chances of making equity partner were starting to seem more likely. Sometimes he was just too depleted to even attempt a move, and Cass still seemed shattered by Percy's death over Christmas. He hated himself for what he had thought the instant Cass called him to tell him that Percy had passed. It was that she'd be so depressed that it could be more than a month before they'd have sex again. After all, Percy was more of a father to her than Dick had ever been, a hundred times over.

Jonathan honestly believed that if they had sex a bit more regularly, Cass's sleeping issues would dissipate. But he was scared to suggest it, thought she'd accuse him of looking out only for number one. They were fast approaching the baby-making start date. Maybe then they'd make up for all the sex they'd missed in the past year. Sure, he'd like their lovemaking to be more evenly spread out, but since when could beggars be choosers?

"Of course, you're right," Laurel said, popping up. She suddenly seemed embarrassed by their talk. Was it something he said? Maybe she was reading his mind, that runaway train. "Sorry I bothered you."

"It's never a bother. Call me Jonathan, by the way."

"Okay." She smiled, revealing double dimples, elongated commas that looked like they'd be fun to trace with his index finger.

When she was out of his office, he thought about closing the door and calling Cass to tell her about the exchange. But he was still too pissed about the dishwasher. And she might say something like, "What compromises have you made?" when he shared the advice he'd given Laurel and then rattle off a list of her concessions to their marriage. Instead, he looked at his watch and was glad to see it was nearly five o'clock. He strolled down the hall toward the well-stocked bar in Jerry's office and pulled a Don Draper. *To wedded bliss,* he thought, silently toasting the anniversary he should have celebrated with Cass.

7. CASS

CASS WAS CONCERNED when her friend Dahlia insisted on meeting her for lunch ASAP. Their friendship had a steady rhythm and this move—requesting an immediate face-to-face—was disturbingly out of sync. The old college friends normally saw each other every two months, and they had just been together for a theater night shortly after New Year's Eve. Cass had ranted to Dahlia about how terrible she thought the play's promo materials were. It was a modern version of *Romeo and Juliet* where the ill-fated lovers lived on opposite sides of the Green Line. "Look at this Playbill cover," she'd said over and over, thrusting the dull imagery in Dahlia's face. "A balcony! Really? Couldn't they have at least tried to be original?" Cass knew she sounded like a broken record but couldn't help herself. Dahlia had patted her knee in sympathy.

They'd talked about seeing another show in March, so Cass was surprised to receive a late-night text from her college roommate, asking her to grab a bite the next day. They met less than twelve hours later at Bella Blu, an under-the-radar Italian spot near Cass's apartment. It was Dahlia's choice, and a surprising one given that she tended to prefer a more see-and-be-seen ambience when she trained it in from Scarsdale. It was freezing outside, the groundhog intent on showing everyone who was boss, and Cass had to layer a vest, coat and scarf before venturing outdoors. Cass had so few plans of late and yet found herself not particularly motivated to leave the house. If she hadn't been so worried about Dahlia, she'd have pushed it off.

"What's up?" Cass asked when she saw Dahlia making mincemeat of a cuticle, already waiting for her at a corner table. There was a half-eaten piece of focaccia on her plate and a thin strand of oregano stuck in her teeth. Cass couldn't recall seeing Dahlia eat a carb since college. She expected to feel a twinge of satisfaction, watching her most high-strung, type-A friend finally succumb to temptation, but instead it just made Cass feel sad. Things must be dim if Dahlia was turning to gluten.

"Harris and I are getting divorced," Dahlia announced before Cass even had the chance to kiss her friend on the cheek.

"Are you serious?" Cass asked, settling into the chair opposite Dahlia. This was worse than anything she had been imagining. Her eyes moved from the precarious water glass getting squeezed to the place where Dahlia's canary diamond used to sit. Now there was just the hint of a tan line, which looked like an albino worm circling her finger. Cass fought the urge to reach out and pinch some color back into the lonely white spot.

"Dead serious. Like we already have lawyers. I'm sorry I didn't tell you sooner. We just told the kids. Brady was sobbing uncontrollably. I don't think Toby had any clue what it all meant."

Cass felt like a balloon inside her chest was inflating and making it difficult for her to draw in air. Brady, her godson, was exactly the age she had been when her parents got divorced. Toby, only a preschooler, had a chance of coming away relatively unscathed. But nine. That huge year where double digits lie on the horizon, when social interactions take on a greater significance, and the first signs of puberty rear their ugly heads (at least they had for her). In other words, a year with enough complications. It was an age when a parent forgetting to call on your birthday is incomprehensible, and yet somehow you are forced to comprehend it. A time when the appearance of half siblings is mind-boggling, and jealousy inducing, and your teachers and your friends' parents ask you too often if you're "doing okay."

And poor Brady had looked so damn happy in the latest Bloomstein holiday portrait. Cass had cleared it off the living room mantel only a few days before, tossing it out along with the dozens of other holiday cards they kept displayed long after the New Year's toasts were a distant memory. She swept most of the cards straight into a trash bag, but had paused to look for an extra moment at Brady in his basketball jersey. He'd gotten so tall and his boyish cuteness was morphing into something different—a chiseled face and actual muscles! Her heart swelled with a surprising shock of tenderness at seeing her godson growing up. It had to be the knowledge that her own "start date" was fast approaching, making her overly sensitive, so quick to succumb to emotion. She'd actually pressed Brady's smiling face to her own before consigning it to the recycle bin.

The Bloomsteins, under Dahlia's auspices, sent a religion-neutral holiday card every year, the outside a collage of family pictures, the inside a rhyming update on their lives. This year's had read as cheerfully as ever:

> *Happy New Year to all from a family in Bloom*
> *May your holidays be all cheer and no gloom*
> *Brady's in fourth grade, shooting hoops night and day*
> *Toby's hit preschool, singing, painting, molding clay*
> *Dahlia and Harris went (sans kids!) to St. Barths*
> *A vacation filled with food, wine and hearts*

And so on and so on, for nine more stanzas!

People with the earnestness and desire—not to mention the time—to compose verse about romantic trips and their children's hobbies weren't supposed to get divorced. Her parents, Donna and Dick, they were the ones for whom divorce was preordained. Those two could barely fill out a mortgage application or send in a permission slip, and lord knows they never took a trip anywhere, with or without Cass. But Dahlia and Harris, the prom king and queen of Scarsdale? It felt impossible. They'd known each other since childhood—and despite what the statistics said about marrying a high school sweetheart, what changes could upend a couple who knew each other inside and out? They had everything: beautiful boys, a white-picket-fenced house on a coveted suburban cul-de-sac, extended families that meshed like peanut butter and jelly.

Maybe the rhyming holiday card was a symptom of their problems. After all, the Wentworths sent a simple card with an embossed wreath and the words "Happy Christmas" along with their names printed inside. Mass-produced and ordered online from Minted. That somehow felt more appropriate than Dahlia's big year-end production, evidence of a couple with nothing to prove. Cass and Jonathan never sent out a holiday greeting; the idea of mailing out a picture of the two of them on a beach with Puddles running between their legs seemed ridiculous. And yet, when the cards started bulging through their rubber-banded mail pile in early December, Jonathan had surprised her by suggesting they send one too.

"Aren't we a family already, even though we don't have kids yet?" he'd said.

"No, we're not," she answered, though she instantly regretted the harsh response. Puddles was like their baby, and even if there was no Puddles, they were still a unit worthy of showing off. Maybe next year she would do a card. But by then she could have a big belly to show, or even a newborn, so the point would be moot.

Looking at Dahlia, who had just drawn blood picking away at the brittle skin around her nails, Cass wondered how she had missed the signs that her friend was unhappy. Cass and Dahlia always did girls things together, but maybe she and Jonathan should have driven out to Westchester more often instead. Brady was her godson after all, and while she Skyped with the Bloomstein kids every now and then, she was pretty sure Toby wouldn't know her if she put a fistful of candy right in his face. What the hell else were she and Jonathan doing on weekends? How many brunches does a childless couple need to have? She'd always thought of herself as a fairly decent godparent, but she knew it would no longer be enough to send thoughtful birthday gifts or score backstage passes to kid-friendly musicals. Cass would have to step things up several notches in the future; Brady was going to need her now. She'd been in the trenches before—she knew there was a way out. At least there was no way Harris and Dahlia would botch things quite as badly as her parents did.

After the *Romeo and Juliet* play, which was rather enjoyable once Cass was able to set aside its dismal logo and signage, Cass had hugged Dahlia and sent her on her way home to the burbs before the two of them had really gotten a chance to talk. Now it seemed laughable, but Cass had come very close that night to confessing her own marital woes and asking for some reassurance. She wanted to tell Dahlia that she sometimes wondered if Jonathan even knew her at all. Was he in love with the real Cass—the girl who once had to bail out her mother from jail for a DUI and whose deadbeat father ditched her like a bad apple at the first opportunity—or was he smitten with a carefully crafted facade? And if Jonathan had somehow managed to mine beneath Cass's surface to touch the truest parts of his flawed partner, did it excuse the fact that, in the beginning, she thought of him mostly as a golden goose? There was no denying that she'd targeted Jonathan—and manipulated him—because she thought he could provide a one-way ticket out of her old life. Hell, she'd even used Google Earth to look up the house Jonathan grew up in—Greek Revival with a half dozen porches overlooking a verdant lawn that stretched on for acres. It had been easy enough to mentally Photoshop herself into the image, to imagine grasping the wooden banister as she descended the grand staircase, heading to the kitchen where a steaming apple pie sat cooling on the counter.

She'd hoped Dahlia would assuage her fears and remind her that lots of women pulled some marionette strings to maneuver a potential partner into place, that all the Scarsdale housewives fantasized about being single from time to time and worried their spouses were often more like strangers than soul mates. Then Cass could cross Central Park in the back of a taxi knowing her feelings were normal. Damn, there was that word again. Well, she hadn't broached it anyway, sensing Dahlia was tired. Plus, in the moment, Cass had been torn about whether she should unburden herself. She'd never admitted to anyone else that she had essentially stalked her husband and orchestrated their meet-cute as though she were planning an FBI sting. The part of her that wanted to finally come clean did battle with—and lost out to—the much stronger desire to keep her cards hidden. It was the same wariness that kept her from asking Jemima about motherhood.

"Well . . . aren't you going to ask me why?" Dahlia asked, sounding faintly bewildered. Cass shook herself back to the present moment with a large gulp of ice water. Whatever it was had to be something big. Bigger than anything she could imagine—definitely bigger than the secret she was holding on to, and drastically more significant than her childish quibbles with Jonathan.

"Yes, of course. Please tell me what happened. Weren't you two just in the Caribbean?" Dahlia's social media feeds trickled through Cass's brain—pictures of Dahlia and Harris clinking glasses, upright toes with the aquamarine sea in the background. The image had made Cass think about how she and Jonathan had let their five-year anniversary come and go without even a celebratory dinner, just some cards exchanged. In some ways she took it as a sign of strength—they were good every day, didn't need a calendar to reinforce it. But in other ways, she saw it as weakness. Had they already given up on milestones? She wondered what Jonathan thought about the lack of fanfare. That's *if* he'd noticed at all.

"Okay," Dahlia said, leaning in closer to Cass. She took up her stalk of bread again for reinforcement. "It's like ripping off a Band-Aid. That's what my therapist said. The sooner you do it, the sooner the pain is over. So here goes: I fell in love with someone else. She's . . . she's . . . she's a she. And she's the assistant principal at Brady's school."

Cass's jaw went into instant battle with gravity. All it wanted to do was drop—badly. *No. Fucking. Way.* That's what she desperately wanted to blurt out, but instead she mustered, "That's great," as though Dahlia had told her that Harris was being promoted. It was a "regional manager" to "East Coast manager" kind of response, but what could Cass do? The shock was so huge that her reaction was inversely related.

Cass flashed back to the night she and Dahlia made out junior year. Wasn't that just to get the attention of the swimmer boys too busy playing beer pong to notice them? Who had even suggested the kiss? Cass could never remember. Now she sized up her friend anew, looking for outward changes. But there was nothing except the bread consumption and a less-than-perfect hairstyle. In any event, it was fruitless to search Dahlia's face and body for insights. Cass's own appearance was unchanged since Percy had died, since her sex life deteriorated, since her brain wouldn't let her sleep. She still tugged on her skinny jeans, slicked on mascara and brushed through her hair enough times to ward off any questions about her well-being.

Besides the shock, there was something else that Cass was feeling upon hearing the revelation. The feeling was relief. The thing breaking down the Bloomstein marriage was monumentally bigger than anything that could fracture her and Jonathan. It was sexual orientation, for crying out loud, not some fib about a chance meeting! She felt her pulse decelerate.

"Just wow," Cass added, reaching for the breadbasket. Now *she* needed a blood-sugar fix. "I did not see that coming."

"Neither did Harris. But I've known forever. And I feel so lame doing this now. Coming out feels very fifteen years ago. I mean we went to freaking Brown. If there was ever a place to leave the closet behind . . ."

"Well, you've got nothing to apologize for. You did it when you were ready. So how do you feel? And who is this assistant principal?"

"Oh gosh, where do I start? I feel really, really good. I mean, I know I look like hell, but that was mostly over telling the kids. I didn't sleep for weeks. We wanted to wait until Brady's weeklong tennis camp in Orlando was over. I couldn't imagine sending him away with a portable fan, an economy-sized Purell and a note that said, *P.S. Your mom's gay.* I'll tell you what's weird about the whole thing, though. As much as I'm happy to be with Roxanna—that's her name—I know I won't get married again. More kids—maybe. I know Roxanna wants at least one; she's already done a bunch of fertility-slash-Franken-science research on how to make it happen."

Cass nodded. *How would that work?* she wondered. She made a mental note not to take it for granted how easy she and Jonathan had it, relatively speaking.

"But marriage? Not a chance in hell. I'm telling you, this situation has turned Harris into the biggest asshole. Never divorce a lawyer. We're looking at a minimum of two years for everything to get finalized, probably longer. We have to work out custody, divide the assets—Harris wants to sell the house. And he doesn't want to see me, so we have to have all of the parent-teacher conferences twice so we can both go alone. A divorce without kids is a breakup with paperwork. With kids, it's a nightmare."

Cass shook her head in vigorous agreement. She'd never heard her own deepest fears articulated so succinctly. In college, she'd heard stories from fellow students about parents who'd had amicable divorces, dividing custody easily and putting pettiness aside for the sake of their children. These anecdotes, shared late at night over beer and pizza and sometimes weed, felt like fables to her. She couldn't help but wonder if these kids had just blocked out the bad stuff or forced themselves to wear rose-colored glasses. Didn't their parents summon the police to demand months of owed child support, send nasty letters to the place of employment of their ex's new spouse (Donna did that twice) and viciously malign the other right in front of their children? Didn't they fight over some shitty piece of furniture that neither of them could remember buying until one of them took a match to it one night in frustration?

"Anyway," Dahlia continued, "what would I get married again for?"

"Because—" Cass started to say, but stomped on the rest of the sentence. *For the kidney,* she continued the thought in her head.

Sometimes, when Cass was up in the middle of the night and looked over at her sleeping, snoring husband, she would think: *No matter what, at least he has to give me his kidney.* Because they were married, and the willingness to part with a vital organ for a spouse was one of the unwritten rules. Being married without kids placed the Coynes in an odd position. Not for the first two years, or even three. But after a while, when the Sunday strolls got old and they'd been invited to more brises and sip 'n' sees than weddings lately, the childless married state had started to feel off. Questions arose in her head, like: *What are we doing this for? Why did Jonathan's parents plunk down a few hundred grand for a legal distinction?* For the promise of grandchildren, Cass supposed. That justified their expense, but what about her own commitment? Was it, in fact, for the promise of an organ if she were ever in dire straits? Or to have someone other than her parents to write down in the space on forms that require an emergency contact? If the answer was yes, she wasn't even sure that was something to be ashamed of. She didn't know if that made her an outlier or just like everyone else.

This limbo state was temporary for them, of course. Once she got pregnant, their union would make all the sense in the world. Little Coynes would dot the beaches of Martha's Vineyard. Their weekends would be jam-packed with birthday parties; their apartment a receptacle for Diapers.com boxes. And Jonathan wouldn't just be the guy obligated to give her a kidney or some of his bone marrow, if, God forbid, she ever needed it.

"You're right," Cass said, because it was always easiest to stand in solidarity with a friend. This didn't feel like the right time to play devil's advocate. "So have you told anyone else?"

"You're the first friend I've voluntarily told. But I can assure you all the moms at Scarsdale elementary and Beth Israel Preschool are buzzing. I'm going to call Alexi and fill her in sometime in the next few days."

Alexi was Dahlia's other best friend from college, godmother to Dahlia's younger son, and someone Cass knew pretty well from theater classes. She was a working actress in Los Angeles, having come a long way from the musical version of *The Vagina Monologues* in which she'd made her theatrical debut at Brown. Alexi was really good in it, actually. The director deserved all the blame—and lots of scorn—for that failed production.

"How are you and Jonathan doing?" Dahlia asked. "I've just been going on and on about myself."

"Really good, thanks," Cass answered, hoping her straightforward and quick answer sounded convincing. It was the truth, but for some reason when she said it, it had the ring of a cover-up. They *were* really good. About-to-start-a-family good. So what if she felt light-headed and sweaty because she couldn't stop thinking about how and why she first pursued her husband? Everyone had secrets, and anyway, didn't the deep and genuine love she now felt for her husband override the artificial nature of their courtship?

The lie wasn't something she was proud of, but in the grand scheme of falsehoods, she didn't think it was completely unforgivable. The problem, as Cass saw it, was that she had waited far too long to confess. Secrets had a funny habit of snowballing, and what may have been a minor infraction on Day One had morphed into something monumental as time ticked on. Maybe that's why she let their five-year anniversary pass without any fanfare. She couldn't bear to acknowledge just how long she'd held her tongue about their origin story. She sank her teeth into the sourdough again.

"Well, that's great. Let's get some wine. We need to toast my divorce and your marriage," Dahlia said. "Plus I need some alcohol before I have to face the bitches at Toby's pickup."

"I'm on it," Cass said, signaling to the waitress. "And D, I'm here for you. Anytime you need me. Text me and I will get my ass to Scarsdale stat. And, of course, anything the boys need, I'll be there in a flash."

"DAHLIA'S A LESBIAN," Cass whispered, almost as though if she said it louder her cell phone would explode in her hand. She'd had a weird pit in her stomach since lunch with Dahlia, the source of which she couldn't quite comprehend. She hoped calling Alexi to discuss the shocking news would settle her. This was news that needed to be picked over with someone else who knew Dahlia as well as she did.

"No way," Alexi said, over the crackle of the Bluetooth. "That's insane." Cass heard a few honks and the zoom of a motorcycle in the background.

"I know. I can't get over it. She's planning to tell you herself soon, but I just couldn't wait."

"Well, I'm glad you called because I could use the preparation. And you caught me at the perfect time. I just left an audition. Speaking of auditions, what happened to the LA-PAC interview? Weren't you supposed to be out here by now?"

"It didn't work out," Cass said quickly, without elaborating further. Her interview with the Los Angeles Performing Arts Center was originally scheduled to take place a week earlier, but she'd called to cancel last minute. On a whim after leaving PZA, Cass had circulated her résumé to a few theater friends, asking that they keep her in mind if good opportunities came up. She wasn't planning to pursue any leads in the near term. It would be a classically bad move to start a new job at the same time as getting pregnant. There'd be too many long hours at the office, maybe even international trips if her shows went on tour—things that weren't compatible with morning sickness and the first few months of motherhood. And she didn't think it would be an issue anyway. It would probably take a very long time to find something worthwhile in her small and highly competitive field. So she was totally shocked when, out of the blue and almost immediately, she received a call from the biggest performing arts theater in Los Angeles. They wanted to know if she would fly out to interview for the head of marketing and sales position. It was definitely a bigger job than she'd had at PZA, and she'd called Alexi to ask her what she knew about the theater. They'd agreed to get together when Cass was out west meeting with the LA-PAC board. One person she never told about the opportunity was Jonathan. His life was in New York City. He'd built a burgeoning career outside of the shadow of his family's success and making equity partner at Winstar was on the near horizon for him. Not the time to discuss a cross-country move. Which meant she should never have spoken with anyone at LA-PAC at all, except to say, "I'm flattered, but no thank you." So why Cass had bothered to set up an in-person interview was a mystery, even to herself.

"What was the audition for? Jonathan told me he saw you on *Law & Order* again."

"Everyone's on *L&O*. You know that. This was for a budget Halloween horror movie, and my next stop is a commercial for a herpes medication. How terrible is it that I'm going to be the face of Abreva? Actually, what's worse is that I'm only just *hoping* to become the face of Abreva. No choice, though, it's a national commercial, and I need money for new headshots. Can we go back to Dahlia, though? How does she seem? What about Harris?"

"They've already started divorce proceedings. She seems happy, but also anxious. Very worried about the kids, of course, and Harris is being a prick. She thinks he's hiding assets. Aah, and I didn't even mention the clincher. Her girlfriend is Brady's assistant principal. Scarsdale hasn't had a scandal like this in decades and Dahlia said it's been like one constant orgasm for the soccer moms since this happened."

"Jesus. Good for Dahlia, though. It's really brave of her."

"It *is* brave of her, isn't it?" Cass said, and it was like a lightbulb switched on in her brain. Dahlia's courage was making Cass feel less than. She didn't want a divorce from Jonathan—of course not. But somehow Dahlia's bid for freedom and self-fulfillment made Cass green with envy. Her friend was finally coming clean, and her life would be better off for it. Since lunch started, Cass's emotions had gone from nervousness to shock to relief and now jealousy—the worst feeling of all.

"Well, I'm sorry to hear about the job not working out. Maybe you should think about coming for a visit anyway."

"I'd love to. I haven't been to L.A. since Percy and I flew out to film those promos for the Grammys a couple of years ago."

"Well, it's settled then. You'll take a vacation out here before you and Jonathan have some gorgeous baby that exhausts the hell out of you and precludes any travel for at least a year."

Maybe Alexi was right—maybe she should go to California and relax for a few days. It would be a bit strange to hang with Alexi without Dahlia for any meaningful amount of time—she was definitely the link between them—but it could be fun to have a little getaway, especially to a warm climate. And there was no reason Cass and Alexi weren't closer. No good one, anyway.

Alexi Williams was physical perfection packed into a five-foot-three frame, defying the logic of her petite stature with her swan neck and longish limbs. She had that ballerina quality that made it seem like at any moment she'd get *en pointe* and pirouette around the room. Add in some white-blond hair, flawless skin and wide-set doe eyes, and Alexi was the rare person who could make Cass feel insecure about her looks. Cass had been dealt many disadvantages in life, so she didn't feel the least bit guilty trading on the one advantage she'd not been spared. So being around Alexi, feeling the power of her prettiness slip through her fingers like sand, well, it made her uneasy.

But there was something else too—a deeper jealousy that made Cass want to keep Alexi at a distance.

Cass had always been tempted by the theater, and she loved the big biannual shows sponsored by the drama club at her massive public high school. Still, she never bothered to try out for anything because there was no one to pick her up from rehearsals or chip in with the other parents for cast parties and costumes. Then she got to Brown, where she didn't have to worry anymore about what Donna and Dick might fail to do. From the moment she stepped foot on campus, Cass secretly hoped that theater would become her "thing," and she auditioned for the first production she saw advertised. The play was *Death of a Salesman*, her favorite, and it felt like a sign when she won the small part of Letta. But, no matter how hard she tried, she couldn't find a way to get comfortable in the role. The problem was that Cass was already playing a part in her real life: the girl who belongs at Brown. She stepped into character each morning before greeting her roommate or even brushing her teeth, and she didn't step out until she closed her eyes each night. It was too difficult, too confusing, to add another layer of artifice on top of the mask she already wore during all her waking hours. She was a good actress, but not that good.

In contrast, Alexi had no such hurdles to overcome in the fitting-in department at school. She was a double legacy at Brown—her parents lived in a rambling mansion in a suburb of Providence that Cass had once been invited to during college. It had a wraparound porch with swinging benches and the inside featured a double-height library with towers of books that looked like they'd actually been read. And while Alexi struggled financially in California, it was only because her parents, both medical doctors, were withholding funds until she "came to her senses" about a career in entertainment. Alexi was cast as Linda Loman in the same *Salesman* production, where she glided seamlessly in and out of character without a hitch.

Over time, Cass found her own place in the theater behind the scenes, working as a stage manager, lighting designer, director and de facto marketer. She had a particular genius for the promotional side, and since that was the job that eventually led her to Percy, she tried not to look back.

"I just might come," Cass said finally to Alexi, realizing a trip to California might be just what the doctor ordered. Vitamin D in non-capsule form. Plus, immersion in a city of shiny, happy people who didn't waste hours each day thinking in what-ifs like neurotic New Yorkers.

Her thoughts returned to what Alexi had said earlier . . . *a gorgeous baby.* Jonathan had a lot of strong, enviable WASP genes to pass on to their hybrid offspring. She'd made sure of that. A well-proportioned jaw, a six-foot-one stature that would hopefully average out her own modest contribution (height was such an easy way to establish gravitas) and a head of hair that was hanging around him longer than many other men his age who were forced into comb-overs or premature head shaves. Cass certainly didn't go weak at the knees at the sight of him anymore, but she appreciated his good looks in a more enduring way. She especially liked walking into a room and seeing the approving glances.

She was a year older than Jonathan. Eight months actually, but it translated into them being a school year apart. It bothered her. She had planned to be a few years younger than her spouse, as much as one can "plan" these things—and if anyone could, it was her—but instead she and Jonathan were growing up together. All things being equal, it'd be better to have your spouse grow up first and then tell you all the mistakes to avoid—unlike her parents, who were both young and dumb about everything, the blind leading the blind. She tried to focus on the positives of growing old *with* her husband, instead of playing catch-up. They could go together for his and her colonoscopies, share a subscription to AARP. Still, the matter of Jonathan's age was made even more irritating by the fact that Cass was starting to show hers and he was not. It was just the normal course of female deterioration outpacing male, but it worried her. Glycolic acid peels could only do so much and she wasn't ready to take any steps that involved needles or "recovery time," *cough cough.* She wasn't a spring chicken anymore—it wasn't the time to risk what she had. Maybe back when her face was still line-free, before cellulite formed those gelatinous blobs that dimpled her thighs. Now she had to play it safe. If she ever were to seek out a new partner—like if Jonathan were to get hit by a bus or discover he had glioblastoma—she'd make sure it was someone comfortably older than her who would appreciate her youth simply as a relative matter. What was wrong with her for even thinking such thoughts? She wondered if Jonathan ever imagined what his life would be like if she were suddenly wiped off the earth.

"Are you still seeing that director, by the way?" Cass asked. "Dahlia mentioned something about that at lunch."

"No, no. He was way too intense. On to the next. Not all of us are as lucky as you—literally bumping into Mr. Perfect. So I'm waiting for my Jonathan and trying to have a good time until he shows up."

"Make a left turn on La Brea Boulevard." Cass heard Arnold Schwarzenegger suddenly in the background.

"What the hell was that?"

"Oh, that's just Waze. See the things you're missing out on in New York?"

"We have traffic here too. You've been to the Hamptons. I didn't realize the Terminator was doing voice-overs. What's next, cold sore commercials?"

"Very funny. I have to go. Arnold just told me there's an accident ahead. I need to detour."

"Drive safely. You just may be picking me up from the airport soon. Stay tuned."

8. JONATHAN

AFTER YEARS OF trying to avoid pregnancy, it would definitely be weird to have sex with the opposite goal. All the worry about having an accident in high school and college was now suddenly converted by the forces of life and age into pressure. Would his boys swim? He had no reason to think they wouldn't. They'd swum once before. It'd be better anyway if it took a while for Cass to get pregnant. More guaranteed sex.

In the past five years, Nate, Jeff and even Russell had all gotten married. Nate and Jeff were already fathers and Jerry and Ginny had four grown children. He was ready to join the club—frankly, he never expected his dopey cronies to get there before him. Nate and Jeff had both married girls without serious professional aspirations. Technically they had jobs, PR-this and fashion-that, but nothing that rose to the level of career status. They were primed for baby-making, according to Cass, from the minute they got someone to put a ring on it. *Attractive incubators,* he thought she may have called them one night when she was feeling particularly uncharitable. Cass was different, which is not to say that she wasn't maternal. One look at Cass with Henry and Jemima's twins or seeing the way she agonized over what to send Dahlia's kid for his birthday, not to mention the excitement he gathered from catching glimpses of the bookmarked sites on her computer when they had been expecting—the ones where the size of the fetus is compared to various fruits (Cass still couldn't eat blueberries anymore)—and it was obvious she'd make an attentive and loving mother. But her career mattered to her deeply, and she had wanted to reach a certain place before a string of maternity leaves (he hoped three) would make advancement more difficult. At this point in time, with "creative director" at PZA on her résumé, when she was ready to go back, Cass would be snapped up immediately by any number of firms. By all accounts and interested parties, the timing was right.

After a fist bump to the doorman and a solitary elevator ride to the sixteenth floor, he turned the key in the door, surprised to find Cass had lit candles and tuned their never-touched Sonos system to a jazz station. They had texted a bit back and forth during the day, somewhat suggestively. They both knew that tonight would be their first night of trying. The day Cass came home from Dr. Levin's office she'd added an event to her Google calendar three months from the day of her appointment and sent him an invite. She titled it "Baby-Making" and inserted heart and baby bottle emojis. He'd accepted the calendar invite immediately: *Jonathan Coyne has accepted your invitation for "Baby-Making" at 9:00 p.m., location (home).*

"Cass?" he called out. Puddles came running, yelping like Lassie with an urgent message.

"Hey, bud," he said, scooping up his beloved pup. "Where's Mommy?"

Puddles led him down the narrow corridor leading to their bedroom. As Jonathan moved farther into the apartment, stopping only to remove his winter gear and drop it on a dining room chair, he heard the shower in the master bathroom running. He made his way into the fogged-up room, Puddles tagging along.

"Hey," he said, opening the glass door to the shower a crack. "Want company?"

"You scared me," Cass said, one of those blasted Le Bristol mini bottles in hand. "I'm almost done."

"Okay," he retreated. He tried not to take it personally. The joint shower literally left someone out in the cold. "I'll be in the kitchen."

Puddles, having uncovered the mystery of who had come through the front door, now refused to leave Cass, so Jonathan went alone to grab a beer from the fridge. He told himself again that Cass's desire to shower alone was no big deal. A shower was a weird place to attempt to conceive a child, anyway, at least on their first try. From a scientific perspective, missionary seemed to be the most reliable method.

Amstel in hand, he returned to the bedroom and mindlessly put on the Knicks game in the background. Puddles loved the Knicks; the sound of the announcer made him ditch Cass and jump onto the bed. Puddles also loved the Yankees, and it was a true testament to how much Jonathan loved Puddles that he could forgive him this transgression. A few minutes later, a robed and turbaned Cass came out, her face rosy and glistening. A gleaming Madonna.

"Let's go out," she said, her voice oddly defiant. "I haven't eaten dinner. Have you?"

"Not yet. But are you sure? It's almost eight thirty. Maybe we should just order in?"

"No, I want to go out," she said. "Is that okay?"

"Yeah, of course," he said, even though it was sleeting, one of the coldest Marches on record, and he barely had an appetite. Jerry had been on edge all day because his bearish call about Chevron had been wrong. Winstar had been bested by several of its competitors and the investor relations team was fielding angry calls all day. This was precisely why he never liked taking credit for the upswings. "Wa Jeal?"

"Perfect."

Why he suggested Chinese on faraway Second Avenue when it was sleeting outside, and why Cass agreed to it, was beyond him. But she seemed to just want to get out of the apartment and he didn't want to retread on their agreement.

Cass threw on jeans, a tight black sweater and motorcycle boots. She was dressing differently since she wasn't going into work anymore, younger, but still stylish—this was Cass after all, and she'd always had an eye for clothes. The rip in her jeans, though? He supposed they were in style, but it seemed strange for a grown woman. Still, he knew better than to share his opinion about the tattered denim or the studs on her boots. He'd noticed just the other day the slightest hint of varicose veins on the backs of her calves. And that was another thing he would never bring up.

"Bye, baby," Cass said, kissing Puddles on the mouth. "I promise we'll be back soon with leftovers." He let out a low growl, voicing his displeasure at being left out.

They walked the entire way to the restaurant in silence, focused on anchoring their umbrellas overhead and keeping them from inverting. When they arrived, the restaurant was empty.

"I noticed Luna hasn't been by," Jonathan said once they were seated. "Isn't she supposed to come on Wednesdays now?" Finding the dishes stacked high in the sink and his dress shirts still in a pile on their club chair had really pissed him off when he got home that evening. He bit his tongue in the moment because he thought sex was imminent. Now that they were out for dinner, he didn't see why he shouldn't bring it up.

"She's in midterms," Cass snapped, twisting her hair into a bun and clamping it with one of those giant clips that were scattered everywhere around their apartment. He thought of them sometimes as Cass's claws.

"Okay. But doesn't she work when she's in school? PhD Housekeeping and all?" He cracked a smile, to show that he wasn't all that annoyed.

"She probably had an exam today. I'll text her and make sure she comes." Luckily, Cass backed off her mercurial stance. On another night, his prodding about Luna could have erupted Mount Vesuvius.

"How's work?" she asked, popping a wonton dunked in orange sauce into her mouth.

"Today was shitty. Everything was down. I heard Russell on the phone with his wife telling her to cancel their trip to Saint-Tropez. High-class problems, I know."

"Seriously. How's that girl you told me about a while ago? She married yet? I'm dying to know what happened with the band-DJ showdown."

Jonathan had ended up telling Cass about Laurel during a weekend stroll through the park with Puddles when he and Cass were out of conversation, something that was happening more frequently than he liked to admit. Once they had children that would certainly change. Then they could analyze the wetness of a diaper or the cuteness of a giggle ad nauseam and never again face an awkward silence.

When he told Cass about Laurel, he left out the juicy part where she expressed worry about being with one person for the rest of her life and him explaining that marriage is all about making compromises. Why open a can of worms? It was hard to see that kind of discussion with Cass going in a positive direction, no matter how cheery his wife seemed at the outset.

"She's on her honeymoon. I never did get to hear what happened with the band. I'll be sure to find out."

"Please do," Cass said, raising her Tsingtao. Jonathan felt like he detected a note of acidity, though he hoped he was imagining it. She seemed off tonight, but it might be him. Jerry's foul mood could cast a spell on the whole office. The investor relations girls click-clacked their heels more quietly; the traders took the circuitous route to the bathroom to avoid passing by Jerry's office. Jonathan suspected his boss's mood went beyond Chevron—something on the home front was probably ruffling his feathers, like one of Jerry's kids having trouble (drugs were rumored to be an issue with his oldest) or Ginny firing their driver—again. Something beyond gas prices was amiss for sure.

"Can I take your order?" the waiter asked, interrupting his thoughts.

Cass took charge, as per usual.

"I'll have shrimp dumplings and garlic broccoli. Honey, do you want the usual?"

He nodded, feeling gratitude for the thousandth time in his life that someone knew what he wanted. His own mother wouldn't have a clue what he'd like. He also felt his insides warm at the term of endearment, which rolled off Cass's tongue like ice cream sliding down a cone.

"He'll have a veggie egg roll and beef lo mein."

The waiter scribbled the characters onto his green pad. "I'll bring extra plates for sharing."

"No," Cass said sharply. She hated to share, but not as much as she hated the presumption that she would be sharing. If Jonathan so much as reached for one of her dumplings, she could turn a chopstick on him. Tapas were literally Cass's worst nightmare. He knew resources were scarce for her as a child, but she should have been able to get over it by now—to let someone have a bite of her cheesecake without fearing starvation.

The food came quickly and they ate without much chitchat. A few comments about the new doorman who'd started working at their condo (Cass complaining he made too much small talk even if she was carrying groceries) and a question about where to go for vacation in July, leading to a brief back-and-forth about the merits of sightseeing versus beach. Then a bout of silence until the fortune cookies arrived with the bill. He guessed they really weren't going to discuss the calendar appointment. Maybe Cass hadn't even seen it. Without work, she wasn't as attuned to things like times and dates. But no, she had to have. It would have popped up as a bubble on her cell phone, which he was sure she'd looked at a dozen times today at least. And there were candles and jazz when he'd walked through the door.

"I still can't believe Dahlia's getting divorced," Cass said when he was paying the check. "We spoke again today for a while. She said the legal stuff is going to be worse than she originally thought. She needs me to write a character letter to the judge. Harris is asking for full custody, can you believe it? He says Dahlia getting involved with Brady's assistant principal indicates her judgment is so poor that she's an unfit mother. Obviously he just feels like a chump. Oh, and he froze their joint accounts. She's trying to dig up some shady stuff on his investments to have leverage. Total mess."

"I'm really sorry to hear that," he said, sliding his wallet into his back pocket. He was anxious to get home. Baby-making had been slated for 9:00 p.m. They were already an hour behind. He wanted to make that joke to Cass but decided against it.

"Shall we?" Cass asked, rising from her chair.

"Let's go."

The sleet had subsided and they walked home through the empty streets, umbrellas flanking them and poking the ground like walking sticks. Jonathan reached for Cass's hand, but she slipped it into her pocket. "No gloves," she explained. He dug his hands back into his pockets and felt the fortune cookies he'd taken with him. It felt like bad luck to leave a fortune cookie unopened, so he'd grabbed both his and Cass's. Tonight was a momentous evening—he was curious to read what the little white scrolls of paper predicted for the would-be parents, even just for humor value.

Upstairs, he watched Cass carefully remove her contacts and slip them into their case. He brushed his teeth alongside her, the buzzing of their electric toothbrushes operating in tandem. Why did he feel so nervous?

They climbed into bed, both of them careful not to disturb a sleeping Puddles. He turned out the bedside lamp, the only light left in the room the glow from their two cell phones. Their screens would go to black momentarily.

He reached for her face, cupping her chin gently, and pulled her toward him for a kiss.

"Jonathan," she said, her voice breathy and quivering. It was a big moment for them. From their first kiss outside Paragon, to running into each other on Park Avenue, to their wedding and the balancing of their families, to what they went through two years ago, to this . . . It had solidified them as the real deal.

"Yeah?"

"I want to take a break."

9. CASS

"I WANT TO take a break."

Her panties were on their way to her ankles when she said it. She and Jonathan were about three minutes away from potentially conceiving a child when the words escaped her lips.

"Huh?" Jonathan rolled off of her. "A break from what?"

She wanted to search his face, to see if he was in fact as clueless as his question implied. But Cass couldn't make herself look her husband in the eye, to directly engage with the anger and confusion he must be feeling.

In those crucial seconds that followed, she still had a chance to stop the madness she was setting into motion. She could say she just needed to get up to pee. Or ask for a break from their missionary rut. The point was, there was time to cap the mess before it unfurled and there was no turning back. She bit down hard on her bottom lip, considering how to proceed, weighing the options as she saw the linear trajectory of her life suddenly forking. The AC, which Jonathan insisted on running even in the dead of winter, cycled to blowing cold air on them and she hopped up to turn it down.

"Cass? A break from what? If I'm not mistaken, we were about to try for a baby. I'd like to know what's going on. If you want me to put on a condom, if you're not ready, it's fine. Just tell me what you're thinking."

She walked over to their club chair and took a seat. Maybe that's why the decorator insisted they have more furniture in the room. Because when two people are about to have a fight, it's unnatural for them to be lying in bed together while they're doing it. The distance, even if it was a measly eight feet, was critical for what she was about to say, though it might have been easier if she could have avoided the eye contact that her position across from Jonathan was forcing.

"I know this is going to seem nuts and completely out of left field, but I want to take a break from us. Not a divorce or anything like that." She paused for emphasis, to let it sink in. "Just some space. A refresher. A chance to think." How many different euphemisms could she think of? And why did she turn down the AC? Now she was sweating like a marathoner, her armpits moist with musky tension. "It's temporary," she added, as though that qualifier should be enough to mollify her husband.

"Are you kidding me?" Jonathan's nostrils flared momentarily but he reined himself back in. With a softer tone, he added, "Cass, what is it you want from me? How can you not be happy? We have everything. Our health. Great careers. I know the thing with Percy was terrible, and you miss him, but you will find another job you love. Don't let that temporary setback upset all the good. We get to make a family. We have Puddles. Friends. Family, for better or for worse. And I think I'm a pretty decent guy. Easygoing, I let things slide, I work hard. You want me to get a nose job, I'll get one, for God's sake. Just tell me where the hell this is coming from."

It was all true. Fact after fact upon which their marriage was built.

Brick and mortar in spades: Puddles. Relative youth, sleek bodies, which should spell virility and desire. Their careers, especially his, which brought in enough that they had the luxury of fighting over nonmonetary things. Jonathan was, as he put it, easygoing, though that wasn't necessarily a good thing when routine and boredom were among the culprits of her discontent. But then it echoed, what he'd said next: *Let. Things. Slide.* What things? Suddenly it was like the car she was driving was now coming at her in reverse.

And why didn't he ask her if there was someone else? When she had rehearsed the conversation in her head, back when she still never intended to say any of it out loud, that was his first question. Isn't that why people left perfectly good marriages—to gamble on a happier life with another person? Or if not happier, at least steamier? She, Cass, was unique in that she was pulling away for different reasons. But how did Jonathan see that so quickly? Why didn't he picture some greasy tennis instructor in white shorts wetting her whistle? Maybe he believed she was more complex than a cliché, though that was optimistic.

Looking across the room at the new landscape of her life, she revisited in hindsight the options that were now unavailable to her. She could have suggested a wanderlust trip to someplace they'd never been—on a beach in Thailand armed with rum punches, nothing could possibly feel wrong. She could have confessed that her joblessness was stressing her and that she just needed to get a new job before feeling comfortable starting a family. Or she could have just stuck with the plan and let her concerns get eclipsed by the wonder of cells multiplying inside her. Instead, she was choosing an escape route. She was buying time. Time she very much needed to evaluate how she felt about her marriage, her deception, and the cold, hard knowledge that she wasn't sure she was fulfilled despite having gotten everything she wanted. This was, in fact, the ultimate now or never. If she did decide that she had to come clean to Jonathan, it had to be before they conceived. He was a loyal husband, and she was certain he would be a devoted father, so if he came face-to-face with the truth about her after they had a child—well, he probably wouldn't leave her. But she'd always wonder if he could see her the same way again—love her the same way again. Or if he did divorce her, then what? They would have a child bounced back and forth like a volleyball, spiked between two angry parents.

So yes, her timing was terrible, but the terrifying horizon of parenthood was what pushed her to this place where she was literally in a corner, facing her husband like an opponent in a boxing ring. She'd been a wreck all day since her cell phone buzzed with the reminder that today was her "Baby-Making" appointment. She'd reflexively clicked to dismiss the reminder. At the time she'd created the entry and invited Jonathan, she'd thought it was an adorable thing to do. Now it made her feel like a fool. Especially with her feeble attempts to get in the mood by lighting candles and playing Sade.

The baby was definitely the central issue, flaming her guilt into a mass that grew bigger every day, but there were other centrifugal forces at play. Watching Jonathan's penis rise like a flagpole in his boxers, knowing she would lie beneath his nearly hairless chest for maybe the five hundredth time in her life, or could it be the thousandth already, and the two of them would push and pull and click and churn against each other and then in five minutes they'd be up drinking water, peeing, flipping on the TV, talking about their upstairs neighbor's penchant for rearranging furniture at odd hours—that might have been the nail in the coffin. The thing giving life to the crazy idea otherwise lying dormant in her subconscious. She suddenly wondered why anyone would name a jewelry company Pandora. There was nothing romantic about opening up boxes meant to be kept shut.

"Calm down," she sputtered, though he had every right to be upset, to question her. Blindsiding him like this was unusually cruel. If she really wanted to do this, she should have built up to it gradually. Picked a few fights back to back, acted distant for at least a month— the old "the cat's on the roof" routine. Instead they went from nudging each other under the table when their least favorite waiter at Wa Jeal ambled over to take their order to breaking up—*excuse me, taking a break*—an hour later. There was a right way and a wrong way to do things, and this was clearly the latter. She wanted to backpedal—to make sure the relationship she was fracturing was intact enough that she could return to it. At the molecular level, she needed to make sure her husband didn't start to hate her.

"There isn't anyone else," she added quietly, just in case he was indeed wondering but was afraid to ask.

"I know that," Jonathan said, matter-of-factly. How *did* he know that so definitively? Maybe he didn't think she could do better, which could very well be true. Or that she'd never be so foolish as to risk losing what they had by giving in to a fleeting, primal urge.

"This is about Dahlia," he said plainly.

How was it that Jonathan was already psychoanalyzing something that he never saw coming and had barely had a full five minutes to process?

"Cass—she's your first friend to get divorced and it's making you freak out about us. You need to be happy with what you have. Dahlia is gay—it's not a case of your parents all over again. And I don't even understand what you mean by a separation. Should I sleep in the spare room? Get an apartment on the West Side? Have you thought this through? Because it sounds ludicrous. Do you love me? Because I love you. And last time I checked, people who love each other and don't have real problems stay together. Yes, we bicker sometimes. If you think you're going to find someone else and the two of you will never fight, good luck."

"Hear me out, Jonathan, please." She was nearly shrieking, with the shrillness that she normally found distasteful in others. "I do love you. This isn't about not appreciating my life or because of Dahlia. I don't think it's the craziest thing in the world to live apart for a time. We are not the same couple we used to be. We argue about the stupidest things.

We have less sex. We don't laugh as much. Can you honestly think of the last romantic date we've had? You are totally wrapped up in your job, and I'm totally out of sorts being unemployed for the first time in my adult life. We both know that what we went through two years ago did a number on us. And your mother hates me. Well, that part hasn't changed, but it's wearing on me. Before we bring some innocent little person into the world, wouldn't we be wise to make sure this is it for us? That we are each other's happy ending? You know that thing where people have a kid to save a marriage. Well, this is the opposite—we're going to save the marriage before we have a kid. As a child of divorce, I can tell you with certainty that—"

"Cass," he said, interrupting her. "What about—?" Jonathan tilted his head over to Puddles and started rubbing his back protectively.

Crap, she hadn't thought of Puddles. And why was Jonathan coming around so quickly anyway? Maybe bringing up Puddles was his way of quashing the entire notion. Neither of them could live without Puddles; ergo, there could be no separation. She felt a momentary sense of relief, but found herself soldiering on. The voice speaking was not her own, or rather it didn't feel controlled by her brain. It wasn't even her heart that was guiding her tongue, because that part of her was wishing she would stop hurting Jonathan. Somewhere, a disembodied voice found the strength to continue.

"We'll figure that out—we can trade off. Don't you ever wonder sometimes if we really know each other?"

Jonathan raised an eyebrow.

"Is there something you want to tell me?"

This was her chance to come clean about the origins of their relationship. The way she'd honed in on him like a sharpshooter at target practice. Not once, but twice.

"I, I just—" she started.

"And how am I supposed to get to know you better by living

apart?" he asked, interrupting her incomplete thought. "Where are you going, by the way?"

"Tonight, a hotel. Tomorrow . . . I will figure out the rest."

"Have you lost your mind?" he asked.

"It's true we'll be living apart, but we'll still speak. Maybe even more than we do now—at least about the important stuff. Let's do this for six months. If at the end, we both decide that we're happier together than apart, that we need each other, we will get back together and appreciate each other more than ever. And start a family. The break will be the best gift to our child because we'll be so sure of our commitment to each other. And if not, we'll . . . we'll . . . you know." She couldn't bring herself to say it. "It'll be a gap year. But half!"

"How delightful," he said, his voice dripping with sarcasm, a device he rarely used. "Will you go to Europe? Backpack perhaps? However will you spend this precious time before you have to buckle down and be an actual adult? The possibilities are endless."

"Fine, poor choice of words. I didn't mean a gap year like for eighteen-year-olds." She knew she sounded pedantic and condescending, but her tone, much like what she was saying, was out of her control. What she and Jonathan needed was to metaphorically stretch. And then the word occurred to her.

"It'll be like an intermission."

"It's idiotic is what it is. Don't treat our life like it's the script from one of your shitty plays." He reached for his pants, draped over their dresser, and retrieved the little folded cookies in their sealed wrappers. And just like that, she watched their fortunes get tossed into the trash.

act two

INTERMISSION

10. JONATHAN

IT WAS HARD to look at the beads of sweat rolling down the ravines of Jerry's hairy chest, but then again it was harder to look away. The tiny white towel wrapped around his boss's waist was quite rapidly coming undone, and since eye contact was really impossible in this situation, the chest was the safest landing spot.

"Son, marriage is complicated," his boss said, raising his thick pointer finger in the air. "You'll see. Life is full of surprises." *Two Jerry-isms for the price of one,* Jonathan thought, though he really shouldn't be nasty. It was awfully considerate of his boss to take him out for a "manly day," as Jerry had put it. Jerry rarely took time away from the office, so it was particularly touching when he'd swept into Jonathan's office insisting they play squash and have lunch at his racquet club.

Jonathan nodded. The towel gap widened. How much longer were they going to *shvitz* for? A similar lobster lunch to the one Cass had had designs on at the Cosmo, before she took off, awaited him and Jerry in the storied, wood-paneled dining room located three floors up in the University Club. Jonathan hated to be so unappreciative, but he couldn't easily accept other people's kindness these days. It felt like pity, and that took the pleasure out of every nice gesture.

"Ginny's going to call Cass. We've been together for thirty-nine years. Four kids. We've been through it all. Affairs, hers and mine, my gambling thing, her drinking. Trust me, there's nothing you can say that'll shock me."

That's for sure, Jonathan thought wistfully. His marriage was falling apart because of purported snoring, his disapproval of Luna, and Cass's boredom from a few months of being unemployed. In a word, minutiae, tiny little pecks that grate at the surface of every relationship but don't penetrate into any real danger zone. Irritations a more complacent person than his wife could overlook. His current working theory: Cass was having a third-of-her-life crisis and he was the closest target in sight. Well, technically their marriage was the target, but it sure felt personal. Why else would Cass have concocted this ridiculous experiment? He hadn't seriously ever doubted that she loved him, but he didn't exactly give it thought on a regular basis. They were in love when they got married, got along decently well (a hell of a lot better than his parents ever did) and had their whole lives together to look forward to. Fifty-plus years, at least, if he considered what they used to write on those wedding napkins. There was nothing to overthink or worry about, though apparently his wife felt differently. Could it all boil down to something as simple as that book people still talked about—*Men Are from Mars, Women Are from Venus?* Because it sure felt like it.

In any case, compared to Jerry and Ginny, he and Cass were milquetoast. Milquetoast on a garden leave. Actually, it wasn't at all like the rules of a garden leave, where ex-employees were forbidden from meeting with any competitors. Because they were expressly allowed to see other people.

"I mean, that makes sense, right?" Cass had said, while she haphazardly threw her belongings into their monogrammed luggage an hour after she announced she wanted a break. The *J* stitched into the leather caught his eye—at least a part of him would be with her during the break. One swooping letter. The heel of one of her shoes was poking into her sweater pile and he resisted the urge to hand her a shoe bag. And to show her the Tumi's inner pockets for accessories. "How can we know if we're happier together or apart if we don't try other things? I just want to be realistic. And I want you to be happy and fulfilled as well." He had wanted to call bullshit on that part, but didn't.

Cass was actually asking him to help design the parameters of the separation. She didn't want to take full responsibility for it—to make the call, so to speak. It reminded him of the way the lesser analysts at Winstar made stock suggestions to Jerry. "This would be a great buy," they said, followed up with, "but the investment committee should do a full study." By asking for his input, Cass was making him a coconspirator. Well, he wasn't so foolish as to become an architect of this plan. It was demoralizing enough to be a signatory.

"This whole thing is your idea. You can decide." That's what he said in return. She only nodded slightly, which he believed meant, *Yes—we can see other people.* Or, *At least I may.*

"Thanks, Jerry," Jonathan said, wiping sweat from his brow. "But I'm not sure that'll be much help. Cass has to work out these issues by herself."

"I'm sure it's a phase. They all act crazy from time to time. You say the word if you want Ginny involved. Let's eat, shall we?" Jerry rose and the terry towel fell to the floor. In a heap on the wet tile, it looked no bigger than a hand towel. Jonathan looked away to save Jerry the embarrassment; Cass might have laughed. She could be kinder than anyone on the planet at times, and then, all of a sudden, exhibit a mean streak. And if he was honest with himself, knowing she had the capacity to be hurtful, he was just relieved whenever someone else was on the receiving end and he was more than happy to tune it out. To think that Cass had suggested they didn't really know each other well . . . Absurd. It was true he couldn't always predict what Cass was going to do, but that was because one of her personality traits was unpredictability! What nonsense could she have been referring to? That he didn't know she used to want to be an astronaut? He knew all about her childhood obsession with Sally Ride. That she thought she might be lactose intolerant?

"Whoops," Jerry said, snatching the towel up and quickly assembling it back as a cover-up, which was ambitious given the girth of his waistline. God, this was a painfully awkward moment, the kind of "detail of the day" he might have shared with Cass during a commercial break when they were in bed watching TV at the end of the night.

"A good woman can be very useful, don't forget it," Jerry added.

Ginny coordinated the Winstar Christmas party; Ginny invited the analysts' wives for lunch; Ginny made sure Jerry's clothes were dry-cleaned (or she told someone to make sure they were). Jonathan wasn't looking for a personal assistant or another mother, and thank God, because Cass wasn't likely to fill either of those roles.

Jonathan tightened his own towel around his waist, looking down at the shiny gold wedding band sandwiched between the puffy flesh of his overheated ring finger. He hadn't taken off the ring, even with the gap. *Especially* with the gap. Because that would give the whole stupid experiment a level of gravitas that he just wasn't willing to allocate to it. Besides, he was still pretty convinced the gap, or the more euphemistically put "intermission," would be a hell of a lot shorter than six months. They were only two weeks in so far and Cass was calling or texting from Los Angeles every day to "check on him." It didn't seem guilt-driven. It felt like pretext, with her trivial news reports following the cursory "How are you?" (*Puddles is probably running low on treats. I saw Jerry on CNBC. Alexi is a psycho exerciser.*) On April Fool's Day, he almost thought he'd get a singing telegram decrying the entire thing a cruel joke.

He saw the separation's end playing out in one of two ways. Either Cass would come charging back to him within the month, blaming her erratic behavior on the hormonal effects of going off the pill or on Percy's death. Or she'd invent some legitimate reason for her behavior, like he never told her she was beautiful anymore or he paid more attention to the stock market than to her. He'd rapidly apologize (because, after all, that would be the easiest way out of this nonsense) and they could bury this episode along with the other unpleasantness they'd weathered since getting married. How else could this intermission play itself out? Cass had said they would take six months to assess how they felt. "That's only two quarters," she'd added, trying to put it in his language. He wasn't an idiot—he knew what six months was. Still, it was hard to tell how literally she meant the time frame. Would they come together at the end of September to weigh the pros and cons? Would each of them write on a piece of paper *TOGETHER* or *APART* and then open the other's simultaneously? Would they flip a coin? He repeated it to himself. *Flip. A. Coyne.* How fitting.

They wouldn't get to that point anyway. The separation would terminate much sooner, most likely with Cass realizing the single world wasn't as great as she'd remembered it. It was chock-full of disappointment and uncertainty, two things he knew his wife wasn't fond of.

When she was packing up her things, the trio of skinny wedding bands she wore stacked like the stories of a shiny skyscraper remained on her finger. He kept his gaze on the tiny tower adorning her left hand while she stuffed jeans, T-shirts and other essentials into her suitcase. When she told him during their engagement that she wanted three thin bands instead of a single eternity band, he'd chalked it up to a style preference. Now he wondered if the idea of an eternity band just wasn't for his wife. Eternal. It *was* a scary word. Throughout the first week of Cass's departure, he thought those rings had made it with her onto the plane. But when he was looking for his anchor cufflinks the other day and opened the safe he barely touched, there they were, along with a yellow sticky note that said in a messy scrawl, "Thanks for understanding. C."

When did he ever say he understood? It was an absurd presumption of hers, not unlike her asking him to help write the ground rules for their separation. To make matters worse, she had thoughtlessly affixed the note to the only photograph they kept in there, of Peanut. The single image documenting the only roadblock in their marriage to date. Well, until this. At that moment he had almost yanked off his ring, but stopped himself.

"Yes, I'm starved," Jonathan lied, rising to join his boss. That reminded him of the last text he'd received from Cass: **Are you eating okay?** Like he was a child and not her equal.

11. CASS

So FAR THE traffic was the thing she regretted the most about her rash decision to split from Jonathan. The most superficial aspect, anyway. But there was so much gridlock, no matter what time of day. Going to the bank was an hour-and-a-half odyssey; the gym a three-hour time drain. Nobody had forced her to move to L.A., although leaving New York for the West Coast after a winter with four major snowstorms just made good sense. But the Northeast was thawing and she could have found a studio downtown, maybe in the Village or Chelsea, and lived out the gap a twenty-minute subway ride away from Jonathan. It certainly would have made the transporting of Puddles much easier. But she knew she'd sense his aura at every street corner, imagine his shadow overtaking hers on the concrete sidewalks. New York City was littered with places of significance to them: the checkered-tablecloth Italian restaurant where they first exchanged *I love you*s, the Pret A Manger where they had their first real fight (tainting all other Pret A Mangers), the subway platform where they drunkenly interrogated a homeless man about his panhandling tactics. The distance, the three thousand miles requiring a five-hour plane ride, it all felt necessary. Alexi had inadvertently planted the seed when she'd suggested a visit. Visit . . . six-month stay . . . what was the difference really when Cass offered to pay more than half of the rent moving forward? Alexi's roommate, Bridget, had barely landed upright, she got tossed out so quickly. And then there was the prospect of a job on the West Coast. Cass looked on the theater message boards and saw the position at LA-PAC she'd been contacted about had been filled. But that didn't mean there wasn't another opening for her—she'd already emailed her HR contact and he'd asked her to come in.

One would think after almost six years of cohabitation, Cass would have jumped at the chance to live alone. And there were parts of her that yearned to eat ice cream straight from the freezer without feeling someone else's eyes boring into her back. She wanted to poop with the door open, pick her nose, masturbate on the couch and rediscover all the other perks that came with living alone. But she was doing her best to treat her separation from Jonathan like a scientific experiment. For the control group to be reliable, she had to cohabit. The other big parameter was the length. Six months felt appropriate. Even the happiest of married couples would relish a couple of months of not having to share the bathroom vanity or turn off the TV when the other fell asleep. But half a year was enough time to miss someone, to get to the place where you actually wanted to see the toothpaste without its cap replaced or the milk left on the counter for the zillionth time, because those things symbolized your partner's presence. Even though she'd surprised herself by asking for the break, the rapidness with which she'd suggested the time frame led her to believe she'd been working out the details subconsciously for some time.

Until that point, she'd viewed their marriage like a car moving along a highway—some patches were rough, others smooth sailing, but still they forged onward with a definitive destination in mind.

Driving forward as if getting off at any random exit and ditching the car was out of the question. Until, suddenly, it wasn't. And she was all the way in California, a detour if there ever was one.

Cass's new place was in WeHo. She learned quickly, from the cabdriver who shuttled her from LAX to Alexi's, that calling it West Hollywood marked her as an outsider. She wondered what other vernacular she needed to thrive in her new surroundings. In every aspect, her accommodations were a major downgrade from her place on East 75th. For starters, the bathroom she and Alexi were sharing. The white porcelain sink dripped all day and night, the tub's oddly ornate faucets were crusted over with rust, and every time Cass flushed the toilet she felt like she was playing Russian roulette. The mismatched furniture had a definite dorm-room quality, glistening stripes of packing tape prolonging life. Worst of all was the refrigerator, which barked like an angry seal for a good five minutes each time it was opened and shut. But the rent was dirt cheap and she would be able to pay for the entire six-month stay with savings she had from before getting married.

Finances hadn't come up at all during their talk of the separation. Jonathan was surely too stunned to consider the economics of the break. But she cared about not draining her husband financially at the same time she was draining him emotionally. It might be wise for her to get used to more meager accommodations anyway. If she left Jonathan permanently, it would mean taking a big economic hit. Their prenup, vaulted in the offices of a stuffy Boston law firm that had been representing the Coynes for generations, decreed it so. She wouldn't have fought them on it anyway. It would confirm everything the senior Coynes thought about her if she did. And while they may have been right about her at some point, they weren't correct now. In fact, things had always been more gray than the way Jonathan's parents saw them. She thought back to their first kiss in college and their first night together in New York City. There was nothing forced or pragmatic about that chemistry.

Now she was on the 405 in a rented Camry with manual seat adjustment and a Christmas tree air freshener dangling from the rearview mirror, en route to meet Alexi at a photographer's studio in Culver City. Cass's willingness to shoulder the bulk of the rent had freed up enough cash for Alexi to redo her headshots. She asked Cass to accompany her, so after an unpleasant morning spent at Avis arranging a long-term rental, she found herself back in traffic heading to another part of town. She hoped Alexi didn't broach her rationale for the separation again, as she was wont to do when they had any meaningful time together. The phrase, "But Jonathan seems like such a great guy," had been uttered at least half a dozen times already and, when Cass couldn't disagree, Alexi just looked even more perplexed. Even Dahlia, from whom she expected an outpouring of support, kept repeating "Really?" when Cass shared what she'd done. Her friends were plainly befuddled, unsure how to react. Were they supposed to take sides? Offer advice? Say "Wonderful!" or "I'm sorry"? If only Cass knew.

Though her car proceeded at a glacial pace, she gripped the steering wheel with both hands at ten and two. She wasn't used to driving after so many years in New York City, and even as a teenager in Hazel Park she didn't get much practice. Donna never thought to lease her honor roll daughter a car when she turned sixteen. No, her mother only lent Cass her cheesy convertible (license plate NO1DONNA) when she needed shuttling to and from House of Shamrocks for ladies' nights. Jonathan's parents handed off their weathered Volvo to him the day he got his driver's license and he still kept that car on the Vineyard, the glove compartment stuffed with mix tapes made by his old girlfriend Brett. When he popped one of them into the tape deck, his face would get this mellow, nostalgic half smile, and she could see the memories of his time with Brett envelop him like a beloved old comforter.

Her hand stationed at two looked normal, but the hand at ten looked out of place, almost like a disembodied arm was steering that side of the wheel. It was the absence of her wedding bands, which she'd sentenced to darkness and neglect inside the wall safe that was bolted to her and Jonathan's shared closet. The whiteness of the spot beneath where her rings used to sit made her hand look sickly, almost like she had a problem with circulation. It reminded her of the way Dahlia's finger had looked to her at lunch: anemic. They should compare photos. In the California sun, hers would soon even out, but still. She moved her left hand down to seven, and when it was still in her sight line, down to her knee.

Cass didn't want to rub it in Jonathan's face, the fact that she was leaving her rings behind. She hoped when he eventually found them he would take it as a positive that she was ensuring their safekeeping. Even though the rings would probably have fit if she shifted them over to her middle finger, it seemed wrong to demote them to being purely ornamental. Alexi's apartment was unlikely to have a safe, and the Hazel Park girl in her just couldn't take any chances with jewelry of a quality she never thought would adorn her body. Her mom's various wedding and engagement rings were always cheap-looking, conjuring the image of a plastic egg cracking open. She kept the "collection" in the seashell-and-glitter-decorated box Cass had made for Donna in daycare a lifetime ago. The box moved with them from home to home, relationship to relationship. It was the only project of hers that Donna had saved, at least to Cass's knowledge, and on her infrequent visits to Hazel Park she always looked for it with bated breath.

Cass's trio of bands was of a different order, with GIA certificates authenticating the value of each individual stone. Of all people, Betsy was the one who had helped Jonathan choose them. She knew a man in New York City with those curly things on the sides of his face and one of those silly black hats (her words, not Cass's) who specialized in diamonds. They were supposed to be Tiffany's quality at half the price. Even a blue blood like Betsy liked a bargain. One had to wonder where the family heirloom that Cass should have gotten was hiding. A family like the Coynes surely had an antique ring sitting in a safe-deposit box somewhere, waiting under lock and key for a more worthy spouse. Perhaps a racquet club girl from the East Coast with tan skin all year long and a PhD in sailing etiquette.

After drinking nearly a bottle of Malbec while Jonathan was at work, she had set the rings carefully in their safe and scrawled "Thanks for understanding" on a sticky note. The alcohol had puffed her fingers so much she had to use cold water and a pat of butter to pry them off. Whatever symbolism there may have been in the struggle, she chose to ignore.

When she reached her destination, Alexi was waiting outside for her on the stoop. The short stucco building housed multiple businesses, all entertainment-related: there were signs for an acting studio, a casting office, a production company, and their destination, Gavin Traynor Photography. Culver City was industrial-looking, not similar to any neighborhood she could think of in New York City. She was still getting her bearings around L.A., doing her best to figure out what the Manhattan equivalents of every neighborhood were. So far she'd come up with the following: Beverly Hills equaled the Upper East Side; West Hollywood equaled the West Village; Santa Monica equaled Tribeca. Many would probably scoff at her comparisons, and seeing as she'd only been stationed in L.A. for two weeks at this point, she had no plans to share them with anyone. Well, maybe Jonathan, the next time they had occasion to speak on the phone.

Her obsession with breaking down the city stemmed from a fascination with belonging she'd had since early childhood. One thing she always knew for certain: she never belonged in Hazel Park. When she was single in New York and a friend would suggest a setup, she'd ask: "If he were a city, what city would he be?" The friend would respond with confusion, "You mean, where he is from?" "No," Cass would say. "That's definitely *not* what I mean." Because in her mind, where you were from and where you belong were, more often than not, quite different. The one notable exception that came to mind was Jonathan.

Thinking of him, she glanced at her watch and did the calculation.

He was likely ordering himself some dinner off a website, probably sushi. She reached for her cell to send off a quick text: Getting headshots. Alexi's, not mine! Hope Luna's been showing up. C. He didn't respond right away, like he would have pre-intermission—what she'd come to think of as act one of their marriage. It was to be expected and she didn't begrudge him his pride. She was well aware that her departure stripped him of a good part of the confidence that comes from believing that circumstances are as you perceive them to be. A classic *the world is flat; no, actually it's round* scenario. Now she saw him slowly building himself back up, feeling shaky but remembering he still had the raw materials to forge ahead. How quickly would a woman come into the picture to help speed along his road to recovery? She'd only said they could see other people as a protective measure. So that if either of them slept with someone, it wouldn't preclude them getting back together. A few dalliances with girls Jonathan met at hedge fund conferences (who hopefully lived in far-off cities), she could handle. Even a cheap one-night stand with a tarty chick from some nightclub would be okay. She knew the guys at Winstar would drag her husband out to party once they heard the news. But something more significant would be harder to swallow. Thank goodness it wasn't likely to happen. Jonathan lived at the office, which didn't leave much time for meeting and romancing someone new.

"Finally," Alexi said, hopping up. She slipped a string bean of an arm through Cass's to guide her inside the studio and Cass felt a jolt from the skin-to-skin contact. "We're almost done. Gavin just ran out for a green juice. I need you to help me choose my next outfit." Alexi still had that pixie-ish quality from her college days, and no matter what ridiculously low weight Cass whittled down to or how short she cropped her hair, she could not begin to approximate it. Cass was just built more solidly, bones thick like Puddles's chew toys. In her short-shorts and tank, Alexi looked almost prepubescent, and Cass felt uncomfortably like she was a stage mother chaperoning her daughter to a casting call.

"I'm no expert," Cass said, "but maybe something a bit more age appropriate?" She let her voice lilt upward and turned the corners of her mouth into a little smile, small moves intended to let Alexi know she wasn't meaning to be hurtful.

Alexi waved off her comment. "I need to get the point across that I can play anywhere from fifteen to forty. Come meet Gavin."

She beckoned a youngish guy, dressed in head-to-toe black with a camera dangling off each shoulder. He stood behind Alexi and started massaging her dainty shoulders. He was remarkably good-looking, though not really Cass's taste. She noticed the tattoo on his biceps when he brushed aside some of Alexi's hair. He looked like the cheesy guys in the porn she and Jonathan sometimes watched. She always wished for something a bit more upscale to get her in the mood. White-collar porn, like *Goldman Sucks* or *B.J. Morgan*.

"You're the friend who's been holding up our last shot?" he said to Cass in a thick Australian accent, though he didn't seem all that upset about having extra time with Alexi.

"Guilty," she said. "This city has a lot of traffic."

"Cass, Gavin. Gavin, Cass." Alexi smiled and her precious chin cleft disappeared.

Alexi lifted her tank over her shoulders, revealing a nude lacy bra strapped tightly across her narrow rib cage. She was maybe a 32A, could probably get away with a training bra or nothing. The jean shorts dropped to the ground and Alexi stood there, as comfortably as if she were fully clothed, in nothing more than a see-through bra and thong. It occurred to Cass suddenly that men other than Jonathan might see her in a similar state. They would hardly miss her bodily flaws, specifically the wavy pockets of cellulite under her ass and the cherry angiomas blooming on her back. Only Jonathan didn't notice the gradual deterioration taking place. She *barely* noticed her husband's worsening overbite (he should have worn his retainer, but who was there to police him in boarding school?) and the graying of his pubic hair. Now she would be scrutinized anew. Someone would see her thighs for what they were—baobab trees, thick in the trunk and disproportionate to the spindly branches. Someone would notice that her veins were creeping toward the surface of her skin, tinting everything bluish. She shuddered in place.

Crocodile Dundee now approached with two different blue dresses: one structured, a wool crepe with a cap sleeve; the other a thin spaghetti strap number, made of silk. He held them up in front of Cass to assess.

"The silk," Cass said definitively.

"Told ya," Gavin said, jabbing at Alexi's itty-bitty waist. She was like a dandelion that would blow over if he leaned too much weight into her. "The other one looks like something an accountant would wear."

"I have that dress," Cass said, eyeing the crepe one.

"Shit, I'm sorry," Gavin said.

"I'm kidding."

"She's funny, isn't she?" Alexi said, and Cass realized they'd been talking about her before she arrived.

"That she is," Gavin said. He winked at Alexi. "Let's get this picture done, love, before my next appointment comes in." Alexi perched herself onto a stool in front of a white backdrop and cocked her head from side to side, twisting her mouth around into a thousand different types of smiles. She managed a full spectrum of emotions by simple adjustments of her eyebrows. It was no wonder Alexi stole the spotlight on stage while Cass retreated behind the scenes. Watching her pose reminded Cass of that song from *Sunset Boulevard*, "With One Look." Her friend had serious talent, and Cass wished she could have borrowed Alexi's expressiveness when she had dropped the bomb on Jonathan. What was the right look for *pity me even though I'm being a jerk*?

"Got it," Gavin said, rising from where he'd positioned himself on one knee. He went over to kiss Alexi on the cheek. "I'll have your gallery posted by tomorrow. Cass, it was a pleasure to meet you. Welcome to Los Angeles." He came toward her and she thought he was about to give her a kiss too. Instead, he snapped a close-up.

"Gorgeous," he said, triumphantly looking at the little window of his digital camera.

In the parking lot, Alexi took Cass by the elbow as they were about to part for their separate cars.

"I'm sure he's not your type, but I'd be withholding if I didn't pass on the message that Gavin would like to call you. I told him your—um—situation and he was intrigued. What do you think? I mean, isn't the whole point of separating from Jonathan so you can see if you're happier with someone else?" Alexi looked at Cass expectantly.

Cass was more than flattered. Undoubtedly Gavin had beautiful women traipsing through his studio regularly—aspiring actresses looking for affirmation that they were pretty enough, thin enough. Delicate girls with radiant skin like Alexi. Women without spouses. And he probably got pretty far with them just on his accent alone. But he wanted to go out with her, Cass, pretty, but with a body that was invariably described as "athletic," a phrase that hovered in that gray space between backhanded compliment and insult.

"You're right, he's not my type. But tell him I'm flattered." She clicked open her locked car with a *toot-toot*. "I'll see you back at home. You looked gorgeous in the pictures, by the way."

Once Alexi's Prius was out of the parking lot, Cass turned the key in the ignition, flipping the radio from AM to FM. She settled on a station playing some happy tune, maybe Taylor Swift or Katy Perry. Bopping her head ever so slightly to the beat, she smiled the smile of a student walking out of his or her last exam, of a teenager finally kissing a crush . . . or, more aptly, of a married woman on the lam.

12. JONATHAN

SLOWLY, AS THOUGH he was working his way through a list of sus-
pects, he crossed off the names of the people he had to tell about the
separation. Cass hadn't returned within a few weeks, or even a month,
as he'd expected, and so the proliferation of the news became un-
avoidable. The first had been Jerry, and he had responded with the invitation to *shvitz* at the club. Then came Jeff, Nate and Russell, who
he told as a group when they were Ubering together to a colleague's
farewell gathering. He had deliberately hopped in the front seat to
avoid looking at them when he dropped the news. They had responded,
predictably, with calling Cass a fool and insisting on getting him
wasted. It was only when they were pulling up to the restaurant that
Russell added, "You know, Jonny. This isn't necessarily a bad thing.
Your wife basically gave you a hall pass." These were the guys who
made cracks about marriage being like a prison, wives like task-
masters, and they weren't necessarily wrong. Jonathan didn't think
that way yet—and if he ever did, he felt more like he and Cass were

sharing a cage at the zoo. There were rules, like they couldn't go out and fraternize with the other animals, but at least they were put in the same cell, given shelter, food and security. People who peered into their cage thought they looked cute.

"I guess," Jonathan said. It wasn't like that thought hadn't occurred to him. Maybe in time he'd come to appreciate it, though one had to wonder what sort of women he could attract under these circumstances.

He was circling the tables at the end of dinner to say his good-byes when Russell grabbed him.

"We're going out," he said, putting his arm protectively around Jonathan. "I just got us on the list at Aura."

"Huh?" Jonathan asked.

"Trust me, dude. Aura always has hot girls and they go crazy for hedge fund guys. You gotta have a little fun. Cass loosened your noose, man." Nate and Jeff had joined their conversation and started egging him on, pushing him toward a waiting car that would whisk them to the trouble late night had to offer. He knew these guys thought he was a bore, the most vanilla dude in the group. They even teased him about his Big Brother commitments, so certain their colleague who was frequently rushing off to see his Little Brother was a saint in their midst.

Twenty minutes later, he and the guys were standing around a crowded bar, doing a shot of Tito's. And then he was dancing to remixes of songs he vaguely recognized with a girl named Ashley, who seemed to appear from nowhere as though his friends had magicked a Cass antidote out of thin air.

"Do you want to sit down?" he asked her over the blaring music.

"Sure," she yelled back, and he walked with this mystery woman toward a velvet banquette in the back, behind a rope for which his buddies had shelled out enough to cross.

"Can I get you another drink?" That was what he was supposed to ask, wasn't it?

"Vodka martini, extra olives," she said, smiling like that was the nicest thing anyone had ever said to her. She was hot. Skinny, but with boobs, and dark hair that fell in waves past her elbows. He could smell her perfume, musky and sweet.

He got the highlights: University of Texas (go Longhorns!), marketing degree, *loving* New York City, dance-cardio addict, sick share house planned for the summer in the Hamptons. Her good breeding was obvious, and he knew his mother would love her—this Ashley von Warwick *of* Fort Worth to be precise. A "von" would please both his parents to no end. And though this random girl he met dancing at Aura with her tits hanging out said things like "ridic" (and also "sick" and "totes"), she held the stem of her martini glass just so, knew to let him go first through the revolving door to get it started when they finally left the club, and was a graduate of the finest all-girls preparatory school in Texas. But Ashley's good breeding was like an anti-boner— when he found himself kissing her on the street, he couldn't stop picturing his mother going gaga for her, flinging this pretty, young thing with the fancy last name around the Cheshire Club to make her friends green with envy. When she asked him if he wanted to come over to her place, he politely declined, only asking for her number as a courtesy.

Later that night he tried to explain this to Jeff at the all-night diner around the corner. Jeff nodded in agreement, stabbing his waffle with the fork like he was spearing meat, saying, "I hear ya, man." But it didn't seem that he did. None of the women Jonathan met before Cass—the Jessicas and the Jennas, and now Ashley—were the type he could imagine sharing inside jokes with or dog-earring *1,000 Places to See Before You Die* together. Well, maybe Brett, but she was nothing more than a ghost from his past at this point. He could barely remember what they used to talk about for hours straight.

After the big reveal to his Winstar crew, the Wentworths were up next to hear the news. He thought Cass might already have told them—or surely one of them noticed that they never ran into her in the elevator or hallway anymore—but the look of surprise on their faces made it clear they had no clue. Jemima hugged him and stroked his cheek like a little boy, saying she had to admit Cass had been acting strange recently. "She didn't even want to try the new blow-dry bar with me," Jemima shared. "And it's right at the corner of our block." This was meant, Jonathan concluded, to assure him that the separation was due to Cass being mentally ill. *Imagine! She wouldn't blow-dry her hair despite the convenience! Bonkers, isn't she?* Jemima only meant to comfort him and put Cass's departure in the context of other erratic behavior, but she wasn't very convincing. Henry took him out for a beer, but two dudes out with a plan to have a heart-to-heart for the first time devolved into a conversation that centered mostly around business.

Random friends came next, Stefania the dog walker, then Luna. Their cleaning lady, whose skill set and reliability made Amelia Bedelia look impressive, for once responded immediately to the text Jonathan had sent out. He wrote: Luna, Cass is going to be living in California for a while. We would still like you to come so please reach out to me for scheduling. The three dots of Luna's response popped up immediately, disappeared, then reappeared and vanished at least five more times. At a loss for words, she finally managed: I hope everything is okay. I'll be there to clean Monday. And she actually showed up. Somehow the idea of Jonathan living alone, ditched by his wife for some self-indulgent soul-searching, induced Luna to meet her commitments.

There were not one, not two, but three platters of food offered to him as a form of condolence, officially turning his separation from Cass into a wake. Luna left a tin of brownies next to a messily scribbled note that said, *You needed Windex. I bought it at CVS. Don't worry about paying me back.* Because of who they were from, he suspected there were some "nontraditional" ingredients mixed in the batter. Three brownies later, he didn't feel remotely high, just nauseous. Jemima delivered a vegetable lasagna. When she handed over the casserole dish with a big smile, Jonathan noticed her forehead didn't so much as move, let alone crease. Cass was right about the injections. He worried this dinner delivery would become a daily occurrence, so he very pointedly but politely explained to Jemima that he ate in the office almost every night anyway. "Uh-huh," she said with her nonmoving eyebrows, and it seemed she had in that instant concluded the source of Cass's departure. Lastly, his secretary, Gloria, the backbone of his professional existence, came to work with an actual carry-on-sized rolling suitcase filled with arroz con pollo and pork enchiladas.

"They freeze great," she assured him. Without asking him first, she rolled her meals-on-wheels into the office kitchen, stacked the aluminum-foil pans and printed out a sign on computer paper that said, "Jonathan Coyne. Do Not Eat." Because his wife leaving him wasn't embarrassing enough.

So the friends, the colleagues, the team (Luna, Gloria, Roger the building super, Derrick the corner barista and others) were all told in succession. Jonathan even shared Cass's departure with his mentee Leon when they were playing chess in Bryant Park on a windy Sunday morning. Leon fixed his eyes on the board and muttered a "Sorry, man, that's rough," and then let Jonathan checkmate him easily as a consolation. Things were bad when a kid who had been to juvie twice described your life as *rough*.

After so many tellings, he'd learned to shorten the story in a way that would eliminate the possibility of follow-up questions. "Cass and I are doing a trial separation. We're going to see how we fare living apart. It's all for the best. Thank you for your support." That last part was key. The recipient of the news hadn't in fact offered any support yet, but by saying so, it showed that the matter was closed, and no particular words of kindness, insight or armchair psychology were welcome.

The one person of significance whom he hadn't yet notified was his mother, whose reaction would depend on a combination of time of day, inebriation and luck. If he caught her in the morning en route to bridge, all hell could break loose. She would need to rush him off the phone because she didn't want to be late for her foursome, but then she wouldn't be able to concentrate on her game, sweating the fact she'd have to tell her friends eventually. Then he'd get a phone call in the late afternoon berating him for the insensitivity of his timing. If he reached his mother after five, she'd have the lubrication of one or two martinis. This could soften her and she'd attempt to coddle him (in her cold, Waspy way) or the booze would loosen her tongue and she'd unleash a murderous string of *I told you so*s. She'd hinted not too subtly that Cass was a gold digger who saw the Coyne firstborn as a cash cow. Jonathan wondered if it ever occurred to his mother that by painting him as the golden goose conquest of some conniving bitch, she was implying that a woman like Cass would never be interested in him if he didn't have money. As if his personality were stale and his career prospects dismal. As though he were ugly.

He couldn't withhold the news from his family much longer. His little brother Michael was getting married in a few weeks, over Memorial Day weekend. His bride, Jordyn, was the sort of woman for whom seating arrangements and place card design were as critical as arms negotiations. She would need to know sooner rather than later that he'd be coming to the wedding stag. Jonathan remembered Cass agonizing over the tiny slips of white paper with each of their guests' names scrawled on them, though her objective seemed mainly to be hiding her family members in small pockets around the room. He reached for the phone on his desk at work, glancing at the computer clock first: 5:09 p.m. Half a martini in.

He grimaced when his father picked up.

"Jonathan, long time no speak. You avoiding us because you have to spend the whole weekend on the Vineyard soon enough?"

"Just been busy at work, Dad. Is Mom there?"

"Hang on." A moment later, he heard "Betsy!" and he could picture his father's deep baritone traveling from his second-floor, wood-paneled study down to Betsy's floral sitting room off the kitchen.

Despite the strain in their relationship, there was still never a question for Jonathan that he would tell his mother before his father. Then she would tell his father in a game of drunken telephone, her gin-soaked lips passing on the message to his scotch-breathed father. But unlike in the children's version of the game, Betsy's changes would be deliberate.

It wasn't just that his mother had a stronger constitution than his father. Even though she wasn't warm and fuzzy in the least, and he had zero memories of her slicking Bacitracin on his scrapes or reading him *Corduroy* (a heavily accented Jamaican lady did that), she was still his mother. And mothers were meant to be the first in line for news, of both a good and bad nature. When he thought of him and Cass as parents, he pictured his wife as the one who would have the first crack at fielding the tough questions and wiping the tears. He wasn't as obtuse as his own father, but he didn't have Cass's emotional landscape. It was all those damn plays she saw. She was "in touch with her feelings," for lack of a better phrase. But there was such a thing as being too in touch. That kind of thing could lead to overthinking and indulging every twinge. That's what got them into this predicament.

His mother came on the line.

"Jordyn is really a piece of work. I thought it was odd that Cass didn't care about the wedding details, and that trailer-trash mother of hers certainly couldn't be trusted to make any decisions."

Jonathan cringed at hearing the phrase "trailer trash." All manner of people went around using it casually, but it stung his wife sharply. She'd lived a good part of her adolescence teetering on the edge of actually moving into a trailer park.

"Anyway, I think this might actually be worse," Betsy continued. "What do they call it? A bridezilla, I think. That's what Jordyn is. But Michael is smitten and it'll all be over in a few weeks."

That was his mother. She was partial to skipping pleasantries, finding the ping-pong nature of "Hi, how are you? I'm good; how are you?" to be a complete waste of time. Despite Jordyn's fine breeding, Betsy didn't seem to like her on a personal level much more than Cass, because he knew his grandmother's emerald ring was still idling in the family vault. Maybe his youngest brother, Wallace, would finally claim it. If he could find a society girl pretty enough, thin enough and with enough composure not to fret over silly things like Jordyn did.

"When are you and Cass arriving, by the way? The house is going to be very crowded. I never thought I'd say this, but if you wanted to take a room at the Winnetu, that might actually be of some help."

How Cass would have celebrated upon hearing that news. If she was in the room, he would have scrawled on a piece of paper, "We're free. Can stay in hotel!" She would have jumped up and down, stifling screeches, prompting Betsy to ask, "What is all that commotion?" He'd answer something about Puddles knocking a bowl over. It was all so easy to picture, and yet it was no longer his reality.

"You there, Jonathan?" He heard his mother take a sip of something. "I saw your boss on CNBC this morning. There's something about him I don't like. Do they pay him to be on the show? He's on practically every other day."

"I'm here, Mom. Jerry is one of their regulars on the show, yes. It's good for business. You might not 'like' Jerry, but he's a pretty amazing boss and we have two billion dollars under management. Anyway, I have to tell you something. About the wedding. I'm hoping you can pass on the news to Dad. And Jordyn." More telephone.

"You don't sound right, Jonathan. What's going on?"

"Cass is not going to be able to make it to the wedding." He let that marinate for a minute before elaborating.

"She's pregnant, isn't she? I thought Cass might pull something like this. I had four children, threw up until my third trimester with each of you, and never missed an obligation. Fine, yes, maybe I skipped a few bridge lessons or some volunteering commitment, but nothing like a family wedding. Is she home now? I'm calling her. Jordyn will have a heart attack when she hears, and who do you think is going to have to fix this? I don't see her father rearranging the tables." Jordyn's mother had lost a battle with kidney disease a year ago. When she passed, Betsy had actually said (with Jordyn's father bent over the casket in the next room), "Well, at least I'll be able to control the wedding details." And now it took a minute for Jonathan to process that his mother thought he was announcing the pending birth of her first grandchild. Her reaction? "I thought Cass might pull something like this"—"congratulations" clearly not a part of her vernacular. Between Donna and Betsy, any kid of his and Cass's could forget about a cozy, cuddly nana.

Despite being taken aback by his mother's harshness, he couldn't blame her for being wildly off the mark. From the outside—hell, even from the inside—it seemed like he and Cass were on the brink of having a child. Cass swore that all their friends would look a second too long at her belly or pay special attention to see if she was drinking. Sometimes she'd order club soda all night just to mess with them. Meanwhile, in her mind, she was packing her bags. Even in her completely unexpected departure, she was being true to her nature. Cass was like sunshine on a freezing day—her presence could give you a false sense of security.

"Cass isn't pregnant, Mom. We are separated."

Silence on the other end. And then . . .

"Separated? Where in the world is this coming from? Everything seemed fine at Christmas." They had spent the weekend in Boston with his parents and siblings, attending the pageant show (as the only married couple there without children, they felt rather foolish) and partaking in a big feast with all of Jonathan's siblings. The weekend was fine, he supposed. Though Cass had disappeared for hours on Saturday without explanation and they had an explosive fight about a comment his father made at dinner about the "blue collars" ruining a resort he and Betsy used to favor in Bermuda after the hotel started offering a fourth night free and rewards points.

"He was looking at me when he said it, Jonathan," Cass had sniped. "You are such a jerk for not seeing that." He *had* seen it, though he pretended to her that he hadn't. And he *had* spoken to his father privately about Cass's sensitivities. His father feigned cluelessness, or maybe it wasn't an act. Some people were truly tone-deaf and Christopher Coyne was likely one of them. At the time of the incident, Jonathan felt just as exasperated with his wife as she did with his dad. Did she really have the right to be outraged when she had fled from her upbringing? This was the woman who preferred to reduce her childhood to a buried footnote. Trips home to Michigan, which were only every other Thanksgiving, usually involved her making snarky comments about the footwear choices of the women that were incomprehensible to him. She'd insist they bolt after two nights for fear she'd start saying "pop" again instead of "soda." A woman full of contradictions could be incredibly sexy, but more often than not, it was cause for a migraine.

"Things were fine then, that's true," he said. "But now they aren't. A marriage doesn't necessarily fall apart over screaming matches and cataclysmic differences, Mom. Sometimes, it's the little things that are the undoing." And for the first time, like someone had waved a crystal ball in his face, he saw where Cass was coming from and felt a momentous breakthrough taking shape. "I'd rather be certain that we are totally sure about our marriage before we bring kids into it. It's not exactly a great environment for a child to be raised by parents who don't like each other." He didn't intend that part to come out as an accusation, but once it landed, it couldn't be taken any other way.

"I'm not calling Jordyn. You can tell her yourself," Betsy said, serving a quick revenge for his nasty comment.

"Good-bye, Mom. I'll see you soon. Please try and be supportive of our decision."

Because he'd be damned if he told his mother it was Cass's idea. From now on, the decision was mutual.

◆ ◆ ◆

WHEN JONATHAN WAS in the sixth grade, he came downstairs one night to get a late-night snack. His parents thought he was fast asleep, but in reality he'd stayed up watching a baseball game on the West Coast and found himself needing a celebratory scoop of ice cream after the Red Sox win.

"This can't happen again," Betsy hissed to his father as Jonathan had entered the room unseen. "I will not be made a fool of any longer." He saw his parents at the kitchen table, though not in their normal seats at opposite heads. His father was in pajamas, rubbing his chin. His mother, in a bathrobe and curlers, had a box of tissues and a bottle of wine within reach. Jonathan tucked himself out of sight in the butler's pantry, but within earshot.

"Betsy," Christopher said. "Let's not pretend this is something other than what it is. I was seeking comfort elsewhere. We have three children together, but not much of a real marriage. It's been that way for quite some time. You know it just as well as I do. Don't pretend this was some big betrayal."

"Well, we are not getting divorced. In fact, I think we should have another child. Jon is off to boarding school soon enough. Michael is nine and Wallace is already six. It might help us to have something to celebrate together."

"You think that's the answer?" Christopher asked, sounding bewildered.

"It's worth a shot," Betsy said. "But no more fooling around."

Less than a year later, his baby sister, Katherine, was born.

13. CASS

THEY VERY RARELY spoke of the termination. Instead they gave air-time to the cracks in their plaster mouldings, the long lines at Whole Foods, the insidiousness of everyone's Internet addictions, but almost none to the thirteen weeks they squealed with joy privately with the knowledge they would be parents and then buried their heads behind closed doors when they learned they wouldn't.

She came to them when they weren't even trying for her. They knew the alien on the screen, the one that looked like all head and a pair of sneakers, was a she, and so much else about her after all the testing. Isabel. That's what they were going to call her, after they briefly considered all the names that would pair hilariously with their last name: *Penny; Golda; Ivana.* It seemed like bad luck to use the real name before she was born, so they nicknamed her Peanut, which seemed a more suitable way to refer to a blurry image projected on-screen by sound waves with no personality or physical features to speak of. At least in this, Cass and Jonathan were in total agreement.

This tiny lady-in-waiting would be Peanut Coyne until the day she came out screaming from the womb, a tiny red-faced thing they would instantly adore.

Cass believed the way people handled disappointment was the clearest window into their souls. Mr. B-positive said everything he shouldn't have said: *We weren't really trying anyway . . . It's for the best . . . At least we hadn't told anyone yet . . . This will make us appreciate our baby so much more when it does happen.* All she wanted to hear was: *This really sucks. Let's drink as much as it takes until we're so numb we can barely feel our limbs, much less our pain.* Jonathan had in spades that thing people were always touting—perspective. Back in junior high, when she'd cry over a bad grade, Tiff would say to her, "Cassidy, there are starving babies in Ethiopia. How can you complain about a stupid biology test?" Cass wasn't a bad person, and she resented the implication that being disappointed about a shitty grade meant she couldn't see that the world had far bigger problems than her GPA taking a minor hit. Of course she saw that. That didn't make her less upset about her grade, it just meant she'd be even more upset if she was a starving kid in Africa. How did Tiffany, and her mother, and Jonathan, and everyone else who didn't share her worldview not see that? Percy got it. When they lost a client, or a show they'd cradled tanked, they'd climb out to their office building's rooftop, smoke a joint together (a habit for Percy, a treat for her) and curse everyone and everything in sight. Percy would quip, "At least we have our health," and they'd both roll their eyes. In retrospect, she was plagued by how flippant they were.

Once she got over the confusion of how she could be pregnant, Cass was overjoyed. The pill was meant to be 99 percent effective, which really meant 100 percent effective; the pharmaceutical companies just couldn't say that because of liability issues. Some dumb teenager would forget to take her pill for a week and would sue for a lifetime of expenses plus pain and suffering. Or so she thought. Because she never forgot to take her pill, gulping it with the same cup of water she used to wash out her morning toothpaste, every single day, like clockwork. And she was pregnant. Two years ahead of "schedule."

By the first appointment with Dr. Levin, with Jonathan at her side, she'd become convinced that this was the most fortuitous way their family could start. How foolish to think they could schedule a baby like a vacation. It was so much more exciting, meant-to-be, fate-inspired that it happened like this, by a fluke of a diluted batch of birth control. Instead of agonizing over the perfect time to have a baby (and when had anyone actually ever felt the timing was right?), they were given one as a gift. With Cass's history of machination, this twist in her plan felt especially significant.

Three months after she learned she was pregnant, precisely on the day of the procedure, she received a letter inviting her to join a class-action suit against the maker of her contraceptive. They had distributed six thousand ineffective pills, leading to countless babies, no doubt. She tore up the letter, even though she was perhaps one of the most affected victims. An unplanned pregnancy and a termination with serious attendant complications. She would have made one hell of a star witness.

They didn't agree on much in the days and weeks surrounding the termination, but Jonathan did wholeheartedly support her decision to shred the invitation to litigate. They both needed a punching bag, her more than him, but some faceless conglomerate based in New Jersey wasn't going to be a satisfying target. She took off two weeks from work, telling Percy she needed to go see her mother, and laid low in her apartment, where every commercial seemed to be for baby lotion. Maybe that's when her hatred of daytime television first came about. Jonathan, on the other hand, returned to work the day after her procedure, trying to seal the deal with a new investor and burying himself unreasonably in developing some new algorithm to track earnings per share. Jonathan was a quantitative guy—he thought in numbers and spreadsheets and formulas—so what did she expect when she sought him out over the emotional theater guys at Brown who had naked parties to prepare for a production of *Hair* and took Ecstasy to get better in touch with their inner selves? Her husband was a math major, then a star at Wharton Business School, and now Jerry Winston's sharpest numbers guy at Winstar. Of course a quant guy wouldn't know how to handle the millions of emotions that accompanied losing a baby you didn't plan to have after finding out the parents' DNA wasn't ideally "compatible." His spectrum of feelings was limited: his angry, a seven out of ten; his happy, maybe an eight. She often thought it would be great to see her husband unhinged, even just once. Even when she told him about the break, he'd remained fairly collected. She'd have thrown the nearest picture frame across the room if the roles had been reversed. It would have looked like a Greek wedding by dawn, smashed plates everywhere, depleted bottles of liquor on their sides.

Every bad thing in life has a silver lining, right? She knew that even the most tragic deaths have a way of forging the survivors more closely together, that heinous mass crimes bond communities and change archaic laws. And she expected that this too would have a bright spot for her and Jonathan. Their experience would be like a shared possession that only they could see, a couple with the same imaginary friend. But instead, it created a wedge, and each of them took their posts on shifting tectonic plates.

"Canavan disease?" Jonathan had asked, his voice flush with certainty that what he was hearing couldn't be possible. "I didn't think I could be a carrier." He looked at Cass, seated in the other chair opposite their OB's desk, for affirmation.

"Like I said, it *is* primarily an Ashkenazi Jewish genetic disorder," Dr. Levin said, looking at Jonathan with a disapproving glance. *Levin.* How dense could her husband be? "And in order for the fetus to have it, you *both* have to be carriers. Now obviously you are healthy adults, which means you are both recessive carriers. Perhaps one of your parents is part Jewish and doesn't know. It happens all the time. Next time around, we will screen very early on. Or test the embryo in advance. There is a work-around."

Betsy, oh please, let it be Betsy! Cass had almost squealed it out loud despite her distress. The woman prided herself on her lineage like it was something she had worked tirelessly to achieve. Maybe that diamond dealer in Midtown Manhattan with the *payot* (Cass made a point to learn the proper name) framing his chubby face, who gave Jonathan such a great deal on her engagement ring and wedding bands, was Betsy's long-lost relative. Cass had vowed to get on Ancestry.com the minute she got home. If it was Christopher, that would also be satisfying, but not to the same degree. His disdain for anyone "other," persons outside his own milieu, flew a bit under the radar, whereas Betsy's was as plain to see as her Lilly Pulitzer tunic collection.

By the time she returned home after a silent cab ride with Jonathan, she was back to hearing the *whoosh-whoosh* of the baby's heartbeat on the Doppler on repeat. How could a baby with such a strong beat, 120 beats per minute crashing through the speaker, have a condition incompatible with life? And why did she feel responsible? Because it was her already-pouchy stomach providing a home for their little princess, their sweet pea, and their blend of DNA would soon be extracted from her body with a vacuum, that's why. And because Jonathan said things to her like, "You'll get pregnant again soon." Like it was *her* fault. Who was this angry person cursing her husband that she didn't recognize in the mirror? An alter ego sprung to life in her thirties, or an echo of the angry child she had been? It didn't matter. The loss of Peanut had changed something in her. She wasn't the person who made lemonade out of lemons. She chucked lemons against a wall and had to clean up the mess.

She and Jonathan had less than a handful of heart-to-hearts about their loss, but Cass returned to it whenever her mind wasn't otherwise occupied. It was the memory that sat on the sidelines waiting for an opening. Like in California, where free time was just too plentiful. She had no friends besides Alexi and virtually zero errands to run without her normal responsibilities like buying dog food and getting clothes for Jonathan. The job she was able to finagle at the performing arts center was only part-time. She was working *for* the person they'd hired to fill the job she was meant to have, a massive bitch who pooh-poohed her Broadway experience as irrelevant to Southern California audiences, whatever that meant. Maybe she *should* go out with Gavin. If nothing else, it would fill her time for a few hours. Educate her about so-called Californians and get her out of the house. She used to like daylight and fresh air.

Alexi had obviously given her number to him anyway and he'd sent off a quick missive asking her to get in touch if she felt like going for a drink. It was early morning on the Thursday before Memorial Day, and it seemed like no matter where she went she couldn't escape the question: What are your plans for the holiday? Like just because there was a Monday tacked on to the weekend, everyone from nail technicians to shop clerks felt entitled to know her schedule. She thought back to the number of times she'd callously asked people what their plans were—lonely singles who had no one to share the holidays with, people without the disposable income to take weekend getaways. Well, now she knew to nip that habit in the bud. It was especially odd to be asked this in Los Angeles, where Monday-to-Friday day jobs were hardly the norm and Tuesday morning didn't feel all that different from Saturday afternoon. Nevertheless, everyone was jazzed about the day off. She wondered what Jonathan would do with it. Probably immerse himself in work. She envied him his job at the moment, because he could always retreat to his office tower and find company, some other analyst on the rise researching new companies, courting investors, analyzing market trends. PZA was a ghost town by four o'clock on Fridays no matter what. The only people traversing its corridors on the weekends were wielding janitorial carts and industrial vacuums. If she had the power to choose how Jonathan spent the next three days, she truly wasn't sure where she'd put him. Hitting golf balls with the doofuses from his fund at one of their snooty Westchester clubs seemed innocuous enough, though she did pity him the firing squad he'd face among the wives. "Where's Cass?" "Los Angeles? So far!" Eventually someone brave enough would ask in a quiet voice, "Can I fix you up?" and gesture toward a lonely divorcée with a rocking body in the distance. Better to tuck Jonathan safely at home with Puddles, away from his demanding job and the twitchy country club women, where man and dog would only surface for walks to pick up coffee and a *New Yorker* from the newsstand.

She shot up in bed, jolted upright like she'd put her finger in a socket. Scrambling, she found her cell phone on the coffee table in the living room and confirmed the date.

Jonathan wasn't even going to be in New York this weekend. He was going to the Vineyard for Michael and Jordyn's wedding. Actually, he was probably already there, charged with keeping Betsy away from any of the hired help, shuttling the groomsmen from place to place as the oldest and most responsible brother. Poor Jordyn. She had to be crying into the ring bearer's pillow at this very moment. Not only would Cass's absence mean havoc wreaked on the symmetry of the table seating, but the cloud of vicious rumors that would drift around her precious wedding weekend would taint the pure, unadulterated rapture she worked so hard to achieve with the recycled parchment programs and the Lucida font on the menus. She had gotten an earful from Jordyn the last time they'd seen each other, over Christmas. Cass's belief in Santa Claus was revived when Jordyn received an emergency call from the wedding planner and had to ditch Cass midway through a description of the bridesmaid bouquets.

And what did Jonathan do with Puddles? The plan had been for Percy's partner, with whom she was still in frequent touch, to take him for the weekend to play with Shirley. She tried not to worry about it. Jonathan would find Puddles a comfortable place to stay so he could focus on the festivities, train his mind on assuring Michael that not all marriages were as erratic as his own and that Jordyn was nowhere near as unstable as his own wife. Had Jonathan forgotten about his brother's wedding when she announced her departure? Surely he would have asked her to stay just through this weekend if he had realized. Or perhaps not. Either way, she felt awful about it. Betsy would destroy him. She'd make it all about her, worse than Jordyn. Cass needed to reach out to him, pronto. She grabbed her phone again.

Hi there. I just remembered it's the big wedding this weekend. I'm so sorry about the timing. Please give your family my love, she texted, resisting the urge to ask about Puddles. She did not want to undermine her confidence in him. Let the poor guy have some dignity.

She threw the phone down and ripped open the barking fridge door and considered the bottle of cheap wine staring back at her. It was the kind that Betsy would sneer at, unless there was nothing else to drink, in which case her mother-in-law would guzzle it down until the last drop rolled into her tight-set mouth. Desperately in need of distraction in a form other than morning booze, Cass went back for her phone and responded to Gavin's text.

Sure. Tell me when and where.

14. JONATHAN

Normally he preferred to fly to the Vineyard—Cass too—but allowed to make decisions totally independently for the first time in almost six years, he opted to drive. He and Cass didn't even keep a car in the city, and when he mentioned renting a Zipcar at the office, Jeff insisted on lending him one of his cars for the weekend. Jeff had two kids, so Jonathan hoped for at least an SUV to store his two duffel bags and garment bag filled with the various Jordyn-mandated outfits he had packed. Nantucket reds were on tap for the Friday night cocktails; seersucker for the rehearsal dinner; a light gray suit with purple pocket square for the wedding on Sunday afternoon. If the dress code was any indication, the wedding was going to be one giant cliché. When he got to Jeff's Tribeca garage, his friend handed over the keys to a Bugatti convertible.

"Be good to her," he said, slapping Jonathan on the back, and he just knew that Jeff waited patiently every day for someone to ask to borrow his car.

He crammed his luggage into the compact trunk and set off, not even bothering to check the traffic. It really didn't matter. He could stop when he wanted to, pull over for a nap if he desired, or visit every McDonald's he passed just for the hell of it. Nobody would tell him he was driving too fast or too slow, that he had missed the ferry exit (even though he knew the route to the Vineyard like the path from his bed to the toilet) or that the air-conditioning was on too high. He was listening to NPR, a *This American Life* about rebuilding homes after Hurricane Katrina, when a text message buzzed, but he told himself that he wouldn't read the message until the segment was over. Ira Glass quieted down as he pulled into a rest stop to take a piss and he saw an apologetic note from Cass about missing the wedding. He appreciated that she'd remembered, though he wasn't sure how to respond.

After a few run-throughs in his head, he settled on: Thanks. I'll pass on your message to everyone. Because what more was there to say? Except there was, because at the next stop, after topping off the tank with premium and buying himself a glazed donut, he pulled his phone from the cup holder and added, Brought Puddles with me. He says hi. Then he snapped a photo of Puddles, crammed into the backseat sleeping, and sent it to Cass. He compulsively checked the message three more times out of fear that he'd accidentally sent it to Jeff, who'd been texting him as well along the way, things like: "How's she riding?" "Great pickup, right?" Jeff was mercifully oblivious to the fact that Jonathan was traveling with a Choodle who suffered from reflux. He had picked up his pooch three blocks from the garage from Maurice, the new permanent dog walker he'd hired to replace the less-than-stellar Stefania. Maurice was excellent with Puddles and totally reliable. Jonathan couldn't help but smile to himself whenever he came home to see his dog nicely groomed, fed and comfortable. *See that, Cass? I can manage just fine without you.*

My boy! Cass responded immediately. Does he seem to miss me? And what car are you in? She dropped in a racecar emoji, which made him blanch. They weren't really on emoji terms, were they?

It's Jeff's car . . . P is sad without you, but says he can't wait to meet all the celebrity dogs in L.A. He hopes you can get him an agent.

The truth was that Puddles didn't seem to notice Cass's absence all that much. He sniffed at a few of her sweaters the first few nights but had cozied up instantly to Maurice, probably because Jonathan had instructed him to give Puddles as many treats as he wanted, like he was a child of divorce who could be mollified with spoiling. If only Cass's parents had done that, maybe she wouldn't be the victim-of-divorce poster child she was. Puddles wasn't the brightest canine, which Betsy was quick to point out, along with a *hint, hint* "You should have used the family breeder," and in fact their dog had earned his nickname because of his inability to avoid any pool of water on the ground. It was Cass who started calling Montgomery by the more suitable name Puddles, and it stuck. So the idea of Puddles having any type of career in the movies was laughable. The simplest instructions, like sit, quiet or fetch, threw their poor pet into a tailspin, and Jonathan couldn't resist making the joke to Cass, even though he was loath to make an overture of intimacy to her. It could make him seem desperate. Or worse, in denial. Some poor sap unaware of what was happening right under his nose.

Of course. Assuming they don't mind him humping the tripods and boom mic, she texted back. Puddles was also unduly amorous.

It seemed Cass was less concerned with employing their shared jokes. There was so much that only they could appreciate—private jokes, knowing glances, a secret language they used in public places where they would only say the first syllable of words and totally get each other's meaning. It wasn't necessarily enough to sustain a marriage losing its luster, but it was something. A foundation, at least.

In six days, Jonathan would meet Cass at LAX to hand over Puddles for his month in California. He got to keep him much longer than his originally allotted four weeks because Cass was getting settled at Alexi's and figuring out logistics, which he later learned meant bribing

Alexi's landlord to overlook the building's no-pet policy. Their custodial arrangement was going to be exhausting, not to mention absurdly expensive, but spending significant time away from Puddles wasn't a concession either of them was willing to make. So he agreed to exchange Puddles every month even though he knew he'd be paying for these bicoastal flights. The funding of their separation was never articulated and he'd just assumed, chump that he was, that a portion of his hard-earned money would facilitate the intermission of his marriage. He made about six times what Cass made back when she was working, and it felt petty to bring up the money, like he was trying to make it seem as though she was financially required to stay with him. To his surprise, he hadn't seen any withdrawals for rent or other expenses from their bank account since Cass had left. It turned out his wife was paying for her crazy intermission all by herself. In retrospect, he wasn't totally surprised. She was a survivor, self-taught from a young age how to get on by herself.

A part of Jonathan suspected that if he'd pressed harder on keeping Puddles for longer stretches, he might have succeeded in convincing Cass to stay. But that felt not only too manipulative but also like a hollow victory. And if they couldn't be amicable about a dog, what type of precedent would that set? He wanted to show himself as reasonable, and besides, this way he was sure he'd see Cass at least once a month. On any given occasion, he could just buy her a one-way ticket to New York and he'd transport both Cass and Puddles back to their apartment, to the status quo, to before their relationship fractured like a child's tibia bone. His younger brother Wallace was studying to be a pediatric orthopedist and analogized everything in life to anatomy, a habit that Jonathan was picking up. Something else Cass had pointed out, like his snoring.

After he caught a short nap on the ferry ride, he was back on the familiar streets of his childhood summers. All at once, the ghost of Cass drifted away and thoughts of Brett flooded his head. He couldn't displace the most recent Facebook image he'd seen of her with her son, who now came up to her elbow. Brett was girl-next-door pretty, kind-hearted, easy to get along with, the sort of woman that, if they'd met at a different point in his life, he'd have had the brains to marry. That wasn't to say she was simple, but her complexity wasn't the nefarious kind. So while he'd known for a long time that Brett was settled and raising a family, seeing it reflected back at him in colorful photographs with seventy-nine comments of the "Adorable!" variety was a different story, especially given his current situation.

Past South Beach and Katama Farm Institute, he pulled into the parking lot of the Winnetu. With Cass gone, he was more grateful than ever to have been given a dispensation to stay out of the family house for the weekend. He checked into his hotel room and found an elaborate welcome basket waiting for him on the desk next to the king-sized bed. Puddles trotted over to it, sensing there might be something in there for him.

"Hang on, buddy," he said. "There's a card here for us. Let's read it before we attack the snacks."

Dear Cass and Jonathan,

This weekend wouldn't be as special without you. We love you and can't wait to celebrate many happy occasions together!

XOXO,
Jordyn and Michael

Even the precise Jordyn with her endless checklists and fancy wedding planner from the Back Bay hadn't remembered to change the card on the welcome basket. He tugged at the heavy lavender ribbon, rescued a granola bar from beneath mounds of tissue paper for Puddles and helped himself to a mini bottle of Mount Gay, which had been repackaged with a label bearing Jordyn and Michael's monogram and their wedding date.

He knew that for girls like Jordyn, weddings were the culmination of a lifetime of fantasizing. No vows were too cheesy, no flower arrangement too fussy and no wedding accoutrement which couldn't benefit from some personalization and a thematic tie-in. Not so for the Casses of the world, who thought fighting about color schemes and petit four varieties was too juvenile to even bother getting in the ring. Originally, this surprised him, given her creative job and attention to detail. Later he learned that it was only after the party hoopla that things got interesting for his wife, tolling the bell for the psychological warfare, where no decision was too small to skip negotiations and no concessions were made that went unnoticed. Until then, you could have your cake any flavor you wanted! He unscrewed the cap of the liquor bottle and let the full contents slide down his throat. Soon enough it would rise back to his head and give his mind a much-needed rest.

Lying on the bed, waiting for the booze to kick in, he reconsidered. What right did he have to complain about Cass? He'd signed up for life with her. Jordyns had presented themselves to him in spades. But then where would he be? Exactly in the same place he grew up, under Betsy's thumb, living the life that was expected of him. He needed some separation from his upbringing, to branch out from the land of embroidered shorts and sunglass tans and trust funds. He'd run to Cass with eyes wide open. The only bait and switch of which he could accuse her was that she pretended to like sushi on their third date and didn't confess her true feelings until after they were married. How could you not love someone with such a big heart, willing to gulp down the abundant raw fish on the *omakase* menu so he didn't feel bad? He'd scored a table at Masa, then almost impossible to get into without connections and deep pockets. He'd gone casual on the first few dates, but then it became time to let Cass see a bit more what a rising tide she had stumbled upon. She didn't seem the type to care—her theater job probably paid peanuts, and she had been more than happy to chow down greasy food on their first date and pop on bowling shoes for date two. But he wanted to show off a little, and he'd liked watching the expression on her face as she appreciatively cleaned her numerous small plates, complimented the famous chef and told him how excited she was to eat there. A year later, when they were newly married and Cass was drunk and naked from the waist down after their umpteenth screw on the living room couch, she'd said out of nowhere: "Remember Masa? When I ate all that *toro*? I actually hate sushi." That was the only outright lie of hers that he could think of, and that felt pretty good. She had been awfully convincing though that night, taking second helpings, and that was enough to keep him on his toes.

THURSDAY NIGHT DRINKS for those guests who'd arrived early were at a casual favorite lobster roll stop that Michael and Jordyn had rented out for the night. As a kid he used to frequent the place with his siblings, knocking their bicycles against the beat-up picket fencing and charging in for lunch. As he got older, he started going at night, and fortunately the summer staff was a mix of college kids and disengaged lifers who couldn't care less that he was underage and that just two years earlier he had been paying for his food with allowance money strapped into a canvas Star Wars wallet.

Mercifully, Betsy had decided the Thursday night event was for the youngsters only, so he wouldn't have to face his parents until the next day. He slipped into his Vineyard gear, essentially a carbon copy of what Jordyn had requested for the next night: reddish pink pants and a pique polo shirt. He added a braided belt and sockless loafers and stepped into the cool, dry air. Five minutes later he arrived and spotted Jordyn and Michael huddled outside the restaurant, near the kitchen's back door. A third person, a woman in jean shorts and a tank top, stood with them. He approached, tapping his younger brother on the shoulder.

"Bro!" Michael exclaimed, embracing him in a tight hug.

"Everything okay?" Jonathan asked, noting Jordyn's look of abject panic. Despite the calamity of the moment, the bride was visual perfection in her strapless sundress, gauzy scarf and flip-flops, the look of the Vineyard nailed down perfectly in a way only someone who'd been coming here all their life could achieve. Jonathan could always tell who had the Vineyard in their blood and who was a transplant or a tourist. It made Cass furious when he pointed it out, though she'd taken to doing the same thing in New York.

"Hi, Jonathan," Jordyn clipped, meeting his gaze for a split second. "We're having a menu crisis." Then, obviously remembering his situation, she looked back at him to add, "I know it's my wedding weekend, but I am totally available to talk to you *whenever* you need."

Really? Because I could really use your advice now, Jonathan was tempted to say. Then he'd see how quickly she was willing to drop everything. He shouldn't be faulting the bride for his ill temper, though. It was her wedding after all—a once-in-a-life occasion (for most)—and he'd promised himself that he'd keep cynicism at bay for the weekend. Like most brides, Jordyn wanted a flawless affair. The one detail she couldn't control—the weather—had apparently been giving her nightmares for weeks.

Michael pulled Jonathan a few feet away back toward the parking lot.

"Don't ask. Jordyn's flipping out because the hors d'oeuvres are too big to eat or something and they don't have the mini lobster rolls she wanted. And there was a tip jar on the bar that maybe like two people saw before she swiped it away, but she's still mortified. Brides, right? How you doing, man? I caught dribs and drabs from Mom. Didn't you get my texts?"

"I'm all right. I don't want you to think about me for a minute. Just enjoy this weekend."

"No, I want to be here for you. You can tell me, seriously." Worry washed over Michael's face and Jonathan was heartened by his brother's concern. Whatever coldness coursed through Betsy's veins, at least she hadn't passed it on to his siblings.

"I swear, I'm fine. We're going to work everything out."

Michael relaxed into a half smile.

"Guess now's not the best time to ask you for marriage advice? It's hard not to have some cold feet when your soon-to-be wife is crying over the diameter of a slider. At least it's not raining."

"No, I'm probably not the best person, but let me give it some thought." Jonathan slapped his brother on the back, offered a salute to Jordyn and headed inside.

Three rum and Cokes later, he was still ruminating about what advice he would give his little brother, even hypothetically. Something about not ignoring the little things because they snowball quickly? Or was it about being a better listener? Maybe it was sex-related, but what? He couldn't think straight anymore. It seemed someone had thoughtfully spread the word about him and Cass before his arrival because nobody who came over to him to say hello asked him where his wife was. Well, that was a pleasant surprise. He'd rehearsed a little one-liner on the drive to the Vineyard, though it was long forgotten by now.

"Can I sit here?" a familiar voice asked. Jonathan swiveled around on his bar stool, dizzy at the sight of Brett waiting for an answer.

"Br—Brett!" he exclaimed, hobbling off the stool to give her a hug. He lost his footing a bit and crashed into her, sending the contents of the cocktail she was clutching onto her dress.

"Sorry," he belted out, grasping for napkins that he swatted at her chest.

"It's fine," she said, smiling at him with a kindness intimating she understood everything he was going through. Or was it the fuzz of the alcohol creating the outline of a halo over her head? "Let's sit."

"I was just so surprised to see you here," he said. "You look amazing." He shifted his head back and then returned it to proper alignment, capturing her like a zooming camera lens. She looked similar to the way he remembered her, though crow's-feet had nestled into the skin around her green eyes and the tan she'd spent her entire adolescence chasing had weathered her to some degree. Her body, though, looked miraculously unchanged from what he could tell. Despite birthing a child, she had the same lithe figure from her high school track days.

"You're too kind. I ran into Jordyn at the nail salon two days ago. I hadn't seen her in ages and she invited me to come tonight. I'm visiting my parents and figured I could use a little time by myself. They're watching my son."

"A son?" he asked, feigning surprise.

"Yes, Lars. He's seven."

"That's great. It really is so good to see you."

"You too. Where's your wife? I ran into your mom a while back and she told me you were married and living in New York."

Apparently word hadn't spread to *everyone*.

"We're separated, actually. Cass, that's her name, is living in L.A. for the time being."

It was hard to judge Brett's reaction. She seemed intrigued, with her wide eyes and slightly opened mouth, like he was telling her about a fascinating article he'd read in the paper. Nervous, he reached into the bowl of monogrammed M&M's on the bar and popped a handful in his mouth. While chewing he added, "I suggested the break to Cass and she agreed. Luckily, it's very civil."

Brett nodded, something like approval, maybe.

"I'm recently divorced myself," she said.

"Sorry to hear that," he said, though he did feel the tiniest bit happy. He hoped he didn't smile. The truth was that he couldn't feel his face. Who knows why he reacted gleefully to her news anyway? It could be a dormant schadenfreude or more simply an expression of misery loving company. Or maybe it was something else entirely. Brett still had those amazing legs, toned, tan and stretching out before him for days.

"It's fine, truly. I have a beautiful son."

"Cheers to that. Should we get another drink?" he asked, noticing just how much of her cocktail he'd emptied on her pale dress, now stained like a Rorschach test. He spun around to get the bartender's attention, knocking over the M&M's, which scattered across the counter like marbles.

He felt the color drain from his face.

"On second thought, maybe I've had enough. I should probably head home. It was so nice seeing you." He leaned forward to kiss her on the cheek, nearly missing her face entirely.

"Not sure you should be driving," she said. "Let me give you a lift."

He nodded appreciatively and followed her to the parking lot, trying his best to walk in a straight line. She clicked something on her keys and headlights on a navy blue Subaru lit up.

"You're right next to me," he said, pointing toward the Bugatti, which looked wildly out of place among the low-key station wagons and Jeeps with their "MV" and "The Black Dog" stickers on the back windshields.

"Wow," she sputtered, but it was definitely not meant as a compliment.

It's not mine, he wanted to protest, but forming complete sentences was suddenly beyond him. He slumped into Brett's passenger seat and closed his eyes.

15. CASS

WHAT DID PEOPLE wear on first dates in Los Angeles? What did people wear on dates? Cass hated that she had to be flush with insecurity all over again, but then again she also loved it. Because she honestly couldn't recall the last time she had had this kind of nervous anticipation. At Burger Joint with Jonathan, maybe.

People got married largely so they never had to go on another date again. At least that's what she and Jonathan would joke whenever they were seated next to a pair on a first date trying desperately to make conversation. Just eavesdropping, feeling the waves of secondhand sympathy, could be excruciating. And what followed was often more painful—the agonizing waiting by the phone, the sophomoric interpretations of text messages, the self-scrutiny—these acts of masochism could make even the most commitment-phobic person settle down. But the mind is a tricky beast, because here she was, actively craving the anxiety of dating. And she couldn't be the only one. The divorce rate would be much lower if she was singular in her desire to risk rejection, objectify herself, frantically go through the motions of sex with a new partner and, quite frankly, take more than one selfie to assess her appearance, all in the hopes of feeling a spark again. She'd read once in some random Facebook post that people would rather electroshock themselves than sit quietly with their own thoughts. If that didn't show desperation to feel something, what did?

She settled on a short white skirt, suede ankle boots and a denim blouse. The ensemble could have been cribbed from a Forever 21 catalog, but she reminded herself that she wasn't dressing to impress other women, she was trying to please a man. She assembled her hair in an "effortless" ponytail that took ten minutes. A cross-body bag sliced her body diagonally. The strap resembled a beauty pageant sash, which seemed fitting, as she felt very much like someone about to be judged. All her parts were shaved, lotioned and tidied, because who knew where the night would end up. She reached for her keys and headed outside, a bounce in her step, not unlike a giddy schoolgirl's.

This was the subplot of her separation, wasn't it? It was the supporting argument she would put forward if she had to bolster her position in a court of law. She put her future in jeopardy to feel a thrill again. To not just wonder what it would be like to screw someone else for a change, but to actually do it. Nearly a decade of working in the theater world had all but taken her out of contact with straight men other than her husband. Sometimes she and her coworkers at PZA would order in salads for lunch and Cass would jump up to be the one to greet the delivery boy. *Do you see me?* she'd want to ask him. *Do you see anything other than my new shoes?*

She was excited.

"WHAT DID YOU say?" Cass found herself shouting over the pulsing bass of the background music. Some type of electronica blared from a huge speaker behind her, making it feel like the nineties were crashing into the back of her skull. Substitute fountain soda for the alcohol and cheeseburgers for the spicy lamb dumplings, and she was back in high school.

"I said, the artisanal cheese here is insane," Gavin repeated himself, shooting a spray of saliva in her direction. "It's all locally sourced. The farm is right near this place I hike in the Palisades." With that he popped a Gruyère onion tartlet into his mouth, washing it down with a hand-crafted beer.

It was the fourth time Gavin had said the word "artisanal" since they'd sat down. She knew because she'd started playing a drinking game with herself. It was already time to order another round.

They'd met at a small gastropub near Gavin's apartment in Silver Lake, which was frighteningly like Williamsburg, where she'd once trekked for a PZA colleague's baby shower. Once was enough on either coast.

"I've got a little hydroponic garden going in my backyard," he continued. "I'd love to show it to you. Hard to pay it that much attention though because my business takes up most of my time. Not sure if Alexi told you, but I just did Pamela Richard's headshots." He rubbed his chin thoughtfully as he referenced one of Hollywood's young darlings. "She's very nice. Super down-to-earth. We have the same yoga teacher."

"Another drink, please," Cass said to the waitress who appeared magically just in time. She had known moving to Los Angeles would mean deep immersion in the "industry." Alexi warned her about it when she first arrived and Cass had shrugged it off. She was hardly a newbie to the entertainment world and sometimes missed the luster of it now that she wasn't at PZA anymore. Her first year on the job, Emmet caught a bad flu, and Percy had taken her as his date to the Tony Awards. She'd air-kissed theater legend after legend that night and didn't think much else could impress her after that.

"I like her," Cass said. "I heard from someone over at the performing arts center that she might be doing a John Patrick Shanley play this year, which I think—"

"Lucy Biele, on the other hand, was a total bitch. Had to reshoot her four times. That's what's nice about working with someone like Alexi. No attitude. No entitlement. Though Biele was a bitch even before she got the CBS sitcom deal."

It was a good thing Cass had decided only to drink at the mention of "artisanal." She'd debated sipping every time Gavin mentioned a celebrity or cut her off, but worried that would mean getting wheeled out of the restaurant before night's end. Thank goodness she'd decided to take a cab.

The date ticked on with more name-dropping and a conversation about gastropubs versus farm-to-table dining. All this while the scene got fuzzier, the lights hazier and the music, unfortunately, climbing even louder. She was still waiting for Gavin to ask her about Jonathan, the cat being out of the bag and all, but the way things were progressing she wasn't in much danger of being asked to speak at all. She just needed to nod appreciatively about the beer, the food, the music, the garden and the new Sony cameras, and time would march onward, toward the point where she could start casually glancing at her watch or feign a yawn.

Gavin held up his end of the bargain in one respect at least. Scruff on his jawline gave him the sex appeal for which it was intended. His long shaggy hair, which kept flopping in front of his face in notably thick clumps, reminded her pleasantly that he was probably a good five years younger than her. And his accent—even when he was blathering on about sun salutations—persisted in its sexiness. Maybe he could be her type after all and she should rethink her exit strategy. Cass adjusted her sitting posture subtly. Shoulders back. Chest out. Legs crossed and recrossed, sending her skirt an inch north.

Gavin motioned for the waitress to return. She couldn't imagine having another drink. The room was already starting to tilt on its axis and her speech was teetering on the edge of a slur. Dating would mean an uptick in tolerance, surely.

"Check, please," he said, and she felt momentary relief that Gavin was finally sick of having to shout over the music. They'd take it back to his place, hopefully with no more booze.

"Where to next?" she asked, astonished by and proud of her bravado. She found herself leaning in closer to him, letting him have a peek down her shirt.

But it was her date who yawned artificially.

"Cass, it was great to see you again. But I've got to be in the studio first thing tomorrow morning. Let me order you an Uber." He pulled out his cell phone and did his thing. "Two minutes," he announced gleefully.

Outside the restaurant, Gavin planted a chaste kiss on her cheek. He didn't even wait for her ride to arrive, just told her to look out for a black RAV4. When the car pulled up, she slumped into the backseat and rattled off her address limply to the driver, who glanced at her sympathetically in the rearview mirror. The radio was playing that same pop song she'd heard the other day when she left Gavin's studio, or maybe it wasn't the same, but weren't all the Kelly Clarkson and Taylor Swift and Katy Perry songs basically all just variations of the same three chords, love ballads that could be interpreted a million different ways? This time the beat made her cry.

IT WAS AFTER midnight when the Uber pulled up alongside Alexi's Prius. She hoped her roommate was sleeping and concentrated hard on entering quietly. Key fit into lock with precision, a soft click and a push, and she was inside, moving about the small space on tiptoe. The lights were off. She set her keys on the mounted ring gently and crept toward her bedroom.

"How was it?"

From the tiny kitchen table a glowing light spilled, where Alexi sat tapping on her cell phone.

"Oh, you're up," Cass said, trying not to sound disappointed.

"Yep. So? Tell me everything."

Cass shuffled into the kitchen, took the seat opposite Alexi, who looked especially precious in her tiny tank-and-shorts pajama set, her legs twisted into a pretzel.

"Truth? I should have thought this separation through more fully. I'm a bit rusty on the dating front. Gavin aside, who is going to date me knowing that I have a husband in New York? It'll be one-night stands at best. I'll be lucky to get back to Jonathan without an STD."

Alexi unbraided her legs and went to the freezer, removing a small pint of organic, stevia-sweetened frozen yogurt and returning with two spoons: a *Golden Girls* hack executed California-style. How Cass longed for New York in that moment, where there wasn't a twenty-four-hour gym on every corner. She even missed Hazel Park, where being a size eight was an accomplishment.

"Stop it, that's ridiculous. Not everyone clicks. If you really want to get out there, if that was the point of the separation, you could try this," she said, sliding her cell into Cass's view and swiping her index finger back and forth over a ticker tape of photos.

"What is that?"

"You don't know what Tinder is?" Alexi shook her head in disbelief. "This is the only way to meet someone nowadays. That Gavin date was a fluke. I'm going to make you a profile; you will get a million matches; it's fun and probably the strongest antidote to marriage one could possibly find."

"Sounds dreadful. I wonder if Jonathan knows about it."

Alexi scraped the slick coating of freezer burn off the chocolate yogurt and dropped it onto her tongue.

"Do you care?" she asked, her eyebrows raised into pointy upside-down *V*s.

"I don't have a right to," Cass responded, a vacuum of an answer. "I'm seeing him in three days when I pick up Puddles at LAX. I don't know if we're going to get coffee and talk or if this is going to be like my parents exchanging me in the Dollar Store parking lot. I guess I'll follow his lead. I miss him." Cass heard the pensiveness in her voice, watched Alexi's doe eyes soften in response. "Things like watching him shave. He's so bad at it, always missing patches, and I point them out to him before he heads out the door. I picture him going into work looking like he has Oreo crumbs on his chin."

Alexi smiled wistfully.

"You're brave, Cass."

"Or crazy."

"One or the other," Alexi said, laughing. She leaned in closer to Cass, conspiratorially. "So, there was really no one else all this time? I know it's a personal question and you and I never got to know each other all that well in college. But, and I hope you don't mind my curiosity, when you called me, I assumed—" Alexi's voice trailed off, and they both finished the sentence in their heads.

"No one else. I swear."

16. JONATHAN

THERE WAS SOMEONE else. That was the ultimate irony of Cass's assurances to him.

He'd been unfaithful to Cass.

Once. Almost twice.

THE TIMING WAS terrible, he knew it.

Cass was passing a lot of blood clots, the cramps were nearly debilitating, and still her HCG level was not going to zero like it was supposed to after the procedure. She was without child and with child at the same time, a state of limbo like something from a Greek tragedy.

But he had to get on a plane and go to San Francisco to court a pension fund. A two-hundred-million-dollar investment was at stake and Winstar was so close to signing them on the dotted line for their new venture fund. Jonathan had been responsible for identifying the potential investor several years ago, and he'd consistently sent marketing materials and relevant news stories to them, called after every profitable quarter and taken several trips out west to meet with the chief investment officer in person. Finally, the trigger was set to be pulled, and if successful, it would be a career-launching move. Jonathan couldn't wait to place the phone call to Jerry the minute he had the signed contract in his hands. Then he'd ask the PR folks at Winstar to make sure this got into the papers—the ones he knew his father read religiously. Christopher had just tried again to convince Jonathan to work for him, and hopefully this would make it crystal clear that he did not need his father to succeed. Cass knew all this.

Besides, he'd specifically cleared the trip with her. Many, many times. Repeatedly, she'd assured him that she had Jemima in case of an emergency. Her mom could be there in four hours if needed. But everything was going to be fine, anyway, so why shouldn't he go, she said. In retrospect, he should have known she didn't mean a word of it. When had Cass ever mentioned relying on either of her parents in any meaningful way? Maybe he had known she couldn't very well call Donna but he'd hung his hat on the knowledge that the Wentworths were next door and more than capable of handling an emergency. Though considering nobody knew about the pregnancy, and his wife was a proud woman, he should have realized how loath Cass would be to call on them. He'd put his career and the chance to show up his father before Cass, whether he liked to admit it or not.

And so he went, deluding himself into believing it was the right thing to do, and settled himself into his business-class seat next to Conor Mathis, another associate from Winstar, and across from Marielle, the investor relations team member who was dispatched to help seal the deal. She was French, limbs as flexible as plastic straws, and what she did with her *r*'s was titillating. Conor, uncomfortable with silence to a fault, kept trying to talk to him about the pension fund while Jonathan was busy memorizing the pattern on Marielle's stockings. When Conor came up for air, Jonathan found himself making bumbling attempts at conversation with her. "What are you writing?" he asked, gesturing at the longhand she was scrawling on her tray table. (Letters to her nieces in Paris.) "Did you order the chicken or the beef?" (Vegetarian.) "Are you beyond sexy?" (Yes, but that one he didn't actually ask.) He was desperate to put the D&C and the pitiful scene in the hospital out of his mind, and Marielle was certainly making it easier.

Back at home, Cass was in bed, sentenced to a week of rest. She made it plain that the termination was happening to her alone. He got it, sort of. There was nothing more noxious than couples who announced, "We're pregnant!" while the man drank scotch and ate sushi and the woman waddled with the weight of a basketball between her legs and downed fistfuls of Tums. In that vein, it was all the more absurd for him to claim an equal stake in their loss—or so Cass indicated. To decode his wife, he really needed one of those feelings charts in doctors' offices for patients to explain how much pain they're in. If Cass could just point to the proper round yellow face with the right-sized frown and the slanted eyebrows, maybe he could come close to understanding her. What was striking, he realized over the course of the flight out west, was how unfair it was that he was so caught up in deciphering how to manage Cass's disappointment that his own feelings were completely sidelined.

Marielle was a graduate of INSEAD, the business school in France, and explained to him and Conor over dinner later that evening that she had wanted to come to New York for a bit of adventure. Did Conor think what Jonathan did? That there wasn't a man in New York City who wouldn't want to give Marielle just what she was looking for? She said she was twenty-six and her translucent, dewy skin and birdlike body didn't contradict her, though her aura was a good ten years older. Maybe it was the French cigarettes she chain-smoked after the meal when they strolled down the Embarcadero back to their hotel. He knew he was flirting with her a little bit, though he crossed no lines that made him feel especially guilty. She flirted back, with a little elbow nudging and a number of hair-tossing laughs. Cass flirted with Henry Wentworth openly, and though he'd never brought it to her attention, he definitely noticed the way she batted her eyelashes at him and went in for playful jabs. His wife was entitled to feel sexy and desirable for as long as humanly possible, and flirting was the most innocuous way to preserve a sliver of one's single identity after marriage. It was probably beneficial to the marriage. What was that expression? It doesn't matter where you get your appetite, just as long as you come home for dinner.

The trip turned out to be a spectacular failure, professionally speaking. Their trio arrived the next morning to the pension fund offices, Marielle a perfect hourglass encapsulated in a black dress, a silver choker and ultra-high heels that forced her to take Jonathan's arm for support. He and Conor were overly prepared and they walked confidently up to the reception desk to announce themselves. All assumed they were there for the client to make it official by signing the FINRA forms, then they would head together for a long celebratory lunch at the ritzy Gary Danko on Winstar's dime. But when the receptionist greeted them she said, "I'm afraid their first appointment is running late. You'll have twenty minutes tops for your pitch. We have twelve hedge funds coming in today to present."

Winstar had been cock-teased.

Defeated beyond measure, unable to stop picturing Jerry's ruddy face doing his spit-yelling, Jonathan returned home on the red-eye and walked into his apartment before dawn, grateful for the chance to crawl into bed with Cass and tell her all about what had happened. He was startled when she wasn't there. Not in the shower or the guest bathroom either. He flew down the hall to the Wentworths' apartment, not caring that it was 4:30 a.m. Henry answered the door after five doorbell buzzes and loud pounding on the door with his fist.

"Do you know where Cass is?" he panted.

"You don't know? She's at Mount Sinai with Jemima. She was bleeding a shitload and called Jemima yesterday afternoon to take her to the ER."

"Jesus Christ," Jonathan said, and sprinted for the elevator.

"I thought you knew, man," Henry said. "I wondered what—"

The elevator snapped itself shut before he finished. In the cab, he checked his phone over and over. There was no missed call, no message.

"Cass," he sputtered, rushing to her bedside after negotiating the hospital's nagging procedures (check in, check out, photo ID, sign here, insurance, insurance, insurance). She was awake when he entered, plugged to an IV and, of all things, on her iPad.

"Welcome home," his wife said with a loaded shrug.

Jemima, who was asleep in a chair against the wall when he entered, now stirred awake.

"You're here," she said, in a tone that made him feel about as welcome as Nurse Ratched.

"I came as soon as I heard, which was only twenty minutes ago. Cass—why didn't you call me?" He looked searchingly at his wife, confused beyond all measure. She'd stumped him before with her peculiar ways, but never to this extreme.

"I texted and called you as soon as I checked into the hospital," Cass said. "When I didn't hear back, I figured I must not get service in here. You know how hospitals are. Bunkers."

Bunkers? What a strange choice of word. More like bonkers. This situation, anyway.

"Thank you so much for taking care of Cass," Jonathan said, turning to Jemima. In case she was too tired to pick up on his signal, he added, "Go home and get some sleep."

She nodded at Jonathan and made a big show of kissing Cass on both cheeks, reminding her to text if she needed anything at all. "I'm always here for you," she whispered audibly.

When it was just the two of them, Jonathan dragged over Jemima's vacated chair and took a seat on the edge. He leaned close to Cass, debated reaching for one of her hands. The only noise between them for a full thirty seconds was the hum of the monitor next to the bed.

"Cass, you did not contact me. If I didn't respond to you right away, you would have asked Henry or Jem to reach me. What the hell is going on?"

"I didn't want to bother you," she said, her voice containing a threatening saccharine note. "I mean, you had that big client to land. I would never want my health or this miscarriage to get in the way of your ascendant career."

He froze. There was a trap here. Or rather the trap had already been laid, and he'd gotten himself stuck but good.

There was no other option but to say what Cass predicted he would: "You told me to go on the trip. I never would have otherwise." Suddenly he felt like the failure in San Francisco had been Cass's doing, even if it wasn't actually possible. Or was it karma?

"You shouldn't have even asked," she said, mock sweetness dropped. Now she was all ice, her voice a jagged edge chipping at him. He pushed his back up against the seat, away from Cass.

"I didn't ask," he finally whispered.

"You hemmed and hawed about how to tell Jerry you'd have to cancel. I'm not an idiot. You were asking for permission to go. So I gave it to you. I didn't know that I would hemorrhage and my blood pressure would drop so low that I'd pass out."

"Cass, please, I'm begging you. I'm stupid. I didn't get it. I really thought you wanted me to go. I felt like things were under control, and if you wanted me to stay, you would have come right out and said it. It was dumb, now I see that, but I swear I wouldn't do anything to hurt you intentionally. I thought that a part of you wanted to be alone. This, this thing that happened to us, it's made me feel like the enemy. Please forgive me. Do you forgive me?"

He reached toward her again, brushed some escaped hair from her bun to the side. *I'm not a mind reader,* he added in his head.

"I'm very tired. We'll discuss it later," she said, closing her eyes as a means of shutting him out.

But they didn't discuss it. Once Cass was discharged the next day, they moved around each other on tiptoe, as shadows overlapping. For the first week, Cass had a wall around her. She was frigid. She was scary. Their home had a carpet of eggshells. He slipped out in the mornings for work, came home and ate a quiet dinner in front of the TV. They slept on their sides facing away from each other, the eyes in the back of Cass's head boring into him, wishing him bad dreams, a rotten day.

Then, a shift. Perhaps tired of the silence, Cass moved on to hurting him by being overly kind, a mind-fuck he couldn't begin to dissect. She said things like: "Would you mind terribly if I didn't pick up the dry cleaning until tomorrow?" "I hope you like the new brand of yogurt I bought. If not, I'll get the Chobani first thing." "I recorded that World War II documentary you mentioned wanting to see a few months ago." Things they'd never said to each other before. Niceties that felt like expletives.

After a month of this dance, Cass opened the door to the shower while he was shaving and said to him, "I'm so sorry for all this. I overreacted. Please forgive me. I love you."

And he did. She came into the shower, they kissed and fondled each other; sex was still off-limits for medical reasons for another few weeks.

But it was too late.

Two days after Cass got home from the hospital, he succumbed to Marielle. Even though it happened in a sad Courtyard Marriott a few blocks from their office, it was the most exciting sex he'd had in ages. Though he tried to suppress it later, he knew that he had pictured Cass watching the whole thing, the anger he felt toward his wife fueling his erection. He'd always said Cass was his power source.

When Cass told him she wanted this intermission, his first thought was that there had to be someone else. There could be no other reason to upend a perfectly good marriage. But he didn't dare ask. No, that question was firmly off-limits for him after the treason he'd committed. Luckily, his wife volunteered on her own that she was not cheating on him, and he believed her. Cass was many things, but dishonest wasn't one of them. He was the one with the secret. Secrets, actually. How ironic that Cass said she worried Jonathan didn't really know her when it was him that was really the mystery to her. His secrets fueled his eagerness to start a family with Cass. That would move them firmly into the next phase of their lives, when they'd be so tethered by their little angel that any transgressions that came to light would be forgiven, or maybe even forgotten.

JORDYN AND MICHAEL'S wedding went off without a hitch. The bride stunned in a creamy strapless gown with a sweeping train, his brother was dashing in a crisp navy suit. Hydrangeas everywhere, like white and lavender clouds. Extraordinary lobster bisque and a decadent coconut cream cake were the talk of the town. Other than his own hangover the day after the welcome drinks, even Jonathan navigated the weekend relatively well. Having Puddles along was a great excuse to dodge unwanted conversations, though he felt surprisingly at ease among the guests. There were a lot of people from Exeter whom he recognized, but as Michael was three years younger, Jonathan didn't have to worry about running into his own classmates and their misperceptions from all those years ago when he nearly lost his chance to graduate. Yet another secret.

His father pulled him aside unexpectedly during the rehearsal dinner and walked him toward the bar. The two men stood at exactly the same height, but it was hard to remember the last time they'd had this kind of direct eye contact.

"Nice party," Christopher said, gesturing toward the one long table glowing with the light of paper lanterns strung above. "Al didn't spare any expense."

Jordyn's father, Alfred Smythson, was a managing partner at Ropes & Gray, one of the oldest and most respected law firms in Boston. He easily made two million dollars a year. The implicit comparison to his and Cass's own wedding was absurd. There was no way Dick, who claimed he was too insolvent to make child-support payments (he probably was), could have put on some grand affair.

"It's nice," Jonathan conceded, wondering where this tête-à-tête was headed.

"Your mother told me about you and Cass. I can't say I'm terribly surprised. It's hard when two people come from different backgrounds. There is resentment. See how seamless this all is?" His father gestured again to the opulence of the setting: the glow from the candlelit tables, the soft hue from the purple flowers casting everything and everyone in a flattering light. Jonathan noted the pearls cascading from the ladies' necks, all shades of white. He had the urge to yank one of them hard enough to break the string, to watch the guests scramble on their hands and knees to gather the loose beads, on a mission to secure the precious orbs that so perfectly symbolized their tribe. *His tribe,* he corrected himself, though less so since he'd married Cass.

"Mom doesn't even like Jordyn," Jonathan said, in the mood to be combative, which arguably his father deserved. "What you're saying has nothing to do with why Cass and I are taking a break. She didn't grow up on food stamps either, by the way. You always treat her like she was raised in a trailer by drug addicts."

Christopher didn't deny it.

"Besides, isn't it a hell of a lot more impressive when someone pulls themselves up by their bootstraps? Most people at this wedding were born with silver spoons in their mouths." As if on cue, a waiter passed by with a gleaming tray of cutlery to reset the tables for dessert.

"That's not quite right, Jonathan. You overgeneralize as usual."

You're being such an asshole. That's what Jonathan would have said to Cass, privately, if she were there. He'd pretend she was his father and reenact the argument for her and she'd play along, allowing him the catharsis he needed, to say the things he really wanted to. Instead of engaging further in a conversation with his father that could only go from bad to worse, Jonathan stalked off angrily, returning to his seat next to his little sister.

There were so many more things he could have added, like, "I can see how great being cut from the same cloth has worked for you and Mom," and reference one of the million muffled arguments he'd heard during his childhood. Or, "At least Cass and I met spontaneously as opposed to submitting to the country club version of an arranged marriage." Or, just to really throw them off-kilter: "Surprise, I have hard evidence to refute our family's double *Mayflower* lineage." But he didn't, because what good would it do to dredge up the past or to compare his romantic run-in with Cass in Midtown to the merger of pedigrees planned by the Coynes and the DeWalts, his maternal grandparents? And the ill-fated pregnancy was still a secret between him and Cass. He stabbed at the tarte Tatin that had been served in his absence with the tiny fork.

"You okay?" Katie asked, eyeing him with worry. His sister was only twenty-two, the product of that fateful conversation between his parents Jonathan overheard as a child. She was a newly minted Hamilton College graduate, building a cupcake business with a friend from high school. Unlike the boys, Betsy kept Katie home for high school, the reasons for this choice never fully articulated. Katie desperately wanted to go to Exeter as well, but instead she attended Field Preparatory in Brookline—a fine school, but not on the level of Exeter. Wallace said it was because their father was more likely to keep it in his pants if there was a child living at home. But perhaps the most proximate cause was that his parents had had to pull significant strings at

Exeter after the incident and they had run dry of political capital by the time it was Katie's turn.

"I'm fine," Jonathan said, kissing his sister on the forehead. "Talk to me about cupcakes."

"We're experimenting with a fermented pumpkin flavor for fall. I'll send you a care package if you promise to give some honest feedback. But I'd rather talk about you and Brett Eddison. I saw you guys leaving together the other night. I've heard snippets of what's going on with you and Cass from Mom."

"Nothing happened with Brett. She drove me to the hotel because I had too much to drink. I promise to fill you in on the rest, but not tonight. I'll be waiting for those cupcakes."

"They're packaged in mason jars, tied with the cutest ribbons. We have our hashtag printed on the box: #letthemeatcupcakes. Clever, right? You need to post with that tag, okay?" Katie rattled on and on, and Jonathan thought, *Oh, to be young again.* Though by her age he was already wracked with guilt, questioning who he was after he'd acted toward a classmate in a way he hadn't known he was capable of.

"Anyway, if your billionaire boss feels like investing his dough in a sweet cupcake business, let me know. And, yes, the puns were intended."

Jonathan rolled his eyes and squeezed Katie's elbow. He loved his little sister so much and wanted nothing more than for her to have a perfect future. If his dad's whoring around was the reason for Katie's existence, well, maybe it was worth it.

She went on, beaming. "Jerry Winston would just be a backup plan anyway. We applied to be on *Shark Tank*."

We love that show, Jonathan almost responded. But who was we? With their separation, he and Cass had lost use of a basic pronoun.

"Thinking about doing a peppermint-nutmeg for Christmas. You're going to be here for Christmas, right? What about Thanksgiving? Would this have been a Cass's family year or an 'us' year? I'm playing around with a savory stuffing cupcake that you've got to try."

The holidays. He hadn't given those any thought yet. This Thanksgiving was technically a Michigan year, but unless Cass came to her senses by their separation's expiration date, he'd be up in Boston with his family.

"I really don't know my plans yet, Katie. I'm operating more on a getting-through-the-day mode at this point."

17. CASS

Twenty-two words.

That was the sum total of what she and Jonathan exchanged during the Puddles handoff. Like a tersely written play, devised to create maximum tension, the script read:

Scene: LAX. A Crowded Baggage Claim Area. Announcements Booming Overhead.
Jonathan: His stomach seems better. *Hands dog crate to Cass.*
Cass: Good. What time is your flight? *She looks up at a clock on the wall, which reads 3:30. There is audible ticking.*
Jonathan: Six.
Cass: Ahh.
Jonathan: How are you? *Looks past her as he asks.*
Cass: Well. You?
Jonathan: Fine.
An announcement for a flight to Houston booms overhead.

Cass: Don't miss your flight. *She plants a painfully awkward kiss on his cheek and walks off with Puddles. Jonathan watches her go.*
Curtain falls.

She played the scene a hundred times in her mind before it actually happened, tried on three different outfits, and popped two Advil to soothe a mounting headache. Coffee, she had decided that morning. That was what she wanted them to get to. A chance to talk for an hour, where they'd be laughing midsentence when Jonathan would look at his watch and realize he had to rush for his flight. They'd continue over text until he boarded. Less than three months earlier, they were having sex somewhat regularly, discussing a last-minute Hamptons rental for the summer, reminding each other to see the dentist like septuagenarians. How could they not sit for a while to catch up? She'd have to ask for coffee. Jonathan's ego would prevent him from being the one to suggest it, and that was perfectly understandable. There was a Peet's in Terminal 3, one terminal over from where they were meeting.

So what went wrong?

Jonathan striding toward her, carrying Puddles, looked nothing like the way she'd imagined. She'd expected to see her put-together husband, who typically didn't dare step outside without a collared shirt and a pair of driving loafers. Instead he cut a grim figure, clad in a faded T-shirt and ill-fitting shorts. He looked exhausted, hadn't even shaved that morning. Most distressing of all was the fact that he didn't smile when he saw her or go in for a hug. She really should have gone ahead and made the sign that said "Puddles Coyne" like the ones the limo drivers hold at baggage claim. That would have made Jonathan laugh, lightened the mood. Her own husband was making her nervous, which was absurd because she was nearly certain that if she told him she wanted to fly back with him, he'd be overjoyed. At least she was *fairly* confident of that fact. Now she reconsidered. Perhaps she had pushed too far asking for time apart, as Dahlia and Alexi had gently suggested.

She had taken care with her appearance: mirrored aviators held back her blow-dried hair, and she chose flattering skinny jeans and a slim-fit white tee adorned with a turquoise necklace. She didn't normally take pains to look good when it was just the two of them alone. This was one of the things about marriage she was already missing. It seemed like Jonathan was deliberating showing Cass how little he cared about the airport rendezvous, although that was too Machiavellian for her husband. Not to mention that he wasn't one to express himself through sartorial choices. Still, it made her freeze, this reality that was so far from her expectations, and that set everything off on a different path than what she'd planned. So, instead of coffee, they exchanged twenty-two words, and she was back in her car within fifteen minutes. Puddles whimpered the entire way home. She told herself it was because her sweet Choodle was exhausted from the trip and not because he was missing Jonathan, or worse, upset from seeing his owners treat each other like hostile strangers.

"I HATE MY job," Cass said, pausing Candy Crush. "For starters, it's only three days a week and the pay is pitiful. And while it's been fun keeping you company on auditions, I can't be your stage mom much longer."

Alexi looked up from her Instagram feed.

"Already sick of being my manager, huh?" she asked, raising a sculpted eyebrow. They were in the waiting room of yet another casting call and Alexi had been given number 122.

"I love being your manager. I just wish you'd sometimes get called within the first three hours of waiting."

"Me too. Isn't your job at LA-PAC pretty much what you were doing back in New York?" Alexi asked.

"Not really," Cass said, sighing. "I've been given almost no responsibility. The job I was meant to interview for was filled by this heinous

woman named Greta and I've become her de facto gofer. I have to exchange Puddles again soon and was kind of banking on at least one
positive thing happening before I see Jonathan again. Never mind me,
though. Let's run through your lines."

Cass moved to shut down their conversation—again. She hated
the whiny undertones of her complaints and was more than aware of
how incomprehensible everything about her situation seemed to outsiders. Alexi must have some urge to settle down, whether she outright
admitted it or not, and Cass was camping out in her apartment on
some indulgent soul-searching mission while a great guy waited for
her back home. At least that's how Alexi must see things. She could
unburden herself to her, confess everything about stalking Jonathan
in college, then in New York City. Explain just how wretched she felt
for using Google as a private eye to learn about his interests, the cost
of his apartment, what his family was like. How her actions made her
a fraud though she did really love her husband, but how could she take
the next steps and have a baby with him if he didn't even know the
truth about her? How she feared Jonathan existed on a higher plane
than she did and that she had never deserved him in the first place?

"No, no. Lines are boring. More about you," Alexi persisted. Cass
wasn't ready to come clean, especially not in a crowded waiting room
filled with actresses rehearsing for a Mentos commercial.

"I'm just feeling a little lost, I guess. I needed time away, for a variety of reasons. But I just don't know where I'm headed." She tried to
lighten the mood. "And what's up with Tinder? I'm worried the guys
are reporting their height in centimeters."

"Do you ever wonder if Jonathan is seeing anyone while you're out
here? Once he gets over the shock of it all—if he hasn't already—I
could see him getting into the idea of having a little fun."

Jeez, Alexi was like a dog with a bone. Cass inhaled and let the air
out in short bursts.

"That's the part I didn't really consider. Talk about being self-centered. When I left, I wasn't even focused on what he would do. I guess I was willing to take the risk, subconsciously."

Alexi nodded, as did some of the women seated around them. Rehearsing lines seemed to have taken a backseat to eavesdropping on Cass's conversation. She lowered her voice considerably.

"Sometimes I daydream about what it felt like when I kissed Jonathan for the first time or when we used to hold hands—that jolt, the butterflies. I really miss that. Once that's gone, and the little things start to get on your nerves, it makes you question everything. The spark went away so quickly. Even if we reconcile, it won't return. Maybe kids would help. We've probably waited too long. I think if you pop out the little ones right away, you're too tired to worry about anything else. Who knows, though? Maybe kids would make everything worse." *And I would feel even more trapped, with only myself to blame, for orchestrating this entire marriage, pulling every string.*

"Maybe you should have had an affair," Alexi said, her tone breezy but not altogether joking. "Probably would have been easier than a full-blown separation."

"No, no. I respect Jonathan too much for that. And I believe in monogamy. It's a sacrifice worth making if you're with the right person. The point of this is to make sure Jonathan *is* the right person. We were on the verge of starting a family. And I'd rather know now than later." The release of *some* of the truth felt like the loosening of a noose. There was something valuable in sharing with an actual person, not just a shower faucet or the invisible call-and-response in her head.

"Just don't forget we're getting old, lady." Alexi used an open palm to pan around the room. "Our reproductive parts are museum artifacts compared to most of the women in this room."

At this, Cass pictured her parts as withered little bits, grapes left for raisins.

"Don't pressure me! My OB says I'm fine."

"I'm just saying. I worry about it. Right now I'm all about career, but what if I wake up one day and decide I want a family and it's too late? And people do get divorced after having children. I mean, your parents did. Look at Dahlia."

Cass inhaled deeply, like she was taking a big pull of a cigarette. "They do."

"Maybe you just need to remind yourself how lucky you are." Alexi smiled, patted Cass on the knee. "From where I'm sitting, your life has gone exactly according to plan. That wedding toast Jonathan gave—I still get shivers when I think about it."

Me too, my friend. Me too, Cass thought.

Alexi was more correct than she'd ever know about Cass's life going according to plan.

ROCKS FOR JOCKS.

It was the unofficial name of Geology 101. Back in college, Cass fancied herself an intellectual and took pride in getting to Brown without an amazing pitching arm or a robber baron ancestor, but her strong GPA had taken a beating last year after she overestimated her ability to perform in Russian Literature in Translation (Intensive): Tolstoy and Dostoyevsky. Now she was looking for an easy A, which led to the discovery of Rocks for Jocks.

She found a spot in the back of the auditorium, which overflowed with a couple hundred other right-brained undergraduates seeking to inflate their averages. The row in front of her was a sea of monochromatic brown and broad shoulders; an athletic team had commandeered it. Well, they certainly belonged, given the class's appellation. She, on the other hand, was alone, as she too often was, though it was already senior year and she ought to have forged more than one or two lasting friendships by this point. Through some combination of feeling like a misfit on campus and not taking the time to let anyone all the way in, she'd been more of a loner during college than she'd hoped for at the outset.

With no pals to chatter with before class, Cass passed the time by trying to follow the athletes' banter. They spoke something like Pig Latin—a variation of her own dialect that she could nearly comprehend if she paid close enough attention. Once she heard "coxswain," she knew; it was Brown's heavyweight crew team blocking her view of the professor. Even though she was able to catch their drift, she felt light-years away from these muscled bodies just inches away from her. These were guys who had grown up in places where boating for sport was a thing. Crew was another one of those mystery sports to her— like lacrosse and field hockey. Athletic programs that seemed only to exist in towns with a certain median income.

"Dude, what time we going out tonight?" a curly-haired blond with sunglasses on the back of his head asked his neighbor to the right, another fair-haired guy with a popped collar layered under his crew T-shirt.

"Pregame is at Coyne's place tonight, right, J-Dawg?" The neighbor reached his incredibly long rowing arm over the backs of two friends to reach the guy sitting on the end of the row, and gave him a good knuckle rub on the head. J-Dawg, Cass supposed.

"Not tonight," the recipient of the noogie said. "I'm going to Paragon instead."

"Is Jon Coyne too good for beer pong these days?" Popped-collar asked. A crumpled piece of paper sailed from one end of the row to the other. J-Dawg, Jon, caught it midair.

"I like Paragon. Different crowd. Better beer." The peanut gallery didn't look impressed. "Hotter girls," he added. Then he reconsidered. "Well, different girls. It's my new Tuesday-night place."

His teammates looked unimpressed.

"They have dollar drafts," Jon added, and finally he earned some approving nods.

Cass studied him, this renegade oarsman opting out of beer pong. He didn't look like someone who made his drinking choices based on economics. His selection of end seat (if it even was a choice) felt symbolic, like he was deliberately choosing to be a part of the group but also separate. A Cro-Magnon among Neanderthals. Her antenna stood up straighter.

The lecture started and Cass watched this person of interest take copious notes while the bulk of his pals napped their way through the hour-long class. Those who were alert made whispered wisecracks. Hard to believe their joke about rocks and testicles hadn't gotten old yet.

Later that afternoon at the library, tucked into a private carrel, she first looked up Jon Coyne's campus address. He lived off-campus in a fancy condo building on Thayer Street, something Cass's scholarship would never allow. Then she googled "Coyne," "Crew" and "Brown," which garnered her a full name, a hometown and a height: Jonathan Edward Coyne, Boston, Massachusetts, six foot one. The rest was a piece of cake; the Internet dumped information on her like manna from heaven. He was the oldest of four siblings, a graduate of Exeter, and his father was the chairman of something described as a family office. She had to look that up. Apparently managing one's own money was a job. Who knew? Images of the parents, Betsy and Christopher, were easy to locate. The mother—statuesque, blond, always with pursed lips—was photographed at the Boston Symphony, at the clambake for the Martha's Vineyard public library, in front of an impressive building at Exeter called the Coyne Center for Cultural Understanding, whatever that was supposed to mean. Christopher was usually a step behind her, looking serious, bored, rich. Yes, a person could look rich even if the photographs were grainy and you couldn't touch the thread count of the suit, just like her parents looked poor before they opened their mouths. Jonathan was the only dark-haired one among the Coyne clan, typically the only tieless one too, and also the only one bearing a look of casual indifference in the pictures. Plus, she liked his last name. Cass Coyne. The alliteration was mellifluous almost to a fault. She couldn't help but contrast the shiny photo of the Coyne family with the one photo shoot she and her parents had ever done. Kmart was running a special where if you spent more than two hundred dollars on other products, you got a free photo session and one 8-by-10 photo, gratis. Donna dressed them up in their finest, rang up a cart-load of goods totaling $203, and then forced them to play happy family while an amateur photographer told them to call out different varieties of cheese over and over again. Through gritted teeth, Cass said "Parmesan," "Cheddar" and "Muenster" until he was satisfied he'd clinched the money shot. A week after their 8-by-10 arrived, Donna returned all the products to Kmart in triumph.

The evening at Paragon was a huge letdown. Jon never showed. She went gussied up in coed cool: scented lip gloss and three coats of Maybelline, tight jeans with a flare at the bottom, chunky wedges. All night she sat at a corner table where she had a perfect view of the front door. In came the townies with their tattoos and piercings, and she had to keep looking down to avoid misleading eye contact. A few RISD students she recognized from her art classes trickled in with their goatees and backgammon boards, and she watched their merriment with envy. At least they had a group. She was alone on a stakeout without much reason other than a sixth sense that Jonathan was worth pursuing, albeit a sense supported by the data. And she'd lied about her whereabouts to Dahlia, not wanting her to tag along or, worse, bring Alexi. Pint-sized Alexi would be a diaphanous butterfly tucked under Jon's enormous wingspan, and Jon wouldn't be the first jock she'd gotten to attend her experimental theater performances. Even Dahlia, who wasn't *as* pretty, had a well-timed wit that more than made up for it.

At first Cass planned to go back the following Tuesday night for another stakeout, but then she reconsidered. Actually putting to use what she had learned in the Modern Consumerism seminar she'd taken sophomore year, she made sure Jon Coyne saw her three times in the most attractive available light before they properly met. It was a course with a name that would have befuddled her parents, had either of them asked what she was studying, but which had proved the most useful to her in more ways than one. She groomed herself carefully before the next few geology classes, inspired by the look of the girls who flitted around the athletes, and once there, positioned herself two rows ahead of Jonathan and did a few back-twisting stretches during the class. She started getting her lattes at the hippie-dippie coffee shop next to the crew house, instead of the hippie-dippie coffee shop closer to her dorm. By the time they met face-to-face at Paragon, he'd probably seen her a half dozen times, though never for long enough to fully place her. It was sufficient for brand recognition, that security you need before you make the purchase. She'd gotten an A in that class, and only a B+ in Geology. Turned out she was far better at marketing than identifying geodes. And that was the first time she'd strategized and plotted and connived to make her future husband notice her.

CRAIG'S WAS A Beverly Hills hot spot. Dimly lit, with a bustling bar scene and wide, leathery banquettes, it was the kind of place Hollywood heavy hitters went when they wanted to be seen. Paparazzi waited out front hoping for a money shot, but the restaurant had a back way out that celebrities could use if they had too much to drink or suddenly felt camera shy.

Alexi and Cass, along with two friends of Alexi's from acting class named JuJu and Zandra, were finally seated after a forty-minute wait at the bar. Cass had had to be coaxed into going, even though it was a place she'd wanted to try since arriving in L.A. But dinner with three actresses talking about auditions while picking at kale salads didn't have much to offer by way of emotional or intellectual nourishment, certainly nothing that could rebound her from her dismal first Puddles exchange. Alexi assured her the night would be more fun than Cass expected, but so far she was underwhelmed. The star sightings were C-list at best (washed-up sitcom stars turned reality contestants) and the wait for the table was downright obnoxious. At least the menu held promise. It was mostly comfort food, a relief since Cass had been expecting microgreens. A burger with fries and a second glass of red wine did a lot to unwind her, and the shortcake à la mode she ordered for dessert gave her serotonin a peppy spring.

The night with Alexi and her friends turned out to be entertaining. She even liked playing the role of single girl out on the town, though it was clear how it could get old fairly quickly. Her dinner companions spent a good part of the evening doing touch-ups and surveying the groupings of single men at the bar, so much so that Cass was sure they'd wake up with sore necks. Alexi, four skinny margaritas deep, was cracking a lot of jokes and Cass couldn't help devolving into fits of giggles. Ironically, each time she let out a belly laugh, it made her think about Jonathan and then she was sad all over again. He frequently said how much he liked to see her "real" smile—told her some nonsense about her brow wrinkling cutely and loving that damn overlap of her teeth, but really it was more like he thought of it as a personal accomplishment.

Sipping the last of their skim cappuccinos, because naturally a group of women orders nonfat milk after a decadent meal without blinking at the irony, they readied themselves to leave. The check landed on the table and Cass seriously considered grabbing it. Listening to Alexi and her friends gripe about making rent and realizing the gray shearling coat she'd bought for herself for Christmas cost more than each of them made last year was causing her to flush, not unlike when Manuela used to iron her underwear. If she didn't reconcile with Jonathan, she'd soon be joining their ranks, but for now she could be a sport and treat.

Cass reached for the bill just as Alexi and her friends gasped.

"It's fine, really," she said, waving her hand dismissively. "You ladies cheered me up."

"Did you see who just came in?" JuJu asked. She'd been quiet for most of the meal after her complaints about being perpetually cast as the kooky friend were not received well by Zandra, who lately wasn't getting cast as anything at all.

"Who?" Cass said. A hush had fallen over the entire restaurant, which a moment earlier had had the buzz of drunken laughter and the clumsy clanking of silver- and glassware. She quietly slipped her card into the black sleeve of the bill. None of the other women protested, either too distracted or just plain grateful. Like everyone else in the dining room, Cass swiveled her head around to see two older gentlemen make their way to a corner booth, which in hindsight Cass realized had been kept empty the entire evening despite the throngs of hungry patrons begging for mercy at the bar.

"Marty Spiegel and Eli Spiegel," Alexi whispered. At tables all around, similar huddles formed. "They're the most—"

"I know who they are," Cass interrupted. "Which one is which?"

JuJu pointed out the taller of the two men. He had a blazer and a thick head of gray hair, the kind of man who might be termed a silver fox.

"That's Eli."

Cass shifted her gaze to the other man, Luna's father, who was semi-reclining on his side of the green banquette. On the heftier side, shirt untucked, he had a hairline that looked like it had been plowed above each eyebrow, resulting in a harshly accentuated widow's peak. She saw him scowl at the drinks menu and there it was, the resemblance to Luna, who made the same face when questioned about not showing up.

"I know him," Cass said. "I mean, I know his daughter."

Alexi gasped. "How did you never tell me that? You do realize he's the most powerful producer in Hollywood? And that I am a struggling actress reduced to eating ramen noodles at times?"

"It's not what you think. Luna's our housekeeper. And she makes a big point of not taking anything from her dad; hence, the cleaning-lady gig. She's an undergrad at NYU and likes to do the Cinderella thing for extra money, probably also to piss off her dad. It wouldn't have been appropriate for me to ask for favors. Besides, I rarely see her."

"Marty Spiegel's daughter is your maid? That is fuuuuuucked up. Well, you've got to go over there now," JuJu said, her expression actually menacing. *She should show that side of herself at auditions,* Cass thought wryly. It would do away with the quirky neighbor/batty friend roles. "You are sitting with three women who would give their right arms to talk to him face-to-face." Zandra nodded sharply by way of backup. Alexi, more comfortable using physical force with Cass, gave her a shove in the direction of his booth.

"I guess it would be interesting to meet him," Cass relented.

She stood up and subtly attempted to pull herself together by smoothing out her silk tank and giving her bra straps a tug in the right direction. Conscious of the many sets of eyes on her and petrified of tripping, she slowly made her way over to the table.

"Excuse me," she said when she was within striking range. Both men looked up at her, a mix of bemusement and curiosity on their faces. "I just wanted to introduce myself. I'm a friend of your daughter's. Well, not really a friend; she works for me. She's lovely."

"Which daughter?" Marty asked, smiling at his cousin. "I have five, so you'll need to be more specific. Though I'm guessing you're referring to Camille."

Flustered, Cass felt heat rise to her cheeks.

"Luna," she said. "I know Luna."

"Ahh. My wayward child," Marty said. "Have a seat, won't you? I'd love to hear how my Luna is doing. We don't speak all that often." He motioned for Eli to slide over. Cass reluctantly took a seat next to the silver fox.

She noticed Marty signal something to the waitress and a moment later a glass of champagne was placed in front of her.

"Um, thank you. I guess you probably know that Luna works as a—well—she's part of a group of students called the PhD Housekeepers. It's really quite admirable how she supports herself. Anyway, she's really amazing, and I just wanted to tell you—"

Eli snorted with laughter and spoke up for the first time.

"Marty, your kids will do just about anything to say 'fuck you' to you, won't they? Does the ice queen know her princess is scrubbing floors and bleaching toilets in her spare time?"

The ice queen equaled Bella Criss, apparently. Luna's mom and star of *Lover's Lane*, a soap opera from days past that Cass's mother watched with a passionate commitment she applied to nothing else in life.

Marty jostled the single oversized ice cube in his scotch.

"I know all about this crazy thing of hers. Kid's got a perfectly good trust fund, but won't touch it. She says she wants to earn her own success. And I say, what's the problem with taking and earning at the same time? Think about it, Eli. Remember how we grew up? Can you imagine us ever declining a handout? We were polishing shoes for dimes outside the R train at her age, for chrissakes."

He turned his attention back to Cass, who was busy processing this unexpected bit of common ground between her and the famous movie producer.

"Unless Luna moved back to L.A. without telling me, in which case I want NYU to refund my tuition, you must live in New York. What's your story?"

Plates overflowing with appetizers arrived before she could answer. Potato skins, tomato-and-mozzarella salad, fried calamari with a trio of dipping sauces, and generously stuffed mushrooms.

"Take some," Marty said to her, and it felt like it wasn't an option to say, *Sorry, I don't like sharing*. She reached for a mushroom, though the waistband of her leather skirt was digging into her abdomen after her last licks of dessert. Marty took a potato skin, fully loaded, and popped it whole into his mouth.

"Go on," he said, his mouth overflowing with bacon bits and cheddar.

"Well, I used to work for Percy Zimmerman at PZA. It's a—it was—a Broadway marketing and advertising firm. Now it's been sold. After he died I took a hiatus from work and moved out to L.A. I'm staying with my friend Alexi, who is an amazing actress by the way." She pointed out their table. Alexi, JuJu and Zandra waved in synchronization at Eli and Marty like Charlie's Angels. "I've just started to work part-time at LA-PAC."

"Uh-huh," he said. "I knew Percy. Brilliant guy. Such a shame." He threw another potato skin down the hatch with his thick fingers. Cass noted Eli using a knife and fork to cut a mushroom. She wasn't sure which form of eating she found less offensive.

"You knew Percy?" Cass exclaimed. "He was my mentor, like family to me."

"We were at Brooklyn College together. You know, Eli and I could use some help in our publicity department. Ever try your hand at movie campaigns?"

"Nope. I've only worked in theater. But I'd be curious." Cass felt her heart accelerate. Just as she had walked out of work on Friday, she'd received an email from Greta aggressively shooting down her suggestion of converting the position to a full-time job.

"Call my office tomorrow," he said. "We want to bring you in for an interview, don't we, Eli?"

"We certainly do," Eli agreed. He had that same smug, amused look on his face as before. Cass wanted to wipe it away with her napkin.

"That would be amazing," she said instead, with a smile—but not her real one.

18. JONATHAN

"So?" JONATHAN ASKED, looking at his wife. She bore an expression he didn't recognize. It had only been four weeks since he'd last seen her, but she was already feeling something like a stranger. After all, he'd thought he knew all her faces, but this one, a mild pout with her tongue running along the edge of her front teeth, was new to him. "Are you happy so far? Figuring things out?"

He had appropriated the decision to separate from his wife with pretty much everyone else by this point, but back with the instigator, he was stuck with the truth. His wife had abruptly left him the day they were meant to try for a baby and there wasn't an obvious way to sugar-coat that. He'd clearly missed some signals leading up to this. While he did leave his wife to recover alone from the D&C (and perhaps didn't tend to her enough after Percy passed away), what should he say about the alleged erosion of their chemistry and the myriad unknown infractions he'd committed to get to this place? Cass didn't know about Marielle, who thankfully was back in Paris as of last year due to an expired work visa, so that couldn't be it. If anything, his greatest sin was over-estimating Cass's ability to just be happy, expecting their relationship to progress on some predictable path to familial bliss.

"Happy is a stretch," his wife now said, and her face morphed into something more familiar. It was her look of deep contemplation, though he preferred seeing it when the variables were Italian or Thai, Bridgehampton or Montauk. "I do miss you. A lot. You should know that. The other day I saw this caption in the newspaper. It had a picture of this young woman, maybe thirty at most, and the caption read: *Julia Gray, founder of the eighty-year-old Mason Button Factory, shown in her office.* I showed it to someone at work and they totally didn't get it."

He smiled quickly, though it took him a second longer than he would have liked to get the misprint. Cass was quick—her mind like a plane on a runway, moving faster than he thought possible. It wasn't feasible to stay a step ahead of her. Just keeping in tandem was an achievement.

"What about you?" she asked.

He sipped his airport coffee, horribly sweet after he'd dumped in two packets of sugar purely to find a use for his twitchy hands. He wasn't going to waste this chance, though. Last time they met up, at LAX, he'd wanted to ask her to sit with him for a while. Instead, he stood there like a stone pillar, dressed like a bum, barely able to hand over Puddles with a steady arm. He hadn't planned to ask her to come back just then. That kind of outright overture was overly simplistic. He knew Cass hadn't picked herself up and gone to California just because she wanted him to beg her to return.

"I miss you too," he said. "Jemima did her god-awful impression of Americans the other day—you know, the one where she mixes Southern and Canadian—and I so badly wanted you to be there."

"Ugh, I hate that accent," Cass said, and she attempted to mimic it, which was even funnier—an impression of an impression. They laughed in unison. These were the essential bits of them. When you boiled their marriage down to its elements, the valuable parts that would collect in the beaker were these shared jokes, six years in the making. That's what he'd miss most. The rest, the detritus of a com-mingled life, would just evaporate if they didn't reconcile. At least that's how Jonathan saw it.

He went on, moved by the groupings of travelers around him ex-changing emotion-packed greetings and good-byes.

"It's lonely in the apartment too. I shouldn't say this, but when you first moved out, I had a fleeting thought that it'd be nice to have my bachelor pad back. I still have my La-Z-Boy in storage. But I don't even have it in me to leave the toilet seat up, you trained me so well."

"Hmm," she said, and her irises floated upward.

"How's Dahlia? Have you spoken to her?"

Even though Cass had denied it, he still couldn't shake the feeling that Dahlia's divorce was the catalyst for their intermission. Yes, Harris was acting like a prick, but to be evenhanded about the whole thing, it was disingenuous of Dahlia to have married him in the first place. Though maybe she had loved him. What the hell did he know about lesbians, other than his certainty that the dynamics of the Bloomsteins' bitter divorce should have nothing to do with him and Cass. He won-dered: If Dahlia and Harris resolved their acrimony, would Cass come floating back to him like a balloon drifting into the hands of a greedy toddler? He bit his lip in anticipation of her report on them.

"Disaster. He hired the toughest attorney that some dickhead at his firm recommended and who is known to just eviscerate the other party. Both the boys are in therapy. And she's got no money—I think she found her lawyer in the phone book. We should really help—" Cass started to say, but the hand she brought to her mouth showed that she caught herself. There wasn't a "we" at the moment, not the kind that would underwrite Dahlia's divorce proceedings, and his wife knew it.

"How's work?" she asked. Clever Cass with her return to neutral territory.

"Busy. Jerry's been really tense lately. I'm assuming it has something to do with our Chinese investors. The economy there is turning to shit and we may have a big redemption. Your mom called our apartment, by the way. Did you not tell Donna what's going on?"

Cass dropped the coffee stirrer in her hand.

"Shit, did you say something?"

"No, just told her to call your cell. Did she?"

"Not yet. I'll call her."

"Puddles is definitely going to miss you," he said, playing the card he didn't want to play. *It sure was nice when we were a family.* Cue the Norman Rockwell painting. Shit, he was better than that.

"Actually, I thought he seemed sad this month. I bet he'll be happy to be back in his home."

It's your home too, he thought.

"He likes the dog walker. I mean, Maurice isn't a film major at NYU, and I'm not sure he even finished high school, but Puddles doesn't seem to mind."

He thought she'd be pissed about his dig at Luna, but instead she interrupted with far more surprising news.

"Actually, speaking of Luna, I went in for a job interview at her father's company. I met him randomly at a restaurant."

He must have looked pretty crestfallen because Cass added quickly, "You knew I was hating that temp job at the performing arts center. I needed a real job, even if it's just going to be for a short time."

His face relaxed and he listened to Cass retell about meeting Marty Spiegel while the aspiring actresses looked on. Then he caught an earful about the insane mangos at the Malibu farmer's market. It was like his wife was describing a girls' trip she'd taken, only she wasn't coming home. And while he knew he should press her to open up and have a real conversation about what was happening between them, he let their chat idle in the superficial. How could he not when any real reckoning between them would be impossible without his coming forward with the things he had always held back from her?

FOR THE FIRST time since her departure, when he jerked off, he didn't think about Cass.

He never *used* to fantasize about his wife before she left him. He either inserted himself into whatever scene he was watching on YouPorn, or he imagined getting blown by the hard-nippled chick with the see-through shirts who worked a few floors below him. But Cass was all that could get him hard since she left, the anger he felt toward her manifesting itself in blood rushing to his penis.

And then, unexpectedly, Brett popped into his mind while he was showering after a workout. It was only the day after he'd seen Cass at the airport, and while his wife had looked damn good, it was Brett he saw when he felt himself getting hard. She was wearing the same dress she'd had on at Michael's party. Sweet Brett, who had stood by him when the going got tough for him at seventeen. Pretty Brett, who had looked so poised and together even when the vodka martini splotched her dress. Big-chested Brett, whose pillowy breasts would spill from his hands when he reached under her shirt at the movies. In his replay of the night on the Vineyard, instead of her dropping him back at his hotel, she came up to his room. Her body was what he remembered it to be: tight, tan, calf muscles as rounded as tennis balls. But her chest was even bigger, tits as big as grapefruits busting out of a lace bra.

When he finished, he stepped out of the shower and dried off quickly. Laptop in hand, still dripping, he opened Facebook and found her. There was a message function somewhere. He diddled around for a few minutes looking for it, letting himself get distracted by the Red Sox game in the background so that he might have time to reconsider. A commercial came on and he forged ahead. Why shouldn't he? He and Cass had been more than civil at the airport and he believed his wife that she genuinely missed him, but she'd done nothing to convince him she was ready to come home. If anything, she sounded almost giddy about her adventures on the West Coast.

> Brett— It was great to see you on the Vineyard. I never did properly thank you for the ride. If you're ever in New York, please let me know. —Jonathan

Postscript: I just jerked off to you in the shower.

He was about to send it when he realized he wasn't Jonathan to her. He shortened to Jon (holy symbolism) and sent, promising himself that he wouldn't look to see if she'd responded for at least one day. A fresh beer in hand, he settled onto the couch to watch the rest of the game.

Ding.

> Jon! So glad to hear from you. No worries about the ride. As it happens I'll be in New York in two weeks and would love to get together.

Ding.

> Whoops. Forgot to include my cell number.

She closed with a smiley face emoji with blush.

Thoughtful Brett. Stable Brett. Funny how those qualities were becoming turn-ons.

He jerked off again.

MOST IF NOT all stories are like onions. Not only are they layered, but when you remove their fragile protective skin, they make you cry.

That's certainly how Jonathan felt about what happened to him in high school. Well, not *to him*, exactly. Just what happened. There, that was better.

It was fall of his senior year at Exeter. He was busy with college applications, crew and dating Brett Eddison, a sophomore on the track team and a girl he'd vaguely known on the Vineyard since he was little. In a nutshell, things were great, not that he knew how much he stood to lose at the tender age of seventeen. Brett was his first real girlfriend. Not his first lay, but his first relationship.

Life had been a bit of a blur since the summer ended. Part of the problem was the uncertainty of everything. He knew he was moving on from the comfortable home he'd known for the past three years—one that was happier and easier to navigate than the actual home he'd shared with his warring parents, whose only place of agreement was that he should become exactly the type of child the neighbors would envy them for. College loomed and he understood he might experience the big-fish/small-fish dilemma that often plagued high school's favored sons. Harvard was his next likely stop. His father and grandfather were alums, both made generous annual donations and, as he kept reminding himself, he had the grades for it too. The crew didn't hurt either.

Daniel Rubia-Mendez was a rookie on the heavyweight team. An unlikely Exeter student, an oddball especially for crew, he was a scholarship kid from the Bronx. His father, who passed away when Daniel was in middle school, had been in the navy. Loved boats more than life itself. With what money he had after he got out of the military and from his job as a security guard at the public school Daniel attended, Emilio Mendez managed a down payment on a small cottage with a river view in the Hudson Valley. And it was there that he taught Daniel how to row. It took. Daniel had a natural ability and his father looked into scholarship opportunities for his son, who was also a gifted student.

Jonathan learned all this about Daniel after the fact. In late October, when everything went down, all he knew of the new kid was his first name. And yes, he did notice he looked different than the other rowers, but he couldn't have cared less about it.

The tradition at Exeter was for the senior athletes to haze the newcomers. How aggressively wasn't specified, and after the incident it became a matter of debate. One to one they got assigned by the team captain, and Jonathan was assigned to Daniel. The freshmen knew what was coming to them—some would wake up with shaved legs, others with warm pee (or worse) on their blankets; the more nefarious plans involved fake love letters to the hot girls on campus or snapping inappropriate photos that got photocopied and dispersed in the dining hall. It was very boys-will-be-boys and the school looked the other way.

It wasn't quite true that Jonathan didn't know *anything* about Daniel. He and Brett worked together on the *Exonian*. She was responsible for writing reviews of the arts performances on campus, and since he was just a freshman, Daniel was assigned the tedious task of fact-checking. Brett had mentioned the kid in passing a few times. *That frosh rower Daniel is unbelievably smart . . . Daniel's the most responsible of the new staffers . . . Daniel said something really funny last night . . . Daniel is probably going to be editor in chief by the time he's a junior.*

Why he was jealous of this freshman was incomprehensible to him. Brett exhibited no signs of attraction to the younger boy; if anything her affection for him was something like a protective older sister. Daniel wasn't particularly good-looking, his clothes were all wrong, and no sophomore girl would trade a senior for a freshman to save her life. On the crew team, none of the upperclassmen paid him any attention; he was just another newbie to be hazed and then ignored for the rest of the year.

Meanwhile, drinking on the Exeter campus was no joke. The school had a zero-strike policy, so Jonathan had virtually no experience with alcohol, especially the hard stuff. He didn't have much of an appetite for it anyway—even in the summertime he stuck to beers he rarely finished. He liked to feel in control at all times. To know what was coming next was the ultimate feeling of peace to him. Later in life, he'd wonder why he chose a career with wildly unpredictable ups and downs given his predilection for stability. Or why he'd fallen for a woman who kept him perpetually guessing.

The night of the hazing, the seniors met in the dorm room of Todd Porter, the team's captain. Todd mixed extra-potent Long Island iced teas, which everyone choked down. The assignments were doled out. Jonathan stared at the piece of paper in his palm: *Daniel Rubia-Mendez*, with his dorm room number scrawled next to it.

His plan had been to do the old eyebrow shave. It was harmless enough, quick, and if he felt especially bold, he'd use the lipstick he took from Brett's backpack and fill in Daniel's lips while he was at it. Jonathan had little opinion on the hazing tradition. When he had been a freshman, the senior assigned to him hung his boxers in the girls' locker room with a note that said, "Dear Mom, I don't know how to do my laundry so I've been wearing dirty underwear. Please help. Love, Jon Coyne." As though Betsy had any idea how to do laundry either.

That whole episode was pretty stupid in his estimation. He had no urge, though, to improve upon what was done to him. The eyebrow-shaving seemed the simplest and easiest choice at first. But the mix of tequila, vodka, rum and gin, which had been passed around at least twice, made him a little nervous to put a razor to the kid's face. What if his hand slipped? Better to do his legs, where there was less room for a dangerous error.

Breaking into Daniel's room was easy enough and he found the kid and his roommate, a boy named Chase Wilde, both sleeping soundly in the tiny space. Chase's older brother had graduated from Exeter the spring before and was now a freshman at Harvard—Jonathan hadn't been close to the guy, but they'd known each other well enough to trade friendly nods in the dining hall. Like the Coynes, the Wildes were an old Exeter family, which meant Chase wouldn't be a problem if he woke up while Jonathan was mid-shave. A relief.

Photos of Daniel's family were tacked up on the wall—Daniel with an older boy and two younger girls sitting on a stoop with melting ice pops; Daniel as a little boy next to his father in uniform; Daniel's mother, so young-looking, wearing a big cross around her neck. A certificate of completion from the Bronx Borough Diversity Talent Initiative was table-tented on his desk. You got the feeling his mother made him bring it: *Show those privileged kids what you're made of,* mijo.

Gently, he lifted the blanket, a Star Wars design similar to what he'd used back home (but only through elementary school), and lowered the razor to Daniel's calf. Around campus, similar things were taking place: bad haircuts, water-filled condoms strung up like Christmas lights, roommates chained together with furry handcuffs. As Jonathan leaned over to make his first scrape, he felt a hand land on his shoulder.

"What are you doing, man?" Daniel said.

Jonathan scrambled upright, landed his fist square in Daniel's jaw. Daniel dropped backward, into his Luke Skywalker pillow. The freshman reached forward with both hands, moving to shove Jonathan off of him. Jonathan ducked to the side, then landed another blow, this time to Daniel's right eye.

"Please stop!" Daniel begged. "Why are you doing this?"

"Quit being a pussy," Jonathan said. A few more hits. Maybe six in total. Daniel hit back a few times, he had to have. "I bet none of the other rookies are being bitches." Daniel's eye swelled up immediately, the dramatic change in proportion noticeable even in the dark. It made Jonathan feel eerily powerful to be able to change someone's body in that way. He'd felt so powerless lately—his father was making calls to ensure his college acceptance; his mother was lining up a dreadfully boring summer job for him in Boston; even his friends were the ones always calling the shots. Finally, he was in control. But the stupid freshman wasn't playing along. He knew he should stop. He had no particular ax to grind against this kid, no desire to actually hurt him. But he went on, the pulse of frightening emotions gushing through his fists like a big, awful catharsis.

Suddenly, the lights flicked on.

Daniel's roommate, sitting upright in bed, watching.

Lawyers, different accounts of what happened, scandal. An administration stressed, very stressed. Everything kept out of the papers, of course.

All the parents involved. An expulsion seeming likely. Very likely. And then, a new building on campus bearing his family's name making everything okay. A cultural center.

It was the insider abusing the outsider. A story with an obvious villain. Except it wasn't like that.

A cloud on senior year, then well beyond that. Jonathan lived every day that followed with a lingering confusion about what lay within him. A constant hum in his subconscious, the always-present question of "why" making infinity loops in his brain. And then fear of a reprisal; fear of a recurrence. Finally, the crucial reminder, to himself, that he was drunk. That night, a fuzzy layer had existed between the real him and the outside world. He wasn't some psychopath with a demon lurking within. No, he was a nice guy who had had too much of a drink that he later found out had also been laced with absinthe.

Brett, angel-like in her compassion, one of the only people at school to really know him on a deeper level, stood by Jonathan in all the ways that counted: sitting next to him in the dining hall, cheering wildly during his races, accepting when he asked her to prom. All those kind acts piling up while alternate versions of the truth were whispered from covered mouths to perked-up ears whenever he walked into a room.

He turned Harvard down in April, but not because he was seeking to be an iconoclast in his crimson-blood family. He chose Brown over Harvard because Brandon Wilde, the older brother of Daniel's freshman roommate, was at Harvard. Chase, likely terrified of Jonathan's clout among the upperclassmen, told the administration and his friends that he had slept through most of what occurred. But the boy had probably shared the truth with someone, and his brother was a likely confessor. The thought of that shadow following Jonathan to college was unbearable, or so it seemed when he was seventeen years old and still a spineless reed, his peer group all just wet pieces of clay upon which everything made an impression. Brown had an amazing crew team and no core curriculum—he used that as his ready excuse for why he went rogue.

Terrible guilt weighed on him when he broke up with Brett his sophomore year of college, but really, it wasn't fair to string her along anymore. Not when he had a campus full of women to explore and couldn't be tied down. She'd been stalwart in her loyalty, caring to a fault, but he'd still dumped her over Christmas break.

Strange the events that determine our futures. Brown led him to Cass. Good rising from bad, the familiar story of the silver lining. He never said a word to Cass about what happened at Exeter and prayed to God she would never find out. His wife was sensitive as shit about class issues and would read in all the wrong inferences. Cass had a chip on her shoulder, even if she would deny it to the death if he ever said that to her. But he knew the situation would have been so much different if he'd kicked the shit out of a white kid with a trust fund—especially in the way Cass would process it. But the team captain gave him Daniel, and his entire future nearly went up in smoke. And that first night, when he'd met Cass in college, he'd made up some bullshit about why he was at Brown. Now so many years had passed and he felt like an idiot explaining everything now. They were supposed to share everything with each other, but they really hadn't come close to it. It took what had seemed like Cass's outlandish suggestion that they might not really know each other to make him face just how much he'd been withholding.

PLANS WITH BRETT were made. Jonathan didn't remember dating ever being this easy, assuming this was going to be a date. She was coming to New York City by chance to visit her aunt, who was having heart surgery. They would meet up for dinner on the day of her arrival, near her hotel. Simple as that.

Finally he did what he should have done months earlier. He slid the gold ring off his finger and put it in the safe on top of Cass's bands. A soft ping sounded as the metal and stone collided.

19. CASS

SHE LOVED THE job at Spiegel Productions and it took *a lot* of restraint not to call Jonathan to rave about it. Only he knew how much she'd worried she'd never find joy in her career again. But she regretted her tone at their last encounter. She should have come across as more somber, but it was hard not to grow animated filling her husband in on the life she was carving out for herself, *by herself*. It had been a while since she'd felt so independent, and instead of echoing the pain of childhood, it was liberating.

Marty Spiegel had taken her call, much to her surprise. For one thing, he hadn't given her a card at the restaurant. So when Monday morning rolled around, she had to google the main number for the studio and tell the operator she met Mr. Spiegel the other night and he'd asked her to be in touch. Four holds and three transfers later, he was on the line and an appointment was made. The Spiegel reception area was minimal, California cool. Orchids whose perfect blooms looked spun of silk were the only adornment on the tabletops. Everything was on a swivel so that when you entered, it felt like you were instantly put into orbit, an alternate universe created in the movies. Cass's interview was with the head of publicity, Aidan Geller. He was a youngish guy, maybe a few years her junior, slickly dressed in skinny trousers and a finely checked button-down and some kind of cool laceless work shoes in gray felt that looked Dutch. His hair was spiky, either highlighted or the most perfectly sun-kissed shade of toffee she'd ever seen, and it framed his chiseled face perfectly. She had assumed he was gay from his coiffed and tidy appearance, but he referenced a girlfriend pretty early on. It was going to be tough to tell in California, that much was already obvious. Not that it mattered much to her. Not after her disastrous evening with Gavin and the headaches she got just scrolling through Tinder. She was looking to clear her head, not find a boyfriend. To see how much she missed Jonathan and to see what a Jonathan-less version of Cass would feel like. In a way she was trying her hand at acting all over again, slipping into a role she hadn't played in six years. A single girl, one with no one to rely on but herself. In other words, her future if she didn't return to her marriage.

Marty didn't meet with her at all. She kept sneaking glances into different offices, but neither he nor Eli was anywhere to be found. There was a tiny part of her that thought maybe he was attracted to her at the restaurant and that's why he was inviting her in for an interview. But their phone call had been strictly business and then he wasn't there to greet her when she came in. The fantasy that in the company of three actresses, she was the one who stood out was quashed. At the very least, she had been hoping for a new mentor. Her job at PZA wasn't just about loving theater and the cockeyed optimism required to mount a show on the Broadway stage. It was about Percy. The first older figure in her life she could truly count on.

Aidan gave her a tour of the studio, showing her the design rooms where the storyboards were created and the drool-worthy screening room, and then introduced her to a handful of people who worked in marketing and publicity. Maybe Marty wasn't going to be the next Percy, but she'd still find satisfaction in her job amidst creative types again. She had reached a certain place in the Broadway world where her job felt a little bit rinse-and-repeat: brochures at the bus terminals; phone booth signage; direct mail to the senior centers in the surrounding suburbs. And still the shows would usually fail, because only about one in ten made their money back. Broadway shows have a far worse success rate than marriages, Percy had once quipped. Movies would present new challenges, and Spiegel was certainly at the center of it. Alexi had primed her on the last two years of movies the studio had put out, but the schooling had proved unnecessary. She couldn't help but sense that her interview was a mere formality.

"You'll be wanting benefits, I assume?" Aidan asked when they returned to his desk, confirming her assumption. The salary was presented to her, and before she even reviewed it or made a counteroffer, Cass was transcribing her Social Security number and filling in her bank account information for direct deposit. Twenty digits later, she was even further from Jonathan.

"Regarding the benefits, I get them from my husband's job. So I'm all right." She thought about having to give up those benefits one day. Winstar let its employees and their spouses use a concierge medical service and paid for three dental checkups a year, up to twenty therapy sessions, even a biennial visit to the Mayo Clinic. The Coynes rarely took advantage, but it was nice to know it was there. The health insurance offered at PZA was pitiful. Before getting married, health care consisted of visits to those doc-in-the-boxes with their glowing red signs advertising "Urgent Care" on dingy side streets.

"I didn't realize you were married," Aidan said.

This wasn't the first time she'd had a bare ring finger since marrying Jonathan. She'd remove her ring before applying self-tanner or getting a massage, and then sometimes, just for kicks, she'd leave it off for a few hours, almost like she'd just forgotten to put it back on. The idea was to see if anyone would hit on her, to explore the way men would treat her if they thought she was available. Wearing a wedding ring was like having a "Do Not Enter" sign on your chest, and wouldn't it be nice, she thought, to shake someone's hand, or buy a cup of coffee, and not say to them *Don't bother* without even speaking? But whenever she did it, she had to face the reality that nothing much happened. The skim latte was handed over without fanfare; the client shook her hand and moved on to the next. Because being married wasn't something you wore on your finger; it was something you wore on your face. And now she knew she had crossed some invisible threshold. Her aura was single.

"I am," Cass responded. "But I'm separated."

"Oh," Aidan said, not quite sure what to do with that information. He looked back down at his form, tapped the paper with the back of his pen. "So you won't be needing the benefits then?"

"Correct. Well, I may end up needing those benefits. But I may not." She found herself rambling on as Aidan looked at her like she was a two-headed alien. One thing she'd noted about being separated: it was a black-and-white world, and nobody seemed to know what to do with gray.

The first movie she was assigned to work on was *The Titans*, an action film based on a comic book series. She was part of a five-person team designing the movie posters; the idea was to roll posters out in succession, each one featuring one of the four stars of the series. These would plaster buses, subways and billboards across the country. She gleaned that while Marty and Eli churned out the big-budget action films to score easy profits, their passion, particularly Marty's, was to make the smaller films that wouldn't be given a chance at the bigger studios—the Disneys, the Foxes. You knew Marty, who was clearly the powerhouse between the two owners, trusted you when you were assigned to work on one of those under-the-radar gems, like the recent subtitled film about orphans in Indonesia or the upcoming one about a musical prodigy and his deaf mother. She was slotted to work on another big-budget project after she finished *The Titans*, but it didn't bother her. She hadn't become Percy's right-hand woman overnight either. Goal-oriented, that was her thing. The budgets at Spiegel were so much vaster than her Broadway projects and the advertising reach just that much wider; she felt like everything around her was supersized. For the cost of *The Titans*'s media budget, entire Broadway shows were put on. It was dizzying, giving her a taste of Jonathan's world, where the numbers were also staggering. At a time when her personal life was shrinking, it was gratifying to feel her professional life expanding, as though one balloon was being let out to inflate another.

Marty still wasn't around much. He traveled often to the sets and went on the road for publicity (she could sense even in his absence he was a control freak), and it was becoming clear that her grand plan to install him as the mentor figure in her life, to fill the immense void created by Percy's death, was unrealistic. Hopefulness, she reminded herself again, was a wellspring of foolery. Like when she started Brown and assumed her life would be a smooth trajectory from that point on. Or when she married Jonathan and was positive she'd avoided her parents' fate by shoring up a stable relationship that would go the distance. We plan, God laughs. It was a saying she'd never really believed in until recently.

At least friends at the office were easy to come by. She'd become particularly fond of this one coworker named Josephine, a California native who eagerly took Cass under her wing. In one aspect, Los Angeles reminded her of Michigan. The people were friendly and went out of their way to hold the door open, give you their parking spot, say good morning. She'd lived in New York for so long it had become routine to pray the elevator door would close before the next person could get on or to pretend not to notice the pregnant lady waiting for the taxi.

If karma was a real thing, she was in trouble. The people she met at Spiegel and in Alexi's apartment complex were genuinely interested in making small talk. Maybe it wasn't even small to them, because they seemed to take it seriously, the *how are you*s being more than rhetorical.

She was building a life for herself outside of Jonathan in California, through a combination of chance and effort. It was a reminder that she could survive without his scaffolding. Still, she updated him regularly via text, like a child mailing home letters from overnight camp: "Hello Muddah, Hello Faddah." She found herself humming the song as she texted her husband. She asked him for a picture of Central Park, which looked positively alive in summer; there was something inherently off-putting about living in a place with only one season. It made her feel as though time was standing still when in fact the six months was creeping forward. When he sent a picture of their favorite tree—a thick-trunked elm as wide as it was tall next to which Puddles loved to do his business—the dense canopy of leaves startled her. When she'd left it had been a huge barren stalk with a thousand tangled, wiry branches hanging off of it.

Her favorite time of year in New York was autumn, when the foliage was devastatingly beautiful, leaves like liquid gold and cherries jubilee. She wouldn't have left Jonathan in fall, certainly not for L.A. anyway, where the seasons bled into each other like grape juice on a purple napkin. Winter was the time for a getaway—had she known that all along? That level of pragmatism was too much even for her.

ONCE UPON A time, a little girl named Cassidy Jessica Rogers lived in a small ranch house with aluminum siding in Hazel Park, Michigan, with her parents, Donna and Richard Rogers. Donna sold makeup at the local department store and Richard—Dick to those who knew him well (barkeeps, his poker buddies, other lowlifes)—was a contractor. Cassidy was a fine elementary school student, had a best friend named Tiffany, kissed a boy for the first time when she was eight and liked how it felt. She desperately wanted a puppy (her mother claimed a dubious allergy) and to go to Disney World; other than that, her life was complete. Her parents shouted routinely at each other, occasionally a glass or plate was thrown, but naive little Cassidy didn't know such things weren't commonplace.

Shortly after her ninth birthday, Cassidy was called downstairs by her parents. She dropped her homework, plucked off her furry pink headphones and walked gingerly down the creaky steps.

"Daddy fixes houses, right?" a younger Cassidy had once asked her mother.

"Supposed to," Donna answered.

"Why are our stairs so noisy then?"

"Good question, baby girl."

Now she sat down and found her mother tapping an empty wineglass with hot pink nails, her father flicking the top of his beer bottle over and over. *Tap tap. Clink clink. Wheel of Fortune* played on mute in the background.

"What's up?" Cassidy asked.

"Pumpkin," Donna said, looking squarely at Cassidy, who heretofore had never been referred to as "Pumpkin." She reached for her daughter's small hand, accidentally scratching it with the tip of her acrylics. "Your father and I are getting divorced."

"Why?" Cassidy asked.

"Because we have problems that we can't fix," Dick said. *Like the stairs,* Cassidy had said to herself. Snarkiness—a defense mechanism she'd discovered in early childhood.

Her parents seemed so lazy in that moment. She was only nine and she already knew that every problem had a solution. She told them so later when she got them each alone. She cornered her father while he was driving Cassidy to sell Girl Scout cookies (she missed so many meetings she had to deactivate eventually); she got her mom while she was showering after work, scrubbing off the scent that the perfume spritzers left in their wake on the cosmetics floor.

Her father's response: "Your mother and I just got married too young, honey."

Her mother's response: "Your father is a lying, cheating bastard." Donna went off script, not the first time, not the last.

"Where am I going?" she asked, back at the table with both parents.

"Your father is keeping the house. It belonged to Granddad and Grandma. We're going to move to an apartment together." *It'll be a grand, glorious adventure for mother and daughter*, is what Donna should have added. But she didn't. And all Cassidy could think about was how her Cabbage Patch would feel about the relocation and whether her new room would have enough wall space for her poster collection. She knew without having to be told that the new place would be smaller, in an even less desirable part of town.

The story ends, in the short term, with nine-year-old Cassidy making up her mind to be different from her parents. By the time she was a teenager, she'd resolved to marry a man from a reputable family and with money—lots of it—and to get the hell out of Hazel Park.

Years later, a college girl named Cass J. Rogers would find a boy named Jon Coyne who perfectly fit the bill.

SATURDAY MORNING, TWO weeks into her new job at Spiegel, and it was Jonathan's birthday. Thirty-four. Mercifully not one of the "biggies," but Cass was still feeling terrible being away from him. If it were during the week, the occasion would make Cass's heart less achy. She'd be occupied with her newest project and would take comfort in knowing Jonathan was busy too. He'd wake up, shower and shave, walk the thirty blocks to his office and remember maybe around eleven o'clock when the first phone call rolled in from one of his siblings that it was his birthday. At lunch, he'd casually mention it to Russell or Jeff and they'd insist on going out to Luger's that evening.

But on a weekend, staring down the barrel of an empty schedule, he'd remember it was his birthday the minute he woke up. Instead of calling early, his siblings would forget the date until late in the day—it being a Saturday and all—and then they'd all call or text within minutes of each other around five o'clock, after the first one remembered and tipped off the others.

Cass and Jonathan never did much on birthdays anyway. Both of them had bad childhood experiences, though he readily admitted his traumas couldn't hold a candle to hers (pun acknowledged by both of them). Jonathan's brother Michael's birthday was two weeks after his so he'd suffered the fate of combined birthday parties with a kid three years younger. And his parents inevitably argued through every single "celebration." Their parties would be these stiff gatherings at the country club and Jonathan remembered one of his friends not being allowed in one year because he wasn't in "proper attire." The boy was eleven. Cass and Jonathan talked, as people without children do, about how they would get it right when they were parents.

As adults, she and Jonathan went out for dinner on their respective birthdays and came home and did it in a slightly more protracted and enthusiastic fashion than normal. Jonathan obviously wanted sex on his birthday, while she would rather have rolled over and had him scratch her back until she fell asleep. But she could never ask that they abstain from sex on her birthday. It felt too cruel, not to mention defeatist, so Jonathan won on both days. This characterization made marriage seem like a game, which of course it wasn't. It just lent itself particularly well to keeping score.

"It's not like we don't have sex when it's not your birthday," she once pointed out to him after he'd joked in the morning that he knew she'd be a sure thing that evening. "You seem so happy about it."

"True, but I just like the certainty of knowing it's going to happen," he had responded. The difference between men and women, simplified: she wanted to wake up in the morning and be five pounds lighter; he wanted to know he'd have sex that day. It was a wonder they had any common ground at all.

Now, three thousand miles from the birthday boy who wasn't going to get laid that night (or would he?), she twisted her stiff neck to face her alarm clock. How she missed that ceiling clock. It was nearly ten in New York, not too early to text him.

Happy 34th J! Hope you have a great day. C. *Light and breezy, light and breezy.* She chanted her mantra silently, wondering if her text would land while he was receiving a "gift" from someone else.

Thanks! he shot back. The exclamation point threw her. He wasn't normally emotive, in written form or otherwise. At least he appeared to be alone.

Then, her Jonathan returned.

Kind of a shitty day. Want to FaceTime?

Yes, give me five minutes. I'll call you.

A hit of bronzer, a swap of glasses for contacts and an application of lip gloss later, she dialed him.

"Hi," she said when his face filled the screen of her iPad.

"Hi."

A moment of silence followed, enough time to see him properly. His hair stood up on end, scruff dotted his jawline, a faded Wharton tee clung to his chest greedily.

"You look great," she said. "Happy birthday."

"You too," he said. "Your California tan is getting darker."

She flushed, feeling more color rising to her bronzed cheeks.

"Any plans for today?" she asked.

"I'm going to eat these," he said, and panned his computer over to their coffee table, on which an open box of cupcakes sat. "Katie's new business."

"Cute." Cass made a mental note to place an order. Maybe she'd send a dozen to Dahlia's boys. "Besides that?"

"Not really. Thought I'd take Puddles to the new dog run near Carl Schurz Park. It's pouring, so he'll be thrilled. Hang on a sec, I'll go get him."

He lifted the computer and she followed the camera's eye to the kitchen counter, littered with a few cereal boxes, then to the open bathroom, where she saw the toilet seat down, and then to their bedroom, where Puddles lay splayed across their comforter.

"Say hi to Mommy," Jonathan said, and Puddles appeared. He started barking, seeing his reflection in the upper corner of the screen.

"Hi, Puddles," she cooed. "Somebody got groomed recently."

"Thanks," Jonathan said, patting the top of his head. "Kidding. The dog walker took him to the new spa on Seventy-seventh Street."

"Well, you both look handsome. Jonathan, I wish I was with you today."

"Me too," he said, sounding wistful. "How's your new job? Do they have any idea you live in New York?" She heard the strain in his voice.

"I was up-front, yes. Spiegel has offices in New York too."

A long pause. Jonathan ran his fingers through his hair, tugged at it aggressively if she was seeing things correctly.

"Or maybe you'll just move out here," she said, joking and not joking. Maybe a change of venue was all they needed. They could always move around the country together every five years, maybe even the world, to keep things interesting. Acclimation would be so exhausting there would be no time left for contemplating secrets, for questioning how life would be with another partner, for developing routines that felt like a prison sentence.

"Uh-huh. Winstar West," he said, rolling his eyes. "Listen, I gotta go. Puddles is scratching at the front door. I'm glad we FaceTimed."

"Me too," she said, holding back "I love you." Knowing that it was the truth, but worried it would be the wrong thing to say. When was telling someone you loved them ever a mistake? she challenged herself, but played out the counterargument quickly enough. It was unfair to say "I love you" when the love came with major strings attached: uncertainty, regrets, secrets. She loved Jonathan, but as trite as it sounded, she wasn't sure love was enough. One thing she was sure of: mature love wasn't anything like new love. If Jonathan questioned these same issues, she couldn't tell. He was so damn good at compartmentalizing; she often pictured his mind like the trays in a cash register.

"Well, happy birthday again," she said instead. "I hope you do something fun."

He shrugged, which killed her inside. How she wished he'd said he was going to play golf, or see a baseball game, or even go out for dinner with the guys. Anything but that defeated shrug.

The FaceTime disconnected abruptly. Had the Wi-Fi gone haywire? Or did Jonathan just hang up? She didn't know and she didn't call back.

MONDAY MORNING, AFTER a weekend of assuaging her guilt with wine and carbs, her office phone rang. The entire design team worked in cubes right around her, a bullpen of creatives. This was literally the first time her extension had lit up since she'd started.

"Cass Coyne?" she asked, inviting the person on the other end to announce it was a wrong number.

"Cass. Marty Spiegel. I'll be in in about ten minutes. I'd like you to come see me about a new project. You can wait for me in my office." He hung up abruptly.

She looked over at Josephine.

"Marty wants to see me," Cass said, hoping for reassurance.

"Then you better go," Josephine responded, giving her arm a gentle push.

Fingertips tingling, Cass gathered a legal pad and pen and strode down to Marty's corner office, watching the others take notice.

Alone in his office, after swooping past Abby, the most frantic of Marty's assistants, Cass took inventory of her boss's photographs. Luna as a small child in smocking, pig-tailed and chomping on a gigantic cookie, gave her a shock. Hard to see the nose-ringed, inked cleaning lady in that picture. Sisters of all ages were in other frames scattered throughout the massive office, nestled between countless crystal awards on granite bases and shiny onyx plaques. One locked glass cabinet held three Oscars. Movie posters everywhere made her feel small and inconsequential. From time to time, the talent from Marty's world came to Broadway, her world, to prove their acting chops, but looking around, it was hard not to feel intimidated. His office was a dizzying display of power. One shelf was devoted to photos of Marty at Cannes over the years. There was Marty with Tom Cruise, here was Marty with Jack Nicholson, there was Marty again with Emma Stone. Red carpets everywhere. Marty looked so much less slovenly in a tuxedo, approximating something like handsome with his cocky grin and well-tailored evening wear. His boyish smile took off ten years at least.

"Cass," he said, entering the room while her back was turned. "Have a seat."

Alert Abby, with her ears pointed like antennae and a cell phone tucked into each pocket of her pants, followed behind him with, of all things, a large pizza steaming in its cardboard box.

"Hungry?" he asked, flipping up the lid.

"Um, no thanks." She glanced at her watch. "I just finished breakfast."

"Suit yourself," he said, lifting two pieces and folding them together to form a pizza sandwich. It was the way her father used to eat pizza. Maybe he still did. She wouldn't know.

"You can go, Abby," he said, and she retreated, walking backward like she was leaving a holy place. If she had crossed herself, Cass wouldn't have been surprised.

After a long pause for chewing, Marty spoke. "Here's the situation.

We're failing in Europe. Especially in the U.K. and France. The movie titles are getting lost in translation, but it's more than that. It's the marketing. Here it's all about flash. It's different there, and we need to know why. Do you understand?"

She carefully considered her words. It was the first direct interaction they'd had since the night at Craig's, where she'd mercifully had the lubrication of two glasses of wine.

"I think I get France," she started slowly. "But the U.K.? No language barrier, and I would assume their sensibility isn't that different than ours?"

"Well, Cass, to be honest," Marty said, and here his face broke into a devious grin, "you may know that my ex-wife is English. Philippa Eastland, the fashion designer. Our divorce was not, shall we say, a smooth one." He reached for something in his desk drawer and tossed it at Cass. A stack of tabloids tabbed with yellow Post-its.

She reached for one, caught the headline and knew where this was going. "A-List Fashion Designer, Ex-Wife of Marty Spiegel, Steps Out with New Man." Below it, a picture. Tall, thin, with a stylish chestnut bob and cheekbones like smooth rocks, Philippa was a striking vision in her all-white T-shirt-and-jeans ensemble. Her boyfriend, identified in the caption as a male model, looked like his body had been chiseled by Michelangelo. They were hand in hand, heading out of a supermarket, toting recyclable bags.

"You see, Cass, I made her career. Forced all the pretty young things to wear her dresses to the awards shows. And I gave our kids everything. Two girls—Olive and Stella. I was making sure to get it right with them after fucking up with my older three. Case in point, Luna has passive-aggressively chosen to mop other people's shit because I was a crap father. But it wasn't enough for Philippa. She needed the looks and youth too."

Now he reached for another double slice of pizza, tipping his head back to angle it into his mouth. *You're not so bad when you aren't shov-*

ing food down your throat, Cass wanted to say. *Look at yourself in these pictures!* As if he could read her mind, he put the pizza down on a plate and reached for a napkin to clean his mouth.

"You would get what I'm saying if you were married. There's an understanding between people. Compromises. I have the money, she has the looks. It's simple arithmetic. You just don't pull shit like Philippa."

"I'm separated," Cass said, and Marty raised his eyebrows. He obviously hadn't known and she witnessed the cogs in his brain processing. Her brain was churning too. Marty put everything so simply. Marriage was a math equation. A sum total between two people, each person coming with a raw score. It was best just to acknowledge it head-on.

"Huh," he finally said, like she'd just told him a neat fact about her, like she was a vegetarian or dyslexic. "Anyway, now Philippa's back in London most of the time, except when she flies over to see this loser." He hit the page with the back of his hand.

"So this is about revenge?" Cass asked cautiously, wanting to make sure she was getting the assignment right. She eyed the yellow tabs. Someone on Marty's payroll was tasked with doing this, obviously.

"Above everything, I'm a businessman. And we are taking it in the ass in Europe. So yes, I want my ex to see my name on every fucking billboard in London, but I also want to make money. And that's where you come in. I looked up PZA's work. Percy ran several successful marketing campaigns abroad for West End shows. And you've got fresh eyes. My old-timers churn out the same product over and over: hero brandishing weapon, opens this Friday; pretty boy and gorgeous woman kiss with skyline in the background, coming this Christmas. You're new enough to shake things up a bit."

"To be totally honest, I didn't work on any of the overseas campaigns."

"Doesn't matter," he said, licking the grease off his fingers. "Aidan tells me you've been a great addition to the team. We leave for London

Wednesday night. We have a bunch of meetings set up with marketing people over there. And then we'll take some time to just to soak things in."

Here again, there was only one option available to Cass. The lack of choice came as a relief. It was the opposite of the intermission.

"Okay."

A business trip with her new boss, who was also her housekeeper's father. If it wasn't happening to her, she wouldn't believe it was true. She had nothing to hide about the trip, but for some reason she wasn't particularly keen to tell Jonathan about it. It would sound as though she was moving farther and farther away from him, slipping deeper into a new life in which he had no part. Yes, she had secrets she kept from her husband, but they were never of the mundane variety. And on good days she could delude herself into believing that a healthy relationship wasn't based on revealing the deepest parts of oneself, it was about exchanging the day-to-day freely. That marriage was trading the bits and snippets that make up a life with someone who cared: what was had for lunch, whose breath was deadly at work. That had been her and Jonathan for years, and until it was time to have a child, it had seemed to be adequate. Now even that part was disintegrating.

20. JONATHAN

THE PROBLEM WITH putting your wife on a pedestal from day one is that she has nowhere to go but down.

Well, strictly speaking, that wasn't quite true. There were higher and higher pedestals to climb until your spouse is deified and you look in the mirror and think, *How did a worthless sack of shit like me get her?* That was *not* the case for Jonathan, though he certainly thought things were headed in that direction when he and Cass first got married. It wasn't that he'd grown to dislike his wife—not at all—it was just that he was no longer as blinded by love as he had been at the outset.

In the beginning, Cass was everything he'd ever dreamed of and more. Conventional wisdom will tell you the first year of marriage is supposed to be the most difficult. Maybe that was true for older generations, before living together became de rigueur, but for Cass and Jonathan, it was pretty seamless. They worked a lot, but when they came together in the late evenings for a ritualistic catch-up, it was with toes nudging each other on the coffee table, hands intertwined, wineglasses clinking each other in self-congratulatory fashion. There is nothing smugger than believing you've found what everyone in the world is looking for.

His attraction to Cass seemed only to grow as he discovered new things about her to admire. She was pretty first thing in the morning, before the makeup and the clothes finished the story. Her skin was a milky white, and in cold weather inky veins surfaced and gave him paths to trace. Cornflower blue eyes, feline in shape, anchored an angular face topped with a sexy shade of blond strands—the kind of hair that made you think this woman just loved to screw. And those overlapping teeth. He loved to run his tongue over the ridge. Small breasts, tiny acorns, but still they fulfilled him. All this on the outside and whip-smart too, an answer for everything, one of those things he thought he was going to love about her forever. And her background? What wasn't there to love about someone who came from nothing and had to work at least 50 percent harder to get to the same place as the one-percenters he grew up with? He was not an elitist, whatever those who misunderstood him said. Just look who he fell in love with. He never saw their relationship as some Henry Higgins–Eliza Doolittle scenario. Except, that is, on lobster night.

It was July Fourth weekend and he and Cass had been engaged for two months. His parents were still treating Cass like she was hired help and he longed for them to get to know her better and show a little enthusiasm about their future daughter-in-law. He thought a weekend of togetherness on the Vineyard would do the trick. His soon-to-be wife had just been promoted at work, she was overflowing with chatter about Broadway shows and up-and-coming playwrights and he was certain she would impress. His mother pretended to be cultured, but she hadn't stepped foot in a theater or a museum for as long as he could remember. Cass could school her any day. This wasn't the gold digger his parents feared. Cass Rogers could easily stand on her own two feet.

His mother reserved a table at the Cheshire for the annual holiday lobster night at 5:30 p.m. It was a ridiculously early time to eat and Jonathan couldn't shake the feeling that she was trying to avoid the regular crowd who would all but give Cass a colonoscopy to suss out her story. If any of his mother's snobby friends looked up Hazel Park on Wikipedia they would cringe at the median income. So no, he didn't buy Betsy's story about being ravenous after a long day on the golf course and needing an early supper.

Cass looked beautiful in a bright pink summer dress and sandals. She easily could have passed for a regular at the club, and Jonathan felt himself relaxing the minute she emerged from his bathroom asking him to zip up her dress. It was one of the tasks he liked best. Cass had a sexy back, and he liked feeling needed. They arrived promptly and were the only ones in the dining room. The waiter took their drink orders and then turned to Cass first to ask which sides she'd like with her lobster. She eyeballed the printed menu card and selected potato salad and green beans. So far, so good. He scribbled it down and then asked, "And can I bring you a bib?"

Jonathan watched Cass's face screw up in confusion, unaware that it was customary to don a bib when cracking open a whole lobster. He knew how much his fiancée hated to feel uncertain, so he waited anxiously to see how she'd respond.

She smiled and then broke into a giggle.

"No, I don't think I'll need a bib. Though I appreciate how much you like my dress that you want to protect it." Then she glanced around the table at Jonathan's parents and siblings, waiting for them to laugh at her witty comeback.

"Okay then," the waiter said, looking just as confused as Cass had, and then turned to Betsy to take her order.

"Bufala mozzarella salad and the insalata mista," his mother said in the voice of a woman who had been to Italy before and wasn't afraid to try the accent. "And a bib for myself and everyone else at the table besides her," she added, looking toward Cass.

"Of course, Mrs. Coyne," the waiter responded, back at ease. Jonathan recognized him as the son of one of the members. It was a rite of passage for many to work as waiters at the club, often between junior and senior year of high school. This kid had been served at the club more times than he'd done the serving, and it showed.

Things got worse when the lobsters arrived along with the tools. Cass eyed the cracker and tiny fork with a mix of suspicion and downright puzzlement and Jonathan desperately wanted to help her with the dissection, like a parent slicing a child's meat. But there was just no way he could do it without mortifying Cass and further satisfying his mother. His father dug into his meal first and Jonathan watched Cass mimic his every move, first starting with the claws, then moving on to the body. She was slow and deliberate, but still as the only non–bib wearer, her dress was streaked with fish juice and butter in no time. And of course, that's when the Coyne friends starting showing up for their more appropriate dinner times. The evening ended awkwardly and they never talked about Broadway, Cass's promotion or anything else that had been on his agenda.

"I'm sorry," he'd said to Cass when they piled into his car to drive back to the house. His fiancée, with more hubris in her thumbnail than he possessed in his whole being, turned to him and said, "About what?" At the time, he'd loved her for not admitting to anything having gone wrong at the meal. Only later did he realize that her reticence was driving a wedge between them. What if instead of Cass saying "About what?" all innocent-like, she had burst into tears and he had comforted her—promising he would make sure she never faced eating another whole lobster again without a private tutorial first. Or they could have shared a big laugh about the whole thing while they dabbed at her dress with club soda, terming the evening "LobsterGate" and adding it to their arsenal of private jokes.

He knew most couples eventually trod a similar path of disillusionment. The midnight snacking once considered cute and childlike becomes a nuisance. The refusal to walk more than three blocks because of high heels? It starts off with feeling proud that your wife stuffs her delicate feet into stilettos to make her legs look sexy, but after a while, you just wish she'd wear flats and stop complaining. Neither of those examples applied to Cass specifically, but he liked to imagine the scenarios that chipped away at other people's foundations. It was maybe the only perk of going out for drinks with the guys from work. After a scotch or two, they were all willing to open up about their pesky wives and Jonathan didn't feel so alone.

The universal question for every married couple was this: How long? How long would it take for the charm to fade? Would the erosion of chemistry be a drawn-out journey, like the gradual evaporation of boiling water? Or a sudden combustion of two incompatible gases? How long would it be before quirks devolved into maddening habits that made you lie in bed and contemplate what life would have been like with someone else? Of course, neither of you was so stupid as to think that your other mythical partner wouldn't have attributes equally—if not more—cloying. So you hope your marriage will have staying power, that you'll both be gray-haired and in failing health before you want to kill each other, and at that point, your lives will be fully commingled with children and grandchildren and a shared history of highs and lows. You would be so dependent on each other for rides to the doctor and reminders to take medication that divorce would be a laughable idea. Something for younger people to do. What you don't do is leave a marriage that's a solid B+ or A− because there's a tiny chance to find something better. Especially when children would likely give it a half-grade boost.

But was he really surprised with the way things were going for Cass and him?

Their relationship, even in its blissful infancy, always had a chesslike quality to it. Chess was Jonathan's favorite game as a child, probably because he was able to beat his father from an early age. One of his greatest accomplishments was teaching the game to Leon, who went on to found a chess club at his high school. In Coyne chess, Cass was the queen, the most powerful piece. And she was out to capture him, the king. This tactical play of their marriage didn't bother him—he suspected more men would be happy with their spouses if they accepted the natural dynamic existing between husband and wife. It was only when Cass moved to California that he returned to the chess analogy with fresh eyes, seeing himself the way Cass must have viewed him all along. As a pawn. Not unique or powerful. He just couldn't figure out what the endgame was. Most days, he questioned seriously if even she, the great and mighty Cass, had any clue.

Cass's contradictions, her unpredictability, had once been it for him. She was hoity-toity *and* blue-collar. Compassionate while clueless. A professional badass who couldn't get to work before ten. An antisocial creature who still wanted everyone to like her. A faithful wife who openly flirted with other men in front of him. These were the puzzles that once flamed his desire. She was the walnut he wanted to crack, preferably with his teeth. Now he saw her differently, though not so extremely that he wanted to make any drastic changes. He believed that as soon as he saw traces of Cass in his son or daughter, he would come to appreciate her again, even more magnanimously than before. Once again her traits would take on a cherished quality; seen in miniature, they'd be infectious again. Especially because their future babies wouldn't just be little Casses—pieces of him would be there too—a collision of DNA would make something else entirely: a Cassathan. A living, breathing human that represented their unity as a couple. Talk about chemistry.

But until then, he wouldn't have minded shouting at her, *Cass, can't you just man up already about how you want to be perceived? Are you the girl from Hazel Park who overcame shit parents to become the savvy Manhattan professional you are today, or were you raised to know the hostess raises her fork and knife first and that seasons are both nouns and verbs? Are you a wife who genuinely loves sex, or do you wish you were sleeping half the time? And, most importantly, do you even love me?*

Over the course of his five-year marriage, he'd imagined an alternate life with Brett on occasion. Like when he split open a fortune cookie at Shun Lee on Valentine's Day a few years ago that said "First loves are eternal," and let the message percolate for a long moment before showing it to Cass. Cass just laughed at him and said, "Lame. Mine says I'm going to learn Mandarin."

Now that he had an actual date with Brett coming up—yes, he had decided that's what it was—the scenario of an alternative life was running through his mind more frequently. He saw Brett insisting he try her pasta, actually foisting it onto his plate; the two of them playing tennis in matching whites—the tennis skirt that barely covered her ass distracting his serve; Brett making him lemon meringue pie on his birthday. When Cass wheeled her suitcase out the door in March, he never imagined he'd feel excited for dinner with another woman just a few months later. ABC Kitchen was almost fully booked when he called for a reservation; he'd requested a table in the corner. If nothing else, he and Brett had a lot of catching up to do.

And then there was the prospect of sex. Except for the one time with Marielle, there had been no one else but Cass for the past six years. Which he knew was nothing to boast about, monogamy being the basis of marriage and all. To his credit, he had had the chance for a repeat with that magnificent French gamine. Before Marielle returned to Paris, she made it abundantly clear that she would meet him again, anytime and anyplace, but he'd declined. Once was a *mistake*; twice was an *affair*. Cass was a better writer than him, the queen of catchy slogans for which Percy adored her, but he was certainly capable of linguistic gymnastics when it counted. Since he'd removed his wedding ring, sexy women goggled him everywhere, suggesting in the least subtle ways he could have them. He was tempted but also nervous, as though sex with one of these unknowns would be the land mine that blew up his marriage.

The thing was, no matter how much he tried to downplay his indiscretion (his colleagues all slept around; it only happened once), he was stricken with guilt. It didn't help that Cass seemed to regard adultery as one step below homicide and was fond of complimenting him on his loyalty. The only mitigating factor was that his wife was unfairly punishing him at the time of his indiscretion. Pushing him away, making him feel like a bystander to their shared heartache. Tricking him. Setting a trap for him like he was a dumb lobster. And he'd been exactly what she'd predicted he would be. Dumb.

He really should tell her the truth. Over the phone, when she was three thousand miles away and her disappointment and anger would have to ping off a dozen cell phone towers before it reached him. He thought back to what Cass said the night she announced her intentions—if they were going to start a family, they should truly know each other. While he didn't take much of what she had said all that seriously—it was the ranting of a woman left reeling from her boss's death and freaking out about becoming a mother—she had a point. They shouldn't keep things from each other. Even the ugly stuff.

"JONATHAN, CAN I talk to you for a minute?"

It was Laurel, his quasi-protégée. He hadn't had much contact with her since he had, laughably in hindsight, offered her marriage advice a few months earlier.

"Yes?"

She closed the door to his office and looked around surreptitiously before taking a seat.

"It's not bugged if that's what you're thinking," Jonathan said, lifting his computer mouse and revealing its underside to her. "No camera. I can't imagine you're here to seek my counsel again? I thought all of Winstar knew my situation by now."

"We do," she said, offering a sympathetic smile. "Sorry. But that's not why I'm here. I have a concern I'd like to discuss with you. Confidentially." She waited for him to reassure her, which he did with a vigorous head nod.

"Okay. My cousin works for the SEC in their Washington head-quarters. She's basically a glorified assistant, and she's in charge of managing one of the regulator's schedules. He had a meeting about Winstar Capital yesterday with one of the most senior directors there. She texted me because she remembered that I work here. I'm nervous. Do you think everything is okay?" She crossed and recrossed her legs, and let out a sharp exhale that ruffled the papers on his desk.

He was startled, because it was rarely a good thing when the SEC came nosing around. He didn't know of any malfeasance, not that it meant the government wouldn't spin something to press Jerry against a wall. The current attorney general hated hedge fund managers, particularly ones like Jerry, who hosted five-thousand-dollar-a-plate dinners to raise money for her political foes. But he knew his boss well, believed strongly he was on the up-and-up. Jerry vetted his analysts like he was recruiting for the CIA and then micromanaged the hell out of them after. No, it wasn't possible anything shady was happening here, though the numbers could lead some to believe otherwise. The returns were compounding daily and his computer screen wasn't showing much red at all. Everything was solid though—strong employment numbers, nice GDP growth, a confidence-inspiring rate hike—and Winstar analysts had just bet on the right horse time and time again. Hadn't they?

He offered a dismissive wave of his hand.

"I wouldn't give it another thought. It's perfectly routine for the SEC to monitor funds as large as ours to make sure we're in compliance with the latest regulations. It's nothing, trust me."

"Thanks, Jonathan," Laurel said, rising and smoothing the fabric of her dress. "I feel so much better."

"No problem. Come back to me if you hear anything else—I want to be able to put your mind at ease, that's all. On another subject, how's being a newlywed?"

"Pretty great," she said, an ear-to-ear grin filling her pretty face. "I can't believe all that stupid stuff we fought about during the wedding planning. We're so happy."

"Nice," he said, but he was already far gone in so many ways.

He ate about fifty spiced macadamia nuts waiting for Brett at the bar of ABC Kitchen, Cass's voice trailing his hand's journey from bowl to mouth repeatedly. *Do you know how many germs that thing has?*

Brett was running late. Her flight was delayed due to winds in Boston and she wanted to stop at the hotel quickly to drop her bags. They volleyed texts back and forth to each other like a Ping-Pong ball and he almost mistakenly wrote to Cass, I'm at the bar. Can't wait to see you, when, interspersed with his Brett exchange, his wife wrote that she needed to put off picking up Puddles by a few days because she was going to London for work.

The restaurant was loudly buzzing with hip people, dating hopefuls and clusters of women in low-cut tops toasting with overpriced cocktails, sharing small plates. He thought he'd left this life behind him five years ago when he and Cass exchanged vows. Jonathan hadn't quite run screaming from the single life, rather he'd comfortably concluded that phase of his life and welcomed the next one with open arms. Now he was back for more, dressed in a close-fitting blazer, dark jeans and driving loafers all picked out by Cass at Barneys.

Brett breezed in, floated like a ghost from his past up to the bar and planted a very non-apparition-like kiss on his cheek. She smelled like the ocean near his family's beach house, salty and crisp, hitting his senses hard with déjà vu.

"This is so nice," she said, hopping on the bar stool next to him. Under the trendy pendant lamp hanging directly overhead, she looked different than Jonathan remembered from the Vineyard—probably on account of his being sober now. He could see the ways the past decade-plus reflected itself on her body—the child she bore stretching her once taut belly into something softer; her worship of the sun freckling her nose in tiny patches; and her teeth, once an army of perfectly straight white soldiers, yellowed ever so slightly from years of morning coffee. Even her eyebrows, which used to stand like pointy tents, had given way to gravity. He was suddenly strongly aware of his own body: wilting, caving, softening so he was roly-poly in the middle with no child to blame it on, hair still thick as a shag rug but meeting his forehead a quarter inch too far back, skin a pasty white from exposure to little else besides the fluorescent lighting in his office. He could go on and on.

"Can I get you a drink?" he asked. "Our table isn't ready yet."

"You mean they gave it away because I was late," she said, raising her eyebrows back up to their former arches. He was able to catch a glimpse of a younger her when she did it. "I'm really sorry."

"You have nothing to apologize for. I'm just happy to see you."

"Me too. And yes, I'll have a drink. Any white wine will do. I'm going to run to the ladies' room really quickly and then I want to hear everything."

She slipped off her seat and headed toward the back of the restaurant, leaving her cell phone behind, trusting or careless. Cass kept hers glued to her person at all times—a third hand. A new text message lighted Brett's screen.

Mom: Are you wearing a dress?

He couldn't help himself—he read the conversation from bottom up.

Mom: Have fun tonight!

Brett: He's married and I'm a recent divorcée with a child. Don't get too excited.

He scratched his head. Brett wasn't wearing a dress. She was in black pants and a sleeveless tank, though to be fair she was fresh off a plane. He was tempted to take the phone and respond, Don't worry, Brett looks great. Which was true, despite everything he'd noticed this evening. His tastes had evolved to where thinking about the private school girls who trolled the streets of his neighborhood in their short plaid skirts, skinny limbs like asparagus stalks, made him feel pervy. Now what he found sexy were the horizontal slices on a woman's forehead and the glint of a lone silver hair. Jonathan recalled his father saying Meredith Baxter-Birney was gorgeous, back when *Family Ties* was all the rage, and how all he could think was—how can you say that when Mallory is on-screen at the same time? Now, he got it.

While seeing the reality of his and Brett's outing distilled to a blunt three-line text exchange was excruciating, he needed sex, a warm body in his bed, and even if his stomach was pillowy, at least Brett would remember the way he looked in high school. He didn't have to worry about impressing her like some blind date appraising his every move. Having settled down before the age of the dating apps, he was far too circumspect now to cozy up to the idea of sexting and swiping and finding a girl to screw in ten minutes based on her global positioning. Somehow a call girl felt more straightforward.

"Did I miss anything?" Brett asked, slipping the cell phone back into her purse.

"Not at all. And our table's ready."

They shared pasta with pine nuts and pesto, lobster fra diavolo, chocolate cake with cinnamon ice cream. Head-on they tackled the weather, the Patriots, Tom Hanks's latest and New York City museums, and avoided anything with a trace of soreness for either of them. Expertly they skidded along the superficial like ice skates on a freshly cleaned rink.

In the lobby of her hotel, he hesitated briefly just before kissing her on the lips. She received his overture happily, applying gentle pressure when she kissed him back, but didn't invite him upstairs. Back uptown, his favorite nighttime doorman Vlad gave him a generous pat on the back. When he went to brush his teeth minutes later, he saw the carbon copy of Brett's mouth that her lipstick had imprinted on his.

21. CASS

THERE ARE CERTAIN dreams so delicious that if you happen to wake up in the thick of one, you try your hardest to fall back asleep, hoping against all hope that you'll be able to slip into the very same story line again before the alarm clock blares. Cass had a lot of those dreams in the months before Percy announced he was sick, after which wakefulness seized her like a plague. Now that she wasn't sleeping, she didn't know what was better—to dream in rich fantasy only to wake up to a life of mundane reality, or to lie awake but not have to confront such a striking contrast.

Jonathan rarely remembered his dreams, but her nocturnal self was prone to especially vivid imagery that left her confused about what was true and what was imagined. A millisecond before her eyes blinked open, she could be in Italy making pasta with a famous chef who also happened to be her lover; or she was back in her hometown, but this time she was in one of the area's few large brick colonials hosting a party where all the kids who'd thought they were better than her were tending bar and lugging tubs of ice; or she was in Thailand, alone, seeking adventure, but her wallet got lost and found by a handsome stranger. These black-and-white adventures, which felt colorful beyond measure even if scientifically they weren't, were always a welcome departure.

The important thing with a good dream was to be okay when the fog of it wore off and reality set its claws into you. By the time you made your morning coffee, the dream should be forgotten and your actual life, staring back at you from your Google calendar in thirty-minute increments, shouldn't seem like a terrifying alternative. Now it didn't matter. She slept in short, stubby bursts that left no time for a virtual getaway.

Many people have "the one that got away." That person they can't resist stalking on social media, who they fantasize about running into when they're all dolled up, and who—and this really would have been terrible for Cass—appears to them regularly in dreams. It pleased Cass immensely that she had no such person, notwithstanding that period of time when Jonathan was beyond her grasp. For starters, it meant she hadn't let anyone slip through her fingers. Whoever was important in her life had stayed put until she felt ready to move on. She even included her father in this roundup. He'd removed himself from her life in all the ways that counted—because showing up for the ceremonial bullshit did *not* count—but she'd made no effort to reel him back in. Ergo, he didn't signify a genuine loss. Most importantly, when she walked down the aisle at her wedding and saw Jonathan at the other end, she could honestly say she'd never imagined anyone else in his place.

Because of this, when the issues Cass had with her marriage began to creep up everywhere she looked—Jonathan's sweaty gym towel on their bedspread, the fact that he listened to the TV louder than she liked, his need to run the air-conditioning all year long, his ability to compartmentalize the stress at work better than she could—she was truly taken aback. She did her best to beat down her grievances like a game of Whac-A-Mole, because, after all, they had to be inconsequential. Two years ago, when she thought they were about to start a family, she had zero reservations at the nuclear level. Her only concern was her place at work—she wanted that creative director title badly, to see the promotion printed on her business cards and in her email signature, to blast it to the universe via her LinkedIn profile, and Percy, whom she loved beyond measure, was kind of an ass when it came to family matters. He and Emmet never had children and he'd snigger about a waddling pregnant lady in the elevator and voice his doubts privately to Cass when another employee asked to leave early for something child-related. When the baby was taken from her, and she and Jonathan orbited around each other like meteors that would explode on impact, her only consolation was the professional advancement that would follow. Otherwise, she was ready to see Jonathan wearing one of those baby backpacks, strolling down Madison Avenue with a to-go coffee cup, she slinging a chic diaper bag over her shoulder and pulling Puddles by the leash. Let the world envy them: a couple in love, with offspring. Yes, ladies and gentlemen, the grass is always greener, unless you were Cass and Jonathan Coyne.

Weakness was Cass's pet peeve. Her mother was weak, allowing men to trample her, the pattern repeated so many times it was like a music track on repeat. Even her father was weak, choosing scams and shortcuts over an honest day's work. The predictable future for Cass would have been to follow the path beaten by her parents, but she'd decided many years ago to take a sharp detour. To master her own destiny through hard work and careful planning, and to always stay the course. So it pained her to see weakness in her decision to separate from Jonathan—to hear the echoes of her parents' behavior and, more troubling, to face the evidence that she hadn't come through her childhood without Donna and Dick fucking her up. She'd chosen a getaway instead of working through their problems together in therapy

(she probably could have convinced him to go) or with forthright conversations between just the two of them without text message dings
and Bloomberg alerts distracting them. Consolation was found only
when she considered the flip side: there was strength in picking up
one's life and moving across the country, in muddling through issues
alone, in being selfless enough to—despite the deafening ticktock of
her biological clock—not rush into having a child who might ulti-
mately end up bounced between homes by the dictum of some judge's
fancy. That had been her fate. Jonathan's was to be raised in a loveless
home: no moving around, a pack of siblings to commiserate with, but
still fraught with its own issues. She wouldn't let either situation happen, not on her watch.

We do what we need to do to make ourselves feel better about our
choices. Oprah said that to her when she was home recovering from
the D&C.

THE PILOT ASKED them to put their cell phones and iPads into airplane mode before takeoff. Not over the loudspeaker like she was used
to. Normally, in the comfort of their business-class seats, she and Jonathan would wait until the last possible second—often after the threat
of confiscation from the flight attendant—to turn off their gadgets.
Today the pilot just came out of the cockpit to greet Marty and shake
hands like they were old pals and make a few announcements about
flight time and headwinds. That's the way it goes on a private jet, apparently.

Disconnecting was harder than it should have been, and Cass
pawed her now useless phone and stared far longer than normal at the
picture of Puddles on its screen. It was taken the night of their condo
building's Christmas party. She and Jonathan had gotten so silly from
the eggnog, they'd ridden the elevator up and down caroling with
their dog in tow. They had been physically apart for months by now,
but always just a text away. This was the first time since she left home

that she wouldn't be able to reach him in case of emergency, and it left her feeling more vacant than she expected.

Cass did her best to appear as nonchalant as possible about flying private. She hadn't been warned that they'd be boarding the Spiegel company plane for their transatlantic flight, and even when they pulled into LAX, and she passed the terminal where she'd been recently to exchange Puddles, she'd had no inkling of what was in store. Only once their SUV glided into the private hangar and two uniformed captains were waiting next to the side of the plane drinking 5-Hour Energy shots did she get it. Her first instinct was to text Jonathan something like: Holy shit! I'm getting on a private plane and insert some moneybag emojis, but she'd sacrificed the ability to communicate with him in that way. She knew as much when he stopped responding instantly to her missives on everyday life (I saw on Facebook that Vlad had a baby! I took a boxing class with Alexi . . . watch out!). Now she'd maybe get a "nice" sent back a few hours later, if anything at all. For someone without much outward emotional range, Jonathan was still remarkably good at communicating his feelings. Besides, with what she was hiding, it was probably best not to bring her enthusiasm for this luxury front and center.

Luckily, she had plenty of practice in making no big deal of things that were in fact very big deals. After a lifetime in the metaphorical cheap seats, she'd managed to keep a perfectly still face when Betsy and Christopher took her and Jonathan to the Red Sox game and they sat in the owner's box—he was an old friend of Christopher's. But small mistakes that she couldn't anticipate sometimes gave her away, and those errors haunted her the most. During the seventh-inning stretch, she'd complained about how long the line for the women's room was going to be. Katie, who was also at the game, had quietly tapped her and pointed out the private restroom in the box. Katie was nine years younger than Cass and she'd hoped her husband's baby sister would worship her as the glamorous Manhattan professional. But after the exchange at the baseball game, small moment that it was, Cass knew it wasn't going to happen. First the lobster-night debacle at the Cheshire, then the Red Sox bathroom incident, plus a myriad of other clashes and embarrassments—she kept getting kicked down each time she tried to climb up.

"First time on a jet?" Marty asked her. There were four of them traveling over: Marty, Cass and two assistants named Minka and Brie who traveled with Marty everywhere. A blonde and a brunette; Cass immediately labeled them the Bobbsey Twins.

Should she lie? Why bother, and then get tripped up having to keep up with the inevitable private-jet slang? Plus Marty was like her, at least in the humble beginnings category.

"Yes," she said, holding back the "It's so cool" that was playing on repeat in her head.

"First time I did it I couldn't stop smiling. I'm a poor kid from the Bronx. Eli too. We grew up in tiny row houses next door to each other—our dads were brothers. We were the scrappiest kids you could find, always hustling to make enough money so we could go to the movies. My father worked for the city as a custodian; my mother was a home health-care worker, which basically means she wiped up old people's crap. Only people who come from nothing can truly appreciate things. Those born with it see their privilege as an entitlement."

Cass nodded, though she felt slightly offended on Jonathan's behalf. He wasn't too entitled, really. Marty had the senior Coynes pegged, though.

"What's your story, Cass?"

Minka and Brie looked at her as she self-consciously lowered the sunglasses that were atop her head.

"Glare," Cass said, and Brie jumped up to lower the window shade. She had no choice then but to return the sunglasses to the crown of her head, forcing eye contact.

"Not too different. I grew up in a blue-collar town in Michigan.

My parents divorced when I was nine. We never had much, and things were especially hard after my parents split. A night out meant the drive-through. I never had the right jeans or backpack; my mom dragged me to Supercuts until I was sixteen and just flat-out refused to go. I wanted to do something creative when I graduated but was also very set on having a stable job. So I compromised, doubled in theater studies and economics at Brown and took a bunch of graphic design classes at RISD. Moved to New York City after college and haven't lived anywhere else until now. I don't know if I was scrappy, but I did a fair amount of lucrative Garbage Pail Kids trading when I was younger."

"My daughter Camille was into those. Luna's older sister."

"Mr. Spiegel, can I get you anything?" An olive-skinned flight attendant in a pristine minidress uniform appeared before them with a rolling cart of food. Sandwiches, fruit and cookies overflowed. "We'll be serving a full dinner in a few hours."

"Just my usual," he said, and a piping-hot corned-beef sandwich was produced from a warming drawer. "And tell the pilot to stop all this fucking turning. I'm getting dizzy."

The flight attendant smiled through gritted teeth, then skulked away toward the cockpit to deliver the news to the pilot that he was meant to get them to England without making turns.

"From the Second Avenue Deli in New York City," Marty said, lifting one dripping half of the sandwich to his lips. "Can't beat a kosher deli. A taste of home." How the sandwich got from New York City to Los Angeles to the plane was not revealed.

He pulled a chunk of corned beef from the center of the sandwich and dropped it into his mouth after a swim in a tub of mustard. Cass's stomach rumbled and she shifted self-consciously. All the fancy meals in the world couldn't compare to a good Detroit-style pizza. She hadn't thought about sinking her teeth into one of those in years. She and Tiff used to be able to put away a whole pie between the two of them.

"I'm supposed to be off carbs," he explained, pointing at the discarded bread of his sandwich. "Ladies, take some food."

She joined Minka and Brie in taking a china plate and plucking a few slices of melon from a silver tray.

Unprompted, Brie produced a metal briefcase from under her seat and handed over several pill bottles and some papers to Marty. She also placed a stack of *Variety*s on the central table. Marty threw back a few unidentified pills like they were a handful of popcorn, pulled reading glasses from a Spiegel Productions canvas bag and started leafing through the documents. He looked over at the magazines, lifted the top one and threw it back down emphatically, and started screaming.

"I want every goddamn article about that asshole who backed out on us for *World War X* flagged. I know we got Tom to step in for the role, but he still has to pay for flaking on me. I want to skewer him."

The getting-to-know-Cass portion of the flight was apparently over. Brief, but she'd shared a more accurate account of her upbringing with him and the Bobbsey Twins than she had with anyone except for Jonathan. Only her husband knew about the McDonald's for her birthday when all the other kids went to Luigi's, the white-and-red-checkered-tablecloth fine-dining establishment she gazed at from the car while her mom whizzed by with a cigarette dangling out the open window. And while Jonathan tried his best to be empathetic, there was just no way he could understand her childhood. Betsy looked at smokers like they were serial killers. She kept about fourteen different styles of cloth napkins in an antique sideboard. The Coynes never discussed how much anything cost—not only because Betsy thought it was crass, but because for them it really didn't matter. Marty could respond to Cass in a way that Jonathan never could. With empathy, not sympathy.

Within minutes of popping the pills and flagellating his copassengers, Marty was passed out, a dribble of drool sliding down his chin like condensation. Clearly he'd taken a sleeping aid, but she wondered what else had been in the stash he gobbled. Everyone was a mystery in some way or another. He was passed out the entire way until they landed, and even she, despite feeling on high alert, nodded off for the last leg of the journey and woke up only when they touched down in London.

THEY ARRIVED AT the Connaught at 7:00 a.m. and were immediately taken to their individual rooms. Rules about no check-in before 3:00 p.m. were fudged for Marty, even abroad where his clout wasn't as massive as it was Stateside.

Her room was large and traditional, with calming watercolors in muted pastels on the walls. She was tantalized by the large flat-screen and the dreamy four-poster bed with its adorable row of boudoir pillows. She lay down with the remote in her hand, hoping to find some *Masterpiece* diversion until it was time to meet Marty and the twins in an hour.

The nap fell upon her like a heavy blanket. She dreamed of a past Christmas morning, when she was about six. Her parents were still together and she didn't know to want any more than she had. Their tree, a fake hauled up from the basement, looked beautiful in their living room, with a shiny angel on top and glossy red ornaments raining down. The dream, wavy and fluid from the jet lag and the champagne she'd sipped on the plane, morphed into a warmer Christmas on the beach in St. Barths, where she'd never been in her life but which appeared to her in sleep as sexy and sun-drenched, with overflowing platters of oysters and magnums of rosé. There, a pink tree strung with twinkling lights stood behind her swarthy French companion.

She woke up disoriented, coming to her senses moments later to remember she was in a hotel room in London on a business trip. And she found, to her surprise, that she had no desire to go back to sleep and reclaim the dream. Instead, she swung her legs over the side of the bed and stood up with purpose.

There was something about being in a hotel room that made Cass feel like royalty. Was it the sumptuous sheets? The ability to order a three-course meal on a whim? The personal movie theater on her TV screen . . . so many options . . . categorized by genre! She supposed it was the fact that she controlled everything about the three-hundred-square-foot space: the temperature, who came in and out (she'd slipped the "Do Not Disturb" sign on the door handle as soon as she arrived), the lighting. As a child, she'd barely traveled. Cass and Jonathan had stayed at their share of nice hotels, often on Winstar's dime, but there was a unique luxury in experiencing it alone. Being king of the castle, so to speak.

She changed her clothes and hastened to the lobby, where she found Marty schmoozing with the hotel manager. Minka and Brie were approaching from the opposite direction.

"We're all jet-lagged," he told them, yawning like a bear. "Explore the city. I'm going to hang with my daughters."

"Hold up, Marty," Minka said. "The AD for *Careful What You Wish For* just called me in a panic. The dailies are apparently a disaster and the director is refusing to cut any of the fight sequences." She produced a laptop from her handbag and set it on a small marble table. Marty gestured for Cass to stand behind him so she could see the screen.

Silently, they watched in a huddle. Out of sequence, with no understanding of the film, even Cass could tell it was bad.

"Call Mitchell," Marty said, referencing the AD, and Brie tapped away at her cell phone until she had him on the line. They crowded around the phone on speaker.

"Mitch," Marty said. "Cut minutes three through five. Show me what it would look like if minute eight started the sequence. And for God's sake, blur the dialogue in minute six and set it to the theme music."

"Hang on," the voice on the other end said. "I need a few minutes."

They waited, nobody speaking. Marty looked like an entirely different person. His face, normally in a half scowl, was lit from within. His irises were laser beams pointed at the computer, transmitting his ideas to the screen. His right knee bounced up and down, a nervous tic perhaps, a way to sublimate his voracious energy. You got the feeling that if the fire alarm went off, Marty wouldn't hear it.

"Got it," Mitchell said. "Open it from the G drive."

Brie leaned over and did as told. They watched the revised version and Cass's jaw fell to the floor.

"Amazing," she couldn't help saying out loud.

"All right," Mitchell said. "I'll present this on set tomorrow. We'll talk later."

"Anyway," Marty said, the scowl back, the fire gone. "Like I said, I'm taking Olive and Stella for the day. Philippa made a stink about them missing the day with their summer tutor, but I just told her to shove it. I'm meeting the girls with their nanny outside the town house that I paid for in the divorce."

Cass nodded to show she was listening but found she had no appropriate verbal response. She noticed Minka and Brie doing the same and felt more at ease with her silence.

Marty wanted her to get a sense of the consumer culture and distill it for him in a few bullet points. It was a vague assignment if there ever was one and Cass bristled a bit at being dragged to another country to satisfy one man's desire to stick it to his ex. The plan was to reconvene the next morning for their meetings.

As Cass pulled up a map on her phone to situate herself, she caught an eyeful of the kid-friendly itinerary that Minka handed to Marty for his review. He was taking his girls to the zoo, the Tower of London, lunch at Harrods and then to the London Eye.

She couldn't remember her father once planning a special day for her after the divorce. Every other Saturday, he would take her to the diner where she would make frownie faces on her pancakes with the syrup dispenser while he made easy chitchat with the waiter, the hostess, everyone but her. While she bubbled her orange juice through a straw waiting for him to tell her to stop, Dick tried to drum up business by asking everyone and their mother if they wanted to finish off their basements or were considering an addition. He was already busy with his second family by then (he and his new wife had triplets, as if Cass hadn't felt left out enough), and Cass was like that last piece of luggage that takes forever to appear on the baggage carousel. Everyone just wanted to go off and start having fun without her. To this day, the sight of a divorced father eating a meal with his kids on a weekend, looking bored to tears and sneaking glances at his phone, made her want to leap from her chair and stab a fork in his arm.

On one of those court-decreed Saturdays, when Cass had packed a full backpack of My Little Pony figurines, Mad Libs and a hardcover Nancy Drew from the library, Donna let her off at the old house and pulled away before Dick came to the door. Her parents had trouble making eye contact without flinging expletives at each other. No one answered the bell, so she lugged her sad overnight bag and backpack to the shed in the backyard where her father kept his power tools and was prone to disappear for hours on end. She heard voices, Dick and his business partner Bruce, and so she stealthily approached, curious to hear her father speak freely in his natural habitat.

"So you're taking the kids to Disney?" she heard Bruce ask.

Her heart leapt. She'd seen so many Disney commercials by that point that she believed with all her heart that it was the place where dreams came true. True, she was eleven, and trotting around the theme park with a trio of two-year-olds would mean Dumbo instead of Space Mountain (she knew all the rides from her classmates), but that was okay. The point was to join the club of children who had been to Disney, which as far as she could tell was a major dividing line between the haves and have-nots. To return to school with pictures from the trip to tack up in her locker would be a serious move in the right direction. If she could only get her hands on name-brand school supplies, she'd have it made. Wait until Tiffany got a load of this.

"Not Cassidy," her father said. "Too much coordination with Donna, and those tickets are damn expensive."

"So you're taking the real family?" Bruce asked. God, she'd always hated Bruce, with his redneck mullet and grease-stained fingernails. He always looked at her like she was fresh meat, and she found herself reaching for a baggy sweatshirt whenever he was around. Her father inexplicably referred to him as a partner in the construction business, but he was more of a hired hand whom Dick had plucked from a plumbing sub. Later she'd learn that Bruce had all sorts of dirt on her father's business dealings, hence the "partnership."

"It's not like that," her father said, but she couldn't hear any fists flying over the question either. She moved closer to the shed.

"Well, I guess it is," Dick added, ripping her to shreds in an instant. If he had turned his electric saw on her, it would have hurt less. Then she heard Bruce and her father laugh together, a dull roar that ruined male laughter for her forever.

Cass admired Marty for making an effort with his little girls, and hated Philippa Eastland for robbing him of his chance to be a proper father. As she set off for the National Gallery, she was distracted by the hope that she'd bump into Marty and his kids. Maybe it was too chilly and rainy for the zoo, so he'd bring them museum-hopping instead. It made sense, though she didn't lay eyes on them once despite her constant crowd scanning. She couldn't stop thinking about how Marty's entire face and demeanor changed while he was working. It was like an electrical force field sprang up around him and the pace of his quickened heartbeat and the rapid churn of his brain became palpable—these were the kind of juices Cass wanted to tap into. Her husband was dedicated to his business, but when he studied a matrix of dizzying Excel boxes, he wore the same expression one might wear to peruse the obituaries. Derivatives, shorts, lockups—the vernacular of hedge funds was so foreign that it left way too much lost in translation between them. Marty's energy, creative in nature, felt like a language they had in common.

She wanted to impress him when they spoke in the morning, let him know he and she were kindred spirits, appreciators of what makes art. But later that evening, cutting into a filet that looked glorious on the room service tray, and coddled by a generous, oversized terry robe and slippers, Cass realized that her main observation from the day was that the English spelled "color" with a "u." She'd have to plunder her bullshit stash to think of something intelligent to say to him. Marty Spiegel was clearly not a man who tolerated being shortchanged. He may have come from nothing, but he was firmly at the top of his game now and he wasn't afraid to let everyone know it.

AFTER A GRUELING day of meetings with every top marketing and advertising firm in London trying to court their business, Marty, Cass, Minka and Brie settled into a booth at Nobu in London's Mayfair neighborhood. Japanese was a cuisine Cass typically avoided, what with everyone using their chopsticks like stealthy tongs to snag a tempura veggie or a piece of spicy salmon from someone else's plate. Not to mention that she still had a hard time with raw fish, having never laid eyes on sushi until college. That *omakase* meal with Jonathan on their third date had been a real pressure cooker. She'd swallowed as much as she could without chewing, because it seemed a better option than admitting she'd never eaten sushi before. But Marty hadn't asked anyone where they wanted to go—Minka just texted her where and when to show up while she was in the hotel room freshening up. Cass would later learn Marty was a silent investor in the restaurant. It made her laugh, this phrasing of the business arrangement. As far as she had seen, Marty didn't keep his mouth shut about anything.

Minka and Brie had grown on her over the course of the trip. Cass never had an assistant at PZA and she came quickly to understand its charms, especially in duplicate form. At first they seemed to regard Cass with suspicion, and she realized that they, despite diminutive frames and only a stash of cell phones as weapons, considered themselves something like Marty's bodyguards—their armor a resting bitch face. She'd passed some sort of test, because both of them softened on her, offering her the seat next to Marty in the booth, and even including her in their stream of office gossip. Gaining their approval wasn't entirely accidental; Cass had made sure to let it be known she knew her place in the Spiegel pecking order—these girls knew Marty liked Diet Coke and eye masks—and she was nothing but an enthusiastic apprentice ready with pad and pen. Not that she was gunning for the role of third travel assistant, or to replace either member of his "dream team" as he called them, but that's how it felt somehow. People around Marty were expected to learn his likes and dislikes and to anticipate what he would want next. Cass, not naturally a pleaser unless the challenge called for her to become one, was up to the task.

Marty had a different aura in London, undoubtedly the outcome of the sea not parting when he walked into a room like it did back home. Here he was charming, inquisitive, still a bit of a slob, but it was endearing in an environment where not everyone was kissing his ass. Cass even found the nerve to announce to her three companions that she preferred not to share and would be ordering her own green salad and miso-glazed cod. Marty didn't say anything, just raised his eyebrows and looked amused. Cass had a tough time reading Marty's plans for her. She was either meant to be a protégée, another daughter, or a friend—she suspected Marty didn't have many of those and that he found some appeal in their random encounter at Craig's, the fluke Luna connection. Cass knew all too well that men put a lot of stock in what they think happens to them by chance—romantics at heart, so much more so than women. Centuries of forced inferiority had turned women into pragmatists; years of coasting let men rest on notions of destiny. When she cast her pragmatism in a historical context, it didn't seem quite as nefarious.

"The Japanese can't do dessert. I'm not eating green tea ice cream," Marty announced after their main courses were cleared. "Let's go back to the hotel for a drink." They shuffled themselves into a waiting town car that glided them back to the Connaught and found the lounge nearly empty when they arrived. A table for four presented itself at the entrance and Cass took a seat, thought to order herself a sidecar, and was about to ask everyone else what they were having when she saw Marty bidding goodnight to Minka and handing off his button-down to Brie. He came into the lounge wearing a faded Nets T-shirt.

"What happened?" she asked when Marty took the seat next to her. Fortunately it was a round table, so they weren't forced to choose between sitting side by side or across from each other.

"I told them to go to sleep. We can talk business."

"Okay," she said, and noticed he had already done that thing he did at Craig's where he subliminally messaged the waiter to bring what he wanted, which was two Grey Goose and sodas.

"You were great today in the meetings," he said, pouring olive juice into both of their drinks. It was almost like he was testing to see at what point she would stop him. She'd provoked something in him when she announced she wouldn't share because he'd taken it as a challenge to test her boundaries.

"Thank you. I learned a lot from Percy."

"It's obvious." He reached across and took her hand, offered it something of a pat and a squeeze, a blurred line of what he wanted from her. She didn't pull away.

"I like you, Cass." Again, a sentence with multiple interpretations.

And then his fingers interlaced hers, and there was no mistaking his meaning.

"Let's go upstairs," he said.

And she went.

◆ ◆ ◆

CONSIDERING SHE HADN'T slept with anyone but Jonathan in six years, and Marty was still something of a stranger to her, the sex was rather good. On top of his body, where she discovered he was more well-built than expected, she felt supple, springy, and light, a veritable sponge cake being released from a springform pan. His fingertips on her nipples gave her a rush and she came quickly and in earnest. She noted a few skin tags on his chest—a sign of the years he had on her. What kind of name was that anyway for a condition of aging, she found herself inauspiciously thinking when they were done. *Tag! You're old.* Looking up at the ornate chandelier glowing above them, she conjured the image of Marty working on his new film, expertly splicing it together like a chef making a filet mignon out of beef stew— the genius he positively radiated. The tags disappeared and instead she saw only his brilliance and boyish arrogance.

Next to her in bed, he reached for his cell phone.

"Texting the concierge to send up some bacon and eggs," he explained.

In plush robes, his wide open, they gorged themselves on a midnight breakfast. She comfortably used her hands to pluck bacon strip after bacon strip from the plate, licking the grease off her fingers. Afterward, she wanted to return to her room for her toothbrush and contact lens case, but Marty again summoned these items by more invisible cell phone magic. They brushed their teeth side by side, and then Cass watched carefully as he opened yet another pill case, labeled with the days of the week, and popped at least four different capsules of varying sizes into his mouth. It was another sharp reminder that they had a good twenty years between them, if not more. A phlegm ball came up with his last pill, a capsule the size of a horse tranquilizer, and he unapologetically deposited it into their shared sink. He was rough around the edges, but somehow she not only tolerated it, she found it enabled her to relax.

Back in bed Marty fell asleep quickly, with his stomach rising and falling under the blanket like a periodically erupting volcano. Within minutes, he was snoring, and Cass wondered, with a dry irony, if her life sentence was to sleep alongside someone whose very breathing disturbed her. She wanted to find meaning in what had just happened between them, to see its place in her decision about a future with Jonathan, but no bigger picture emerged quite yet. It had all happened so fast— the disappearance of the Bobbsey Twins, Marty's hand slipping through the space between their drinks to touch hers, the ride in the elevator where she already felt herself pulsing—that Cass had had no time for calculation. At the very least, it was unexpected, and that fact alone pleased her. It wasn't a total surprise that she'd be intimate with other men during the gap; she'd known that going into it, but actually doing it was surprisingly anticlimactic. The sky didn't fall, Jonathan didn't subliminally know what she'd done, and her confusion about the future wasn't immediately vanquished. And while she did feel some amount of guilt, she was awash with a stronger feeling—it was sadness for her marriage, like it was a living, breathing person in need of a hug.

She needed a reminder of what brought her here. Quietly, she slipped from the bed and went for her cell phone. She scrolled toward one of the first messages she'd received since creating her new email address with her married name, five years ago. The subject read, *Wedding Toast.*

Dear Cass,

Noticed you tearing up quite a bit during my toast. Here is a copy as a reminder of how much I love you. J.

She darted her eyes over the opening remarks, where he thanked wedding guests from near and far for joining them and made a joke about his bungling the first dance.

Not all of you know just how lucky I am. Not only do I feel so incredibly fortunate that Cass agreed to marry me, I feel especially lucky given the fortuitous circumstances of our relationship. Back at Brown, when I was a junior and Cass was a senior (sorry Cass for outing you as a little bit older), I first met this gorgeous, interesting woman at a little-known bar called Paragon. It was pure coincidence that we started chatting there, as that was a place where almost no undergraduates went. Cass was there because she was meeting with some art students from nearby RISD and I stumbled in looking for a change of scenery. We instantly hit it off and I remember thinking of all nights, of all bars, how great it was that I'd chosen to be there at that time.

Cass swallowed hard and kept reading.

Now, here I beg forgiveness of Cass because I was a total idiot and never called her after that. I thought of her from time to time as the super-cool girl from Paragon, but doubted we'd ever lay eyes on each other again. And then, as my tremendous luck would have it, we bumped into each other on a crowded New York City sidewalk five years after graduation. Thank God I'd grown up a little since college and knew not to squander this chance meeting again. We had coffee, then our first date, and the rest is history.

 Two chance meetings in unlikely places. That's what I call fate.

 Cass, I don't know where I'd be without you. I thank my lucky stars every day that, years after we met at Paragon, I was lucky enough to find you looking for a cab on 52nd Street at lunchtime on that excruciatingly hot day. Now let's all raise a glass to love, to fate, and to my beautiful bride.

When she set down the phone on the room-service table, next to the debris of their foolish midnight snack, Cass noticed she'd started to cry. She wiped an eye, tried to collect herself quickly. This was nothing new. She'd read that speech a hundred times by now and could practically recite it by heart.

What would her husband do if he knew the truth? She slipped back into bed and let this question torment her until finally the snoring of the stranger beside her lulled her into a state of unconsciousness.

BACK IN LOS Angeles, Cass said nothing to Alexi or anyone about sleeping with Marty in London. There were so many question marks surrounding the whole thing and a part of her was dying to dissect the entire episode with her roommate. But the stakes were simply too high. Cass was a grown woman with an estranged husband and a job to protect. She couldn't just revert to her college self, pulling Alexi into some giddy postgame analysis not unlike the sessions she and Dahlia used to have after every big frat party. And then there was the fact that Alexi, a struggling actress, would happily cut off one of her diminutive limbs for a screen test at Spiegel, assuming said amputation wouldn't mess up her chances. She wanted to help Alexi but needed a little bit of time for things to shake out before she went asking Marty for favors.

From London, Marty flew to Toronto with Minka and Brie to check in on a period film that was set in what was supposed to be colonial Mumbai. It was hemorrhaging money because of a temperamental director who claimed that he could only work if he was high and that the pot in Canada was shit. Cass was sent home on Virgin Atlantic (business class), though she was a tiny bit crushed that Marty didn't send the jet back for her. She marveled at how quickly she'd managed to grow accustomed to new heights of luxury. Was that everyone, or just a particular weakness of hers? She hoped it was very much the former, that she wasn't some materialism octopus. Like teenagers, she and

Marty exchanged cell phone numbers the morning after their rendez-vous and Cass was admittedly excited to receive a text message from him in Toronto. It was a selfie on set, the larger-than-life producer seated in a director's chair. She returned the favor with a selfie of her own: lace nightie, Brigitte Bardot bun, a pout copied from a study of Alexi's facial movements. The only difficulty was blocking any traces of her surroundings. By putting the camera close up, she was able to cut out the worn-out sheets, the headboard-less bed, the peeling paint on the walls. When had she last sent Jonathan a selfie? Maybe never. Married people didn't do things like that. Not after the first year anyway. She cued a figurative sigh in her head.

Whereas in New York she'd taken to stealthily peeking into baby carriages, now she found herself observing couples out and about in Los Angeles, especially those with noticeable differences in age or attractiveness. She attempted to decode their body language like those "experts" who get quoted in gossip magazines. Cass and Jonathan walking down the street together raised no eyebrows. They were well-groomed yuppies with flush bank accounts—people knew this from their matching Moncler vests and Cass's well-tended highlights—of equal attractiveness give or take some small margin of error. Marty was a different story. He was just so much older than her that even when he was dressed in a casual tee and tennies, he was always going to look more like her father than her boyfriend. What did that say about what she was looking for? It was hard to imagine this whole experiment boiled down to unresolved daddy issues. It was more important to focus on why she cared what passersby would think. The years of her ill-fitting clothing, her tacky mother, their dented car with its dice hanging from the rearview mirror were a lifetime behind her, but they had taken their indelible toll. She still believed that everyone was sizing her up unfavorably, that she was a play that would get skewered on opening night.

When she returned to the office after a weekend spent replaying the trip to London in her mind, Aidan told her she'd been reassigned to working on a small but important film about a group of Nigerian mothers who start an underground school to educate young rebels. It was projected to be the main event at Sundance. Aidan looked at her askance when he handed over the draft press kit. Success at Spiegel and in just a short time—yes, it was eyebrow raising. Cass tried to beat back her doubts about why she'd gotten the assignment.

The new film was called *School of Rebels* and she went at it day and night, tinkering with some of the imagery that she'd previously designed for an off-Broadway play set in the Congo. Aidan approved of her drafts, often making no suggestions for improvement or just the smallest comment, and so she forged onward, gaining confidence with each passing day. She deserved this job. She deserved this assignment. If it wouldn't have been so obscene, she'd like to have called Jonathan to lay out the case for him. He'd help to suppress any of her insecurities. Besides serving as Puddles's playroom, the spare bedroom in their apartment was where Cass worked on her storyboards. Sometimes she'd see Jonathan in there looking at her work, a big smile on his face. But that was then and this was now. She wasn't even sure she could call on him for that kidney anymore, let alone an ego stroking.

22. JONATHAN

ABOVE EVERYTHING, JONATHAN was a rational guy. Whether that made Cass love him or hate him was unclear—she had bits and pieces of an artist's temperament, had accused him of being unfeeling more than once, with which he took serious issue. Wasn't making a rational choice—weighing the pros and cons on the scales of justice in your mind carefully until you could see one side starting to tip—the very proof of how sensitive you were? In fact, when Cass spelled out her argument of why a separation would be healthy for them, she'd sounded like the rational one, not him.

His way of thinking, the careful consideration of options until a course of action revealed itself, led him to call Brett a few days after she returned home to Boston. The way he saw it, why should two people who clearly want to have sex, who've done it together a hundred times before, not do it because they are worried about what the other will think? He didn't put it to Brett like that, but he did say he'd like to take the train up to see her that weekend. She would connect the dots.

There was something else that made him reach out to Brett again. Something that had really pissed him off, rendering his decision to call his ex three parts logic, one part impulse. He had been rummaging around Cass's night table drawer looking for his Swiss Army knife. Normally he kept it in his travel case, but she was always swiping it to cut a loose thread or snip a hangnail, and she never remembered to put it back. In the drawer, pushed to the back, he found a letter from the director of human resources at the Los Angeles Performing Arts Center. Attached were brochures from half a dozen shows they had put on. The letter was dated January, two months before Cass had asked for the break. Could this be what Cass was alluding to when she said he didn't really know her? He dialed Brett's number as he crumpled the letter into a ball and swooshed it into the garbage can.

And wouldn't you know it? Brett accepted and a few days later he was ringing the doorbell of her home in Beacon Hill, where she lived on the second floor of a narrow row house.

Sex with Brett, which they wasted no time getting to after a quick dinner she'd prepared, was like time traveling. For a brief, shining moment, they were sweaty, careless teenagers, basking in the glow of an orgasm achieved not with their own hands. Weightless, their bodies glistened, miscarriages and divorces evaporated, Daniel Rubia-Mendez was a name with no meaning, cheating didn't exist, and life was magically simple. Brett wasn't the woman with tense shoulders who opened the door to a home littered with finger-painting projects and refrigerator magnets. She was the girl who did her homework in short shorts with her legs positioned in a figure four, a scrunchie tying up her naturally wavy hair, the gum in her mouth forming gigantic bubbles that landed adorably on her nose when they popped. And he wasn't the guy with a wife in California likely in bed with other men, with a job that could blow up any day if Laurel was onto something with the SEC, with secrets that could crush everything he cared about. He was the guy who wore sunglasses on the back of his head, rotated his crew

T-shirts like day-of-the-week underwear and had a set place in the school cafeteria where no one else would dare sit.

The moment passed, as he knew it would, and cell phones started dinging simultaneously. Lars had thrown up, was running a very high fever. No need to panic, Brett's mother wrote, just letting you know. Cass texted: What is wrong with Puddles??? I had a voicemail from Dr. Strouber's office to call ASAP. Freaking out!!!

The high school sweethearts couldn't help themselves, their screens were bright and buzzing, begging for stolen glances. They saw it all— the realities of having a child, a spouse, a complicated life in which the other person played no role. And he saw in his mind what he hadn't wanted to see moments earlier. That when he kissed her stomach, inching lower and lower until he was going down on her, his lips passed a silvery scar about three inches wide—the place where she had been opened to remove her son. The indelible proof she wasn't who she was fifteen years ago, and neither was he. Now they pecked each other on the cheek and said rushed good-byes.

It was much ado about nothing with Puddles.

Jonathan had boarded him in doggie daycare, a place called Groomingdales on Second Avenue that was practically as expensive as a night at the Four Seasons. He left careful written instructions about Puddles's medication with the manager, which got blurry after a nervous dachshund owner knocked over her coffee on them. The manager at Groomingdales was able to decipher the phone number for the vet, where the receptionist passed along Cass's cell number.

"Why is Puddles at a hotel?" Cass asked. She wasn't being accusatory, though Jonathan felt his defensive impulse kick in. In the background, his express train to New York was being called and he struggled to hear her over the stream of announcements.

"I had to go out of town for work," he found himself yelling back, and realized in his cover-up the reason Cass was so nonchalant. That's exactly what she'd assumed—a business trip. Not that she expected celibacy from him, but he doubted she thought he'd traveled four hours to meet up with his ex-girlfriend. Especially the one whose name cued Cass's famous eye roll. Who could blame her, though? Betsy seemed to relish mentioning Brett in front of Cass. Just last Fourth of July, Betsy announced how delightful it was that Brett had been promoted at her publishing job, where she designed book covers for young adult novels. Brett's mother was a confidante of Betsy's from the bridge club and Betsy just couldn't say enough good things about how creative and talented she must be to do that kind of work. Three feet away, Cass attacked her hot dog with the tip of her knife, piercing the skin with sharp little gestures, then cross-attacking the flesh. Jonathan reached for her back, stroked it gently, though she wriggled out from under him.

He couldn't imagine Cass wanted him to say something to Betsy like, "Mom, you know Cass works in a creative field as well?" Needing to prove herself was beneath Cass, and they'd both agreed that Betsy's opinions didn't matter anyway.

Jonathan wasn't deliberately choosing to reconnect with Brett to wound Cass. In fact, he prayed she'd never find out. If and when they reconciled, he didn't expect they'd give each other a full accounting of the six months apart. It should only matter that they chose to commit to the marriage, not what occurred to make them realize it.

"How's work?" Cass asked, once the matter of Puddles was settled.

Jerry might be getting indicted.

"Great," he said. "You? How's Luna's father?"

"Really good."

He didn't know if she was referring to her job, or Marty Spiegel the legend, and he didn't probe.

"Happy to hear it. Cass, I gotta get on the train. I'll text you a picture of Puddles later with a copy of today's newspaper so you won't worry."

She laughed her Cass laugh. She was naturally more of a chuckler, letting out a "haha" from the back of her throat that sounded like she was throwing him a bone. But every now and then, she truly giggled, and it was light and giddy and as airy as freshly spun cotton candy. Getting that laugh was a mark of success. He recognized this feeling of victory not only in himself, but in the faces of those around Cass who could also make her laugh—Percy was the most capable, but also Jemima at times, even his little sister. His wife would laugh more often if she could learn to laugh at herself.

From the train he texted Brett to ask about her son. He was fine, a nap and a lollipop seemed to have done the trick, and she asked if everything was okay on his end. **Doggy drama**, he wrote back.

I had a great time, she wrote. There were no ellipses, but he felt the effect of one. Thoughts left unsaid were often weightier than words spoken out loud.

Me too, he wrote back, but didn't suggest making another plan.

She sent him a smiley face emoji with hearts for eyes and he was immediately reduced to being a teenager again—not that such forms of communication existed when he was pimple-faced and hormonal, but in feeling that every word and gesture exchanged mattered, that he couldn't just speak with ease, even though it was all so silly when you took a thirty-thousand-foot perspective. He'd felt young and virile in Brett's bed, but this was a different kind of déjà vu, the kind that made him grateful his high school years were behind him. Maybe it was her habit of making sad puppy dog eyes at him, the way she looked at him like he needed coddling. Being around her made suppressing the Daniel episode more difficult. He realized that was another reason why he'd never shared the story with Cass. Because then he'd have to look at her and know that she knew what he was capable of at his worst. So he'd kept it to himself, even if it meant he wasn't as up-front with his wife as he should have been. At least now he knew, after finding the L.A. job materials, that his wife was no open book either.

◆ ◆ ◆

LAUREL WAS BACK in his office the next day, after scurrying rapidly down the hall when he'd gestured for her to come inside. She looked petrified, closing the door behind her without him saying to do so and bracing herself stiffly.

"Is it the SEC?" She was whispering again, eyes bulging from her head like a bullfrog.

"No, no, nothing like that. You can relax," Jonathan said. "I need your help with something non–work related. Have a seat. Or rather, come around here." He motioned for her to join him on his side of the desk.

"I'm something of a Luddite when it comes to social media," he explained. "I have a Facebook account, but I barely check it. Let me ask you something. If I look for someone on Facebook, will they know that I did?"

"Depends," Laurel said, obviously relieved this was purely a social call. This was something she could handle—a favor she could easily pay forward from her generation to his. "They say you can't tell who looked you up, but I think you can because the most random people that I've met only one time will get suggested to me as friends and I think the only way that would happen is if they searched for me. So I'd say if you don't want someone to know you tried to see their page, don't search for them."

"Got it," he said. "Thanks so much."

"Although," she said, and her eyes now lit up like fireflies, "you could try Instagram. If the person doesn't have their privacy settings on, you can see their pictures without them knowing. I'm sure of it."

"Okay, how do I do that?"

"Give me your phone."

He handed it over and her index finger feverishly punched at his screen, a look of concentration on her face like she was performing laparoscopic surgery. Russell had suggested that during his temporary single status he should dabble with younger women. "Twentysomethings love finance dudes," is what he'd specifically advised. It hadn't seemed particularly appealing when he'd said it, and now, watching Laurel at work on his iPhone, he believed it would be like trying to find common ground with a different species.

"Done," she announced proudly, handing back the phone in her open palm like a tray of hors d'oeuvres. Pure alien.

"Who are we looking up?" she asked, hopeful that her role in the mission wasn't yet complete.

"Nobody, now," he said. "I've got to get my Q2s ready for Jerry. Just show me how this thing works really quick."

She took the phone back from him and placed it on his desk, and the two of them watched the screen as she navigated him through Followers and Following and searching for tags, people, and places.

"Simple," he said. "I think I got it."

"All right, but let me know if you need anything else."

She slowly backed out of his office and when she was safely a few yards down the hallway, he typed in Cass's name. No entry matched, which wasn't surprising because neither of them were huge social media people. As far as Cass was concerned, there was no one she wasn't in touch with that she had any interest in finding, or having find her (read: people from Hazel Park). He too kept a low profile, and so while the two of them wasted some amount of time surfing the web, they weren't sucked into the rabbit hole of posting and stalking like many of their friends.

After the Cass search turned up empty, he successfully found Brett Eddison. Member since 2013. Thirty-eight pictures. He scrolled through and found most of them were solo shots of her son: Lars in a swing, on his grandparents' boat, at baseball practice, in a class play, blowing out birthday candles. Brett was in a few of them but there was no trace of Lars's father. Her feed had the distinct essence of something that had been sanitized, like a crime scene. He buzzed Laurel at her desk.

"Can you delete pictures from Instagram?" he asked.

"Of course. It would be terrible if you were stuck with everything you posted forever. I thought you weren't going to do that now," she teased.

"You got me, Inspector Gadget," he said, and slid the receiver back into its place.

Online images were so easily expunged, much more so than physical pictures and mementos. Of course it was natural to erase pictures of an ex from a Facebook profile or Instagram feed where hundreds of people, maybe more, would review your life as recorded in pictures and captions and determine that was who you were. But what about a physical picture? He and Cass had both decided to hang on to the sonogram image of Peanut (their pet name for the bundle of cells that was supposed to have become their raison d'être) after the termination, but it was private, locked in the safe where only the two of them knew the combination and now their wedding rings served as paperweights. Still, they had chosen to hold on to the painful memory for some reason, and Jonathan wasn't even sure what that was. What did Brett do with all the printed photographs of Lars's dad? Torch them one night after her son went to bed? Shove them all in an envelope in the back of a drawer in case one day she got sentimental? His thoughts moved rapidly to Cass.

She wasn't hugely nostalgic—people avoiding their pasts rarely are—and he remembered watching in horror as she sorted through her things while packing to move into his apartment. Like they were used tissues, she tossed her college face book (the carbon one), a certificate from RISD, and loose photos from opening nights into one of those huge gray trash bins that they'd hauled up five flights of stairs from her building's laundry room.

"What? The certificate? The pictures?" she asked when he must have let his incredulity show. "I don't need to keep those things."

If they didn't come through this separation together, what would they do with the remains of their marriage? Could their six years be sanitized in the same way an Instagram feed was scrubbed clean of historical hiccups? Their apartment had a dozen photos of them together—black-and-whites from their wedding, candids shot by friends, pictures with Puddles at Christmas—all gleaming, smiling faces surrounded by silver frames that had gotten polished regularly when Manuela was still in play. They would need to divide their things: the coffee table they bought together in Milan, their modest collection of art and tchotchkes, the Christofle silverware from their wedding. Would the pictures end up in a different pile altogether—the up-for-grabs pile? Or would one of them step up and admit to wanting to keep them?

Embarrassed to call Laurel again, he emailed her.

You sure nobody knows if you're looking at them on Instagram?

Yes! But you will only be able to see their pictures if their profile is public. All celebs are public. Many regular people are too, but some are private. You sure I can't help you?

No, I'm good. Thanks.

Daniel Rubia-Mendez was one of those people who kept their profile private, Jonathan discovered. It was the first time he'd typed his full name since writing the apology letter that was in both of their sealed academic records.

He was about to return his phone back to his pocket when he remembered that celebs are public, at least according to Laurel, who seemed to know everything about everything in this world.

Marty Spiegel, over three hundred thousand followers, was indeed public.

And there she was. His Cass. In a picture with three other people he didn't recognize, all grinning like clowns and pointing to a poster for *Zombies Attack . . . Again!*

She looked tanner, trimmer, sillier. Like she'd gone straight from Hazel Park to L.A., with no evolution of self at Brown or sophistication captured from her years in New York City. It was only a picture and probably whoever was behind the camera had said something funny to get them all to laugh, but he had to admit, Cass looked really happy. It hit him like a sucker punch.

23. CASS

IT TURNED OUT they were *a thing*.

Marty came back from Toronto, catching everyone off guard by returning a day early. Bare feet propped on desks returned to the ground at lightning speed; personal calls were dropped midsentence. Instead of walking straight to his office like usual, he strutted up and down the aisles of cubicles like a security guard doing rounds.

"Cass," he said, reaching her workstation. "I'd like to speak to you about *School of Rebels*."

"Okay," she said, searching his face for clues as to where things stood between them, but his expression was a startling blank.

"Now."

She popped up from her chair, sneaking a glance at her watch. Jonathan and Puddles were landing in an hour and she had planned to leave for the airport in five minutes to meet them. Hopefully this would be quick, or she would just tell him she had to leave. They headed toward his office, Marty a pace ahead of her. At PZA, Percy was fond of linking arms, and they'd amble around the office like school chums ready to break into a skip.

Behind the closed door, Marty reached his hand around her waist and pulled her in for a long kiss.

"I missed you, Cass. Did you miss me?" he asked, the upward lilt of his voice unmistakable.

"I did," she said. And simple as that, by saying she felt the same way, she was part of a pair that didn't include Jonathan. It was terrifying and thrilling all at once. She was unaccustomed to having so little agency. It was like reading from a script for the first time, uncertain how to modulate her voice because she didn't know where the story was going.

"You know, Aidan emailed me your mock-ups of the *School of Rebels* posters and the web banners. You are a major talent, Cass Coyne. The one you did with the machine guns stowed in the lockers was genius. And I don't throw that term around lightly."

She beamed. He had singled out her favorite. It had come to her in the middle of the night and she'd gotten out of bed to sketch it.

"It'll probably be the one we're going to use for the Tribeca Film Festival and for Sundance." He patted her on the back, now all business. "I'd like you to join the team working on *Home Is Where the Heart Is*. Their concept is too saccharine. I tore their mock-ups in half at the last marketing meeting."

"Um, sure. I'm happy to see if I can help. I'm around to meet with them today, I just have to run out of the office for a bit to pick up my dog from the airport. My husband, I mean Jonathan, probably just landed and I know he has to catch a—"

"Cass?" He cut her off, not even flinching at the sound of Jonathan's name. "Do you have a black-tie dress here?"

July, July, July . . . Which awards show was in July? The Tony Awards had just passed. None of her shows were winners this year, but she enjoyed watching it at home with Alexi. Out of habit, she had scanned the crowd for Percy's face only to be cruelly reminded that he wouldn't be there. She continued to rack her brain, heart pounding. The Golden Globes were January and the Oscars were February, but maybe this was something abroad? The BAFTAs? Or something more insidery, like the Directors Guild or amfAR?

She didn't have any formal wear in Los Angeles and there was no way anything Alexi owned would fit her. She didn't want to say no, fearing a *Pretty Woman* scene unfolding if she did: Marty calling the managers at the upscale boutiques on Rodeo Drive, her being treated with the forced courtesy of a charity case as a result. Or he'd just retract the invite and take one of the Bobbseys instead.

"I have something that could work," she fibbed. "Why do you ask?" She was already calculating how quickly she could get to the stores. If there was no traffic getting to and from LAX (ha!), she could potentially make a quick stop before coming back to work.

"Mr. Spiegel," came a voice from the doorway. It was Abby, his most sniveling assistant.

"Anything yet?" Marty asked her, looking up from his desk.

"Nothing," she reported. "I combed every website and magazine. So did Minka and Brie. It'll come."

"Call Diller over at Tower Media. Find out what the fuck is going on. Tell him to call his Eurotrash friends and get this done already. It's been more than a week."

Cass had no idea what they were talking about, but their mysterious exchange gave Cass the necessary moment to consider Jonathan's feelings when he flipped on the TV and saw her dangling off Marty's arm, photographers snapping pictures. She ought to prep him in advance with a text saying he'd asked her the favor of accompanying him because he needed a "civilian" to avoid media spotlight. Jonathan might buy it, the idea of her and Marty together so unlikely that her alternate story was far more plausible. Then there was poor Luna to consider, who would probably faint if she saw.

"Okay, I'll update you in an hour," Abby said, and did her backward-walking thing again.

"And Abby," Marty called out. She dashed back inside. "You need to pick up Cass's dog from the airport. Better yet, get Minka to do it. Cass will give you all the information in a moment."

What? Cass literally shook her head in disbelief. Was this meant to keep her from seeing Jonathan or just because he was trying to be helpful? She'd better text Jonathan to give him the heads-up.

"Of course," Abby said, and retreated again.

"Well, I'm glad you have a dress. I'd like you to be my date to an upcoming event. What do you think?"

"Of course, I'd love to," Cass said, hearing her words come out in a gush. "When is it?"

"Next Sunday evening at the Beverly Hills Hotel."

"Can't wait," she said, dialing back some of her enthusiasm. "What's the event?"

Marty gave her a mischievous wink. "My youngest daughter with Bella, Jasmine—it's her bat mitzvah. I hope you have another dress to wear to temple in the morning. It's L.A., so don't worry if your tits are showing."

CASS: What the hell do I wear to a bat mitzvah? It's black-tie.

Dahlia: Excuse me?

Cass: I've been invited to a bat mitzvah . . . by someone famous. SOS.

Dahlia: I will not continue this conversation over text. Calling you now.

"Hi, D," Cass said when her phone rang a second later.

"Can I get some details, please? Whose bat mitzvah? Where are you?"

"I'm in a dressing room at Brentwood Gardens, deciding between a sequined black strapless and a one-shoulder gray lace. Basically a toss-up between looking like a cocktail waitress or a bridesmaid. I don't need to tell you this is my first bat mitzvah."

"Back up. Whose is it?"

"Marty Spiegel's daughter. You know I've been working for him, right? Well, we kind of became involved, and he wants me to go with him to his daughter's bat mitzvah this weekend."

"You're serious?"

"Completely."

"Aren't you part Jewish?"

"I'm about as Jewish as your freshman-year roommate was Native American. You know how she said she was one-sixteenth Iroquois because of her fifth cousin named Winged Foot?"

"Right." Dahlia chuckled. "I don't think Maria DeSouza had much tribal experience in Parsippany, New Jersey. Text me pictures of your options and I'll figure it out for you. And Jesus, you're dating Marty Spiegel now? Isn't his daughter your cleaning lady? Does Jonathan know?"

"Yes, she is, and no, he has no idea, and I'm hoping to keep it that way. I have the perfect dress back home, the silver Valentino I wore to the Tonys, but of course I can't exactly ask Jonathan or Luna to ship it to me. Hence, my call to you."

"Gotcha," Dahlia said. "At least I'm not the only one dropping bombs."

"Speaking of, how are you? And the boys?"

Cass heard Dahlia blowing her habitual raspberries, the way she released her frustration into the world.

"The divorce proceedings continue to be a nightmare. Roxanna transferred to another school, which is great, but Harris is out for blood. He is taking my sexuality as a personal assault on his masculinity, which is ridiculous because he has a slew of twentysomething girls lined up down the block. He's the Caligula of Scarsdale. I swear only women age. I wanted to thank you for FaceTiming the boys so much the last few months. They love seeing their Auntie Cass. I've been so worried about Brady."

"Is he still obsessed with the Golden State Warriors?"

"Beyond. Why?"

"Just asking." She made a mental note to send Brady a new jersey. Team swag wasn't going to make everything better, but it couldn't hurt. A care package from just about anyone would have gone a long way with Cass back in the day.

"Listen, Cass, I've actually been meaning to call you about something. You know *The Real Housewives* show, right? Well, one of the producers lives in Scarsdale and asked me to be on the Westchester edition they're getting ready to film."

"You've got to be kidding. You wouldn't consider it, would you? Those shows make everyone look despicable."

"Cass, I already owe my lawyer a hundred thousand dollars and Bravo pays really well. It's not that easy to dust off my degree after twelve years and get a job, not to mention that I'm always tied up in depositions during the week. Harris is slowly poisoning me with paperwork. Do you know what discovery is? Trust me, you don't want to find out."

"I'm not telling you what to do, Dahlia. I just want you to consider it carefully before you make a decision. Brady and Toby, they are at a tough—"

"Well, how much consideration did you give your separation?" Dahlia interjected. "I feel like it came out of absolutely nowhere, unless you just weren't being totally honest with how things were going all these years."

"That's different. My marriage isn't getting broadcast on television," Cass deflected, though the thought crossed her mind now how easily her trial separation would translate to prime-time entertainment: *The Coynes: Better Together or Apart?* Or better yet: *Coyne Toss.* Viewers could vote after each episode on whether they should stay married or get divorced. The final tally would determine their fate. In some ways it was appealing to hand off the decision to the American masses, whose collected sense might be better than hers and Jonathan's meek attempts at choosing their future.

"And, to be perfectly honest now if I wasn't before, I probably didn't think about it enough. You talk about the women lining up for Harris. I'm sure Jonathan isn't living like a monk either. I'm nauseous when I picture it, even though I'm the genius who said we should be free to see other people as though we're a couple of horny teenagers."

She said that partly to make Dahlia feel better. Maybe she was being naive, but Cass still believed her husband wasn't taking much advantage of the freedom she'd bequeathed him. When she pictured him in New York, it was tethered to his desk. And if he wasn't working, he was devoting his spare time to fantasy football and the Big Brother program. Speaking of which, she had to make sure to secure the free tickets for Kids Night on Broadway for Jonathan's chapter. She'd told her husband that this year she'd arrange a meet-and-greet with some of the stars. No matter what, she'd still deliver on her promise, even if it meant FedExing the tickets to Jonathan at his office while she lived another life apart from him.

"You know I'm here for you, right? Cass—if you want to talk, I mean really talk, not just in sound bites and platitudes. You've always been private about your parents, but I have a feeling this has something to—"

"Miss?" There was a knock on the dressing room door. "Everything all right in there? Can I bring you another size?"

"I really appreciate that, D. I do. But I gotta go. I've been in the dressing room for twenty minutes. I'll call you soon."

JASMINE'S NAME WAS reflected on the dance floor in sparkling lights. The entire ballroom of the Beverly Hills Hotel had been transformed into an Arabian palace; all the servers were dressed in either turbans with Nehru jackets or midriff tops and harem pants. They were serving toothpicked bites off of gold trays. The bat mitzvah girl was dressed in a teal blue Herve Leger dress, four-inch gold Louboutins and a jeweled tiara. While a tarot card reader floated among the guests "predicting" their table assignments, a bare-chested man played the sitar during the cocktail hour, taking requests. He then joined a twenty-piece band that welcomed the guest of honor and her parents into the ballroom to the tune of "A Whole New World." Marty caught sight of Cass in the waiting crowd and gave her one of his customary winks.

She headed off in the opposite direction from Marty to where the snake charmer was performing and did what she knew she had to do.

"Luna," Cass said, breathless with anxiety as the two of them met face-to-face. They'd made eye contact early on despite Cass's juvenile efforts to hide from Luna behind a flaming torch.

Marty's daughter stared back at her coldly.

"Um, mazel tov," Cass said. She'd nailed down that that was what she was supposed to say at this event, though she kept confusing the "bar" and "bat" before the "mitzvah."

"I'm not the one having this incredibly cheesy thirteen-year-old's birthday party," Luna said flatly, looking Cass up and down.

After some back-and-forth with Dahlia, Cass had settled on a black strapless sheath that hit her legs just above the knee. It certainly wasn't the nicest dress Cass owned, but there was no way she would use her and Jonathan's joint American Express card to splurge on couture for the benefit of another man. Instead she used cash from her freshly deposited paycheck. Marty's ex Bella Criss, the mother of the bat mitzvah girl, had muddled the Arabian theme and looked like a cross between Cleopatra and a 1920s flapper with her gold-sequined headdress and many strands of knotted pearls around her neck. She had breasts the size of floatation devices and lips that could double as airbags, her body obviously anticipating some type of accident before night's end. At the very least, Cass was sure she looked better than Bella.

"Right," Cass said. "I like your dress." Luna was way off theme in a pink taffeta dress with a full skirt, irony dripping from each ruffle.

"Okay," she answered.

Jesus, this was like pulling teeth.

"So I hear Puddles loves the new dog walker." Cass prayed talk of her pet would neutralize the other issues silently dancing around them like a thousand waving arms flailing for attention.

"He's happier than ever," Luna said, finally animated. She took a big swig of her Jas-tini. "Puddles is *obsessed* with Maurice. He's much better than that Stefania chick you hired off the street."

"Great," Cass said, through gritted teeth. Nobody dared insult Cass's care of Puddles. "Have you seen Jonathan?"

Luna raised one eyebrow, suggesting she couldn't believe Cass was really going there. A silence that felt endless followed, and then Luna offered a lazy shoulder shrug. It was either I-don't-know or none-of-your-damn-business. Cass got the feeling it was the latter. It occurred to her that in the court of public opinion, *she* was the villain. That could explain why Jemima was barely texting her back. Why did nobody recognize the benevolence underlying her seemingly callous actions? This experiment was for Jonathan's benefit as well—in the long run at least.

"Well, I hope he's doing well. You're not going to mention that you saw—"

Luna snorted.

"No, I'm not going to say anything to him. But not to protect you, trust me. I don't want to hurt him. You must think you are really something special because the all-powerful Marty Spiegel is—"

"Luna, Cass," Marty said, approaching them from behind. He awkwardly put an arm around each of them, squeezed them tightly so their profiles were almost touching. "Forgot you two knew each other. Cass, I'd love to introduce you to my mother. She's sitting down over there." He gestured off in the distance, near where the Bengal tiger was stationed in a cage alongside a worried-looking trainer with an exposed pistol. "And Luna—you could say hello to your grandmother at some point before she drops dead."

Luna rolled her eyes and stalked off toward the bar.

"Having fun?" Marty asked Cass as they glided across the dance floor, which was now projecting baby pictures of Jasmine.

"It's an experience," she said, still shaky from the interrupted conversation with Luna. Had she been totally naive to think of her and Luna as friends in a way, the two of them occasionally blathering on about diet trends, Netflix shows and the Kardashians? When Luna straightened up the kitchen, Cass always helped bring the plates and cups to the sink—a gesture that they were in it together. "You certainly went all out."

"Party cost half a million," Marty said. He was indisputably bragging, like a small child hoisting a trophy in the air. While she was mostly turned off by the ostentatiousness of it all, a part of her liked how freely Marty talked about money. Betsy would sooner cut out her tongue than be so tactless. Jonathan too. When he and Cass would meet with Carmel to discuss furnishing their apartment, her husband would point to a table he liked and say, "Tell me more about this. Is it an important piece?" Anything to avoid, "How much does it cost?" Carmel seemed to catch his drift. It was like they spoke in code and Cass was left wondering why everything had to be so oblique. She didn't like the way the Coyne clan was so formal and militant about being understated, but she also hated the gaucheness of tonight's affair. What was wrong with her? When did she become this person who had a problem with everybody and everything? If preteen Cass with the bad glasses and terrible clothes could see glamorous, successful Cass now, well, she would slap her across the face for being so ungrateful.

"I didn't want Jasmine missing out like you and I did." Marty tucked a piece of Cass's hair behind her ear. "You really look beautiful tonight." Cass beamed. Next to Marty, she felt amazing in her own skin for the first time in ages. The other night after a late-night swim in the nude, after they had toweled off and were enjoying a glass of wine in his study, Cass had told Marty a bit more about her childhood. After he showed her a picture of the tiny house he'd grown up in, with its vinyl siding and air-conditioning unit dangling precariously out the window, she had decided to open up more to him.

Marty bent down to kiss the elderly woman examining her manicure a few feet away from the tiger. Mrs. Spiegel was that bizarre, surgically enhanced combination of old and young, what her own mother would look like if she had the money for this battery of cosmetic procedures. "Mom, this is Cass. Cass, this is my mother, Adele."

"Sit down, honey," Adele said to her. Her voice was croaky and coarse, what sandpaper would sound like if it could talk. "It's nice to meet you."

"I'll leave you two to get acquainted," Marty said, and headed in the direction of Ron Howard.

"It's nice to meet you too," Cass said, pulling up a chair next to Adele, who took Cass's hand in her own.

"My son loves shiksas," she said.

"Excuse me?" Cass said, leaning in closer. The music was blasting.

"And I understand," Adele continued. "Look at you with your blond hair, that tiny little ski-jump nose. And I bet you're not mouthy either. No matter what, you've got to be better than the last one—that fashion designer with no talent. Who would wear any of her *schmattas* if Marty hadn't made them? And this one?" Adele said, pointing at Bella with a hot-pink nail sailing half an inch past her fingertip. "Washed-up trash." She eyed Cass again. "You're very young, but it's to be expected."

"Mom, I think that's enough," Marty said, returning just in time to catch the tail end. "I'm going to steal this one away now. The show is about to start."

"Show?" Cass couldn't imagine what came next. The entire evening had felt like some kind of tacky performance art.

"Ariana Grande," Marty explained. "She's doing a short set after Jasmine lights her cake."

"Let me tell you something," Adele said, pulling Cass toward her just as she was rising to join Marty. Despite her expensive jewelry and designer suit, Mrs. Spiegel's perfume had a cheap, old-lady scent. Inhaling it transported Cass to Hazel Park. It was the smell that Donna brought home with her after a day of work at the mall.

"Yes?" Cass asked, trying to breathe through her mouth.

"The champagne at this shindig cost three hundred dollars a bottle. I suggest you drink up." She looked at Cass as though she were waiting for her jaw to drop. "And bring me a glass while you're at it."

"Sure," Cass muttered. *Might as well be a waitress too,* she thought. She had enough different identities, so what was the trouble in adding one more?

THE NEXT MORNING, Cass and Marty stood side by side in his master bathroom, she applying makeup and he clipping nose hairs. CNBC blared in the background.

"It was fun last night," Marty said. "I thought Jasmine's friends looked like a bunch of hookers and Bella was shit-faced by the end of the party, but all things considered, I'm—"

"Shush!" Cass said, dropping her eyeshadow. Purplish-gray powder flew in charcoal bits across the milk glass vanity. She put her hand in Marty's face to keep him from talking and ran into the bedroom, where the seventy-inch TV was mounted on the wall.

"—welcome Jonathan Coyne," the morning anchor, Becky Quick, said. The camera panned to Jonathan, who looked like he'd been spray-tanned before going on air. He had on one of his slick suits, gray with a subtle windowpane pattern, narrow, expertly tailored, twenty-first-century Gordon Gekko. "Your boss, Jerry Winston, is in a lot of hot water. Can you tell us what the atmosphere is like at work?"

Jonathan looked confused as to whether he should look at Becky or the camera. His head darted side to side like a turtle checking if the coast is clear.

"To tell you the truth, Becky, it's just business as usual. I cover natural gas, which, as you know, is having a tremendous quarter. We've been lucky, but we also do our homework. The allegations against my boss are absurd and totally without evidence. The SEC has it in for hedge fund managers and this is just simple vindictiveness and dirty politics."

Becky's cohost, Andrew Ross Sorkin, chimed in, further confusing Jonathan's eye contact.

"You're considered by many to be Jerry Winston's right-hand man. Are you worried at all he might set you up to take the fall, like what happened to some of the top managers at Steven Cohen's fund? It's easier to go after the smaller fish, you must know that, and the SEC wants a win."

"Jerry would never do that to me, and I have nothing to hide."

Becky addressed the viewers.

"All right, you've just heard from Jonathan Coyne, senior analyst at Winstar Capital, two days after the SEC launched a major investigation into the fund due to allegations of fraudulent reporting, insider trading and price-fixing. Jonathan—thanks for joining us, and good luck."

"Thanks, Becky," Jonathan said, looking directly at the camera. Cass cringed. They should have prepped him a bit instead of bronzing him like a *Jersey Shore* cast member. The hosts probably wanted him to look like an idiot—better for ratings.

"So that's your husband?" Marty asked. "Looks like he's in deep shit."

"I have to go to him," Cass said, fumbling for her cell phone to book a flight. Jonathan had spoken confidently and kept his composure, but she saw the fear and hurt in his eyes that no other person watching CNBC would have been able to discern. She needed to support him. To tell him face-to-face that no matter what happened with Winstar and his career, it wouldn't have any impact on her feelings toward him.

As HER TAXI barreled through the streets of the Upper East Side heading to 75th Street, Cass kept her eyes glued to the window like a child. She breathed in the city smog, dizzied herself at the sights. The bodegas on every corner with the freshly cut flowers, the sidewalks thick with pedestrians weaving about like Tetris pieces, the blare of car horns making a symphony; God, she had missed home.

Like a burglar, Cass donned a baseball hat pulled low over her eyes to enter her apartment building. She didn't want to be forced into chitchat with the doormen, who would gossip on their smoke breaks about her unexpected return. She slipped into the building with a group of nannies pushing strollers and went unnoticed into the elevator. At the front door she paused, running her finger over the grooves of the keys in her hand. She hadn't turned that lock in months, or set her bag down on the coffee table, or grabbed a handful of pretzels from the jar on the kitchen counter. Foolishly, she considered if her key would still work. She didn't waste too much time wondering, for fear Jemima would emerge from her next-door apartment at any second. Cass's plan was to drop her overnight bag off and head to Midtown to see Jonathan, then buzz his beloved Gloria to ask him to come downstairs. She didn't think he'd be shocked to find out she'd come. It was an unspoken rule of the separation: if the shit hit the fan for either of them, they'd be there for each other.

She expected to find the apartment returned to bachelor status: empty fridge, inside-out dirty boxers, depleted beer bottles stacked in the garbage. To her surprise, the place was neat and well stocked, the refrigerator and pantry filled with fresh produce and a wide variety of cereals and pastas. She felt a fleeting surge of pride that Jonathan was taking such good care of himself, until a feeling of being unneeded soured her mood. She went to see the state of the bedroom, which was also tidier than expected.

Exhausted from the flight, she lay down on her side of the bed for a short recharge. Removing her sweater and socks, she slipped under the covers. As she tossed and turned trying to get comfortable, her foot became entangled with something in the bed. It felt silky. Maybe it was one of the pocket squares Jonathan sometimes sported in his breast pocket. When was the last time these sheets had even been changed? Cass looped her big toe around it and shimmied it out from under the blanket.

She gasped.

Hanging off her foot was a lace thong. One that was definitely not hers. It had to be a size XS—with scalloped edges in the front and a strand of spaghetti in the back.

"Jesus," she said, flinging them off of her. She staggered out of bed. What else had she missed? She swept the apartment a second time, collecting evidence. In the bathroom, she uncovered a cherry-flavored lip balm she couldn't remember buying and a Venus razor. Years ago, Cass had lasered off every hair on her body other than the ones on her head and, until recently, a well-tended triangle below. In the kitchen, on second glance, she noticed an out-of-place container of soymilk. She and Jonathan were a strictly dairy couple. The hallway closet had a floral Vera Bradley bag tucked in a corner. Who was this lactose-intolerant, chapped-lip slut Jonathan was screwing in *their* bed?

She needed to sit down or she'd faint. The nearest landing spot was the chair tucked under their desk. She flopped onto it, noticing that their wedding photo had been nudged behind a stack of magazines. She shook the mouse to bring their computer to life. Minka or Brie could probably get her a flight back to L.A. for this evening, or maybe she'd nudge Marty and he'd send the company plane for her. With jittery fingers, she clicked open Gmail. As she went to log out of Jonathan's account and into her own, she gasped again. On the screen she read the words: *Are you sure you want to sign out of BrettGEddison @gmail.com?*

Fuck him.

Fuck her.

Fuck everybody.

24. JONATHAN

THE SHITSTORM STARTED a week earlier when he went to bring Puddles to California. News of the investigation had reached Winstar's shore. It turned out Laurel had been dead right. The SEC was probing their fund after an unidentified whistle-blower contacted them with alleged evidence of wrongdoing.

Jerry called in all his top guys, which included Jonathan, Russell, Nate, Jeff and Liz—the head of investor relations, whose phone was ringing off the hook—for a meeting with a team of lawyers from one of the city's premier white-collar firms. Jonathan knew not to assume that hiring legal representation was an admission of guilt, but he couldn't help feeling otherwise when he saw eight men in suits looking grim, armed with legal pads and surrounded by towers of brown boxes stuffed with file folders.

Jerry swore up and down the firm had done nothing wrong, that everyone should stay calm and continue to work, that clients calling should be put at ease. Liz chortled and the boss shot her a menacing look. He asked if anyone had any questions and slowly the hands shot up. Jonathan looked at his watch nervously—he had only one hour to get to LaGuardia for his flight. The dog walker was already downstairs with Puddles in his airport bag. He briefly thought about asking Gloria to go in his place, but dismissed it. When the dust settled and the investigation proved fruitless (he still believed the SEC was on a vindictive fishing expedition—he, Jerry and his colleagues all operated aboveboard), the only thing that would have an impact on his life was Cass remembering that he couldn't be bothered to meet her at the airport, for one of their, give or take, six meet-ups. This absurd dog exchange had always felt pretextual. Yes, they adored Puddles beyond measure, but the blueprint for their handoffs was so convoluted and expensive it could only be interpreted as a calculated excuse to see each other.

Hours later, he stepped off the escalator leading to baggage claim at LAX and did a double take when he saw a striking, dark-skinned woman holding a sign with his last name. She smiled at him and he approached cautiously, assuming there had to be another Coyne in the airport.

"Jonathan?" she said. "I'm Minka. I'm here to collect Muddles. Cass got tied up in a meeting. I believe she texted you."

"It's Puddles."

"Sorry," she said, eyeing the doggy cage like its handle would scorch her hand.

He looked down at his phone. It was still powered off from the flight, but when he booted it up he saw Cass's message. Stressed, and feeling rather the fool for crossing three thousand miles in the wake of a crisis, he texted her back: Really appreciate you making the effort.

She wrote back right away. Marty wouldn't let me get away. Big deadline looming. I'll be there next time. Wish it had been a different day. He reread what she wrote, feeling heat creep up the back of his neck.

The response was so Cass. She'd type a million extra words just to avoid saying the simple one needed: *sorry.* Over the years they'd had their share of spats and in the beginning he'd go at her until he heard the magic word he was seeking. It became obvious after a few years of marriage it wasn't going to come easily. When Cass was angry at him, he'd blurt out an apology before internalizing what she was even upset about—sometimes while she was still midsentence. Like when he forgot to cancel the mail before a vacation (which, honestly, was not a capital offense), he'd heard the first beat of her rant and said sorry a dozen times just to put a muzzle on the forthcoming lecture. By contrast, when Cass wasn't friendly enough to Ginny Winston at the company holiday party, he'd pressed until she was flattened like a pancake in order to extract an apology, when all along she'd been giving him one, albeit in her special Cass way. "I had a terrible headache . . . Work was so stressful today . . . I'm getting my period." These were all variations on a theme, and the theme was *I'm sorry*. He had thought it was childish of her to be so parsimonious with her apologies, but had come to consider that his pursuit of them made him the juvenile one. Or maybe they were both complete babies.

Jonathan slipped his phone back into his pocket.

Boy, was he happy now that Brett was coming for a visit the next day. When he was with her, his shoulders could actually relax into their proper alignment, muscle memory from a simpler time in his life kicking in. He used to think that Cass brought out the best in him, a figurative good posture, but maybe it was Brett, with her straightforward nature. If they couldn't decide where to eat after having sex, Brett would say it was up to him and actually mean it. It wasn't a trick or a trap or a test. There was no "right" answer.

The publisher Brett worked for had its main office in Tribeca and she was able to go into work when she visited him. She could even work there full-time, if that was in the cards. Lars was only seven, pliable still, and his father had moved back to Germany. The only hitch was that Brett's family was in Boston and they, particularly her mother, looked after Lars frequently when Brett had to work. It was hard to believe he was actually noodling logistics with another woman when Cass was still sticking to the script—in the fall, they would reconvene and make a decision. Unless he were to call off the intermission early, tell Cass that while she was figuring shit out he had found someone else. It was premature to do anything like that now. He and Brett were just barely reacquainted. But it was nice to think that he might be the one to pull the plug on Cass and not the other way around.

Before his return flight even took off, the flight attendant brought him a scotch and soda. He tried with each sip to regain his calm. Even if there was some malfeasance at his company, it had to be at a lower level, some junior analyst cutting corners to get ahead. The investigation would be stressful, and it was unfortunate that the media would pounce on the story when the SEC went public in a few days, but it wouldn't amount to anything. And Cass, well, she was a pain in the ass. As he got a little drunker, he toyed with the rhyme. Cass—Ass. Cass—Ass. Cass—Ass.

HE MAY HAVE been right about Cass, but he was way off the mark on the work front.

Jerry was indicted on charges of embezzlement, insider trading and market manipulation two days later. The SEC had been collaborating with the attorney general's office, and what at first seemed like a probe that would amount to nothing more than some fines and a public spanking turned into something far graver. The idea of Jerry being carted out in handcuffs went from a ridiculous notion to something that could happen at any second. Jonathan literally jumped every time the receptionist buzzed him. He imagined a scenario where he'd have to create a diversion while Jerry did a perp walk.

And he, Jonathan, was chosen to go on CNBC and Bloomberg and the *Wall Street Journal*'s streaming web channel to represent Winstar the next morning. Why him and not slick Bugatti Jeff or silver-tongued Russell was a mystery.

It was Brett who was tasked with the uphill battle of keeping him calm. In high school, the age difference between him and Brett had seemed monumental. Jonathan had felt light-years ahead in everything: she was a virgin when they had sex; she had no idea that the cafeteria pantry was unlocked every night and students could stockpile snacks for their rooms, or that there was a group of seniors doing mushrooms regularly. Now she was older in every way *but* age. Being a parent and having been through a divorce, she outpaced him by a mile. She talked him through the worst-case scenario and then listed the dozens of reasons why it would never happen.

That night he woke with a start at 3:00 a.m., filmed in a cold sweat. There was all this talk of a cover-up at Winstar: false filings, fraudulent investor reports, payoffs to lower-level SEC employees. This was rapidly turning into yet another disastrous episode in his life, a moment in time when he could feel the floor beneath him turning to quicksand. What if, in some twist of fate uniting the worst times in his life, Daniel came forward to the press and shared what had happened in high school? That story going public could set him up as the perfect fall guy—the privileged prep school kid who'd known scandal before and had used his family's wealth and influence to cover it up. The heartless jerk who beat up a scholarship student surely wasn't above perpetrating white-collar crime, depleting pension funds of teachers and firefighters in the name of self-enrichment. He couldn't go on national television and put his face in front of Daniel.

"What's wrong?" Brett asked him, sitting up in bed. "You're panting."

He awkwardly reached for the water glass on Cass's night table. Brett was sleeping on his side of the bed. It would be too strange to see her in Cass's spot, so he'd done a swap of the night table sundries. Whenever Brett slept over, he moved clumsily about his makeshift side. It was like retraining himself to be a leftie after a lifetime of right-handedness.

"I've been thinking about Daniel." He turned to Brett, but her face gave nothing away. "I know this is probably irrational, but I'm worried he's going to see me on the news and use this to get back at me somehow."

"Jon, that's insane. He doesn't want revenge. It was a high school prank. He knows that."

"Brett, I beat the shit out of him. All these years I've tried to make sense of it. I was drunk. I was scared about going off to college. Peer pressure. But I honestly don't know how I could have done it."

"This is crazy talk, Jon. You beat him up because he wasn't playing along with the prank, and you were wasted. It wouldn't have mattered who was in the bed that night. And none of that is relevant to Winstar in the slightest."

But there was also the locker room talk, which Jonathan remembered more of than he cared to admit. He wasn't the instigator of it, but he didn't shut it down either. Tom Lazarus called Daniel a "spic" once and everyone had laughed. Jonathan may have cracked a joke of his own. He didn't think so, but who could remember so many years back, especially since that would have occurred before the incident. Afterward, he didn't mutter a sentence without thinking it through twice.

"I realize Cass is the elephant in the room at all times when we're together, but what does she have to say about what happened with Daniel? I'm sure she agrees with me."

"She does," Jonathan mumbled. "Agree with you." He didn't express what he thought next. Had he married Cass to prove something to himself? To his family? No, not possible. Who wouldn't have wanted Cass? She was gorgeous and brilliant and could be witty as all hell, not to mention that she fucked like a porn star, at least in the beginning. And then Leon, as the nine-year-old boy he was when they first met, came into his head. Why had he lunged at the chance to join the Big Brother program after getting some holiday mailing from them that everyone else probably just tossed in the trash? Cass once asked him what got him started in the program and he remembered feeling on the defensive for some reason. He'd said that he knew his job wasn't exactly focused on helping people, and this was a way to give back. But was that really the whole story?

He handed Brett her cell phone, which was charging on the nightstand. His nightstand.

"Will you friend Daniel or whatever it's called so that you can see his pictures?"

"What? Why?"

"I just want to know where he is. How he's doing."

Brett looked at him askance but played along, opening Instagram and typing.

"Actually, he and I are already following each other. I didn't even realize because I don't go on so much anymore."

Jonathan recalled Brett's profile, sanitized of her marriage and maybe more.

"Here he is," she said, handing over the phone.

He scrolled through the pictures. Things didn't look too shabby. Quite the opposite, really. Daniel lived in Silicon Valley, worked for Google, and had a pretty wife (redheaded, smiley) and three young children, including a newborn. In various pictures Daniel was on beaches with his family, fishing with friends, thumbs-upping at a Giants game. He didn't have the look of someone with an ax to grind. Life had been good to him, at least the social media version of it, and Jonathan had no reason to suspect otherwise. The knowledge that Daniel was thriving calmed him somewhat, enough to where he slipped his hand into the waistband of Brett's thong, gave the string in back a tug. She wore the sexiest underwear to bed. Tonight's were black, just a series of strings and a patch of lace.

"I know my situation is a mess. With Cass, I mean. You are just incredible. It was so lucky that you were at Michael and Jordyn's party that night."

He expected more from her, but she just responded, "Mmm," before turning on her stomach to go back to sleep. In the morning, she rushed out the door, fretting about missing her 6:00 a.m. train. It was visiting day at Lars's day camp and she couldn't be late. When she was gone, he went to make himself coffee and noticed Brett hadn't thrown out the used filter. He pinched it and carried it to the trash, musing that cohabitation meant putting up with other people's shit no matter what.

He checked his cell phone for the twentieth time that day and it was only 1:00 p.m. Back in the office after his series of television interviews, Jonathan couldn't concentrate on anything at all. Investors, who were supposed to call Liz first, were bypassing her and calling him directly. He let most of the calls go to voicemail. Truthfully he had nothing to say to them other than reassuring platitudes, which, if they were savvy at all, they wouldn't buy. Jeff, Nate, Russell and the other senior guys felt the same way and together they congregated in the kitchen to bite their nails collectively.

As the minutes ticked on, it was becoming harder and harder to come to terms with the fact that Cass hadn't called, emailed or texted him. News of the investigation of Winstar and Jerry's indictment *had* to have landed on the West Coast. His father was already combing his gigantic Rolodex and putting out feelers to his business cronies in New York to land him a new job. His brothers texted a few times— Wallace emailed him some dirty jokes—and his little sister messengered a box of cupcakes, a flavor called Chill-Out, peppermint icing piped onto a dark chocolate base. He tried to eat one of them but was too nauseated.

Then it was 4:00 p.m., then 7:00 p.m., and still no word from Cass. Where was she? If she wasn't reaching out to him, then their separation was nothing more than a precursor to a divorce, not a trial separation at all. It was down to principle at this point. He was owed a modicum of respect on account of their shared history. The woman texted him about trying kickboxing and drinking kombucha, but nothing when his longtime boss and friend was facing jail time and the financial blogs were suggesting he or one of his colleagues might become the sacrificial lamb. She knew how much his job meant to him. She knew Jerry was *his* Percy. So why was she radio silent?

AFTER A RESTLESS night, Jonathan arrived at work feeling the need to be proactive. Cass would talk about something called *agency* when she would criticize a play. "That character was so passive," she'd moan. "He had no *agency* for anything that happened to him." Well, Jonathan was going to have agency. So he did something he hadn't done in at least five years: he sent flowers to a woman. When he was dating Cass, he had flowers delivered to her office regularly—cool moon cacti he knew would impress the creatives at her office, orchids in rare breeds, even quirky Venus flytraps because the juxtaposition of smoothness and spikes reminded him of her. Once they got married and their finances comingled, Cass told him, in one of her sweeter tones, that it was truly unnecessary for him to continue sending them. "They just die so quickly," she explained, looking pained at the thought of a withering blossom. In hindsight, maybe it was another test of hers. He had assumed it was because she didn't want to be wasteful when the money was coming from their shared pot, but now he thought maybe she was seeing if he'd still continue to woo her after she said, "I do." By telling him not to send flowers, she'd upped the ante. Would he send them despite her insistence not to because he just couldn't help himself?

Gloria found him a florist in Boston. He didn't tell her what it was for and the fact that his family was there hopefully cast away any suspicion that they were intended for a woman. His assistant was like his office mom, except more attentive and helpful than his birth mother, but still he wasn't ready to fill her in. Drafting a note to accompany the flowers proved a struggle. He hemmed and hawed on the telephone with the lovely woman who answered his call at Mayflower Florals, who was initially charmed by his indecision and then quickly lost patience. She offered her email address and told Jonathan to send her what he wanted printed on the card when he was ready.

Finally, he put together:

Dear Brett,

Wanted to thank you for everything. I can't wait to see you again.

Jon

Not a staggering work of genius, but he thought it expressed everything he wanted to say. For the arrangement, he selected pink tulips. Something in season, fragrant, in a feminine color would be just right for Brett. No finger-snatching plants required. For the rest of the day, between grappling with the bleak situation at work and breathing fire over Cass's negligence, he delighted in thinking about Brett's reaction when the bouquet arrived on her doorstep. At least someone appreciated him.

25. CASS

THREE WEEKS HAD passed since the bomb dropped and Winstar was appearing less in the papers. Or at least it was no longer making it to the cover or the front page of the business section, and Cass purposely avoided digging deeper. She rationalized that if Jonathan had been carted off in handcuffs or Winstar had been forced to shutter, the news would reach her somehow. Osmosis. Telepathy. Paper airplane. It was more plausible that the SEC had given up after the probe turned up nothing of any real significance and Jonathan was back to business as usual.

Still . . . she hadn't spoken or even written to him since the story broke. Of course, she did fly three thousand miles at the drop of a hat to see him, but *he* didn't know that. How would that slight ever be undone? They were due for another Puddles handoff in about ten days. After Minka did the pickup at LAX last time, there was no way she could miss this one. A few options whirled before her: she could pretend she didn't know what happened (not the most plausible, but she *was* living in Southern California, and they didn't call it La La Land for nothing), or she could say that she wanted to give him space and not make things more stressful with her reappearance, or, the most daring option, she could confess. She *did* have her regrets about fleeing after she realized Brett had been there. It was sanctimonious of her to feel wounded that Jonathan had brought another woman into their bed. What was he supposed to do—rent a hotel room every time he wanted to have sex? And the fact that the owner of the panties was Brett? Cass had been the one to define the parameters of the break— never did she say that they could only see people with whom they had no past entanglements. Why *had* he chosen her, though? Familiarity? Availability? To please Betsy? Maybe there was no single answer— certainly there wasn't one when it came to why she'd let herself get involved with Marty Spiegel.

Marty. While the feelings of regret and confusion regarding Jonathan tap-danced on her superego, Marty worked her id. Dinners at the hottest restaurants where waiters and bartenders practically lay prostrate when he entered, a weekend away in Napa at a famous director's winery, a Cartier watch that had a waiting list a mile long. With each new luxury item he gifted, her level of excitement diminished. Things were easy for Marty to give, and that made them less special. He did throw Alexi's name in the ring for a supporting actress role in one of his new films, and for that Cass was the most appreciative. She wondered if this was what growing up felt like, or if she'd always been someone for whom material things weren't as fulfilling as she'd thought they would be. Or was it that she was less deprived now, so she didn't relish the next bracelet or the court seats at the Lakers? She still hated basketball, even when she was close enough for the players to drip sweat on her, and she still forgot to put on jewelry when she left the house.

Across the country, she wondered if her husband was making any changes to please Brett. Evolution or regression? The thought of him reviving his pink polo shirt collection, or reading the books Brett suggested, or the two of them getting hooked on a TV series (somehow she pictured Brett liking *The Bachelor* or something else dreadfully lowbrow) made her ill. But it also made her feel less shitty about what she was doing with Marty. Which was, by the way, still not entirely defined. It was hard to picture a man of Marty's vintage asking to have "the talk" with her. He was fully aware of her situation back in New York and never brought it up, leading her to wonder what kind of future he was imagining with her, if any. She vacillated between feeling that they were an item and that he could have six other women on the side. Strangely, both swings of the pendulum made her feel woozy. If he wanted things to progress even further with her, what would that mean for the future? Marty had five children already. It was hard to imagine him wanting numbers six and seven. She was ambivalent about some things in life, but not about wanting her own family. Her wish to have babies felt like breathing to her—not even a choice. The only question mark was when, but never *if.* For the raw simplicity of her desire to be a mother, she was grateful. And she didn't want just one child. No, she wanted at least two. Often she'd thought how much better things would have been during her parents' divorce if she could have had a sibling or two to commiserate with.

And then came the email that halted everything. It appeared on her iPhone while she was lounging at Marty's Olympic-sized pool, feeling like an extra in a rap video. The boss was off in the distance, shirtless and barking on a conference call, uniformed attendants bringing him a steady stream of Diet Cokes.

Cassidy,

We haven't spoken in a long time and I know the next time I will see you is Thanksgiving. You will be surprised when you see me. I have stage-one lung cancer. Guess I shouldn't be shocked after a lifetime of my Camels. The doctors discovered it after I had a blood clot a few months ago. I know I wasn't the best mother and for that I am sorry. You are the person that makes me the happiest when I look back on my life. Seeing the life you and Jonathan have, knowing one day you will become parents (much better ones then your father and me), makes me smile.

Love, Mom

P.S. I know its bad that I'm doing this over email. Sorry.

Devastation struck Cass on many levels: that her mother was sick, that she'd never hidden Donna's cigarettes like she'd thought about doing a million times in high school, that her mom didn't even know what a disappointment her daughter actually was, and that she, Cass, had turned into such a pretentious snob that she couldn't help cringing when she noticed the grammatical errors in her mom's message. The blood clot must have happened around the time Donna had called and spoken to Jonathan. She hadn't even called her mother back, believing it was just some nonsense—gossip about a Hazel Park neighbor or Donna bragging about winning a few bucks at the casino. Why had she taken that chance?

She dialed her mother's cell.

"I guess you got my email," Donna said, her voice sounding like it was funneled through a vaporizer.

"I want to come see you," Cass sputtered, swallowing the lump in her throat.

"It's fine, Cassidy. I know you're busy. I'll see you and Jonathan in November. I'm not going anywhere before then, at least that's what Dr. Shore told me."

"Dr. Shore? Are you kidding me? He's got to be ninety by now. You can't seriously be going to him. Mom, this is serious. You need better care now."

"He takes Medicare, and when the balance is more than what it covers, he looks the other way if I don't send in the rest. I'm not going to run to the oncologist for every little ache and pain."

"I'm coming to Michigan," Cass said, defiantly.

"I would like to see you and Jonathan. You got lucky with that one. I never found a man half as good."

"We'll be there within a few days, Mom." Cass hung up, staring at her phone in disbelief. One of the helpers who orbited around Marty day and night must have told him that she was crying, because he made his way over to her and swung an arm around her.

"My mother is sick. Lung cancer," she said softly.

"Shit," he said. She leaned her head on his bare shoulder, her tears mixing with the sweat slicked on his skin.

"That is fucked-up," he added. She nodded solemnly. "If Pedro can't manage to shoot a war scene with three hundred extras, he can kiss my ass. I am not paying for a thousand extras. Tell him to use the fucking peasants from the village I plucked him from. I'm sure they'd be glad to be in a movie."

Cass looked up, confused, and saw the wire dangling from Marty's other ear. It blended in with the curly black hairs that grew in patches on his chest and shoulders.

He was still on the phone.

TEXT OR CALL, text or call, text or call?

She asked herself, and then Alexi, that question at least a dozen times before settling on email, the middle ground between distance and closeness. She purposefully sent it at 3:00 a.m., grateful for once for her insomnia. By dispatching the message in the middle of the night, she was saved the agony of refreshing her Gmail every two minutes waiting for a reply. At least she knew that when morning rolled around, an answer would be waiting.

Jonathan:

I hope you are doing well. There is no beating around the bush.
My mom is sick. She has lung cancer and I know how much a
visit from us would mean to her. Would you please consider it as
a favor to me? She basically said our marriage is the only good
thing in her life. Yes, I see the irony. Anyway, it would mean a lot
to me.

Cass

"What are you doing?" Marty asked, rolling over unexpectedly.

She was hunched over her iPad. The light cast a whitish glow in the bedroom that brought out the bluish-black bags under his eyes.

"Working. I had an idea for the social media promotion of *End of the World.*"

"Show me in the morning," Marty said, and rolled back over, blasting his orchestral snores within seconds.

Sleep was hopeless. She slipped out of bed and into the pile of clothes that were heaped on the floor. On tiptoe, she padded out of the house and entered the alarm code to open the iron front gates, knowing it might rouse Marty again but having no choice, then got into her car. Loosely, she knew she was headed in the direction of the apartment she shared with Alexi, but she chose a circuitous route, hoping the calming purr of the engine on an open road might pacify her.

On Mulholland, the traffic lights shifted from green to yellow to red seamlessly, and no matter how hard she focused, she couldn't pinpoint the exact moment of change. It gave her pause. Personalities weren't fixed either. She could be one way with Jonathan and a totally different person with Marty, and both sides of her fit like a glove. It either meant she was a chameleon, which made her feel like the careful development of her identity over the past thirty-four years was a fiction, or that everyone chose personalities like prizes in a grab bag. Don't like what you got? Throw it back and take another. Feel like reinventing yourself? Follow these three easy steps. One of the greatest doubts about her marriage was that she and Jonathan didn't really know each other—too many secrets between them, inner selves buried under protective shells. But maybe there was no fixed Cass or Jonathan to know anyway; they were fluid, not static. And secrets weren't secrets; they were just stories not yet shared. Though even as she considered that, she knew it was a sliding scale, and felt at once that her husband was more an open book than she'd ever be. Things would be different if he had some sinister side to him, but he was like the human version of vanilla ice cream.

And her mother being sick? How was she supposed to feel about that after they had been basically estranged since she left for college and not even close before that? Throughout Cass's childhood, Donna had put herself first—choosing to spend whatever extra money there was on makeup and lingerie instead of getting Cass new glasses or fixing her teeth. She'd say things to Cass from time to time like, "You can always talk to me," but then never seemed to be around for a heart-to-heart. And yet still, Cass was rather sad thinking about her mother suffering alone, knowing she would face more trials after a lifetime of disappointments—men leaving, jobs lost, money tight. Now she and Cass might never have a chance to build a relationship. She'd harbored a below-the-surface notion that maybe a grandchild would unlock something in Donna: responsibility, generosity, maturity—qualities that were dormant in her mother all along that only a cherubic, cooing grandchild could summon forth.

Would Jonathan come with her to visit? If not, she doubted she'd choose to be honest with her mother about the reason. Cass kind of enjoyed the superiority that came with showing Donna just how well she'd turned out in spite of everything. It would be easy enough to fib about Jonathan having a work commitment that prevented him from visiting. Maybe she'd even send a box of Godiva from him. Donna considered anything in that gold-and-brown box to be top-shelf. Once Cass offered her a truffle from La Maison du Chocolat on Madison Avenue and Donna teased her about not springing for the good stuff. Cass and Jonathan had exchanged a look. That single confection from their favorite chocolatier had cost seven dollars. God, they could be snobs sometimes.

She made it all the way to the Santa Monica Pier before deciding to drive home. She thudded into bed as heavily as a wet towel and didn't wake until after nine. Lunchtime in New York City. She reached for her cell phone and scrolled through her new messages, bottom to top, looking for Jonathan's certain response. A message from Emmet startled her. He was planning a memorial service for Percy. It was timed for early September, around what would have been Percy's fifty-sixth birthday. He asked that she and Jonathan please attend and would she consider speaking—she was Percy's favorite PZA employee after all. Another visit to New York. She could scarcely draw in breath. Where would she stay? She didn't want to be forced into a hotel like some interloper in her own city. But did she have a place in her own bed, wrapped in the linens she and their interior designer picked out at Pratesi, when Brett was keeping Jonathan warm at night? Perhaps the answer would become clear after a weekend with Jonathan in Hazel Park.

Of course, she responded to Emmet. I miss him so much.

Unfathomable, really, the way cancer could just appear out of nowhere and dismantle life as she knew it from the inside out, molecule by molecule. Percy's death had shattered her like a vase into a million shards. And now her mother. Jonathan would help. Her stable, reasonable husband would bring order to chaos. Not Marty, for whom she was probably just a shiny plaything, but Jonathan, who loved her to the core.

She continued scrolling through her inbox, imagining what she would find. That plane reservations were already made, a caring voicemail left for Donna. And yes, Godiva purchased.

But instead, there was nothing, nada, zilch. Not even an "I'm sorry" or a "Call me." Radio silence, and there was no way Jonathan hadn't checked his email for the past ten hours. Not when Winstar was imploding and more than half of the investors were demanding redemptions. Okay, fine, she did peek at the news to see what was happening.

What a jerk. Screwing his high school ex like some middle-aged guy having a midlife crisis. Why did he have to run to Brett the minute she'd closed the door behind her?

She called him at work.

"I guess the server is down at Winstar?"

"Excuse me?" he answered, already on defense.

"Don't tell me you haven't checked your email. You know, you could have just said no to coming with me or at least offered a bit of sympathy. Unlike your mother, who treats me like trailer trash, my mother has always regarded you as some type of royalty from the kingdom of New England."

On the other end, she heard papers shuffling, taps on a keyboard, a drawer being slammed shut, but no words.

"Hello?" she prodded.

"Cass," he said, his voice loose and wild, like a spilled vial of poison. "You have some nerve talking to me about support. Everything's always been about you. I dance around your moods, trying to figure out how to keep you happy. And I don't complain. I don't expect you to do the same for me when it comes to the little stuff. But honestly, my fucking career is collapsing and I don't even get a text from you. You're selfish, Cass, and I'm sick of it. No other man on the planet would stand for what I've stood for with your childish 'intermission.' This isn't some dark play where the characters act like a bunch of little crybabies. This is my actual life."

She expected the click of the receiver meeting its cradle after that tirade, but Jonathan didn't hang up. It meant there was still time. The simplest route out of this mess was for Cass to admit she flew to New York to see him as soon as she heard about Winstar. She'd cop to leaving when she saw Brett's things. It would humanize her, give her a fighting chance of redeeming herself in Jonathan's eyes, of making their separation an actual experiment and not just a placeholder until the divorce.

Instead, she went coward.

"What are you talking about?"

"Do you expect me to believe that you haven't heard about Winstar? That Jerry was arrested? That we've had half of our investors pull out already? That I'm not sure I'll have a job tomorrow?"

"Jonathan, you've got to believe me. I had no idea, I swear. I've been crazed with the new job. Nobody talks about finance here. It's only about entertainment—you seriously can't imagine. I promise, this is the first I'm hearing of it."

She had to do it. Because telling Jonathan that her pride was more important than his well-being was not an option. He would never look at her the same way.

"Humph," he said, and she didn't know if he was buying any of it.

Still, Cass committed to the lie. She peppered him with questions about what was going on, which he answered with discernible aggravation and, to the extent he could, monosyllabic answers. They did their dance, Cass with her repeated "Oh no, that's terrible" and Jonathan with his series of *yep*s.

"So I'm guessing that means you can't get away for a few days to see my mom?"

"I don't know, Cass."

She felt herself starting to hyperventilate, wishing for a paper bag to catch her shallow breaths. It was far, far worse to lie in a bed of her own making than to deal with a mess that was handed down by fate alone.

"I understand," she managed.

SHE DIDN'T ACTUALLY deserve any more from Jonathan than she got. After all, their initial relationship was based on a lie of her fabrication. And for a long time, it hadn't bothered her. She barely acknowledged it to herself for the first few years of their relationship. Then something irreversible snapped and the deception became too much to bear. She knew it was the specter of a child from their union that tested her ability to push away the past. Parenthood would force a dependency on Jonathan like none she'd ever known, raising the stakes of him knowing the truth about her infinitely. And even if he never did find out, it would be hard enough just listening to Jonathan tell their little ones a thousand times over—*Daddy was so lucky that Mommy was at Paragon . . . Daddy was so lucky to run into Mommy on Park Avenue . . . Five minutes' difference and you guys wouldn't be here.*

The truth: it was no coincidence that Cass ran into Jonathan on Park Avenue outside of his office building. She knew exactly where he worked and that he'd been in New York for six weeks and change. He was an analyst at Winstar Capital; had attended business school before that at Penn. His apartment was located on a well-regarded Upper East Side block in a posh, doorman high-rise. His office was in Midtown in a building not too far from the graphic design firm with which her team would be pairing to represent the Roundabout Theatre Company. It was only a matter of time before they ran into each other during the workday. Cass was going to be doing a lot of on-site work there (she'd make sure of it) and Jonathan was bound to take a lunch break. Loitering outside the office would be a cinch. She could always say she was looking for a cab.

And there it was. The chance meeting Jonathan referenced so lovingly in his wedding toast, that he marveled at repeatedly on their anniversary, was actually a carefully orchestrated lunge at the financial security she knew he could provide for her. First in college, then years later. Jonathan had been marionetted, not once but twice, and he was none the wiser. More than that, he was blissfully taken with a fiction that fate had kissed him. He could crumble knowing that his life was just following the script written and directed by his cherished wife. And he might never forgive her for it.

26. JONATHAN

To BE MARRIED, you have to be willing to accept certain fictions. His mother accepted that his father was done cavorting with other women after Katie was born. Russell's wife did her best to believe that his lower back could only be properly treated by this one particular Swedish masseuse in Hoboken who needed at least three hours to release his sciatic nerve. And his brother believed Jordyn when she said she was only acting like a frenetic, high-strung bitch because of the wedding stress and that after it was all over she'd chill out.

Accepting a fiction isn't the same as ignoring a proven lie. When you choose to stop asking further questions, to cease picking at the Jenga blocks upon which the fiction rests, you are preserving the sliver of a chance that it isn't fiction after all. That your partner is being honest, that you were the paranoid one for doubting them to begin with.

He called Cass back the next day. It was genuinely upsetting that his mother-in-law was sick; she'd never said an unkind thing to him the entire time he'd been with Cass. He'd gotten a hero's welcome whenever he visited Michigan. The littlest things he'd do, like pick up the check at the diner or fix Donna's computer, were met with an embarrassing amount of gratitude.

Cass's appreciation was palpable when he told her that he'd go with her to see her mother. She was high-pitched and obsequious, repeating a string of thank-yous. The whole exchange was so un-Cass that it made him nervous. He just wanted her to stop babbling. It felt good to have some upper hand, but not necessarily at the expense of losing the version of the wife he married.

"My mom basically told me how much it means to her that I married you and that I'm settled. I guess it helps her feel less like a total failure as a parent," Cass said just as they were about to hang up.

"Cass, listen, I'm glad to hear that our visit will be nice for Donna. But you created this rift between us and I don't want to get back together just because you want your mom to be happy."

And then a pause. He knew he'd overreached. Had actually done it on purpose. The best time to make headway with Cass was when she was down. They coexisted on a seesaw. Cass up meant him down and vice versa. And he felt definitely up now, at least vis-à-vis his wife. After all, just last night he had been having sex with Brett, who never said a word about his snoring or the TV volume. Not that things were perfect between them. He and Brett were living in no-man's-land relationship-wise, the place on the tennis court where you miss every shot. The purgatory seemed to be working for the time being, but only a fool would think it could continue that way indefinitely.

"I didn't suggest getting back together right now," Cass said, not quite emphatic, but with enough bristle that he jumped. "Our six months isn't up. I said I want us to go visit my mom together. We need to do a Puddles exchange soon anyway. We'll do it there."

"Tickets?"

"Already reserved them."

"Forward me the confirmation."

Had Cass really reserved him a ticket before he'd acquiesced? Apparently she knew he'd come around before he did.

WHAT DO YOU pack for a trip to visit your mother-in-law who may soon be estranged from you forever? Jeans and button-downs, boxers, a toothbrush and an iPhone charger. Oh, wait, and condoms.

In his master bathroom, standing in front of the mirrored vanity, he actually smiled at himself. It was possibly the first time he'd seen his own teeth in ages. It happened the moment he dropped three Durexes into his Dopp kit. It was the lunacy of having to wonder whether you're going to sleep with your own wife, the idea of packing protection when she could have been in her second trimester by now. That's what made him grin at himself in the mirror like a goofball. His smile eased up when he thought about Brett—the reason he was even flush with condoms these days. Would he be cheating on her by sleeping with Cass in Michigan? Or was he cheating on Cass by sleeping with Brett in New York?

Cass had decided not to bring Puddles along on account of her mother's allergy, so they set a date to do the next exchange for right after the trip. He knew she believed it was bullshit that Donna actually had any intolerance to animals, that it was just the easiest excuse to give her puppy-crazed daughter for why they couldn't get a pet. But obviously Cass had decided not to be confrontational about it. It wasn't deserving of the Nobel Peace Prize not to bring a dog around a cancer patient with a hypothetical allergy, but for Cass, these gestures weren't a given when it came to her mother, who brought out the worst in her. He got it, though. As much as he complained about his parents, at worst he was fighting systemic coldness and golden handcuffs.

Their planes were due to land within an hour of each other and they were supposed to meet up at the bookstore in Terminal A. The flight was smooth and he managed to sleep, which was easier than re-visiting Brett's expression that morning when he told her over Face-Time (with spotty Wi-Fi) where he was heading. Up until that point, Jonathan hadn't seen the situation for what it was in Brett's eyes: a competition for him. Probably because he didn't feel like there was a woman out there, let alone two, who would be particularly motivated to fight for his affections. But maybe that was the case. After all, how broken up would Donna really have been if Cass had revealed her sep-aration to her? Jonathan smelled a ruse.

His flight landed ahead of Cass's plane. Maybe that was the way it had to be, maybe not. He didn't bother consulting Expedia to see what options there had been for Cass to choose from. Why bother when the answer could infuriate him? He told himself that when she arrived he wouldn't rush toward her and envelop her in some heroic-slash-pathetic hug. That he'd tilt his chin upward in acknowledgment of seeing her and wait for her cues. But when he spotted her struggling with a wheelie suitcase that kept turning on its side and a heavy tote slung over her shoulder, he pounced, gallantly swooping in to relieve her of her bags and stroking her hair like she was a child retrieved from a burning building.

"Hi," she said meekly.

"Let's go," he said with a hand positioned on the small of her back, finding the generous dip in her spine. It was a dent from untreated scoliosis and the perfect place for his palm.

He led her toward the taxi line while juggling his own luggage and hers. Cass looked thinner, like her outer layer had been slogged off with an aggressive loofah. She wore cropped silk pants in beige, a white tank, taupe moccasins with beads. He wasn't used to seeing her so lithe and in soft, unstructured clothing. It made him want to touch her bare arms again, to rub his palms on her skin and see if she still felt the same.

"Any more news?" he asked her when they were seated in the back of a cab. Cass gave the driver an unfamiliar address. Donna was a gypsy and it drove Cass crazy that her mother had a hard time planting roots. Did his wife recognize the irony now? That Cass had become the pot, Donna the kettle?

"Not really. She sounded better this morning when I called." She turned to look at him, sliding her cell phone back into her purse. He had tried to see what her home screen was set to. It used to be a picture of the two of them in Miami together, away for the wedding of a couple from Brown they hadn't spoken to in years. He couldn't muster a glance, though he did see that her lock screen hadn't changed. It was still Puddles, wearing a Santa hat from last year's holiday party in their condo building. It had been a great night, the furthest thing from a precursor to where things stood today.

"Thank you for coming. I know you have a shitload going on at work. Do you want to talk about that, by the way?"

"Eh," he said with a shrug. "It's becoming clear that the SEC has real evidence. Emails with public company executives, particularly with this one pharmaceutical CFO detailing when a certain drug was going to be FDA approved. Mostly I'm upset about Jerry. He just wasn't who I thought he was. Maybe nobody is." He looked at her through the corner of his eye, thinking about the papers he'd found in her night table.

She reached over and put a hand on his leg and kept it there until they pulled into the parking lot of Donna's complex. It looked like a shitty motel with its outer corridor and aboveground swimming pool. Cass owed him.

She took back her hand from his thigh and was now fiddling nervously with the cord from her earbuds, wrapping and unwrapping the wire around her index finger so tightly it looked like she would lose circulation. He didn't know if it was the sight of where Donna was living giving her angst or the two of them doing this together as a couple, but something was making it look like Cass could jump out of her skin at any moment.

"Let's go," she said, looking again at her cell phone. "My mom said she's in Unit 209. Remember, we're acting totally normal, okay?"

"I got it," he said, resentfully. Hadn't he acquiesced to coming along fairly easily? She didn't have to treat him like an imbecile, someone who would offer Donna a kiss on the cheek and then inadvertently let it slip that he and Cass were living on opposite coasts.

They ascended the steps, both of them avoiding the dilapidated railing with the peeling paint and wads of chewing gum pressed into the grooves. He knew full well that if he and Cass got divorced, this would be the last time he'd lay eyes on Donna. One of the realities of a divorce without children was the ability to make a clean break from the supporting cast of characters that each of them came in with. Cass's family would be history to him, but he'd feel Cass's absence forever, like a phantom limb.

Cass tapped on the door gently, calling, "Mom?" through the peephole. Footsteps could be heard approaching. Heavy ones, the thud of work boots. The door swung open and they were faced with a bald man in an open flannel shirt that revealed a tangle of wiry chest hair. He looked to be in his forties; a cigarette dangled out of his mouth.

"Uh, sorry," Cass sputtered. "I think we have the wrong unit." Jonathan saw her fishing for her iPhone again.

"You must be Cassidy," he said, his twang hitting the *a* like a high note. It was jarring to hear anyone other than her parents call her by her full name. If his wife could have burned the *idy* at the end of her name, she would have.

"Yes," she said hesitantly. "And you are?"

"Come on in," Donna's voice beckoned loudly from inside. His mother-in-law had a tendency to shout even when she was perfectly calm. Cass, in her defiance, had adopted an aristocratic timbre and sometimes Jonathan had to lean down to hear his wife. It seemed important to her that they be at the same level.

Slowly, they trudged through the front door, stealing confused glances at each other.

Donna was seated in a large armchair with fraying fabric, her legs spread in a V to accommodate a tray of food propped on a makeshift ottoman. She wore royal blue leggings and an oversized T-shirt that read, "Don't Hate Me Cuz I'm Beautiful." Her hair was flaming red, a new color for her, and she used her long nails painted in bright pink to summon them over for a kiss.

"Who is this?" he heard Cass mutter in her mom's ear. Donna brushed her off and laid her sights on him.

"Jonathan, give Mom a hug." Mom? He nearly shat himself when he heard it. Never had he called Donna by anything other than her name. Could this be a show to impress this new guy? Or to endear herself to Cass? He wanted it to stop.

He crossed the living room, where the television blared NASCAR, and bent down to her. She smelled like alcohol, the one thing his mother and mother-in-law had in common. Donna had her signature gold cross around her neck. Cass said once that her mother was not religious enough to behave like a morally sound adult, but just enough of a believer to think she'd have a place to repent.

"I'm Billy," said the bald man, reaching out to shake Jonathan's hand. Billy's hand felt like one big callus. It reminded Jonathan of the way his hands felt during his rowing days, though it was pretty obvious Billy's skin wasn't coarse from too much boating.

"I wanted you kids to meet Billy in person," Donna explained. "We've been together now for, what, eight months, is it?"

"Think so," Billy said, picking up his beer from the coffee table for a swig.

"Billy works at the meatpacking plant," Donna said proudly. Jonathan saw a tattoo on Billy's left leg, a shape that looked rather like a ribeye.

"I don't think you should be smoking around my mother," Cass said firmly, coughing for emphasis. Jonathan had to agree. He felt like he was on the set of the Maury Povich show, like a bouncer was waiting off in the wings in case this family reunion got out of hand. If any-one met Cass in New York, watched her command a room of powerful producers while she pitched a marketing plan or trailed her as she nav-igated a snooty cocktail party, they wouldn't imagine in a million years that her mother was holed up in a three-hundred-square-foot shithole wearing a shirt she probably got for free at a used-car dealer-ship, screwing a redneck meatpacker with a missing tooth.

"It's fine, Cassidy," Donna said. "It's not like I can get cancer twice. Besides, Billy is very considerate. He puffs out the window or he smokes in the bathroom with the door closed when it gets cold. We were just about to make up the pullout couch for you two."

Jonathan shot a look at Cass that he hoped indicated that this was not what he'd signed up for.

"We can't impose," Cass said, message received. "I booked us a room at the Townsend."

"Fancy," Billy said.

Donna shrugged.

"Suit yourselves," she said.

The four of them spent the next twenty minutes making awkward conversation. Jonathan was relieved when he saw Cass reach for her purse.

"So I'll see you in the morning," Cass said. "You booked the ap-pointment with the doctor, right?"

Jonathan couldn't help but cringe hearing his wife ask this. He knew for most children and parents, a role reversal was inevitable. But Cass never had the chance to be the recipient and Donna the caretaker.

"I did. You kids need Billy to give you a ride?"

"We're fine," Jonathan said. Lord knew how many Natty Lights he'd put away before they arrived. "It's good to see you, Donna." *That's right,* he thought. *I said "Donna." No "mom" bullshit.*

He reached for Cass, put his hand on her arm to guide her out of the apartment. When the door was closed behind them, he felt his wife fold into herself like a Chinese fan. Condensed, she turned toward him and buried her face in his armpit. Soon the sleeve of his button-down was drenched.

"Let's go to the hotel," he said. "You should rest."

"No. There's a place I want to show you."

He looked back at her blankly and she, perhaps remembering he wasn't necessarily hers to boss around anymore, added, "If that's okay with you."

"Of course."

HE'D HEARD SO much about Luigi's it felt surreal to be there. Cass said the restaurant hadn't changed a bit since she was a kid. Twice she'd gotten to eat there when she was invited along with other families. She remembered the meatballs and spaghetti being amazing (they weren't) and the soft drinks being free refills (they were).

Cass finished two glasses of Chardonnay before the breadbasket was even set down. The wine, five dollars a glass, was no less potent than the double-digit glasses they swilled in New York City and soon his wife's head was bobbing.

"You okay?" he asked.

"Yes," she said, putting down her drink. "I'd better stop with these. Our appointment is first thing tomorrow morning at the hospital. Can we not talk about my mother, though?"

"Of course," he said. "What should we talk about?"

"Well, Dahlia was invited to join the cast of *The Real Housewives*. She might actually do it."

"You're kidding. Did you try to talk her out of it?"

"Yes, but no one is taking advice from me all that seriously these days. Can you imagine?" She looked at him sheepishly. "Oh, and Alexi might get a part in this new sci-fi movie that Marty—that Spiegel Productions is putting out. What about you? What's going to happen to your job?"

"Who knows? I'm the third most senior guy there, after Russell, who I think is toying with the idea of trying to take over, though he doesn't have the name or track record. I really just don't know what the future holds."

"You always did love throwing yourself into work," Cass said. "I'd hate to see that disappear for you."

"So did you," he said. "I guess we both did."

She smiled and twirled her fork into her spaghetti.

"First carb I've had in a while. The only thing I miss about living in the Midwest is the different body standards. I'm a ten here. In New York and L.A., a seven at best."

"It's not true, Cass. You're a ten in any state. You know that."

He reached across the table for her free arm, started to stroke the inside of her wrist.

"I'm not really that hungry anymore," he said. "And I'm exhausted. Did you really book us at the Townsend?" It was where they stayed on their infrequent trips to Michigan, and Jonathan had been surprised Cass had been planning for them to brave a night at her mother's this time.

"Yes," Cass said. "I realized staying with my mom wasn't going to work out. I just didn't anticipate the chain-smoking hillbilly."

Jonathan left two twenties on the table (when had he last ordered dinner for two that cost less than a hundred dollars?) and stood up. They waited outside on the desolate street for their cab, Cass standing so close to him he thought she might lean her back into his chest any second. When they arrived at the hotel, Cass approached the front desk. He had still not asked her if she had booked one room or two, knowing the answer would reveal itself in time.

"Checking in," Cass said. "It's under Coyne." She added something more quietly to the clerk that he couldn't make out. The clerk then handed over two keycards to her and guided them to the elevator. As the doors slid open the clerk asked, "Ma'am, did you still want me to hold that second room for you?"

Cass shook her head from side to side.

The sounds of the key sliding into the slot and the click of the door opening were the only noises for the next few minutes, as though the king bed taking up most of the room filled the silence. Cass plugged in her phone, scrolled it with her thumb, then fished around in her roll-away suitcase for something or other. He mimicked her with his phone, reading but not really absorbing his stream of work emails, and texting his sister a thank-you for the latest box of cupcakes.

"So?" he asked her when he couldn't take the silence any longer. Cass had slipped into the bathroom but the door was open.

"So," she responded.

"Why did you leave your wedding bands on top of that photo?" he blurted out. It had been driving him crazy since he'd discovered it, but he couldn't raise it over text message. This moment was his best opportunity, in person but not face-to-face. "The sonogram."

"I did?" she asked, sounding genuinely surprised. "I'm sorry. I really wouldn't have done that if I'd realized. You know me better than that."

Do I? he mused. *Do I know you at all?* And what was with Cass apologizing directly? Something was afoot. He shifted on the bed from side to side nervously; it was like the mattress was filled with simmering coals.

She emerged from the bathroom, completely naked. He scanned her from head to toe, noticing bones he'd never seen before jutting from her frame. Skin more golden than ever. He'd never known Cass to tan like that—maybe it was fake. And she was fully shaved, just a slice of flesh where a neat triangle had once been. The two of them used to joke that her pubic hair was shaped like a downward arrow, guiding entry. Had someone asked her to get rid of it? Nipples, the cherry pits on her nearly flat chest, stood at attention.

"So," she repeated, and walked toward him, reached her hand down his pants, found the state of what she was looking for to be acceptable. He saw this from her satisfied grin.

He thought about the condoms he'd packed. They were still in his suitcase, which he'd yet to open. Luckily, it was only a few feet away and he could grab one and be back under her in no time.

"I need a second," he said, scrambling to free himself from her grasp.

"No, it's fine," she said, reading his mind. "We're good."

That either meant she was back on the pill, or that she was okay with them chancing a baby, or that she was in a place in her cycle when conception was highly unlikely. He'd lost track of her rhythm, she'd been gone that long. And right now it just didn't matter.

But it was something else. She got on all fours and guided him behind her.

"You've wanted to try this, right?"

"Yes," he said, nearly exploding. He'd only done that once before, with Marielle, ironically also in a hotel room. Maybe that was where such things were meant to take place. It was frantic and fast, and the room was so dark he could only make out the outline of his wife as he pushed into her. When it was done, they lay side by side, their puffy breaths in perfect harmony.

In the middle of the night, they came together again. He reached for her and she spryly submitted to him. It felt so natural to be back with her; it was like they were jigsaw puzzle pieces. When he entered her, she moaned so loudly with pleasure it was like the walls, the blankets, even the air disappeared and it was just them.

MORNING CAME TOO quickly, the sunlight blinding them both into unattractive squints. They hadn't remembered to draw the shades. Hadn't even brushed their teeth, or at least Jonathan hadn't. Cass was already up, propped against the headboard, on her phone again. He slipped into the bathroom quickly to clean away the stink in his mouth.

"I gotta go," she said, coming up behind him suddenly. She put a hand on his waist. "My mom's appointment is in twenty minutes."

"Okay," he said and watched as she threw on a sundress and applied makeup. She kissed his cheek, leaving the stain of her reddish lip gloss on his face.

"Good luck," he said.

And she was out the door. He looked back in the mirror to wipe off the makeup she'd left behind. It looked like his wife had taken a bite out of him.

After Cass departed, he read the paper on his iPad for a bit, then ventured outside for a walk. It made him feel like a tool, but he couldn't beat back the grin that kept creeping up the corners of his mouth. He marveled at how good it felt to have something back that he'd lost. The plan was to meet Cass back at Donna's place around lunchtime. They would get a bite together (Cass had been militant last night about taking her mother to a decent restaurant) and then head back to the airport. It was a quick visit, but enough to show their concern and for Cass to straighten out Donna's treatment plan.

He headed off in the direction of a shopping center that the concierge had suggested. Maybe he'd pick up something nice for Donna, a sweater or a scarf, earn some brownie points from his wife and mother-in-law. Or better yet, maybe he'd see a Godiva store. He was three blocks from the hotel when his cell phone dinged three times in a row. Three messages from Brett, which arrived out of order. His head began to spin and he found a nearby bench where he could piece together the messages.

(2/3) okay with it, I've had more time to think. You need to sort out your life before I can see you again. My son is upset with how often I've been traveling to New York and I can't lie to him anymore about why I've been

(1/3) Jon—I hope all is okay in Michigan, or as good as can be expected. While I appreciate that you were truthful with me about you going to visit Cass's mom with her and I was initially

(3/3) going. Please don't be in touch with me until you are certain Cass is out of the picture. I fear otherwise I will become collateral damage. B.

He took a deep breath and began to type.

B: You have been so understanding of my situation and reconnecting with you has been a lot of fun. As it turns out, I was going to get in touch with you because Cass and I did reconcile on this trip to Michigan. I truly was planning to tell you as soon as I got back to New York. Please forgive me for everything. Best, J.

He sent it off like a hot potato and then made the mistake of re-reading it. "Reconnecting has been a lot of fun?" Even he hated himself for writing that. But a follow-up message apologizing for his insensitivity seemed like it would only make things worse. Instead he turned off his phone, even though he knew the chance of her responding to his message was minimal, and continued on his errand. He chose a Chanel perfume from a cosmetics store because he knew Donna would be impressed with the label.

He walked back happily with his package to the hotel, where he put on a fresh polo shirt and powered up his phone again. Nothing from Brett (no surprise), but a message from Cass saying she and her mother were going to be late, at least a few hours. He should get lunch himself and then they could just meet at the airport later to say goodbye if the timing allowed. He looked down at the Sephora bag in his hand. He'd give the perfume to Gloria tomorrow at work.

He texted back: Got it. Hope it's going okay. Call if you need anything. xo

27. CASS

SHE COULDN'T STOP staring at the text from Jonathan, specifically the *x* and *o*. Two letters, one consonant and one vowel, and her stomach was in knots. She didn't bother deluding herself that it was just a casual reference meant to offer some nourishment during a difficult time. Why *would* it mean only that when she'd given Jonathan every indication that they were now back together? In one night she'd undermined the gravitas of the separation, and for what? Jonathan certainly didn't deserve any more sudden drops on the roller coaster she'd forced him on. And to make matters worse, she was physically suffering as well. She couldn't sit comfortably for a week, her own body punishing her for recklessness. The flight back to L.A. was particularly brutal. She walked up and down the aisles for most of the four hours like a parent with a crying toddler.

Though she tried, it was impossible to pinpoint what drove her to eschew the extra hotel room and to offer the kind of sex that had never been part of their repertoire. Leave her husband for six months to fig-

ure things out—that was daring. Have porno sex, toy with said husband's emotions and confuse the hell out of him—that was audacious
and borderline cruel. Now she was Icarus feeling the burn.

She didn't want Jonathan to think she'd done what she'd done as
a show of gratitude for his accompanying her to Michigan—that felt
coldly transactional—so when he'd made another move in the middle
of the night, she'd played along, moaning and groaning like it was the
best screw of her life. It *was* good, their problems didn't specifically lie
in that sphere, but her theatrics were overblown.

Why had she done it?

Maybe it was about outdoing Brett.

Maybe it was desperation for release after being around Donna.

Maybe it was because she really missed her husband.

And maybe it was just because she knew she could. That possibility
was the worst. The least excusable.

While she didn't understand her motivation, she was certain that
it wasn't part of any nefarious plan. Would Jonathan get that? And
now what? Thank God he hadn't seen the flowers Marty sent her
mother. Or rather that Minka or Brie sent, but they were signed from
him: *To Donna, Wishing you strength. Marty Spiegel.* Donna had almost shit herself when she read the note, leaving Cass to explain that
her boss did this kind of thing for all of his employees. It was after the
bouquet of lilies arrived that Cass realized she couldn't face Jonathan
again that day without risking a nervous breakdown, and so she texted
him that the doctor's appointments were going to run late. Then she
switched her flight to a later one to avoid any chance of an airport
run-in. But still it was only a tiny stopgap, because they were scheduled to see each other again almost immediately to exchange Puddles.
She was booked on a red-eye to New York in a few days to hand off
the dog at the crack of dawn.

What she wanted now was to reenter her L.A. life for a day, even if
it was an escapist cop-out. She wanted to immerse herself in the shiny

people, watch the obsequious assistants zigzag around and listen to the buzz of *Variety* columns setting the office ablaze. This alternate life was so abstracted from anything she'd ever predicted for herself that she could try to pretend that everything between her and Marty was simply part of a made-up script. Opening credits: *The role of "Girl-friend" will be played by Cass Coyne*. Or better yet, live theater, where she could hand off the role to an understudy if necessary.

The next morning she woke up earlier than usual and avoided her email and phone like the plague. To have gotten this far into the inter-mission only to have risked everything in one reckless night was going to kill her, unless Jonathan murdered her first. She certainly wasn't prepared to tell him Michigan was all a big mistake and that she wanted a definite split. But she also wasn't ready to cut the separation short and attempt another stab at domestic bliss just yet. How many more chances would her husband give her, especially when another warm, waiting body with cherry-flavored lips and a sexy thong was available to him?

At least one good thing did come out of Michigan. When Jona-than was talking about the possibility of his career cratering, she didn't flinch, on the outside or the inside. The idea of him having to start over didn't scare her and she'd been tempted to tell him so—that she wouldn't care if they didn't have a lot of money. But she was afraid to because it might require admitting to Jonathan just how important to her that had once been.

She couldn't overlook the fact that in the midst of a major profes-sional crisis, Jonathan had picked himself up and gotten on a plane to be there for her. He'd left Brett behind, explaining his departure God knows how, and had been every bit the supportive husband any woman would dream of. She didn't know what the hell her problem was. Here was a man with everything to offer: hardworking, smart, handsome, and faithful too—before the intermission anyway. How often had she eavesdropped on the Winstar wives and the ladies at her gym saying they didn't mind "looking the other way" because "he's such a good provider and father." The problem, she reasoned, might lie in Jonathan's goodness. He wasn't a man who deserved to be deceived in any way. So if she went back to him, it would have to be with all the cards on the table this time.

Cass found herself yawning repeatedly during the morning commute. Tension, coupled with a confused body clock, woke her before dawn. At least she had slept for a decent stretch, though her dreams were a terrifying montage of treachery: rocky cliffs she tried to scale without shoes, downpours with broken windshield wipers, fires smoldering everywhere. She fiddled with the radio tuner in the Camry, but it was Taylor Swift on every station and those lyrics were like horoscopes—you could find some way to relate them to your life no matter what and it was just too vexing. She switched to the news, letting talk of stocks, terrorism and political corruption occupy her until she cruised into the parking lot.

Marty was at work early, catching the worm. She knew he was there the moment she stepped off the elevator and saw his door closed. It was kept open when he was out of the office and closed when he was there, like the flag flying outside of Buckingham Palace when the queen was in residence. She needed to thank Marty for the flowers he'd sent to her mother. Maybe he'd suggest dinner that evening. If not, she'd sleep over. Her appetite for sex wasn't normally so strong— she sometimes wondered blithely if one forgettable fuck with a hot trainer at Equinox could have quenched her thirst and rendered the intermission unnecessary. But now, oddly, sex had become like medicine. It offered the briefest but most effective of reprieves, like a lozenge for a sore throat. Ten minutes of blankness. Of transparency.

She knocked gently.

"Hang on," Marty called. A moment later the door swung open. He had a guest, the tawniest and lankiest woman Cass had ever laid eyes on. The woman's bronzed collarbone protruded into the room flagrantly and she wore a denim miniskirt with gladiator sandals that coiled around her calves until the kneecap.

"Thanks for coming in, Tamara," Marty said, walking her to the door as Cass entered. "Minka will show you out." He turned to Cass. "How is everything?"

"Thank you for the flowers. That was truly generous."

"It was nothing," he said. "Took a little effort for Abby to find your mother's address."

"Yeah, well, she moves a lot," Cass said, wanting to brush aside this conversation. This wasn't the distraction she needed. "So Aidan told me he did the ad buy for *School of Rebels*. Back page of the *New Yorker* and banners on the People.com homepage? I'm happy you're putting so much muscle behind it. I caught the dailies in the screening room the other night before I left work and they were intense."

Marty walked over to his mini fridge and reached for a Diet Coke and a cold package of M&M's, keeping his back to her.

"I'm glad you brought that up, Cass. You know how much I admire the work you've done for that film." He paused to shovel some ice into his drink, which cracked and fizzed with the hiss of a snake. "Unfortunately it didn't play well with the media." He whirled around. "I had to make the call and go with the alternate campaign that Josephine created."

"Josephine? I didn't even know she was on the *Rebels* team. I could have redone the posters. What about the bus ads? I mean, no one ever suggested I make any changes. All I heard from you and Aidan was that my campaign was exactly on point."

"I'm sorry, Cass."

"What about the Sundance submission? Were my materials used for that? They don't cater to subscribers like the *New Yorker*. And the buses," she repeated, though she sensed she already knew the answer.

"This is a tough business. It takes a long time to get a feel for film advertising. It's different than live theater. You will get there, Cass, I have no doubt. We'll talk more about it tonight. Did you want to have dinner?"

She acquiesced wordlessly.

"Now I'm sorry to cut this short, but the girls have been buzzing me for the last half hour." He walked over to her and kissed her gently on the forehead. "And you didn't tell me anything about your mother. We'll talk later."

She retreated from his office and watched the Bobbsey Twins flock in like hungry seagulls. Neither of them looked at her when they passed, which made Cass question if they knew about the *Rebels* situation. Probably not, since they mostly fielded phone calls and organized snacks for Marty. Cass was just getting paranoid. Another troubling emotion to add to her growing list of maladies.

Something didn't add up about what Marty said about her work. The *New Yorker* wouldn't have a problem with the art she created— there was nothing controversial about it, and even if there was, it was the *New Yorker*!

She managed to stumble back to her seat and found her cell phone lit up with texts.

Jonathan: All good? Can't wait to see you in a few days. xo

Dahlia: I signed with Housewives. They start filming me later this week. Don't judge!

Cass dropped her head between her knees, heavy as a bowling ball. Aidan looked over at her curiously from his neighboring cube, but she ignored him. It was the perfect storm. The steady train of praise she'd received since day one at Spiegel had spontaneously derailed. She knew her concept for *Rebels* was strong, though she couldn't say that Josephine's wasn't better. The question was why, unbeknownst to Cass, another person had been tapped to work on the same movie in the first place. Marty strategically placing Cass on the *Rebels* team to get in her pants was a big pill to swallow, but he wouldn't be the first man to treat a woman preferentially at work because he wanted to sleep with her. Or maybe there was no conspiracy, and it was just her paranoia at work. Cass was new—Marty had given her a chance, but had a backup just in case. She just didn't know what to believe. Her confidence was quicksand.

Then there was Dahlia, selling out to pay legal bills and Cass powerless to stop her. And Jonathan, her husband under fire, whose only solace in life was that he thought they were back together, firing off *x*'s and *o*'s like rounds of ammunition to her heart.

Aidan's head appeared again over the partition.

"Don't let it get you down. Marty can be very erratic."

She rose to face him. "Were you surprised when I was assigned to work on *School of Rebels* so quickly after I started here?" she asked, in a whisper.

Aidan scratched at the scruff on his chin with slow, deliberate strokes.

"Not really," he said finally, though Cass didn't know if that was because it was an open secret she and Marty were sleeping together or because Marty routinely allowed rookies a chance to prove themselves early on. "Matcha cookie?" He held out a bakery box, as though Cass were a small child whose grievances could be mollified with sugar.

"No thanks," she responded, and sank back in her chair, turning her attention to the blinking cell phone. She ignored Dahlia's message for the moment and responded to Jonathan, without letting deliberation slow her down:

I'm truly sorry and feel terrible if the other night was confusing.
I wasn't in my right frame of mind. Please be patient with me—I
still need time to work things out. I'll see you soon to swap
Puddles. C.

Then she added something else, even though she knew it was a mistake.

But thank you so much for everything. I love you.

And she did mean it, in her own way.

AFTER WORK, CASS called Marty to cancel their dinner plans. He clearly interpreted the cancellation as sulking over her *Rebels* campaign not being used and let it go easily. Alexi left for a date. Alone, Cass erupted in her first body-trembling, cathartic cry since the separation. She wasn't one for dramatic tears, but her insides felt like they would rupture if she didn't get some release. She lay on her stomach in bed and drowned her pillow in tears until there was nothing left to expel.

In this state, she took a stab at her speech for Percy's memorial. She had a ton of light stories at her fingertips: getting trapped backstage after too many cocktails at *Hamilton*, stealing props from *La Cage* for the PZA talent show, disastrous typos in Playbills. But the words flowed from a darker recess inside her and she wrote instead of unexplained loss, needless suffering and quashed plans. Finally she fell asleep with the laptop on her thighs and woke in the middle of the night to move the computer to the rug. She made the mistake of glancing at her phone. Midnight in California, 3:00 a.m. in New York. There was a text from Jonathan, a response to her message:

Screw you.

28. JONATHAN

WHEN HE WAS growing up, his mother was fond of the expression "Fool me once, shame on you. Fool me twice, shame on me." She used it mostly in reference to bridge, but it obviously had implications beyond cards.

What should he say for himself after Cass treated him like Play-Doh, like a circus monkey, like a puppet whose every movement she manufactured and he went along with willingly, like some cult member following an insane but charismatic leader?

He should know better. He *did* know better. When he got on the plane to see Cass's mother, in his heart he knew Cass didn't really need him there. It was a test, like everything his wife did. It wasn't designed to measure how devoted he was to her, like after the D&C; it was to see how much control she still exerted over him. And he failed the test by passing.

When it came to dating, people fell into two distinct categories: those who analyzed whether they liked the person they were out with and those who spent the time worrying if the other person liked them. Cass was the former and he was the latter, and that match generally worked. One hopes that after the initial courtship period is over, those roles soften and the liking/being-liked dichotomy blurs into a more natural give-and-take based on actual events. But with Cass and Jonathan they never really had. She was still sizing him up, and he was still trying to please her.

But the sex. He couldn't figure out what that was about. After he made the mistake of being at her beck and call, Cass should have given him the cold shoulder in Michigan, made him feel like an interloper. Instead, she stripped and offered herself to him in a way she never had before. She was outsmarting him at every opportunity; each time he thought he had her figured out, she was one step ahead. He just had to determine the significance of it, because there had to be one. And then it occurred to him. The sex was his last chance to redeem himself. He'd come running like a puppy to her side and so she'd given him one final opportunity to stand up for himself. By refusing to sleep with her he could have reconstructed his backbone, but instead he'd let her filet him like a sea bass. Of course, in classic Monday-morning-quarterbacking style, *now* he had a thousand responses to the sight of her naked body. "Cass, is this really the time?" . . . "I'm seeing someone" . . . "No fucking way" . . . "Not unless we're back together." Or, if he'd really had courage: "I'm too tired."

But like a lamb to the slaughter, he'd entered her willingly. Only to receive a fuck-off text from her two days later. Well, technically it was a fuck-off followed up with an "I love you." Because Cass couldn't be straightforward about anything. She'd confuse him until he waved a white handkerchief and submitted to her treaty.

Another one of his mother's expressions he now ruminated over, proverbially kicking himself: "Don't throw out the dirty water until you have clean water." Cruelly and impetuously, he'd kicked Brett to the curb when he believed his marriage was back on. As though two rounds of enthusiastic sex with his inebriated wife could reassemble the crumbling bricks.

And despite everything she'd done to him, he found himself feeling sorry for Cass. It was hard not to, walking into that nasty apartment that Donna was living in with its musty tobacco smell and secondhand furniture, with her loser boyfriend who would leave her the minute the chemo meant she couldn't give him what he wanted. You had to feel for Cass. Her parents really were trash, though he hated to use that word. It wasn't money they were missing; it was basic empathy and responsibility for the only child they had together. Donna should have waited for another opportunity to debut her latest boy toy, and Dick—that aptly name piece of shit—could have treated Cass at least a fraction as well as he did the three kids he had with his second wife. He could have avoided cheating her teachers and friends' parents when they hired him to do contracting work, making Cass persona non grata in school and on playdates.

Screw you. Even as he reflected on his wife with compassion, he didn't regret it. Yes, it was late at night and he was drinking a little bit when he wrote to Cass, but now it was the morning after, and in the sober light of day he'd write it again. No matter how much he found he could sympathize with Cass, he was still sick of being toyed with, frustrated that he'd cast aside Brett for the chance to be flogged again.

He pressed the speaker on his office phone.

"Gloria, I know it's a weekend, but I need you to pick up my dog at the airport this coming Saturday from Cass. You can take off the following Monday."

Without hesitating, she responded that she would. At least someone was on Team Jonathan. Actually Luna more than ever had seemed to take sides. Though they still never saw each other, he'd find notes from her on the dining room table saying things like, "I had the building super clear the shower drain today. Looked nasty full of Cass's hair," and, "Decided to put Cass's clothes into storage bins. You deserve a bigger closet." He had assumed Luna would ally herself with Cass from some neo-feminist impulse, but he'd been wrong. She was smarter than he'd given her credit for—taking his side in the War of the Coynes made it obvious. Maybe he'd give her an extra fifty bucks next week.

There was something else he knew from his night in Michigan: Cass was sleeping with someone else. Maybe multiple people, but he suspected there was a specific person. He knew it from the way her body responded to his touch, the way she carried herself naked, the rhythm of her moaning. It had the imprint of someone whose essence Jonathan couldn't begin to conjure, who was filling Cass's cup with whatever he'd failed to provide her.

For his part, he'd chosen to retreat to the familiar with Brett, even though he wondered how well he still knew her. The details of her divorce remained a mystery and she kept details about her son under lock and key. Frankly, if Brett told him she'd spied a UFO or was waiting for Mercury to be out of retrograde to decide on a future with him, he couldn't even claim that was out of character. Maybe there wasn't more to Brett than what was on the surface. At sixteen, she'd seemed fascinating and complex, but that was mostly due to her having a vagina. Now he wondered if she had always been a bit too straightforward for him. Simplistic, maybe that was a better word choice. Cass was too much; Brett was too little. Perhaps there was a woman out there who was just the right combination of sugar and spice. Or maybe he'd be better served adjusting his palate. In any event, he was sick and tired of trying to read the blueprint of any woman. It was a fool's errand if there ever was one.

While he reached for his phone, he mentally expressed his gratitude to Laurel for introducing him to Instagram. On impulse, he pulled up Alexi's feed, thankfully public. Headshots, headshots and more headshots. He almost closed out of it when a picture caught his eye. It was Cass, Marty and Alexi seated at a table together in an outdoor café. Well, it did make some amount of sense—Cass told him Marty had given Alexi a part in a film. Cass was in the middle, flanked by Alexi and Marty, though her chair was edged ever so slightly closer to her boss than to her friend. Jonathan brought the phone closer to his nose, accounting for everyone's limbs. Marty and Cass were each missing a hand. As he tried to stretch the picture to see if they were holding hands under the table, as he suspected, a heart appeared in the center of the picture. What had he done? He had just been trying to zoom in on the image. Rather than ask Laurel again for help, he texted his little sister.

What does the heart mean on Instagram?

That you liked the picture.

And that's public?

Yes.

How do I zoom in?

Carefully, dummy! Why? Is this about Cass?

He didn't answer, just placed the phone down on his desk and let the last few months stream through his mind like a movie on high-speed rewind. Cass's new "fabulous" job with Marty. Luna staunchly taking his side. Cass's trip to London. Alexi getting that part. These revelations felt liked repeated stabs in the neck. He had spent the last six years trying to figure out how to make Cass happy for nothing. If fame and Hollywood glitz were what she was after, he had been doomed from the start. He gave Cass financial comfort beyond anything she'd ever anticipated growing up, but having paparazzi snapping pictures and turning heads when they walked into a room, that was never part of the equation. Did Cass genuinely want these things or was she just that bored with her life? That bored with *him*?

Marty had to be a good twenty years older than he and Cass. Maybe that meant his wife had been seeking a father figure all along, though Marty Spiegel seemed to be more of the sugar daddy variety. And for all of Cass's mind games, she was still a relatively fragile person (and hadn't he just adored that about her way back when) who needed scaffolding. Did Marty listen to her blather on endlessly about the virtues of one-man shows? Did Marty sympathize when she cried injustice over the fact that 80 percent of Broadway ticket buyers are women but all three major *New York Times* critics were men? Did Marty not snore? Did he praise her daily? Did he make her laugh?

By liking Alexi's picture, which at first felt like the worst possible thing he could have done, he was acknowledging awareness of what was going on. Doing so made him ever so slightly less of a cuckold. He could picture Alexi running over to Cass and showing her the latest like, the two of them huddled over the phone trying to see how much it revealed.

He did a full 360-degree spin in his office chair. There had been an undeniable sea change. Since the moment Cass declared the intermission, he'd nurtured a gut feeling that his wife would eventually return to him. Some weeks he felt it more than others, but the basic idea was always there, migrating between the deepest recesses of his brain and his outermost thoughts. Now the certainty evaporated. Especially the part where something he might do or say would be just the thing to reel her back in. He now believed that he was powerless to determine his future with respect to his wife.

For type-A sorts, like him, that moment of relinquishing control is freeing for just a fleeting moment, but then the focus needs a desperate reallocation. For Jonathan, he knew that thing would be work, and he'd do his part to put the broken pieces of Winstar back together.

He'd also focus on getting Leon into a good four-year college. Fuck— he'd learn squash and bridge and improve his tennis game too. He would do whatever it took so that he was left with virtually no free time. The plan reminded him of his sister's eating disorder in high school. Really she wanted the popular girls to include her, and when she couldn't make that happen, she shifted her focus to severely limiting her caloric intake. Reaching for the coffee on his desk, he took a long gulp and imagined the caffeine reaching his nerve endings, giving him the jolt he needed to propel himself into the next phase.

HE WASN'T DELIBERATELY holding Puddles hostage, but a few weeks had passed since Gloria had collected him at JFK and no arrangements had been made to get him back to Cass. It had become de facto protocol that the person who had Puddles for the month would initiate contact about the exchange, and Jonathan hadn't done so yet. To be fair, Cass had a calendar—she was fully aware it was nearly Labor Day weekend—and she hadn't reached out either. If she missed their dog so much, she'd be in touch.

Jerry had reached a plea deal with the government that would spare him a jail sentence, which had created quite the outrage in the media. Jonathan had to appear on CNBC three more times, and even though he wasn't there specifically to defend his boss, but rather to comment generally on the fate of the company, the fact of his employment at Winstar made him feel like the secondary villain. After his second appearance, Becky Quick complimented him on his improved television demeanor. You'd think she'd handed him an Academy Award the way he crowed afterward. A week later he received a call from a producer at CNBC asking him to return to the show, but this time to speak only about market trends in the energy sector, not about his workplace catastrophe. He accepted happily and chose his favorite suit and tie to appease his mother, who'd chastised him for having a wrinkled shirt on his last appearance.

It was true he was getting the hang of the whole television banter. A little humor, some sports analogies, a friendly smile—it wasn't rocket science. Hours after his last guest spot when he was in line getting his lunch at Dishes, not one but two people stopped him to say they'd seen him on-air earlier that morning and to ask him some follow-up questions about his market theories. The recognition was surprisingly intoxicating, but even more so, the fact that it was his face spouting knowledge instead of Jerry's made him feel like he could be the front-runner for a change. He'd always seen himself as a behind-the-scenes guy, but the turn of events at Winstar had forced him into the spotlight. During commercial breaks, the anchors would keep grilling him and he realized he wasn't just filling airtime for them—they thought he had something valuable to offer. Maybe he'd have the balls to do what Cass had long ago suggested and start something on his own. Probably not, though.

There was a lot of hullabaloo over which bank or rival fund was going to buy Winstar and who would keep their jobs after they did. He knew raising his profile with the media appearances would help shore up his chances of staying employed after a takeover. For the moment, Goldman Sachs was the lead contender in the contest to swallow the fund, and although the idea of working at Goldman would once have made Jonathan euphoric, he had soured on his industry lately— and he knew why. The entire business was created on the premise that you could make money with money. He sometimes imagined his job as taking dollar bills and putting them in a photocopy machine. And that was when things went well. Often it was like taking dollar bills and running them through a shredder. Marty Spiegel created art. Yes, he made people rich with his business (the actors, the coproducers, not to mention himself), but he brought entertainment to hundreds of millions of people too. Jonathan pictured Cass's glazed expression on the occasions he tried to tell her about his work and shuddered. How she must love working with Marty, the two of them feeling so superior for contributing to "culture."

His office phone rang. Jonathan scooped up the receiver when he saw it was his brother Michael calling.

"You're calling to ask if Becky Quick is hot, aren't you?"

"What? No. I'm calling to see you if you've spoken to Mom today."

"No, I haven't. Is everything okay?"

"I'll let her tell you. You'd better call."

Jonathan immediately pushed for an open line and dialed his mother's cell.

When she answered after four rings, her voice was raspy. She sounded a million miles away.

"Mom, I just got a call from Michael telling me to call you. What's going on?"

She snorted.

"News travels fast. Your father left me. After thirty-six years together. One day before the Cheshire clambake, he packs himself up and tells me he rented an apartment in South Boston of all places. And do you know why?"

"No," he said, but assumed it had to do with his father's favorite pastime. During Jonathan's childhood, Christopher took more "business trips" than a traveling salesman. He thought his father had slowed down in his old age, but perhaps not.

"It was you and Cass. You inspired him." Jonathan could hear his mother putting air quotes around "inspired."

"He said to me, 'Betsy, I'm taking a page from Jonathan and Cass. They separated to see if they could be happier apart. I'm going to do the same. I should have done it decades ago.' Can you imagine? Who's going to want him, with his limp penis that he can barely get up and his all-night flatulence?"

Jonathan flinched at his mother's lack of decorum. Not offended—just shocked to hear her this unhinged.

"Mom, you can't blame me and Cass. We didn't make you have a bad marriage." He wasn't automatically on his father's side, but he could understand where he was coming from in wanting a woman who didn't try to crush his balls daily, whose judgmental gaze wasn't crippling. Even though his father had told his mother this was a separation à la he and Cass, was there really any chance they would reconcile? It was hard to imagine absence making the heart grow fonder for Betsy and Christopher.

"You put ideas in his head. Your whole generation thinks marriage is about being happy every second of the day. It's childish."

Well, she was somewhat right about that. It *was* childish. He'd thought that about Cass and her grand plan many times, especially after she first departed. Life wasn't about choosing to be single on Mondays and married on Tuesdays, or getting to be a parent every other week. It was picking a lane and committing to it. That sounded awfully rigid, but it was the truth, unless you were Cass Coyne and married to a chump like him.

"I'm sorry, Mom. I'll call Dad if you think it'll help."

"Don't you dare," Betsy said.

She hung up abruptly and he found himself numbly holding the phone in his hand. He wasn't ready to hang up, even from his mother, who was probably off to spread her wrath to Wallace or Katie.

Jonathan needed to talk to someone. And he knew just who that was.

In high school, he and Brett would trade stories about their dysfunctional parents, and then in the summer, when both families were on Martha's Vineyard, they'd elbow each other when said dysfunction was on display. They hadn't spoken since he dispatched that terrible message from Hazel Park.

He texted first because he knew there was no shot she'd pick up the phone otherwise. Choosing to be as direct and succinct as possible, he wrote: I'm about to call you. Please, please, please pick up. He added the praying hands emoji for emphasis.

"Well, this is unexpected," Brett said after three long rings. Her voice, normally as velvety as tomato soup, was strained. At least she'd taken the call.

"I really appreciate your answering," Jonathan blurted out. "I'm so sorry, Brett. About everything. I handled things terribly. Cass and I aren't back together, by the way, but that's not why I'm calling. I just got off the phone with my mother and she shared with me the fact that after thirty-six years of marriage, my dad is leaving her. Technically a trial separation, but not really. You were the first person I thought of. Remember how much we used to make fun of our crazy families?"

There was such a long silence that Jonathan almost told Brett he was sorry he called before hanging up.

"Of course I do," she finally said. "Your parents have hated each other for ages. What took them so long? I bet your mom is going to have some bohemian sexual awakening now."

Jonathan heard the tension melting in Brett's voice and he found his body responding in kind. His rib cage must have dropped three inches.

"That I don't need to picture. She says Cass and I are to blame."

"Betsy never did like your wife, did she?"

"Nope," Jonathan said simply, this time not filled with anger toward his mother but a resigned détente.

"So?" Brett asked.

"So. I am beyond sorry about the way I handled things. I just needed to say that."

"Hang on a second," Brett said, and Jonathan heard a trail of sirens and the blare of car horns that could only come from New York City traffic.

"Where are you?"

He could hear Brett hesitating, letting the fading sound of the fire trucks buy her time.

"I'm in New York. Doing a girls' weekend with college friends in the city. We're downtown."

"Can I see you?" he asked. The loneliness became the blood in his veins, running through him in repetitive loops. "I know it's asking a lot."

"You know, I don't even blame you, Jon. I kept tabs on you, a little bit anyway, since we broke up. By all accounts, Cass had a pernicious hold on you. Trust me, if I could figure out how to have that effect on people, I'd do it too."

He almost started to defend his marriage and say things weren't really like that, but he stopped himself. Brett didn't even know the truth about the separation. Lies were everywhere he looked, in coffee cups and mirrors and the wind that flapped at his collar.

"Will you meet me for coffee? Take a few minutes out of your wild girls' weekend and see me?"

"Let's do a drink tomorrow night."

"Drinks it is."

When he hung up the phone, he closed his eyes, actually dizzy. He felt like a yo-yo, released and pulled back, released and pulled back, over and over and over.

29. CASS

IN THE OFFICE screening room, Cass was with Aidan, Josephine and a few others watching a screener of the Indiana Jones reboot. Not the movie she would have chosen. It reminded her of watching a tape of the Harrison Ford original with the volume on full blast to drown out one of her parents' epic fights. And then the VCR broke midway through and never got replaced, so she was at the mercy of friends if she ever wanted to see a movie from that point on. To make matters worse, Jonathan was an Indiana Jones freak. She hadn't communicated with him in over a month—not even by text since the "Screw you"—and now she was heading to Percy's memorial service without him. Of course she wanted him by her side when she went, but she was petrified to reach out. If he rebuffed her again, it would be him hammering the final nail in the coffin. No second act for their relationship. Baby steps were needed to get back in Jonathan's good graces—not asking for another favor.

It was early September; Labor Day was around the corner. The final squeeze of summer was in full force and nobody even jumped when Marty sauntered through the lounge and saw their group sprawled out in front of the screen in the middle of a workday. Cass longed for a challenging project to throw herself into, but post-*Rebels*, her assignments were a steady stream of second and third installments of franchises that would kill it at the box office even though they were prepackaged, predictable, and almost impossible to watch. If she wanted to get ahead at Spiegel, in earnest, she'd have to commit herself to learning more about the film industry and reaching a different demographic than she was used to. The only problem was, she wasn't entirely sure she wanted to adjust her professional self. There had been too much adjusting lately, the line between the "old her" and the "new her," and the "real her" and the "reinvented her" like a scribble drawn in disappearing ink. When she was with Jonathan, there was significantly less fluctuation, though she suspected—with a certain amount of resignation—that she'd never have the luxury of being wholly fixed.

"Should we pop in *Raiders of the Lost Ark* for good measure?" Josephine asked when the credits started rolling.

Cass glanced at her watch. Her flight to New York wasn't for another five hours. She was about to voice her agreement when Minka burst through the swinging door with a hand truck overflowing with magazines and newspapers tied up with twine. Brie trailed behind, carrying a large cardboard box that nearly outsized her.

"Finally!" Minka exclaimed.

"Cannot wait to show Marty!" Brie squealed.

The others in the room barely glanced in their direction. Everyone was accustomed to the Bobbsey Twins flitting around in varying states of hyperventilation. But Cass's attention was piqued. A feeling she couldn't name came over her and demanded that she take notice. The girls headed off to Marty's corner office and Cass excused herself a moment later, ostensibly to confirm her flight status, but really to skulk behind them and see what the fuss was about. A feeling of dread was upon her inexplicably. For the past few weeks—since Jasmine's bat mitzvah if she had to put a date on it—she'd known there wasn't much longer she could go on cavorting with Marty. She knew what it felt like when a relationship had substance. It was like a weight you could hold in your hand, and this wasn't it.

His door was already shut when Cass approached, but fortuitously Abby was away from her post, so she was able to position herself close enough to eavesdrop. She was lucky that news of the Indiana Jones marathon had spread around the office, which left most cubicles abandoned. If anyone saw her, she'd make like she'd just arrived and was about to knock.

Cass heard Marty's muffled exclamations first.

"Finally, goddammit! I thought these pictures would never go to print. Paid that dipshit paparazzo two thousand pounds."

Cass peered down the hallway furtively. Still nearly empty. She leaned closer to the door, her earring scratching against the wood.

Next she made out Minka's voice in fragments. "Fresh off the Federal Express truck . . . forty advance copies of *Hello!* magazine. They ran three half-page photos."

Then Brie. "And *Daily Mail* . . . the one of you and the girls at the zoo was priceless."

Minka: "Next to a picture of Philippa and the boyfriend at a nightclub . . . both of them totally wasted."

Brie: "Was so worth it . . . stalking the editors . . . Took forever to run them but paid off. We should . . . champagne . . . call Stefan Diller."

Marty (loud and clear—his voice boomed when he was happy): "Well done, ladies. Philippa will be hysterical. I look like father of the year, and she looks like a washed-up stripper partying all night. Brie, that photographer you found turned out to be perfect. The girls look so happy with me. The picture of the three of us in the Harrods toy department is fucking priceless. Had to bribe Olive and Stella with a shitload of new clothes to get them to smile like that. Fuck, wasn't it just one of their birthdays? I have too many fucking kids to keep it straight."

"I'll deal with . . ." Brie said. "Now it's . . . celebrate."

"To screwing over Philippa!" Her boss cheered. Cass pictured Marty raising a glass.

"Let's see if we can't find a good picture of me and Cass to send over to Perez Hilton. While Philippa's with Zoolander, I'm dating someone substantial. Fuck, I think Cass went to Princeton or something. Have that detail put in. Just make sure they don't mention she's married."

"On it," one of them responded. "What if Tamara sees the picture?"

Tamara? The Aussie actress. *Of course.*

"Not gonna lose sleep over it."

In unison came evil chuckling, like villains in a cartoon.

Cass started to back away slowly. Acid was working its way up her esophagus, and she thought she might throw up on the spot.

The door flew open unexpectedly.

"Cass!" Marty said, sweeping her limp body into a hug. He kissed her on the lips, his breath steamy and full of garlic. "It's a good day."

Nothing could be less true. There was only one way to get her life back on track. One person who would never do anything so cruel. One person who was loyal to a fault, until she'd pushed him away so much that he had no choice but to lash out at her. That person was in New York City, hating her.

SEVERAL HOURS LATER, she gulped down a Xanax she had filched earlier from Alexi as the plane took off, enabling her to sleep for most of the cross-country flight. Cass wasn't normally a pill-popper, but anything not to think about where she was headed.

After Marty kissed her brusquely outside his office, Cass had freed herself from his embrace and muttered something about getting on an earlier flight and needing to run. He called something after her, but

Cass pretended not to hear. By the time she reached her car in the studio parking lot, she'd ended the relationship with all the pomp and ceremony someone like Marty deserved. She dialed his private office line and left a voicemail with a terse "It's not you, it's me" message. She knew with near certainty that Marty wouldn't fight for her. He had Tamara, and if not her, then a dozen other options. She, Cass, was fungible when it came to feeding Marty's appetite.

She landed in the very early morning and breezed into the city from LaGuardia, arriving at her hotel before seven. Emmet had specifically chosen a long weekend so that Percy's siblings would be able to make it. Staying in a hotel in her own city felt excruciating, especially when Puddles was a stone's throw away from her, but she was too afraid to ask Jonathan if she could stay in the apartment when they hadn't spoken since the Michigan debacle. What a mess she'd made of her life. And not just hers.

After fueling up on caffeine and purchasing a price-gouged umbrella on the street during a sudden downpour, she checked into a hotel in SoHo. There was little chance of running into Jonathan, as his office was three miles north of her and the husband she left behind didn't cross below 42nd Street without good reason. The memorial service was going to be in the Tribeca loft Emmet and Percy had shared. She'd refined her notes from the first draft (which, in retrospect, made her seem suicidal and might have had the same effect on the other guests) and ran them by Alexi and Aidan, who both approved of them. Matters were simplified when Emmet didn't ask why Jonathan wasn't coming. He probably assumed it had something to do with the mess at Winstar, which, for all she knew, was still going on. She had purposely avoided the morning financial shows after seeing Jonathan's smiling face too many times. She'd cringed when he was awkward on-screen, but somehow seeing his newfound polish was even more disarming.

The thought of kidnapping Puddles during the day had crossed her mind. But what if she ran into Luna, or the dog walker, or if the doorman stopped her? If she did see Luna, it would be hard not to collapse in her arms and say, "I understand why you clean houses now! I wouldn't want to take anything from that man either." Later that day, she had plans to see Dahlia and her girlfriend, who were coming in from Westchester to have dinner with her. They said they had a big announcement and Cass had an inkling what it would be. Dahlia had warned her the *Real Housewives* cameras would be at the restaurant but that "honestly, you forget about them after twenty minutes." That seemed hard to believe.

"What about text messages?" Cass had asked.

"They read them," Dahlia answered.

"Paper airplane notes?"

"They'd be intercepted."

"Okay, see you at dinner. Only for you, Dahlia."

THOUGH SHE'D REHEARSED her speech numerous times, when she filed into Emmet's apartment for the service, her stomach was burbling. Public speaking was never her thing. Emmet was slated to go first with a welcome and his remarks, then it was Cass's turn, then Percy's siblings, then two college friends, and that was it. Many of her coworkers from PZA were there, which she'd been expecting, and she engaged in pleasantries that she steered to the superficial. Only Percy's former assistant, Nancy, chipped away at her with question after question like a woodpecker: "What do you mean you're working at Spiegel Productions? Aren't they based in L.A.? Does that mean Jonathan relocated? But I keep seeing him on TV talking about Winstar? Are you doing that long-distance thing? How is your sweet dog? The one that always played with Shirley." Cass finally excused herself to use the restroom and made sure to station herself far away from Nancy when she returned.

Emmet approached the podium that had been set up in front of the fireplace and asked everyone to take their seats. He looked different than the last time she'd seen him, gray around the edges and wearing spectacles, a far cry from the chorus boy he'd once been. Had Percy been the one who insisted he dye his hair and wear contacts? She couldn't tell if the physical change was a symbol of freedom or neglect.

He spoke poignantly about his thirty-year relationship with Percy, from meeting at a bar in Chelsea when they were both wearing cutoffs and cowboy boots, moving in together and getting Shirley, making it legal when they could, the pain of the diagnosis, fighting it together. Cass knew most of the story and shifted her focus to her own notes, which she rehearsed in her head until something Emmet said caught her attention.

"I admitted to Percy pretty early on that the only reason I went out with him in the first place was because he was *the* Percy Zimmerman, Broadway Big Shot, and I was Emmet Nobody from Manalapan, New Jersey, wishing for stardom. I figured this guy could be my big break. I'd go out with him a few times, land a great gig and say buh-bye. But wouldn't you know it? I fell head over heels in love with him. By the fourth date, I didn't care if I never got another part again. I just wanted to be with Percy. And the rest, as they say, was history."

It was that simple for them. Cass looked around the audience. Down every row, up every aisle, nobody was tsk-tsking, nobody was silently judging. Just sympathetic smiles and some drying of eyes. Why had she occluded her motivations for so long? Why had she ever let this snowball with Jonathan? She should have realized so much sooner that she could tell him the truth. She put her palms together and rubbed them back and forth until the friction became too much, feeling acutely alone.

"Next up to say a few words is Cass Coyne. She had the joy of working very closely with Percy for ten years. I know he saw her as some combination of a daughter, a best friend and a mentee. She was very special to him."

Cass sucked in air to the pit of her belly and rose, running her hands nervously through her hair. She was skeptical of memorial services generally, even Percy's. But as she headed for the podium, she felt her skepticism fading. Look what she'd just learned. Percy never mentioned what Emmet had admitted to him—had it really been that inconsequential? She just wished she had Jonathan in the crowd to make eye contact with. He'd have flashed her some silly thumbs-up to which she would have rolled her eyes, but felt that much sturdier at the podium. She was a full and capable person without Jonathan. She was just a better person with him.

Her remarks seemed to go over well, and while the siblings and friends spoke after her, she found herself staring at the back of Emmet's head, wanting to swim inside what he now knew from looking down the barrel of his relationship from its end point. During the refreshments she tried to corner him, but he was busy mingling, telling one Percy story after another to his guests. She edged close to one group he was speaking to and overheard Emmet saying, "I swear sometimes Percy and I had nothing to say to each other aside from what we needed to order from FreshDirect. And you know what? That was enough for me. To have someone like Percy to make a grocery list with . . . that was enough." Cass thought about Jonathan—how he loved coffee ice cream, Oreos, had an endless appetite for bananas. She waved her good-bye to Emmet and poked around until she found Shirley, crated but happy to see her nonetheless. She pulled out her cell phone and showed her Puddles's picture.

Outside, in humid air as thick as the facial cream she spread on at night, she reached for her phone again. She would call Jonathan this minute. Ask him to meet her. The worst thing that could happen was that he said no. As she was about to dial his number—the first name in the list of "favorites" saved in her cell phone—she remembered it was a holiday weekend. Jonathan was most likely with his family on the Vineyard, maybe holding hands with Brett while his parents cheered from the sidelines. She stuffed the phone back in her purse.

Four hours remained until Dahlia and Roxanna were due to arrive in the city and she wandered the streets endlessly, attempting to shop but staring listlessly into the distance when clerks came over to offer help. A visit to the new Whitney downtown was foiled by long lines and even the pizza she craved at John's was impossible to get. When had New York gotten so crowded? She'd only been gone a few months. Now she felt frightened by the magnitude of change she perceived everywhere she looked.

Finally it was time to meet Dahlia at a downtown restaurant that was paying the show a fortune to film there. Nothing was pure anymore.

Cass settled herself into the booth that was being held for them and ordered a Manhattan sour. Dahlia texted they were stuck in traffic. Two cocktails in quick succession strengthened her courage and she texted Jonathan. If she didn't do it now before the cameras showed up, she wouldn't have a chance until much later, and her urge to be in touch with him felt suddenly all-consuming.

Jonathan, I'm in New York. It was Percy's memorial service today. I'm missing the hell out of you. If you're in town, can we please get together while I'm here? I fly back to L.A. tomorrow night. And . . . I'm sorry. xo, Cass

30. JONATHAN

PUDDLES WAS LOOKING at him funny as he got dressed for his date, or whatever it was. Maybe it was the fact that he sprayed cologne, which he normally never did, or that he was in the bathroom fiddling with his hair for longer than the usual fifteen seconds. It was almost as though Puddles sniffed the magnitude of what Jonathan was doing. Brett was willing to meet him. Maybe it was just as a friend, maybe she was horny, he wasn't sure. But he wasn't going to disrespect her again. If she was willing to explore a relationship with him, he'd give it an honest try. If she wanted a friend, he'd be the best one he could be. If she wanted a fuck, he'd give her a good one. Cass was history. She'd made it abundantly clear that she didn't care about him, and even as it pained him to realize it, he had no choice but to move on with his life. The woman he loved didn't love him back—at least not enough to want to stay married to him—and he had to accept it.

He and Brett were supposed to meet at Bar Italia on Madison Avenue, ten blocks from his apartment. It was hot and sticky outside,

August in September, but he was ready early and felt far too fidgety to wait at home, so he decided to walk instead of cabbing it. He checked his reflection in the mirror approvingly before stepping out, blanching at the irony that he was wearing the "cool jeans" Cass had bought him in order to impress another woman.

Cass. Why did she keep infecting his mind? She was like a song he couldn't get out of his head. Where was she now? What would her face look like if she could magically see where he was headed? Proud of her boy for not being a pussy waiting around for her? Or crushed beyond measure, biting down on her bottom lip so hard that those crooked front teeth left an impression?

He was crossing 73rd Street when he felt the buzz in his back pocket. A text message from Brett. Running a drop late. Order me a glass of white wine. He responded with a wineglass emoji and slipped the phone back in its place.

On 72nd Street, it started to rain. First a few drops, then in full sheets.

He was crossing 71st Street when his phone buzzed again. Smiling to himself, he reached back in to see what Brett had written now. But it was from Cass.

> Jonathan, I'm in New York. It was Percy's memorial service today. I'm missing the hell out of you. If you're in town, can we please get together while I'm here? I fly back to L.A. tomorrow night. And . . . I'm sorry. xo, Cass

The taxi making a right turn came out of nowhere. He flew into the air, as though he'd been sprung from a giant trampoline. Then all he felt was pain. Asphalt burning his skin. Shattered glass stabbing at him. Shooting pains in his legs and arms like he'd never known before. Darkness everywhere. Ringing in his ears so loud it was actually making him feel deaf. Then nothing.

31. CASS

WHEN THE CALL came in, they had just finished ordering dessert and Cass was in the restaurant's vestibule getting repowdered by Tina, the show's makeup artist. "Bronzer!" "Contour blush!" "Lip stain!" The artist was yelling to her assistant like a surgeon demanding a life-saving scalpel. Did she look that awful?

The screen showed an unrecognized 212 number. Likely a wrong number, Cass thought, but answered anyway, happy for a break from getting spray-painted.

"Excuse me," she said to Tina, who was losing patience with Cass quickly. She held up her ringing phone with an apologetic expression. "Hello?"

"This is Nurse Sharon Carella calling from Weill Cornell Hospital. Do you know a Jonathan Coyne?"

Her entire body froze.

"Yes, I'm his wife. What's going on?" She instinctively walked away from Tina, knowing she needed quiet and privacy.

"He's been in an accident. You are listed in his phone as his next of kin."

"Is he okay? What happened?"

"Ma'am, I can't release any of that information over the phone. Can you please come here as soon as possible and bring identification?"

"Yes, of course," she said, and darted back over to their table, where two enormous cameramen were hovering along with a full lighting crew.

"Cass, you look much better. The TV really washes you out, trust me," Dahlia said.

"Jonathan was in an accident. I have to go."

Both Dahlia and Roxanna jumped up and followed her as she dashed outside, her arm already outstretched for a taxi.

"We'll drive you," Dahlia said. "It's Saturday night and it's raining buckets—you'll never get a cab. We're parked half a block away."

"Okay," Cass agreed. "But I'm driving." Only she would feel the urgency to weave through traffic and plow past the red lights.

"Fine," Roxanna and Dahlia said in unison. The three of them shuffled quickly into Dahlia's black Lincoln Navigator. Roxanna took the back, Dahlia sat shotgun next to Cass. And they were off, Cass gunning the engine like it was the Grand Prix.

32. JONATHAN

WHEN HE WOKE up again, he was alone. He knew he'd seen Cass's face in the last twenty-four hours. Brett's too, possibly at the same time, appearing fuzzily before him like the angel and the devil. He was also aware that he was in a hospital, that his limbs were mummi-fied. There had been an accident with a taxi, that much he remem-bered. Everything after was a blur. He tried to move his right arm but it felt Krazy-Glued to the bed. Same with his left. Mercifully, he was able to wiggle his toes, the first sign that his body was able to do what his brain was telling it. There was a call button for a nurse within reach. If he could manage to shimmy his body over a couple of inches, he had a shot of reaching it with his elbow. No—too much effort.

His sense of smell was intact and he breathed in the antiseptic stink of his surroundings, a cocktail of baby powder, rubbing alcohol and Ly-sol. He tried to piece together a timeline. He knew it had something to do with Cass. And that he'd called Brett, possibly from a gurney.

Outside his room, voices. Female voices chatting softly. Familiar ones.

Cass and Brett, conversing. His heart started to race, another sign that this wasn't a postmortem nightmare. The heart monitor to which he was attached reflected the uptick, but not enough to warrant any alarm bells.

"I just don't understand. I thought he'd be on the Vineyard for the long weekend." Cass. "When I texted him, I expected to get back a picture of Puddles at the Pooch Parade." The annual Labor Day weekend dog walk was the only thing Cass approved of at the Cheshire golf club. Having gotten Puddles on Halloween, their dog had more costumes than the average toddler.

"Nope. We were supposed to meet for a drink." Brett.

The longest pause Jonathan could imagine in a conversation between two people followed.

"I see." Cass.

Footsteps shuffling by.

"Doctor!" Cass called. "Can you give me an update? I understand he lost a lot of blood. We have the same blood type if it's needed, B positive."

"I'm a universal donor, so I can give as well." That was Brett, chiming in.

A pissing contest over giving him blood. Crazy the turn his life had taken. He remembered joking with Cass when they found out they had the same blood type, saying something to her like, "I thought you'd be more of a B negative."

"Ladies, thank you both. Mr. Coyne did lose a lot of blood. We've already transfused him, but the nick in his spleen is presenting a slow ooze. He will need more blood over the next week. If either of you does want to give, you'll have to get screened today."

"I'll do it." Both of them at once. Either Brett was a saint or a masochist. Cass was, well . . . Cass was competitive.

"As I explained earlier, Mr. Coyne also has a number of broken bones. He'll likely need months of physical therapy, but your husband is very lucky."

And here Jonathan couldn't see which woman the doctor was

looking at. Did he know he was married to Cass and therefore direct that comment to her, or did he size up Brett as the more likely spouse?

"The orthopedist will be in shortly to examine his X-rays and set him in the permanent casts. By morning we'll have the balance of the test results back. Hang tight."

"I think I'll go check on him now, see if he's up yet," Brett said.

"Me too."

He immediately shut his eyes, certain beyond measure he was not ready to interact with anyone just yet, let alone those two. Playing possum was easy enough because he couldn't move a limb if he tried.

He heard their gentle footsteps pad in and back out of his room while he attempted the even breathing of a deep slumber.

"I just feel so terrible for him," Brett said. "He's had such a difficult year."

"I suppose a great deal of that is my fault," Cass said.

No shit.

"He never really said why he felt he had to ask you for the separation. I imagine he wouldn't have said he needed space unless you were, well, never mind. It's not my business."

He flinched internally. How was Cass reacting to his portrayal of the separation?

"Uh-huh."

In those two syllables, he could make out his wife processing the new information. Her husband wasn't the slouch she thought he was. He wasn't going to take it lying down. If that meant saying he'd orchestrated the separation, so be it.

"And well, it wasn't just that, right?" Brett continued. "The Winstar thing was horrible. To have his professional life unravel suddenly. Jon is so hard on himself, you know? I had no idea until we reconnected how haunted he was about the incident with Daniel Rubia-Mendez."

Though he couldn't move his exterior limbs, Jonathan felt his insides work themselves into the tightest possible coil of veins and organs. How would Cass handle this latest bit—the shameful secret he'd never shared with her? Like a defense attorney in a courtroom, Cass in particular didn't like being presented with evidence for which she hadn't been adequately prepared.

"Yes," Cass agreed.

"I mean, it was back in high school, for God's sake."

"You know, Brett, you're so right about *Jonathan* being too hard on himself. His version of that, um, episode has always seemed really outsized to me. I'd love to hear it from your perspective."

Smart cookie, Cass. Way to extract the information without letting on that you are in the dark. He was turned on, despite being paralyzed.

"Oh, sure," Brett said, and he heard the details slide from her mouth. He more or less agreed with her accounting of the events, though naturally she didn't touch on what plagued him most—the electric charge that ran through him when he landed his punches. The dominance. It occurred to him that maybe that was another reason he'd fallen so hard for Cass—someone he had no chance of dominating . . . ever.

"I blame his family. Betsy is so tightly wound. She expected perfection from Jon, as the oldest. She practically was in mourning when he turned down Harvard," he heard Brett say.

Cass's voice interspersed:

"So, Daniel was not your typical boarding school kid, right?"

"Nearly expelled, huh?"

"Yeah, of course Jonathan told me about it when we first started dating, but he didn't like to talk about it much."

Then finally, Jonathan heard Cass say, "You know, I'm suddenly feeling like I need coffee desperately. I'll be back." Jonathan listened to the *click-clack* of her heels receding.

Then only Brett remained. He pictured her sitting patiently on a folding chair outside his room, holding a vigil.

33. CASS

SHE WAS DIZZY.

New information, so much of it, zapping her brain like a Taser against the skull.

Jonathan had a secret that he kept hidden from her. A big one. That explained his commitment to the Big Brother program. He wasn't the Boy Scout she thought he was. He was repenting and proving to himself, to her, to anyone who would take notice, what a good person he was.

And he'd told Brett *he'd* asked for the break.

She wanted to be upset, to charge into Jonathan's hospital room and demand complete honesty. But she had secrets too. Secrets that had gotten them to this exact place. And she could rewrite history with the best of them. She and Jonathan were far more alike than she'd realized.

She needed to get Brett out of the hospital. To speak to Jonathan alone. It was clever of him, pretending to be asleep when the two of them entered his room. Too bad for him she knew the exact rhythm of his breathing. If he'd been sleeping, he'd have been snoring. If she honestly thought Brett was the woman whose presence would help Jonathan's bones heal and whose encouraging smile would make him work a bit harder every day in physical therapy, she'd leave the hospital in a mad dash and let the high school lovers have their happy ending. But she didn't believe that, especially after learning Jonathan was more nuanced and deliberate than she'd ever appreciated. She and Jonathan needed to give their marriage another try, but this time, with complete honesty—his and hers. If, after full disclosure, her husband still preferred Brett, well, at least she had tried her best. The real Cass and Jonathan would be making the decision, not some fraudulent, manufactured versions of themselves.

The ex was prettier than Cass expected, that much she had to admit. The Vera Bradley bag and the cherry-flavored ChapStick left behind in their apartment had really thrown her. She thought in person Brett would look like an overgrown teenager. She'd never bothered googling her, that's how firm of an image she'd conjured of Brett after finding her belongings in their apartment. But Brett was light-years evolved from her high school yearbook photo, and she wore her white jeans with the strategic rips at the knees and the asymmetrical silk blouse quite well. The shoes, well, Cass didn't know who made them, but they were expensive and spot-on. Brett spoke in that cool, confident tone of the upper class; sentences slipped from her mouth in pithy little punches. And a universal donor to boot? Of course she was. But the blood type said it all. Brett had something to offer to everyone, whereas Cass was uniquely matched with Jonathan.

So why did that stupid resident look at Brett when he said, "Your husband is very lucky"? It had hurt so damn much. She had wanted to shout from the rooftops, "It's me, it's me! I'm Mrs. Jonathan Coyne!"

Coffee, a few moments to collect herself, and then she'd head back up to Jonathan's floor and force the reckoning they should have had six months ago. If she had been brave enough to be honest back then, they wouldn't be where they were now. In a hospital. At the breaking point. It was time to tell him she'd been to New York, in their apartment, but that she'd fled like a coward. Time to say that and much more. There wasn't enough caffeine in the world to mask how tired she was. She'd run a marathon only to return to the starting line. But perhaps that's what she needed all along. To see her life come full circle and feel grateful to end up back where she started. Hopefully it wasn't too late. *Please, please, let it not be too late for us.*

34. JONATHAN

DOWN THE HALL, he heard Brett on the phone with someone who had to be her mother.

"Accident . . . Yes, she's here too . . . No, I don't know what's happening . . . Kiss Lars for me."

He was so thirsty, his throat felt like sandpaper. He'd have to ring a nurse to bring him a drink or he'd expire, even if it meant alerting the two women in his life that he was awake. Just as he was about to shimmy for the buzzer, Cass appeared in the doorframe holding two bottles of his favorite: raspberry-flavored Perrier. She entered quietly and closed the door behind her, finding space on the far edge of his bedside for her bottom.

For a minute they didn't speak. She unscrewed the cap of one of the drinks and it released its telltale fizz. Cass rose again to fish in her purse for a straw and brought the drink to his lips. He took a much-needed sip and found his throat in working order again.

"Hi," he said.

"Hi." She sat back down. "How do you feel?"

"Like hell. Is Puddles okay?"

"Totally. Jemima's got him for the week."

"Good."

"So?" she asked poignantly.

"So," he responded, sidestepping the doorway she'd opened for him.

"I'm sorry," she blurted out.

"Cass," he began.

"No—let me. I freaked. The baby, my job. Worrying that we were turning into roommates more than lovers. I think you think I'm a certain way, but I'm not really the person you think I am."

"I could say the same, Cass."

"It turns out you could," she said. "Did you really believe I would think you were some kind of bigot because of something that happened when you were seventeen years old? You think I don't know you better than that?"

"I was worried, Cass. I didn't want to risk you misinterpreting. What if you couldn't understand?"

Cass nodded, like she got it. Enough to make him go on.

"Remember that night we met in college and you told me you chose Brown because of RISD? Years later I heard you telling Leon's buddies that it was because of the financial-aid package. Which was the truth? And after you left for California, I found a huge stack of programs from some theater in Los Angeles in the back of your night table drawer. We both have things we've kept from each other for too long."

"I agree. There's mystery and there's deception. It's a fine line, but I think we both know which side of it we're on."

Cass stood up again and came closer to his face. He thought she might kiss him or brush aside his hair.

"You're so banged up," she observed, like he was a damaged work of art.

"I haven't looked in a mirror yet. But I can feel it."

"Are you hungry?" she asked. "I can run out to get you a sandwich or pasta from Elio's if you're up to it."

"Not yet. Maybe later," he said.

"So . . . Brett?" she asked, settling herself back on his bed. He noticed her stiffen as she sucked air forcefully into her lungs. "I came to New York when the news first broke about Winstar. But then I found her things in our apartment and I ran."

"Really? I had no idea." So she was human after all. "What about you and Marty Spiegel?"

"It was a thing. But it's over. You guys?"

"I don't know. Your leaving was like a Mack truck mauling me. And then an actual taxi did maul me. I can't think straight right now. We've both made mistakes that need sorting out."

They sat in silence for a while, listening to the background noises of the hospital. Brett's voice sounded intermittently, broken fragments that were incomprehensible but still difficult to ignore.

Cass finally spoke.

"We should be more up-front with each other. About the big things. And some of the little things that were pissing us off. No married couple is perfect, right?"

"I don't think anyone would ever accuse us of being perfect."

She laughed heartily and he knew that if he never saw those overlapping teeth again, he couldn't go on.

"Cass, I cheated on you. Right after we lost Peanut."

Her face fell, like she'd been hit from behind.

"I'm so sorry. Cass—there is no excuse, I know, I just—"

"Jonathan, stop. I have to say something too. We didn't meet by chance. Not in college. And not in New York City either."

Heightened senses shook them as the room flooded with anger and the deafening echo of truth.

act three

AFTER

35.

THE LAWYER'S OFFICES were located a few blocks away from his new office. He'd rented a cube in a WeWork office, where he shared a printer, secretary and copy machine with a dozen others trying to make something of themselves one day at a time. He had avoided working for his father—but just narrowly. Instead he was trying to build a new fund, though with the stench of Winstar following him, it was proving tougher than expected. He'd hoped to parlay his TV experience into a weekly gig, but so far nothing had materialized. Money was tight. He'd sold the apartment and was moving a few avenues farther east the following week, where a comparable apartment was much cheaper. It turned out the Coyne trust he'd assumed was growing at a steady rate had been mismanaged recently, and there wasn't much there.

He'd spent a lot of time in lawyers' offices over the past four months. The recovery was quicker than the doctors had first anticipated (he'd had a good nurse), but the minute he was back on his feet he was called into depositions regarding Winstar. This was different, though. The law firm to which he was headed now, hopefully for the last time, specialized in family law. The others were white-collar specialists. They were basically the same, though, with their sterile atmospheres, enormous panes of glass, pin-drop quiet—decor designed to intimidate.

Outside, he was blasted by the cold February air and bent down to zip his puffer. A group of young guys in Steelers hats was crossing the street en masse. The Super Bowl was on Sunday. Jemima and Henry weren't even neighbors anymore—they had decided to move to London before Christmas. This year would be very different from last.

He was too cold to remove his gloves to check his phone, though he felt the text messages buzzing. It was probably just Cass, letting him know she was running late. But when he arrived, she was already seated at the long conference table. She looked fresh and glowy on the outside, a peach peacoat draped over her shoulders and her hair blown out smoothly, but he didn't know how she felt on the inside. For his part, he was a wreck. He nodded at her and she looked up from her phone and gave him a surprising smile. Couldn't she be stoic, just for his benefit?

"Hello, Jonathan," Mark Hemmer, the senior partner, said when he entered. "Please have a seat. You and Cass are just here to finalize the documents and look things over one last time. Everything should be in order, I think you'll find."

"Let's do this," Cass said, a bit too eagerly. She already had a pen in her grasp—an orange one that said Spiegel Productions on it. Or did it? He looked more closely and saw that it said Superior Podiatry, from that time Cass had bunion surgery. What was wrong with him?

Mark slid duplicate copies of the papers in front of him across the table and asked one of his associates to bring in a notary.

"Take your time and let me know if everything makes sense."

Cass pulled out reading glasses from her purse and ran the capped side of her pen under every line, gently nodding her head. Jonathan tried to eyeball his copy, but the words looked blurry, monsters with dots and crosses and slashes. He assumed it was all right. The lawyers hired were the best and all the terms had been agreed upon already.

"Here on page three, this dictates where the property goes, right? And what about the stock accounts? Where is that detailed?" Cass was all business.

One of the associates jumped from his chair to explain everything over her shoulder. Jonathan was barely listening.

"Makes sense. Okay, I'm ready," Cass said, uncorking her pen as sprightly as a champagne bottle. "You?" she said, looking at him expectantly.

"Yes," he said, and scribbled his name, barely legible, on all the places flagged with the yellow sticky arrows.

Mark and the rest of the lawyers stood when they were done, hands extended.

"That's everything. Good luck," he said, looking slowly from Jonathan to Cass and then back to Jonathan again.

They walked out of the conference room in silence toward the elevator.

"Well, that was pretty painless," Cass said, once the elevator doors slid closed.

"I guess," he said, watching the numbers of the floors illuminate as the elevator eased down the shaft.

"We had to do this. You know that," she said, struggling with the buttons. "Ugh, this is tight."

He nodded.

Outside, Cass raised her hand for a taxi.

"You're going to your office?" she asked him. He was looking down at his phone. Stocks had fallen while he and Cass were getting their lives in order. Money was shrinking and his obligations were expanding.

"Yep." He started to stalk off in the direction of his office, once he saw that Cass had gotten a free taxi's attention. "Wait a second," he said as her hand reached for the car door. "First this."

He bent down toward her waist and planted a kiss on her stomach, finally taking the shape of a curvy mound.

"Bye, baby," he added. "See you tonight."

She smiled, the corners of her eyes crinkling into a million tiny pathways.

"Yes, you will." She patted her tummy affectionately. "We'll see you later tonight."

SHE STIRRED THE spaghetti after stealing a strand and returned the lid to the pot. The best part about being pregnant was the nonstop carb party. She and Jonathan both ordered dessert when they went out and had started a ritual of going for bagels on Sunday mornings. She was even, at times, willing to share.

"I know this afternoon was weird, but I'm so happy we got our wills over and dealt with. Dahlia told me she didn't get around to it until Brady was nearly one and every time she and Harris got on an airplane, she'd be in a full panic. All she could think whenever the pilot announced turbulence was that her crazy sister would get custody instead of her brother and his wife. She and Roxanna made their wills a day after Dahlia got pregnant this time around."

"I know it's smart. It's just not fun to think about our mortality. Especially with her on the way. Let me rub that genie lamp one more time," he said, approaching her from behind.

"It might be a boy," she said, elbowing him back. The carbonara sauce was bubbling over. She didn't want him to get burned.

"No, it's a girl. Cass 2.0. Buyer beware."

"Hilarious," she said, but she found herself really laughing. They both looked down at her stomach, appraising its curves, portending its contents. "Listen, I need to talk you." She saw Jonathan's face freeze when she turned to him. PTSD from the intermission, something she'd inflicted on him and something she'd have to work hard to alleviate. She squeezed his hand protectively, watching the color rush to his fingers. She liked thinking about the three pints of her blood that swam through his veins since the accident, feeding his parts and nourishing his tissues. It was the physical manifestation of everything they'd confessed in the hospital room. A true commingling.

"We're low on groceries. Can you buy mint chocolate-chip ice cream and two dozen eggs? I thought maybe you could grab that on your way home from work tomorrow? I'm going to try to be in the library working all day tomorrow." She had decided to take up playwriting, at least while she was pregnant and had an infant at home. Both she and Jonathan were starting over and it was new beginnings everywhere in sight, even in the signs of an early spring.

"Sure thing," he said.

"Can you watch the sauce for now? I think I'm going to get a bit more packing done."

She reached for a small wooden box on the bookshelf and sifted through its contents. A sonogram, dated two weeks earlier, was on top. Underneath were some candids from their wedding, Playbills from her favorite shows and two Red Sox shot glasses. A glimmer of bronze in the corner caught her eye. A key. It opened the shallow drawer of the desk in their bedroom. She hadn't unlocked it in years.

"Look at this," she said, showing Jonathan what was in her hand. "We should check that the desk is empty. I sold it on 1stdibs."

They walked into the bedroom together and Cass slid the key into the lock. The drawer opened with a light tug. Inside there were paper napkins in all shades of the rainbow, metallic monograms in flourishing script printed on each. Cass unfolded one.

"*J D R*," she read aloud. "You said fifty-plus, I said ten years tops. Now I can't even remember who they are."

"A guy from my business school class," Jonathan said. "No idea what happened to him."

Jonathan smoothed out the next one.

"*A C M*. I think that was that girl Alice from your office, right? We both wrote thirty years."

"She moved to Chicago and I saw on Facebook she's divorced." Cass looked down at the rest of the napkins. "I can't believe we ever did this. Can you?"

"It doesn't matter now," Jonathan said. "What we once did. We're not the same couple we were then."

"We're better now," Cass said, knowing her husband agreed. "Much, much better. Onward."

"With the packing?" Jonathan asked.

"Yes. And, also, just for whatever our future holds."